King's Highlander

ALSO BY JESSI GAGE

Highland Wishes Series

Wishing for a Highlander

The Wolf and the Highlander

Choosing the Highlander

King's Highlander

Love Under Construction

Hurt You

Tempt You

Keep You

Arouse You

Turn Back Time

Terror Undone

King's Highlander

A HIGHLAND WISHES NOVEL

Jessi Gage

To each and every wonderful reader who demanded this story be told. Magnus would not have gotten his happy-ever-after without you.

Acknowledgements

Thank you to my wonderful friends and critique partners, Amy Raby and Janice Whiteaker for your brainstorming help, critiques, and good company. Thank you, Shane for your love and support. I couldn't do this without you. That goes for you too, Mom. Between babysitting, plotting help, proofreading, laundry, and just listening when I need to talk, you make it possible for me to follow my dream. Thank you, Piper Denna for editing this manuscript and Damonza for the gorgeous cover. Thank you, beta readers Michele Engebretson, Patti Kilcullen, Mina Waldron, Sarah Wallhauser, and Paulina Woods for your enthusiasm, comments, and patience as I know each one of you waited for EVER for this book. You all helped me make this finished product the best it can be.

Prologue

FOOTSTEPS SOUNDED ON stairs of stone as Danu's jailor descended to her.

Within her cell, she drew herself to her full height. All she had left was her pride. It was the one thing Hyrk could never take from her.

"Good morning, my fair goddess." His voice slithered through the silence. The torches in the walls, ever glowing with crimson light, caused slashes of shadow where rocks jutted from the dungeon floor. Hyrk sailed gracefully around the obstacles, so familiar with the path, he could no doubt walk it blindfolded. Clothed in his usual finery and smelling of lavender baths, he reminded her of the luxuries she'd once taken for granted.

Hatred pulsed in her chest. If she weren't surrounded by bars of cold-iron, she would use that hatred to sear him where he stood. The immortal demigod wouldn't die from it, sadly, but it would take him time to heal, time during which she would not have to suffer his presence.

"I have the most wonderful news, my dear." Framed by hair the color of fresh blood, his pale face beamed.

What would he crow about this time? Had he acquired a new follower? Had the population of her precious wolfkind dropped more quickly than usual? In the absence of her blessing, her people had steadily declined in number, especially the women. Each death added thickness to the bars of her cell. Soon, wolfkind would be extinct, and she would be worse than dead, forever sealed inside a box made from her failure as a goddess. Lest she forget her inevitable fate, Hyrk reminded her daily.

Whatever his news, she did not encourage him to deliver it. Anything Hyrk considered good was sure to displease her.

"A battle is afoot!" he said, clapping with glee. "My King Bantus and his traitorous, little helper are about to usurp the throne of Marann. What's left of your wolfkind will soon be under *my* complete control! No more will your pesky followers stand in my way. At last, I'll have free rein to shape them into the bloodthirsty race they should have been from the beginning. Isn't it fantastic?"

Her fists clenched at her sides with the effort to remain quiet. Over the past two thousand years, she had learned that her rage only fueled her enemy's excitement.

"Of course, it doesn't have to be this way." his tone sank to slimy depths. "You have the power to free yourself. To save them. We will rule them together. As one flesh, joined by Sacred Tradition. What say you? Is this the day you hold to your word and become my wife?" The question was the same every morning.

As was her answer. "No."

Chapter 1

"HEAR MY PRAYER, Goddess. Answer the plight of your people. Shine your favor on us once more, I beg you." Smooth marble cooled King Magnus's forehead as he prostrated himself before Danu's altar.

He'd greeted each new day of his reign thus, at the temple where generations of Marann's kings had sought their creator's wisdom and truth. Of late, his prayers had grown in urgency, but the news he'd woken to this winter's morn' caused his plea to pour forth with even greater desperation.

Along with the expected handful of male deaths this week, a lady had gone to Danu's breast.

Her name was Massabel. Mother to eight sons, granddame to twelve, great granddame to eight, and great-great granddame to one, she had lived one hundred thirty-seven years, leaving behind her pledgemate, a governor in Chroina's Financial District. Aged but not ancient, Massabel had been the very definition of health until a tooth abscess had caused her to stop taking food. Fever had claimed her life only days later.

The most skilled tooth surgeon had gone to Danu's breast years ago. His two apprentices, who had been thrust into the trade out of necessity, had done all they could for Massabel, but without their master, they had not been able to restore her health.

Soon the last remaining master physicians would return to the goddess, leaving behind apprentices and texts, but taking with them their long years of experience. It was this way with masons and smiths, bakers and cheesemakers, farmers, tailors, parchment makers, and jewelers. No trade was unaffected.

It was the way of extinction.

The number of women remaining was a mere one hundred forty-nine. Those young enough to breed a terrifying thirty-five, none of whom had produced young in more than eleven years.

Today's population, unless another death was reported before the breakfast hour, was five thousand nine hundred ninety-seven. With so few women left and none of them producing young, five years would see their numbers reduced by a thousand. Then another thousand. Then another. In twenty years, the world's population would fit comfortably in Chroina's city center and there would be no females of breeding age left.

Unless Danu saved them.

Two moons ago, hope had surged.

As autumn had yielded to winter, he'd led his men to victory in Larna and there saw the slaying of his sworn enemy, King Bantus. Twelve women of breeding age had been miraculously discovered in Bantus's dungeon. But the victory swiftly gave way to chaos.

Lawlessness abounded in both newly conquered Larna and the far reaches of Marann. Insurrections cropped up more quickly than his dwindling army could put them down. Revolutionists lurked in the royal city of Chroina, eager to place a king of their own choosing on the throne—it would have been his cousin Ari if Magnus hadn't discovered the plot and executed Ari for his betrayal.

As for the women, the joy of their discovery evaporated as word spread that they were not wolfkind, but human, a race with shortened lifespan and delicate build compared to theirs. Some lobbied to include the women in the breeding lottery regardless of their weaker blood. Some wanted to rent the women to men desperate for female attentions. Some, like Magnus, wished to return them to their human realm, for they'd suffered unspeakably at Bantus's hands and owed wolfkind nothing.

Except for one woman. Seona.

Here in this very temple fifty years ago, Danu's priest confirmed the sacred vision Magnus had experienced the night of his coronation. For his entire reign, he'd waited for the chestnut-haired beauty with a paw print on her cheek, the special lady Danu had promised to him in a dream. For fifty years, he'd anticipated loving her and being loved in return. For fifty years, he'd prepared to make her his lifemate. His queen. She would bear his heir, and, ruling together, they would save wolfkind.

Only, now that she had been found, she wanted nothing to do with him.

After the abuse she had suffered in Larna, Seona seemed to hate all wolfkind, especially men—*most* especially him, a king like the one who had horribly abused her for more than a year.

With his face pressed to the temple floor, he remembered her panicked shrieking the one and only time he'd entered her chamber. Anya, Seona's sister and the only individual Seona permitted to tend her, had advised him to give her time. But time was one thing he did not have.

At twenty-nine years of age, Seona was nearing the end of her pitifully short human breeding period. In order to make his vision a reality, he needed to breed her within the next few years. That left him precious little time to woo her, especially considering she pressed Anya daily for access to the magical gemstone that brought the humans over from their realm.

He had committed to using the gemstone to send the other eleven home once they had physically recovered from their captivity. That time had come. Physicians had seen to the mending of their wounds, and their frail frames now carried healthy weight. He could stall no longer.

Indecision ripped his insides to pieces. Return his promised lady to her home, where she longed to go, or keep her and have faith that the goddess who had been silent for decades would open the human's heart to him, and open her womb to his seed? Keeping her while he sent the others home felt like the wrong thing to do, but how else could Danu's plan unfold?

Breath fogging the polished floor, he poured out his heart. "I've kept your laws. I've honored your name. I've cut down your enemies. I've sought your wisdom in every matter from large to small, but you have not blessed me with a vision since my coronation. I've given you my whole life. What more can I give? Will you not answer me, my Goddess? Will you not guide your servant?"

Despite the chill in the air, sweat beaded on his forehead. A few drops splashed onto the marble. A temple servant would come with a rag and clean it up once he finished praying.

Speaking of temple servants, where were they? The sanctuary had been deserted when he'd arrived with his guards. Normally, a youth tended the candles, ensuring none went out during his morning prayer. And where was Assaph? The high priest met him each sunrise for communion. True, Magnus had come early today, as he often did when sleep eluded him, but it was well past sunrise. Assaph should have met him at the foot of the altar by now.

A thread of unease tickled the back of his neck. He got to his feet.

"Assaph, I am ready for communion." He projected his voice toward the priest's quarters. A door of oak stood between Assaph's residence and the sanctuary. Usually, it hung open a crack, no doubt so the priest might observe Magnus's prayer and know when to serve communion. Today, however, the door was shut tight.

Hearing no response, Magnus strode to the carved wood and rapped. "Assaph." Perhaps he had overslept.

Riggs, Magnus's newest knight, and Anya's lifemate, left his post by the temple doors. Coming into the sanctuary, he said, "Shall I check on him, Sire?"

"Yes." It was unlike Assaph to keep him waiting.

Riggs tried the latch, but it was locked. "Please stand back, Your Majesty." With a few steps' start, Riggs forced his shoulder into the door, which gave as if it had been slammed by a boulder. Magnus was not surprised, since Riggs was the largest of his personal guard, the Knights of the Crescent Moon, not to mention one of the tallest and strongest men he'd ever known.

Magnus allowed Riggs to enter Assaph's apartment first. No lamps were lit, suggesting Assaph remained abed. He called the priest's name again while Riggs, axe at the ready, rounded a corner.

"Sire," Riggs called. "He's here."

Magnus followed the call into a sleeping chamber littered with overturned furniture. On the pallet was Assaph, bound and gagged but seemingly unharmed. His wide eyes reflected the gray light from an open window. Its shutters hung crookedly, as if someone had torn them open in haste.

Riggs drew a hunting knife. He sliced the ropes binding Assaph's hands before releasing the gag.

Magnus hurried to fetch a cup from the cabinet. After filling it from the ewer, he crouched by the pallet. Once Assaph had rubbed the feeling back into his hands, Magnus passed him the refreshment.

He could not imagine anyone brazen enough to raid the apartment of Chroina's high priest. Whoever had done it would suffer. He would make sure of it.

Striving to keep the anger from his voice, he said, "What happened? Who did this to you?"

Assaph drank deeply and wiped his mouth on the back of his arm. A simple nightshirt covered all but his legs and bare feet, and

Magnus reflected he had never seen the priest without his robe or spectacles. Riggs handed the spectacles to Assaph, having plucked them from the floor.

Assaph accepted them with a nod and dragged a hand through his close-trimmed hair. Unlike most wolfkind males, priests and temple servants shaved their faces daily. They took pride in their appearance, showing deference to Danu in their morning rituals. A shadow of beard along Assaph's jaw struck a note of discord with Magnus. Not being allowed to attend his daily ablutions was an insult, not only to Assaph, but to the crown as well.

Magnus could not help grinding his molars as he awaited Assaph's answer.

The priest swallowed the water, cup shaking in his hands. "I wish it were not so, Your Majesty," he said past chafed lips. "But I swear on the writings of Danu it was your promised lady and a man I did not recognize. They left me like this well before dawn. Perhaps two hours ago."

Like a blow from a mace, shock rocked him onto his heels. "Seona? In the custody of a man?" He would have said such an accusation was impossible, but he trusted Assaph implicitly. "But how? She is well-guarded, as are all the women." Wolfkind or human, it didn't matter. All were protected like the precious jewels they were.

"Not in custody, Sire," Assaph said. "They worked together. She was active and willing in binding me and searching my apartment."

He could scarcely believe it. Not only had Seona rarely left her bed since her rescue from Bantus's dungeon, but she did not tolerate the company of men.

Riggs said, "Describe the man, please, Your Holiness."

Assaph nodded and moistened his lips. Addressing Riggs, he said, "Tall, though not as tall as you. Slender. His hair was not unlike yours with black curls. He wore tattered clothes beneath a gray cloak, and one shoulder hung lower than the other."

"Tattered clothes," Magnus mused. "That could only be a prisoner." With the population so low and commodities like cloth in abundance, most residents of Chroina possessed fine wardrobes.

"I know of only one prisoner fitting that description," Riggs said.

"The messenger." Magnus recalled the injured man who had ridden into Chroina two moons ago. Bilkes. He'd falsely accused Riggs of kidnapping Anya when, in fact, it had been Bilkes who'd attempted to steal her. He'd failed in the attempt, resulting in his shoulder injury when he'd been trampled by horses. Anya had wound up in the hands of King Bantus's trackers and would have become a prisoner of Bantus, like Seona, if Riggs hadn't overcome incredible odds to rescue her.

A member of Breeding First, Bilkes had been part of the conspiracy to usurp the throne and hand it over to Ari. Now, it seemed, he had Seona in his possession. His shoulder injury and the two moons he'd spent in the dungeon were just the beginning. Bilkes would suffer once he was found. He would suffer greatly.

"Guards!" As Riggs's three companions arrived at a run, Magnus dispatched them, one to search the dungeon for Bilkes, one to confirm Seona's absence, and the last to bring Anya to the parlor for interviewing. She was Seona's sister. Perhaps she knew something.

To Riggs, he said, "Search the apartment. We must discover whether they took anything."

"No need to search, Sire," Assaph said, pulling a dressing robe over his nightshirt. "They took my keys and nothing else, then left through the sanctuary door." He motioned toward the door Riggs had forced open.

Keys. Bilkes must have planned to raid the temple strong room. The writings of Danu were kept there, along with priceless symbols of the goddess and offerings made in her honor.

"Assaph, if you are recovered, please gather your most trusted temple servants and inspect the strong room for missing items. When you are finished, please find us in the library."

"Of course, Your Majesty."

A quarter hour later Magnus paced the front room of Glendall's library. Named for his mother, Queen Abigail, the series of rooms contained thousands upon thousands of volumes relating to Marann's history and people. Every trade and academic subject was represented, preserved for what he hoped would be future generations. His knights arrived and confirmed that Seona and Bilkes were both missing.

"Impossible," he said, even though he knew his guards would have double and triple checked before reporting such news. "I greeted Brom and Drustan myself only an hour ago when I left my chamber. They reported not a peep from Seona's chamber all night."

He had always kept the room adjoining his for the ladies with whom he'd attempted to breed over the years. Since Seona had been found, he'd ceased his attempts to breed with other women and made the posh chamber hers and hers alone. His night guard kept watch over the doors to both his chamber and the adjoining one. They would have known if she'd attempted to leave.

"She might have gone through the tunnels." Anya's alto voice met his ear. She stood wringing her hands by the fire. Riggs's big paw rested protectively on her shoulder.

She referred to the secret passage leading from his chamber to a few useful locations throughout Glendall. When he'd wrongly assumed Anya to be his promised lady, she had used the passage to flee a Breeding First attack, but due to her crippled legs, she hadn't succeeded. Fortunately, Danu had been on their side and had led him to find her before she'd come to harm.

To one with intimate knowledge of Glendall, accessing the tunnels from the Orange Blossom chamber was a simple matter of crossing into the king's chamber, lifting a tapestry, and pressing a specific stone. If, in fact, Seona had used the secret route to escape, someone had to have shown it to her. Someone he had trusted. Would these betrayals never cease?

Anya's face, lovely despite the claw-like scars on her cheek, mirrored his worry. She could not bear to lose the sister she'd so recently been reunited with. He could not bear to lose the woman Danu had promised him.

His people could not bear to lose their savior. He would not allow it.

"I'll search the tunnels," Riggs said. Receiving a nod from Magnus, he made haste as he left and nearly collided with an out-of-breath Assaph.

With a temple servant at his heels, the priest came to an abrupt halt. "They took the red gemstone," he wheezed. "The one I blessed in the name of the goddess. It was the only thing missing from the strong room."

Maedoc, the commander of his knights, growled a curse.

The gemstone in question gave the wielder the power to open a portal to any destination desired, even if it happened to lie in another realm. Ari had used it in the name of an evil god by the name of Hyrk to bring the human women over from their realm. Under Danu's blessing, it had hastened the rescue of those same women from King Bantus's dungeon in Larna.

A sharp intake of breath made him look at Anya. She paled before his eyes. "She means to return home."

Magnus's blood chilled in his veins. His promised lady had not only declined his offer of safety and luxury, but she had run away from it. She had run away from him. Unfortunately for Seona, he had no intention of letting her go.

12

from it. She had run away from him. Unfortunately for Seona, he had no intention of letting her go.

Chapter 2

FIRST, ONE DAY had passed without a visit from Hyrk. Then another. Then another.

The span of a mortal moon came and went with no sign of Danu's jailor. This was strange, in and of itself, but even stranger was the stasis of her bars. They hadn't thickened so much as a hair's breadth since she'd last seen him.

This would seem to suggest none of her people had died in that space of time, but that was impossible. Death was a part of life. It was the way of mortality. The way of all things created, her creation especially, since wolfkind's population was now skewed toward the aged.

Perhaps Hyrk had somehow been weakened. If the demigod had come to harm, he might siphon power from this cell for temporary aid.

Or perhaps he planned to keep the cell open enough that he could taunt her eternally, thus depriving her of the one silver lining of being sealed within: freedom from his self-important ramblings. At the moment, she would give a lock of hair for a visit from him. She would bear his vile presence if it meant discovering the reason for the cell's stasis.

Her snort disturbed the silence of the dungeon. Never would she have imagined *desiring* to lay eyes on her enemy.

"There is a first time for everything," she muttered.

"Don't tell me you've begun talking to yourself, love." A male voice rose above the quiet. Not Hyrk's.

Her pulse sped. Only one being in all existence possessed the skill to enter, unseen and unheard, a place as secure as Hyrk's dungeon. "Duff? Is that you?" She squinted past the bars, searching every patch of blackness untouched by torchlight.

"Aye, 'tis me."

She followed his voice with her gaze, not seeing him, of course, but finding the shadow he'd donned as his cloak. He'd chosen a pyramid of darkness at the base of a nearby rock. If the space between the bars weren't so narrow, she might be able to reach through and touch him.

Oh, to touch another! It had been so long since she'd known the silk of another's skin, the warmth of another's life. And Duff wasn't just any other. He was her friend. And former lover.

"How did you come here? Why have you come?" Shock stole her composure. Tears stung the corners of her eyes. "I thought I'd never see you again." Or anyone, for that matter.

He chuckled. "Story of my life, love. No one will ever see me again."

A sound that was half-laugh, half-sob escaped her throat. "You know what I mean. It is—" She had to swallow and begin again. "It is good to hear your voice. It has been so long." So long since she'd heard anything but Hyrk's taunts.

"Likewise, dear goddess." Duff must have heard the longing in her voice, because he said. "Here. Feel my breath."

She pressed her cheek to the bars and forced herself not to recoil from the frigid pulse of Hyrk's power. The sweet wind of Duff's breath made her eyelashes flutter.

A pang of remembrance brought her back to long before her imprisonment, when Duff had warmed her bed. They'd shared good times, but being mere Fae, Duff had known better than to seek anything beyond satisfaction of the flesh with a deity.

Their affair might be long over, but that didn't mean her caring for him had ended. "You should not be here. Get away, before

Hyrk returns." Just because her jailor hadn't shown himself in recent days didn't mean he couldn't appear suddenly. He would show no mercy to a perceived rival.

"Have you forgotten, love? '*He shall abide forevermore in deepest shadow, where no being, mortal or immortal, shall gaze upon his ensnaring beauty ever again.*'" He mimicked the Fae king's imperious tone. Duff had always done well at impersonating others. If he'd been born a mortal, he would no doubt have joined a troupe of entertainers. "Just as you cannot see me, so will Hyrk never see me. I am safe. I vow it."

"He might not *see* you, but he will sense you. If you won't leave for your own wellbeing, do it for mine. He will assume I summoned you, and punish me for it."

Hyrk could not harm her physically, for the cold-iron bars that nulled her power also prevented his from reaching her, but he had other ways of causing her grief. With her imprisoned, there was no one to stop him from manipulating her people with his half-truths and temptations. He tormented her by describing in horrifying detail how some of her people had begun raping and mutilating wolfkind women and, recently, women Hyrk claimed were from a parallel mortal realm, the human realm. She couldn't bear the knowledge of her wolfkind inflicting such suffering. More, she couldn't bear Hyrk's jubilation at such despicable acts.

"Do you really think I would have come if I posed any danger to you? I remember your command well."

Two thousand years ago, Duff had risked a single other visit. It had been the very day she'd fallen victim to Hyrk's scheme and been thrust into this wretched cell. Using rocks from the dungeon floor, she'd shorn off her hair and created from the strands a relic to hold the portion of her power that sustained her people. She'd disguised it as an ordinary amethyst and used glamour to replace the appearance of her hair until it regrew. Tossing the moonstone into a shadow outside her cell, she'd willed it to summon Duff.

The magic had worked, and despite knowing his trespassing might cost him his life, he'd come to her, faithful friend that he was.

"Take it," she'd told him urgently when he'd found the gemstone on the dungeon floor. *"Keep it safe. Should I escape, I'll find you and reclaim it that I might restore myself to my people. If I am to remain here forever—"* She'd pressed on despite darkest despair. *"At least I'll know a piece of me remains free and my people will live on. Hyrk will never be able to rule them as his own. Now go and never return to this place."*

Separated from her people, she had no way of blessing them, not even if she managed to break free from Hyrk's dungeon. She was effectively a demigod and would remain so unless she reclaimed her power from her moonstone. The difference between her relic and Hyrk's was that his *made* him a demigod. It was the source of his power. Its destruction would mean his destruction. Hers held only the portion of the power she'd used to create wolfkind. If destroyed, her relic would return its power to its origin, and she would be a full goddess again, though one locked within a cursed cell.

"How can you be certain Hyrk won't discover you?" she asked Duff.

"Because His Self-proclaimed Darkness has gone missing." Duff snorted at the name Hyrk favored. They both knew Duff was far better suited to the name *Darkness*, having been one with it for so long.

"Missing? How?"

"No one knows for sure, but it might have something to do with your king, Magnus."

The wolfkind realm she'd shaped and breathed life into for her own glory lay utterly beyond her reach. She knew nothing save what Hyrk chose to share with her.

During his visits, Hyrk liked to crow about a tall, pale king he had at his command. *"You should see him, darling. A virile specimen seven feet tall. He bears lupine strength and cunning in measures far beyond your intent, thanks to me. He will show no mercy to those few who still hold you in regard. Pity you won't be privy to the battles to come. But never fear. I shall regale you with the tales. Over and over again, I shall remind you of how your followers fell to my Bantus."*

This Bantus could not be who Duff meant. He'd clearly said Magnus, a name she'd not yet heard, because Hyrk had not mentioned it. "*My* king Magnus?" she asked.

"The most loyal of your followers," he replied. "Since the time of Lachlan, the kings of Marann have kept a temple and priests for your honor. The current king is no exception. You would be well pleased in him, I'd wager."

"I'm through with wagers." A wave of regret crashed over her at the mention of Lachlan, the last ruler of her people she had known. Not only had he been brave and true, but he had fought for her glory even after she'd foolishly made him the object of a wager with Hyrk.

She'd let Lachlan down. She'd let her people down.

Her knees hit the rocky floor, bleeding then healing. She relished the brief sting. "They worship me still, but I cannot hear their prayers. I cannot send them aid or blessings. What a pitiful goddess I am!"

"Whist, love. Enough. No good can come from self-pity. Now listen. I will tell you all."

She scowled at his rebuke, but Duff took no notice. As if they had sat down together for tea, he summarized the last two thousand years in her realm. From Hyrk, she'd learned only those facts that had suited him, but Duff, a stealthy and curious Fae, had observed all, having taken an interest in her realm since he carried her moonstone.

Where Hyrk only told her of his victories, Duff recounted several defeats the demigod had suffered, including the most recent. It seemed the battle Hyrk had anticipated during his last visit had never come about. Once again, according to Duff, her enemy's attempts at evil had been thwarted by Lachlan's descendants, including this Magnus her friend told her of.

Duff's lilt took on a teasing tone as he described King Magnus's physical attributes. "He stands a head taller than most males and has the lean build of a stealthy hunter. His skill at spearing prey is matched by his prowess on the battlefield. Did I mention he is a young king? His predecessor sired him late in life and went to your breast while Magnus was barely more than a— what do your wolfkind call their young?—a pup?"

Her bosom swelled with pride to know this king honored her and ruled justly. But as Duff described his physical characteristics, a stirring of something other than pride caused warmth in her stomach. She hadn't felt anything like it since before her imprisonment. The unsettling sensation grew the more Duff talked.

"Even though he has ruled for half a century, he is still in his prime. Silver streaks his temples, but his royal crown sits upon a head of hair as golden as a lion's mane. They call him the Lion King for his resemblance to the wild beasts from the southern climes. Rumor has it he's every bit as skilled at bedsport as he is at hunting and skirmishing. Seems he's given his seed to every remaining woman of childbearing age in an attempt to gain an heir, and none have found his attentions lacking."

Duff's words had her imagining a golden-haired wolfkind male rutting female after female. The warmth inside her grew to a tingle of carnal awareness. She pictured him training every ounce of power in his well-formed muscles on the primal thrust of his cock into willing wetness.

Longing made her fists clench. How she missed the basest and most rapturous dance of life! "Enough about this king," she said more sharply than she'd intended. "Tell me about Hyrk. What happened to him? Where did he go?"

"No one knows where he is, only that he must be lurking in a mortal realm since no immortal has heard a whisper from him. What I do know is that he had two of your wolfkind at his beck and call, both men of power. Ari was second in command to your King Magnus. The other was—"

"Let me guess," she interrupted. "Bantus." The king who found pleasure in the pain of women.

"Aye." Duff sounded surprised. "How did you know?"

"Hyrk likes to boast."

"Ah. Of course. He likely left out the part where your Magnus defeated Bantus's army in a war twenty years past and had every last female removed from Larna's borders."

Danu found herself liking this Magnus more and more. "You are correct. He did not regale me with this tale of his defeat." She stored the information away for next time Hyrk taunted her.

"Unfortunately," Duff said darkly, "Once Hyrk finished licking his wounds, he resumed his wickedness. He taught his followers how to replace the women Magnus took from them. Using his relic."

She gasped. "He wouldn't!"

It violated the Sacred Way of All Things to allow mortals access to a relic, like the one she'd created to keep her power. Like the one that gave demigods like Hyrk their power. Even demigods were far too powerful for mortal comprehension. In the wrong hands, a relic could destroy an entire realm. She dared not even imagine what could happen if a mortal got hold of her relic, bestowed with the power of a full goddess.

"Oh, he would, and he did," Duff assured her. "Hyrk's followers used his relic to steal women from the human realm. Twelve of them."

The ones Hyrk had crowed about. "Those poor creatures."

She had never troubled herself over the affairs of humans, having dismissed the ancient race long ago for their short lives and fragile health compared to her wolfkind. Nevertheless, hearing about their suffering sickened her just as much as when Hyrk had described the abuse of wolfkind women.

"Do not worry for them, love," Duff said gently. "Your Magnus rescued them in another victorious battle, a recent one at that. The human women are safe, at least for now. Though I would not put it past His Sniveling Shite-Licker to fix his target on them if given half the chance."

"Why would he seek to harm the human women? Why not take revenge on Magnus for his victories?"

"Oh, he hates Magnus. You can be certain of that. But he hates the human women nearly as much. You see, it was a human woman who slew his servant Bantus. Her interference gave Magnus the advantage and cost Hyrk his relic. And a human woman is said to have appeared to Magnus in a vision as the mother of his future heir. Wherever Hyrk is, I'd wager he's plotting to reclaim his relic and prevent this vision from unfolding."

She waved away the notion of a vision, knowing she had not granted one since before her imprisonment. Even if she'd wanted to, the bars made such a thing impossible. What concerned her more was the mention of her enemy's relic.

"So. Hyrk is without his relic." She tapped her chin. "That would make him next to powerless." It also explained the stasis of the bars. He was surely diverting power from her cell for sustenance until he secured new followers. She sniffed. "That's what he gets for entrusting the source of his power to mortals. The fool."

"Yes, well—" Duff cleared his throat. "Not only does your Magnus have Hyrk's relic in his possession, but he had it blessed by the priest who serves your temple. *That* is why Hyrk has gone into hiding. Not only has he lost his most faithful followers, but he has been cut off from his source of power. Even if he manages to get his hands on his relic, it won't work for him unless he can find a mortal to put faith in him."

If not for the evidence surrounding her, she would find Duff's news too good to be true. One thing didn't fit, though. "My priest would have no power with which to bless Hyrk's relic. I am captive." She motioned around herself. Being Fae, Duff ought to know the properties of cold-iron. "What you suggest is impossible."

"Is it?" Duff sounded smug. "Have you considered the possibility of your power moving in the mortal realm and working your will even without your active participation?"

"Of course not. What power I have left cannot pass through the bars." Was Duff acting dense simply to annoy her?

"Have you forgotten our last visit?" Duff said. "Hyrk is not the only one with a powerful relic in the mortal realm."

She stilled. Even the breath in her lungs froze in time. Not a molecule shivered in or around her. "Tell me you have not lost my moonstone." Her voice reverberated with a trace of power. Though faint, it was enough to make the bars hum. The relic contained a portion of her very soul, the portion that sustained her people. Any mortal seeking to use it in her name, even for good, could unleash unprecedented destruction on their realm.

"Easy, love. I have not lost it."

She began to relax.

"I gave it away."

Chapter 3

DREAD CLOAKED MAGNUS as his stallion galloped after his finest tracking wolves. He had taken every conceivable precaution to protect Seona from outside threats. He'd never imagined she would pose a danger to *herself* by fleeing Glendall. Why *would* he imagine such a thing? Women prized safety and comfort. What could be safer or more comfortable than the king's palace?

"She means to return home." Anya's words repeated in his memory.

Apparently, she'd wanted it badly enough to ally herself with a felon and betray all Magnus had offered her. If any harm befell her, the fault would be his. He should have taken precautions to prevent this.

He would discover how Seona had stolen out of Glendall with Bilkes, but first he would find her and cure her of the faulty notion that anyone could be trusted with her wellbeing above him, certainly not the very criminal who had attempted to kidnap Anya.

A hair-raising howl sliced through the mist. Newell, the swiftest and strongest of his tracking wolves, had picked up Seona's trail.

"Hi-yah!" He twitched the reins and flattened himself along Taranis's mane as the stallion streaked through the royal hunting grounds. Dense steam billowed from his snout, hot breath colliding with wintery air. Behind him, the pounding of hooves meant the two knights who had mounted up with him kept pace. The rest of

his knights were organizing multiple search parties and scouring the royal city for any trace of Seona and Bilkes.

He no longer believed Seona to be in the royal city. If she were, his tracking wolves wouldn't have led him beyond the wall. What he couldn't guess at was why she had fled with the gemstone instead of using it immediately upon obtaining it. Her goal was to return to her human realm, but the trail he followed proved she was still among them. She hadn't used the stone yet. But she could at any time.

Perhaps she didn't know how it worked. But she was with Bilkes, and he would know the stone's secrets. At least, he would have observed Ari using its magic in his attempt to usurp Magnus's throne. Many members of Breeding First had witnessed Ari using the stone, and, like Seona's escape, it had happened beneath Magnus's nose.

His fury had spread through Glendall like wildfire. While he could not countenance putting the plotters to death with the population so low, he'd seen them imprisoned for their crimes. They would not see the light of day again. But Bilkes had been captive with them, and he'd managed to escape.

Magnus *would* find Bilkes, and if he had harmed Seona in any way, Magnus would make an exception to his stay of the death penalty.

He followed the call of his wolves, urging Taranis up the gravel-strewn slope leading to Lachlan's Promontory. The stallion knew the ground well, the landmark a familiar meeting place for Magnus and those he invited to hunt with him.

As Taranis carried him nearer the promontory, the mist broke. Cool sunshine kissed away the frost on the ground. They were a full morning of hard riding from Glendall. The safety of Chroina's walls had fallen away an hour ago. To have come this far in so short a time, Seona and Bilkes must have secured horses. Which would have required planning and help.

By the moon, if he had to interview every servant in his keep once Seona was found, he would discover how Bilkes had stolen away with her. He would ensure nothing like this ever happened again, even if he had to keep Seona with him at all times, her hatred of him be damned.

As the cleft of the canyon came into view, another wolf call rose on the air. Newell's victory call. His tracking wolves had Seona circled.

Commanded to isolate and protect the quarry whose scent they followed—in this case Seona's—the wolves would attempt to separate her from Bilkes. The only reason they would stand down and await further instruction was if Bilkes posed a threat to her. As Taranis rounded the final switchback before the promontory, Magnus witnessed that exact scenario.

Named for Magnus's ancestor, an ancient King of Eire, Lachlan's Promontory was a flat, triangular rock jutting over a canyon. Normally, he stopped to rest and pray here before descending into the canyon to hunt sweet mountain goat or a rare lynx, but today, Bilkes occupied the rock, and in his grip was the rarest prize of all: Seona.

Bilkes stood with his back to the ledge, feet planted for battle. Struggling against his arm across her throat was the small human. The sight of her frightened eyes roused a surge of protectiveness. She had betrayed him, but that did not alter his duty, which was to protect her and return her to Glendall at any cost. Whether she wished him to do so was irrelevant. His people needed her.

He nudged Taranis forward to where gravel gave way to table-flat rock. Another few steps, and he'd be near enough to swing his sword and remove Bilkes's head. If Seona were not in the way.

"That's close enough," Bilkes said, his voice dripping with an unfamiliar accent. "Close enough for you to see the fear in her eyes and to understand that I hold over her the power of life and death."

A small movement of Bilkes's arm made Seona's face redden. She struggled for breath.

Magnus had heard Bilkes's voice twice before, once when he'd falsely reported Riggs as Anya's kidnapper and again at his trial, which had occurred only the week before. The voice he used now was not what Magnus remembered. Further off-putting was the way the man no longer appeared disabled from the trampling injury he'd sustained two moons ago. Rather, he easily overpowered Seona as if he had full use of both arms. A closer look explained how such strength was possible.

Clutched in the dirt-streaked hand near Seona's throat was the stolen gemstone, and glowing from Bilkes's eyes was the red light of demonic power.

Understanding cut through him like a sheet of ice. This was the voice of the god Ari had chosen to serve, the one he'd betrayed Magnus for. This was the god whose power had imbued the gemstone before his priest had blessed it in Danu's name. Hyrk. Could he have power over the stone again now that he possessed it?

Danu, help us.

So this was where the evil deity had gone after his most loyal followers, Bantus and Ari, had fallen. He had been lurking under Magnus's very nose inside the body of a prisoner. Now, Hyrk could create a doorway to anywhere at any moment and take Seona from him forever.

Magnus must tread carefully. "Release her!" he commanded, but as he did so, he backed Taranis a step.

The distance did not encourage the imposter to loosen his hold.

Magnus's wolves waited in a semicircle around the pair. Despite their raised hackles, they would make no move unless Magnus commanded it. Unfortunately, Seona was in too precarious a position to risk setting the wolves on Hyrk. He was betting Hyrk knew it as well.

"You lied!" Seona choked out, her lilting brogue so much like Anya's. "You vowed the stone would send me home! You vowed to escort and protect me! I trusted you!"

Hyrk clucked his tongue. "Females are so simple to deceive, are they not? So easy to manipulate." He leveled his chilling red gaze on Magnus. "You know who I am. I see hatred in your eyes."

"I know who you are," he confirmed. "You are the one who deceived my cousin. You sanctioned the kidnapping and torture of many women." Despite knowing the name of this god, his priest had been able to uncover next to nothing about him. All they knew was that this vile being had brokered a deal between Bantus and Ari. Ari provided human women to Bantus using the gemstone in exchange for the use of Larna's army in overthrowing Magnus. "You sought my destruction, but Danu gave us strength to prevail. Now, it is *you* who shall be destroyed. Release her!" His command echoed in the canyon. Somewhere nearby, a hawk screeched and took flight.

A chuckle seeped from Hyrk's sneering lips. "How quaint that you think your goddess has any power to aid you. It is *I* you ought pray to. It is *I* who shall soon rule your entire world. And your precious Danu shall be my servant for all time."

Rage filled him to hear this blasphemy. "Speak ill of my goddess at your peril, demon! Release the woman!" His hands shook with the need to end this miserable being.

"You mean this *thing*?" He shook Seona, making her whimper. "I think not. She has yet to fulfill her purpose."

"Her purpose is no concern of—"

"I shall be the one to speak." Hyrk interrupted him, all mirth gone from his countenance. "You shall be the one to listen."

No one dared interrupt Magnus, but he had never spoken face to face with a deity before. He tightened his grip on his sword. "Say what you must. Then give her to me. She is mine."

"No!" The protest came from Seona. She coughed and sputtered, "—rather die than be yours." Her words sliced through his pride. She yet despised him, even though he attempted to rescue her.

Behind him, the scraping of hooves on gravel meant his two guards restlessly awaited instruction.

Hyrk appeared unhurried. "Fear not," he said to Seona. "He will never touch you."

The nail in the coffin of his pride was the relieved drop of Seona's shoulders despite the reddening of her face as Hyrk's grip slowly suffocated her. She truly preferred the abusive captivity of this beast to *him*.

From the satisfied glint in Hyrk's eyes, he knew just how deeply Seona's reaction had cut. But he gave Magnus no time to dwell on it. "I've been meaning to have words with you, *oh King*." Mockery dripped like boiling honey over the title. "One moon ago, I held in thrall two powerful men." He referred to Ari and Bantus. "Thanks to your interference, both are gone. Do you know what happens to mortals who stand in my way?"

Magnus refused to answer. Seona was in danger, and he had to do something. Quickly. But his hands were tied. Any action he took to save her would be too slow. Hyrk could transport them out of his reach or worse, snap Seona's neck. "What do you want for her?" His only hope was to bargain with Hyrk.

"What do I want? What do I want?" The prisoner's lips peeled back with Hyrk's cackling laughter. Seona's tiny fingers dug furrows into the arm choking her. Her face purpled.

Hyrk seemed not to notice. He threw back his head and laughed even harder before sobering in an instant. All mirth dropped from his face as he locked gazes with Magnus. "What I want," he said clearly. "Is for you to suffer."

Quick as a flash, he spun around like a man throwing a disc. His cape flared in a tattered arc. When the fabric settled, the view beyond it gouged panic through Magnus's chest.

At the tips of Bilkes's outstretched fingers, Seona went over the ledge. The shock in her eyes and the swell of her hair as she fell out of sight were the last things Magnus saw before rage propelled him off Taranis's back, dagger drawn.

§

"YOU WHAT?" THE bars shook with Danu's bellow. Her chest heaved with indignation. Power whirled around her, stirred up like silt at the bottom of a loch.

Duff went on, unperturbed. "I said, I gave it away. If you'd like to calm yourself and listen, I shall explain."

Her power crackled and spun. Her hair swirled upward as if caught in a stiff wind. But the bars contained her fury.

How intolerable it was being shackled thus! Her power longed to break free. She wished with all her being to lay hands on her moonstone and return to her people.

If only she hadn't failed her people! Failed her father, who had trusted her with the power of Creation! He had given her the greatest imaginable gift, and what had she done with it? She'd made a beautiful realm filled with beautiful mortals only to allow all that beauty to fall into the hands of evil incarnate.

She would give anything, *do* anything, to repair what her foolishness had wrought.

A rush of wind assaulted her out of nowhere. It sucked the breath from her throat before she could unleash the tirade she had ready for Duff.

With no warning, the chaos of screaming air filled her ears. Daylight assaulted her eyes. Turbulence like clawing hands ripped at her clothing.

She was falling.

Instinct had her thrusting out her power to halt her descent, but her power didn't come.

Panic gripped her like the talons of a dragon.

A collision sent shock waves through her body. Bones shattered. Pain sluiced her from her toes to the tip of each hair on her head.

She'd landed in a heap, her body crumpled. She stared at a hand that looked like her own but not. Though its position was unnatural, she somehow knew it was attached to her broken body. In its death grip was a red gemstone she recognized in an instant. Hyrk's relic.

It was the last thing she saw before blackness claimed her.

Chapter 4

SHOCK DOUSED MAGNUS like icy loch water. Numb to all but rage, he charged his target. Mindful of the cliff, he dug his fingers into Hyrk and threw him to the ground.

In a heartbeat, Magnus was on top of him, hands locked around the throat of what used to be one of his subjects.

Hyrk put up no fight. His attention was on the cliff. "That bitch! She stole my relic!" He writhed and scrabbled for the edge of Lachlan's Promontory, like he would throw himself over to retrieve his gemstone.

Magnus could care less about that hideous stone. He cared only about vengeance. A fall to his death was too good for the murdering bastard.

"You killed her!" He poured every ounce of his strength into squeezing the life from his foe. "She was to be our salvation!"

The former messenger's face reddened, like Seona's had mere moments ago.

Hyrk's eyes bulged, and he finally shifted his focus to Magnus, as if he'd just realized the vessel he had possessed was dying.

Overhead, a hawk screeched. Its shadow passed over them.

Hyrk's mouth curved in a sickening grin. Magnus's efforts should have made it impossible for Hyrk to speak, but apparently, the normal way of things did not apply. Bilkes's mouth said, "You'll all die now. Your supposed vision will never come to pass. And once the last of you is gone, your precious Danu will be locked in my dungeon for all eternity." Spittle flew into the air with his taunts.

"Go to hell, Hyrk!" Magnus squeezed with all his might and felt something crack inside Bilkes's neck.

Vaguely, Magnus was aware of his guards surrounding him and of his wolves circling. He could have let either finish Hyrk for him, but he would not be deprived. Black satisfaction filled him as he squeezed the life from a wicked deity. The enemy of Danu. The enemy of wolfkind.

But what about Bilkes, whispered his conscience. The messenger had betrayed the crown and broken many laws, but had taken no life that Magnus knew of. He didn't deserve a death sentence.

Magnus released his grip as if he'd been burned. The feeling of Bilkes's windpipe collapsing was a memory on the skin of his palms. There would be no washing it off. He had acted rashly, and the messenger paid the ultimate price.

Bilkes should be dead, but Hyrk continued to taunt. "Foolish, sentimental mortal. You are a weak race. But not for long. I will have my way in the end." He fixed his gaze on the hawk circling the canyon. Then the blood-red light went out of Bilkes's eyes.

Cackling laughter echoed off the rocky walls. That awful sound had not come from Bilkes's body but seemed to ride on the air all around them. The hawk swooped out of sight, seeming to chase the laughter.

Bilkes, at last, lay still. His eyes, back to their color of the harvest moon, stared into the sky.

Woodenly, Magnus sat back on his heels. Regret crushed him. He'd lost Seona and taken out his fury on one not ultimately responsible for her death. "What have I done?"

"We both saw, Sire," said Cadeyrn, one of his knights. "He killed your promised lady." The knight's face reflected Magnus's grief. But there was something more. An acknowledgment of what they'd just witnessed: a deity possessing one of their kind. "You did what had to be done."

Perhaps. Perhaps Bilkes had been dead from the moment Hyrk had taken him. *Dearest Danu, take his soul to your breast. Forgive me.*

He got to his feet and half-heartedly praised his wolves for their work.

"There's still Lady Anya," Cadeyrn said. "And her babe."

He shut his eyes against a wave of jealousy. As much as he celebrated with Riggs and Anya, he wished it could be his offspring, his heir, to be the first child born to their people in eleven years. Still. Cadeyrn's words brought a faint ray of consolation. He nodded his acknowledgement, throat too tight to form words.

Speaking of Anya and her mate—Magnus scanned the shelf of rock. "Where is Riggs?" He and Cadeyrn had given chase with Magnus. Riggs's horse stood ground tied beside Cadeyrn's, but the man himself was nowhere to be seen.

"He's gone down into the canyon." Cadeyrn frowned and averted his gaze. He didn't have to voice the reason. Riggs had gone to retrieve Seona's body.

Magnus should weep for her loss. His heart should be broken. All he felt was heavy despair for his people. And for Anya, who just one moon ago had rejoiced at finding the sister she'd thought lost forever. They knew now why Seona had gone missing. Ari had used Hyrk's relic to invade the human realm and lure females to Bantus's dungeon. Seona, Magnus had learned from Anya, had been the first. Of all the human women rescued from Larna, Seona had suffered the longest.

May she find peace at your breast, he prayed, gazing out at the canyon. Countless shades of gray and lavender striped the rock on the far side. Yellow moss grew in places where water trickled down to the river below. A treasured hunting spot, the canyon had provided game for generations of Marann's kings. How cruel that the source of such beauty and provision could be so deadly.

Distantly, he heard shouts and the clatter of hooves on rock. More of his men were on their way.

He toed off his doeskin shoes. "When the others arrive, help them build a litter. I'll bring her up with Riggs."

Cadeyrn nodded solemnly. "Yes, Sire."

He'd made the descent countless times, first as his father's quiverman, then as a hunter in his own right. Always before, he'd navigated the narrow ledges and outcroppings with anticipation. Each handhold and foothold led the way to the sweet meat and luxurious pelts waiting below. Only a careful, patient climber could descend safely, and only a skilled hunter could fell the beasts that prowled the riverbanks and caves below.

On today's descent, there was no anticipation. No excitement. He felt only regret.

He'd let this happen. He hadn't protected Seona well enough. Perhaps if he'd loved her the way he was supposed to, she would still be alive.

"—Rather die than be yours."

Her words had been too quiet to echo in the canyon, but they echoed in his mind. She'd gotten her wish. Poor lady.

She'd experienced such pain in the past year. The horrors she'd endured had blinded her to the honor that awaited her as his queen. Danu would soothe her pain now.

And I will bear mine with dignity and courage.

He must not lose hope. He must not let his people lose hope. They would scrutinize him in the days to come. How he responded to Seona's death would set the tone for all Marann. If he let them see his despair, they would despair.

He would have to make a decree. There would be a service to celebrate Seona's life and to bid her safety on her journey to Danu's Breast.

As his soles met the bed of the canyon, he spotted Riggs's dark head. The knight was picking his way through dormant pitberry shrubs toward where Lachlan's Promontory cast its shadow.

He followed the trail his knight had made. His stomach turned in on itself at the thought of the terror Seona must have known in her final moments. Her body might very well be broken beyond recognition. Anya was going to be grief-stricken.

Up ahead, Riggs shouted, and a hawk took flight from the bushes. The knight's head dipped from view, signifying he'd found Seona. The hawk had found her first and thought to make a meal of her. Danu bless Riggs for chasing it away.

With every step toward his fallen lady, his feet felt like blocks of stone. At last, he rounded a thicket and saw what had become of lovely Seona.

Blood soaked the ground beneath her head. Tangles of hair lay across her face, part of which was collapsed. Her arms and legs jutted at impossible angles, her pelvis obviously crushed. The evergreen nightgown had torn along the side, partially exposing one of her pale, hairless breasts.

He fell to his knees beside his knight and righted her nightgown before lifting his gaze to the mocking blue sky.

Doubt crept in where only thoughts of Seona should be. Fifty years ago, Danu had given him hope in the form of a vision, but Seona had never stirred his heart the way she had when he'd dreamt of her. Now she was dead. Clearly, she was not to be his queen. The dream vision he'd received from Danu had been wrong.

Are you listening? He asked the goddess in his heart. *Are you watching? Do you care for us at all?*

A feeling of sharp betrayal cut into him, more wicked by far than the pain Seona's rejection had caused. Danu had created them only to abandon them. He had loved the goddess his whole life, but she had no love for him. Perhaps she had never even noticed him.

He bent over Seona's broken body. The amethyst gemstone he'd planned to give her, the one Anya had given him and that he'd named the Translation Stone, slipped from the collar of his tunic. The bejeweled chain hung from his neck, dangling between his heart and the one he'd needed so desperately to win.

"I am so sorry," he told her. She deserved great honor, but she had gotten death. It was his fault. If he'd sent the human women home, and her with them, she would be alive now. "I do not deserve your forgiveness. But I am sorry, sweet lady."

A single tear slid down his cheek and landed on the gemstone. It glistened like a liquid star before plummeting from the stone and landing with a splash on Seona's cheek. Directly over the purple paw print Bantus had branded into her.

Her cheek moved.

Flesh that had been sunken with injury filled out. Delicate facial bones that had been broken fit back into place like a puzzle solving itself. The changes spread from the place where his tear had landed over her entire body.

Her arms righted themselves. A loud snap came from her pelvis as it expanded to its normal shape.

An instinct to jump back from whatever unnatural thing was happening warred with his fascination.

"Sire?" Riggs said. "What's—by the moon, she's—" His knight sounded as mystified as he felt.

Seona was a broken doll, and unseen hands were mending her.

Her legs straightened. Her chest rounded. Her lips parted, and with a sound like a bellows, her lungs filled with air.

"By Danu." If Riggs weren't with him, Magnus would wonder if he'd gone mad. "Are you seeing this?" he asked.

"Yeah." A shaky breath came from his knight. "Is she—alive?"

Blood still soaked the ground around her halo of silky walnut hair. Her nightgown was still torn. Otherwise, she looked completely hale. She might be a woman asleep in her bed.

He cupped her face carefully—oh so carefully, and he felt warmth. Passing his thumb over her lips, he felt breath.

"She lives."

§

ONE MOMENT, DUFF had been preparing to explain to an irate goddess how her relic had ended up in the hands of a mortal. The next, he watched through the bars as her fury ruptured with a hair curling scream.

Danu's shriek echoed off the dungeon walls as she flung her arms out. She flailed as if she were on fire.

Duff shot to his feet. Only the curse kept him from breaking free from the darkness and rushing to her aid. "What is it? What's happened?"

Danu fell to her hands and knees, gasping for breath. Panic made wild moons of her eyes.

"What is it, love? Is it Hyrk? Is he coming?" He swept the dungeon with the senses he'd honed for millennia, detecting nothing out of the ordinary—except for the fact that Danu was suddenly deathly afraid.

"Wha—what's happened? What is this place? Did you say Hyrk? Who the bloody hell is he?" Danu seemed to have forgotten where she was and who had put her here. And her voice had taken on a decidedly Scots affectation. Interesting.

"You're in a dungeon, my dear, locked within a cursed cell. I did indeed say Hyrk, for that is the name of your jailor." While he spoke, he scrutinized her reaction, a narrowing of her eyes as she peered toward him, seeing nothing but the shadow that chained him. It was the look of prey assessing the capabilities of a predator.

Whoever this woman was, she was not his friend and former lover. Of that he was certain. But the body the woman inhabited most definitely belonged to Danu. He knew that body well.

He began to suspect Danu's moonstone had worked some mischief. And mischief was one thing no Fae could resist.

"Is this hell?" the woman asked. "Is Hyrk the Devil? Does he imprison everyone he murders?"

What intriguing questions! "This is not 'hell,' love." He recalled the word as one of the names mortals had given to the low realm. "But you're not far off. Tell me the last thing you remember." If his suspicion was correct, this woman's memory might help him confirm where Danu had gone.

"I was falling," the woman said. "That bloody bastard Hyrk threw me over a cliff, but I thought he was someone else. He deceived me, that good-for-nothing, lying wolf man. None of them are to be trusted. Not a single one." The venom in her speech would flay the skin off a lesser man.

Her accent and her mistrust of wolfmen strengthened his suspicion. There were but a handful of women with this accent who were privy to the existence of wolfkind, one of whom he'd had the pleasure of meeting. This one reminded him of that one. Strongly. "What name are you called by, lass?"

His memory supplied the name at the exact moment she spoke it. "Seona."

She was Anya's sister, the one he had helped Anya search for all over the Highlands while she was in his care. It seemed the magic that favored him was at it again. But what broken circle did the magic seek to repair this time? Wouldn't separating Seona from King Magnus have the opposite effect? Seona was meant to save the wolfkind people, to be Magnus's mate, was she not?

If Seona was here in the body of Danu, that had to mean Danu was now in the body of the mortal. Wait. Had Seona said Hyrk threw her over a cliff? Worry for Danu strung him tight. It would take more to end a goddess than a fall from a great height. But if she was in a mortal's body…

He must learn more. Something magical was afoot, and he demanded more than a spectator's role.

"Tell me everything, love. If I am to help, I must know all you know." Like where Hyrk was and whether Danu might be in danger from him.

Seona scoffed. "Help, indeed. No man offers aid to a lass without taking somat in return."

Such a jaded view of males, not unlike the views of her sister. Except in his dealings with Anya, he'd never experienced an urge to prove her notions of men faulty.

For some reason, he longed to show Seona that goodness and maleness could coexist. True, he intended to help himself—he was Fae after all, but he was determined to help Seona as well, whether she wanted his help or not.

"Astute of you, my dear. What will you give me if I vow to free you from this place?" She expected him to bargain with her. He would not disappoint.

"Have you a key to this cell? You said Hyrk was my jailor." Her tone dripped with suspicion.

"Unfortunately, this is not the sort of cell that can be opened with a key." He doubted it could be opened at all, since Hyrk had formed it from his power. The fact it remained standing meant that wherever Hyrk was, he still possessed power enough to hold a goddess captive. But perhaps there was another way, if one was clever enough to find it.

"Then how do you propose to aid me?"

He'd given the subject much thought in the centuries since Danu had been imprisoned. "There may be a way to free you, but you must tell me everything you can recall about Hyrk."

Seona's sigh of acquiescence was a pleasant sound in his ear. "Very well, but there isna bloody much to tell. I only heard his name moments before I came to this place."

Duff would be willing to wager she knew more about Hyrk than she suspected. She'd lived as a captive in Bantus's dungeon, and Bantus had been Hyrk's most loyal follower. And, apparently, she'd been within striking distance of the shite, though it seemed she'd thought he was someone else, a wolfkind male.

"Begin with your rescue from Saroc. King Magnus would have placed his most trusted guards around you. How is it you wound up with Hyrk?" If he learned how Hyrk had infiltrated Magnus's keep, he might be able to find the bastard before he could harm Danu or her people. "But first, you must agree to what I desire." No Fae worth his immortality offered help without securing something for himself in the process.

"What is it ye desire?" she asked, resigned. This was a woman who had bargained much in her life, but whom he suspected had rarely come out on top.

"Why, your hand in marriage, of course."

Chapter 5

MAGNUS'S HEART BANGED in his throat as he crouched at Seona's side. His breath came in heaving bursts, but he forced himself to stillness long enough to assure himself of the rise and fall of her chest.

She had been dead. And now she lived.

"It's a miracle." Riggs gave voice to the conclusion Magnus had formed. Clearly, he had been wrong. The goddess had not forgotten them. Nothing but divine intervention could explain what they'd just witnessed.

"Danu be praised," Magnus said, a tremor in his voice. Wonder coursed through his veins.

"Danu be praised," Riggs echoed.

Magnus couldn't tear his gaze from Seona. Never before had he been granted an opportunity to view her so closely while her face was peaceful. Between Anya's fierce protectiveness and Seona's hatred of him, he'd developed an impression of cold, untouchable beauty where she was concerned.

His days were filled with duties that kept him from dwelling on his lukewarm interest in the human, but during his oft sleepless nights, worry chased him in endless circles. A sense of wrongness hung over him like a storm cloud. He did not feel the way he was supposed to feel toward Seona.

In the vision Danu had blessed him with the night of his coronation, he'd experienced an overwhelming flood of adoration for her. The child she'd held in her arms meant salvation for his people, but even in his dream, he'd understood that a barren womb would not have decreased the measure of his love for her. It was *her* he loved. Her essence. Her moonsoul.

Nothing like that had come upon him when Seona had been discovered in Bantus's dungeon with the other human women. He'd felt no differently for her than for any of the others. It was only due to the vision that he'd treated her any differently, cosseting her in the chamber beside his while the others recovered from their captivity among the wolfkind women in the *Fiona Blath.*

For fifty years, he had anticipated an incomparable love for the woman in his vision. For fifty years, he had planned for her arrival. For fifty years, he had longed to finally hold her in his arms, to join with her in the tradition of old and make her not only his pledgemate and queen, but his lifemate. Together, they would restore the sacred, ancient tradition, done away with when women became too scarce for a man to have one all to himself. For the first time in centuries, one man and one woman would pledge their moonsouls to one another while joining in body beneath the full moon. Danu would bless their union, sealing their moonsouls together for eternity. He and Seona would be celebrated far and wide, bringing hope to their people. When she grew with his child, that hope would be strengthened. Through them, wolfkind would be saved.

That was how it was supposed to have gone.

Instead, since the discovery of the human women, Magnus had despaired at his failure to love Seona the way he ought to. He'd despaired at her hatred of him. How would they bring new life to the world when she could not even bear the sight of him? When she demanded each and every day to be allowed to return to her native realm?

As he bent over her on the canyon floor, something changed. He drank in the miracle of her renewed life and something moved inside his chest.

His feelings for her had been like a polished boulder resting in a basin. The visible face held no markings of note, only a duty-filled affection, no more or less remarkable than what he felt toward the other women in his care. But as he marveled at her in the wake of her rebirth, it was like a pair of massive hands rotated the boulder to reveal hidden treasures set into the stone. Diamonds, gold, silver, and gems of every color sparkled to life inside him. He was suddenly awakened to a precious bounty he'd not noticed before.

Her parted lips released puff after puff of steam into the cold air.

He yanked off his cloak and flung it over her for warmth. Then he searched her form with careful hands, looking for non-obvious injuries. He would not take this miracle for granted.

Gentle squeezing of her arms and legs produced no movement of the bones where there shouldn't be. Pressing fingertips along the back of her neck and what he could reach of her spine, he found no obvious deformities. He would have his physician inspect her when they returned to Glendall, but, incredibly, she showed no sign of damage. Not even a bump on her head where blood matted her hair to her completely healed scalp.

"How will we get her up?" Riggs asked. Palming the back of his neck, the knight squinted up the canyon wall. "Shall I make a litter?"

Magnus shook his head. The thought of trusting her wellbeing to sticks and twine left a bitter taste on his tongue. "I'll carry her."

Riggs ventured a step closer. Magnus didn't blame him for keeping a small distance. What they had witnessed had been jarring. Magnus would never forget it as long as he lived. He would never forget that he had doubted his goddess only to have her prove her faithfulness in the most powerful of ways.

"How will you climb and keep her safe?" His knight's brow furrowed with doubt.

Magnus grinned as he lifted her into his arms, the most precious bundle imaginable, more precious than all the game he'd brought up since his youth put together. "Have a little faith," he said. Cradling her to him, he led the way to a hidden, gentler path a furlong east of where they'd descended.

The ascent ate up the rest of the morning. By the time Magnus mounted Taranis with Seona still clutched to his chest, his buoyant mood had faded. At long last, he had discovered the sort of affection for her he had longed to feel, but that did little to soothe the anger building behind his breastbone.

During the return ride to Glendall, his thoughts were plagued with the circumstances that had led them to Lachlan's Promontory. Seona had not only betrayed the safety and luxury he had offered, but she had entrusted her fate to another man. A prisoner and member of the Breeding First rebellion. This lawless rebel was her choice of ally in place of the king who had rescued her?

His arms tightened around her delicate form. Anger gave jagged edges to his protective urge. She'd misplaced her trust and nearly been killed—had been killed, for the love of the moon. He would not stand for any more of this foolishness.

Magnus had honored Anya's request to give Seona time. He'd kept his distance when he'd wanted nothing more than to be close to her in hopes of sparking his dormant affection. No more.

Seona was his, damn the moon. No one would keep him from her again.

§

"I WANT MY OWN realm someday, Papa." Danu tugged on her father's beard, pleased to be on his lap, the focus of his adoring attention.

"Is that right, little one? You know ruling an entire realm is not a simple matter." The warning was gentle, his smile transcendent.

"I know. But I shall study hard and learn everything so I can be a good goddess."

"You already are a good goddess, my precious one." He made her feel so loved. More than anything else in all the realms, she wanted to make him proud. He kissed her head, his beard tickling her ear. "As long as you treasure love, as you do now, I will always be proud of you."

She liked when he understood her thoughts. He was her papa, and he knew her. She liked being known. "I will, Papa. I will treasure love forever and ever."

Wisps of memory taunted Danu.

In one memory, she was a young goddess on her father's lap in his study, which overlooked the sparkling Sea of Realms. In another, she was plunged into darkness and consumed with anger, but couldn't remember what had upset her. In yet another, she was falling and unable to command the air. She searched the milky gray sky above for something to grab onto, finding no handhold, no answers. Her most recent memory was of darkness.

Darkness was familiar. For a very long time, she'd known only darkness and cold.

Why did daylight suddenly push at her closed eyelids? Why did her head ache and her ears ring with noise?

She called forth her power, an act as natural as breathing, to heal what ailed her. Her power did not respond! With more intention, she summoned relief for her pain. Still, it did not come.

Panic fluttered like a wounded bird behind her breastbone. Where was her power? Why was she hurting so?

Despite her discomfort and confusion, she felt oddly safe. Warmth supported her on all sides. *Papa?*

Gentle rocking eased her panic and lured her away from her cares. She might be hurting, but she had an unshakable feeling she was protected. Whatever had transpired before didn't matter. She was safe now, and she was loved. This assurance filled up a dry place in her soul with rushing, cleansing waters.

The illusion lasted a few precious minutes. Then recollection rolled over her like a storm.

Hyrk's dungeon. That was the darkness that had become her world. Duff visiting her. Bringing tidings of her captor's disappearance.

Her moonstone! That trickster had given it away! To a mortal!

"What have you done, you sly mongrel?" Her voice sounded weak. And the tone of it was all wrong. Huskier and lower than it should be.

Her cocoon of warmth tightened. "What have *I* done?" said an authoritative male voice. Not her father's. "If anyone has the right to ask that question, it is I."

She opened her eyes. The brightness of a cornflower blue sky made her wince. Slowly, a bearded face came into focus above her. Hair like flames of gold licked at a strong brow and fierce cheekbones. As the strands shifted in a cool breeze, silver streaks showed at the man's temples. The pleasing bulk of teeth behind the man's lips marked him as wolfkind.

My realm!

Somehow, she had come to be in the mortal realm she had created. But how? Why couldn't she use her power?

As she worked the problem through, her aches and pains took on new meaning. The evidence suggested she was not only among her mortals but that she was *one* of them.

The rocking she felt was the movement of a horse at a brisk walk. She appeared to be a lump of cargo on the rider's lap. Winter-bare trees surrounded them, and a handful of other riders rode ahead and behind.

What a way for a goddess to be transported! She ought to have chariots and trumpets, an army to escort her on streets strewn with flowers. Instead, she got a small contingent of riders making their way through a cold, gray forest. Fitting, perhaps, since she had failed so miserably at being a goddess. And since she appeared to be mortal at the moment.

She glanced over her body. The cloak she was wrapped in made it difficult to ascertain much detail, but breasts made plump mounds beneath the wool. Clearly, she occupied the body of a woman. She ran her tongue over her teeth. They were small and even, like those of her truest form.

Having created her people from the immortal Fae and the mystic wolves she so adored, she'd carefully molded them into a mortal race that reflected her favorite qualities from both. Beauty and long life came from the Fae. Fierce protectiveness and strong community ties came from the mystic wolves. Their physical appearance was, in her opinion, the perfect marriage between grace and power. This body she inhabited did not belong to one of her precious wolfkind. It was too small, for one, and as her legs rubbed together beneath the silky undergarment, she could tell they lacked even the light coat of hair typical of wolfkind females.

Strange, since the only intelligent life in her realm was the life she had created.

Except the humans Duff had mentioned.

His words from what seemed like only moments ago filled her memory. *It was a human woman who slew Hyrk's servant Bantus . . . Another is said to have appeared to Magnus in a vision as the mother of his future heir. Wherever Hyrk is, I'd wager he's plotting to reclaim his relic and prevent this vision from unfolding."*

If Duff's assumption was correct, she might not be the only immortal present in her realm. Hyrk might be here.

Her pulse kicked at the terrifying thought. In this mortal body, she would be easy prey. But wait. According to Duff, Hyrk had lost his followers. And his relic. He would be next to powerless. Depleted of power, he wouldn't be a danger to her, but that didn't mean he wasn't a threat to her realm.

She must learn where he was and what plans he was making, for if she'd learned anything from the last two thousand years, it was that Hyrk never gave up. But thwarting Hyrk would have to wait. First, she must understand her surroundings and work out what in all the realms had happened to her.

She expanded her attention to the regal specimen holding her. With his shoulders pinned back and his chin jutting confidently, his air of command was clear. A man like this could only be a king. Since Hyrk's king, Bantus, was dead, this must be the one Duff had told her about.

My king, she thought, recalling her friend's teasing. "Magnus." It came out as a whisper.

Piercing, gold eyes narrowed on her. "Which is it, Lady Seona? *Sly mongrel* or *Magnus?* I admit I prefer the latter."

Lady Seona. He'd just given her the name of the mortal she inhabited. And he had no idea who she really was.

Heavens, if she was here, where had this Seona gone?

Magnus interrupted her thought. "I regret to inform you your coconspirator is dead. You are once more in the care of the man you would rather die than belong to." He ground his teeth. "Thanks to Hyrk, you almost got your wish. But it seems *my* goddess has other plans for you."

My goddess. She felt her eyebrows rise. He truly had no idea he held his goddess in his arms.

Putting the strangeness of that aside, she tried to make sense of all he'd said. It was Hyrk she would rather die than belong to, not Magnus. But, of course, he thought he was speaking to the mortal, Seona. This woman must have hated Magnus to have uttered such words. Odd, since Danu could find nothing displeasing about him. Odder still was his emphasis on *my* goddess. Perhaps Seona had allied herself with Hyrk in some way, thus pitting herself against Magnus. But why would she do so? Hadn't Magnus rescued the human women from Hyrk's Bantus? Then Magnus had said that thanks to Hyrk, Seona had almost gotten her wish—to die rather than belong to Magnus.

Of course! The fall.

Duff had said Hyrk hated Magnus and the human women, since one of them had killed his Bantus. Hyrk must have tried to kill Seona. In fact, the fall should have been fatal, but somehow, she'd survived. And her body was not broken, as it had been when she'd hit the ground. Whose power had healed her? Not hers, because she had no power at the moment.

There was so much she didn't understand. So much she must learn if she was going to stop Hyrk once and for all.

Clenching the muscles in her abdomen, she pulled herself up straighter. "Tell me all that has happened."

Magnus's arms tightened around her. "Easy, Lady. Do not struggle. I know you would prefer death to my touch, but I will not allow it. You'll not flee from me again. I swear it. If I must keep you by my side the rest of my days to prevent your harm, I will do so. You may not be one of my subjects, but make no mistake. You are mine in every way that matters." His voice held no room for compromise. The strength in it thrilled her. The words themselves thrilled her, for no man had ever spoken to her thusly, claiming possession of her.

She should find such a claim repellent, but to the contrary, something feminine and greedy sparked to life within her. Longings that had lain dormant a long, long time began stirring.

She ignored the feelings. This was no time for frivolities. Magnus had mentioned Hyrk. She must learn all that he knew. "Tell me about Hyrk, mortal—Magnus," she corrected, remembering he did not yet know her true identity.

"You think to command a king? In this way, you are like your sister." His mouth twitched in an almost smile. "However, I shall be the one conducting the interview, and I shall wait until we are safe in Glendall."

Glendall. The palace in Chroina. She remembered it from the days of Lachlan.

It rankled to be scolded by a mortal, but she bit her tongue. Keeping her deity a secret might give her an advantage, especially where Hyrk was concerned. Once he caught wind of her escape, he would stop at nothing to find her. What better place to hide than in this human skin?

"Very well," she said. "Will you tell me this? You said 'safe in Glendall.' What danger do we face outside the palace?" Besides Hyrk, what other players were at work in her realm? If she'd been a proper goddess and not fallen into her enemy's hands, she would already know. It was time for her to stop failing her people and begin saving them.

"Too many to count," Magnus said grimly, his gaze sweeping the trail before them. "And the number seems to grow with each new day."

Chapter 6

MAGNUS'S FEELINGS TOWARD Seona were not the only thing that had changed. The woman herself had changed. She no longer curled her lip at him or glared when in his presence. She didn't fight to free herself from his hold. Her hatred of wolfkind had disappeared, or so it seemed. The most dramatic change of all was that she chose to speak. To him. Since her rescue from Bantus's lair, she'd said not a word to anyone save Anya, and even then never in the presence of another.

Perhaps her ordeal with Hyrk had made her see her situation in a new light. Or perhaps she was regrouping and preparing for a new attempt to flee from him. He would get to the bottom of it soon enough. In the meantime, he would not let down his guard.

As his knights escorted him past Chroina's walls and through the city to Glendall, Seona seemed to grow stronger and more alert. Tawny, doe-wide eyes took in the crofter buildings, the shops, the men in the streets, and the five-story *Fiona Blath* that stood on the castle grounds.

This was her first time seeing the city, he realized with a start. Like the other rescued women, she'd been brought directly into Glendall through the magical doorway opened by the red gemstone—Hyrk's gemstone. The other human women had been shown to the *Fiona Blath* soon after their rescuing. They would have at least seen the grounds separating the castle proper from the stately manor where the ladies lived. But Seona had been placed under guard in the Orange Blossom chamber adjoining his. She had not been outside as yet.

If she had asked, he would have allowed it, under guard of course for her protection, but she had not. Or at least, Anya had not passed along such a request to him. Perhaps, once they sorted out that she would not be running from him again, he could escort her on a tour of Chroina. But such pleasures would have to wait. There was much to do in light of Hyrk's attack.

Holding Seona secure with one arm, he dismounted. She made it easy for him by wrapping her arm around his neck. Tingles raced up and down his spine at her touch, but he had no time to dwell on it. Cradling her close, he commanded his guards while stablemen took care of the horses.

"Riggs, Cadeyrn, you shall accompany me and Lady Seona. The rest of you, inspect the dungeon. Find out how Bilkes escaped. Then round up all my knights, and summon my war chieftain. We'll conference in my solar in one hour." He felt Seona's gaze on him and liked being the center of her attention. Perhaps he stood a little taller as he found Daly, his head of household, awaiting instruction at his usual spot by the kitchen door. "Have a bath prepared in the Orange Blossom chamber then summon my physician."

"Right away, Sire." The elderly man raised his brows at the sight of Seona docile in his arms, but his manners were too impeccable for him to comment on it. Daly disappeared into Glendall, and Magnus followed. He strode to his private quarters with the footfalls of his knights in his wake.

It was no surprise to find Anya pacing his solar. As he passed the large, private sitting room, she bolted out and stopped short. Her mouth dropped open—probably because Seona still held on around his neck.

He did not acknowledge her as he continued into the Orange Blossom chamber and laid Seona on the high, elaborate bed.

"What happened? Is that blood on Seo—?" Behind him, Anya's questions were cut off. He heard Riggs quietly assuring her, but his attention was all for the lovely, rebellious miracle before him.

Seona settled into the bed pillows. Her hair cascaded over her shoulders in waves of glossy walnut. Dried blood streaked sections of it but did not mar her beauty. The paw print scar stood out starkly lavender against her porcelain cheek. Her eyes, much like Anya's but lighter in color, fixed on him, inquisitiveness in place of their usual hostility. Despite her torn dressing gown and blood-caked skin, she held her head at a regal angle.

She looks like a queen.

Never before had she so closely resembled the portrait he'd commissioned after his prophetic dream. There was no doubt in his mind she had changed. But how much of it was an act meant to gain his trust until she chose to run again? Her betrayal stung anew.

By Danu, he'd almost lost her. He couldn't bear for something like this to happen a second time. He wouldn't stand for any more of this foolishness.

He paced alongside the bed. "Have I not fed you? Clothed you? Lavished upon you every imaginable luxury?" He motioned at the finery all around them before raking both hands through his hair. "Have I not saved you from that vile cell and the depraved whims of a madman?" His voice broke at the memory of how he'd found her and the other women. Huddled in the filthy dungeon beneath Castle Blackrock, tattered clothes hanging off bony bodies, faces branded with Bantus's paw print marking. Worse was the fear in the eyes of some of them. And the abject nothingness in the eyes of a few, Seona included.

"*Haud* your *wheesht*! I'll not have you raising your voice to my sister!" Anya's voice cracked through the chamber like a whip, but just as quickly, Riggs made apology and whisked her out. No easy task, for Anya was not as fragile as her smaller human body suggested. Magnus would never forget she'd slain four of Bantus's trackers and the king himself two moons ago, all to protect Riggs. Now she would fight to protect her sister.

He would assure her when he was finished here that no one— no one—would keep Seona safer than he would. And not just in body, but in mind. Just as he would not forget Anya's bravery, he would not forget Seona's suffering. Out of respect for all she'd been through, he reined in his temper.

Magnus turned to see the door close, leaving only Cadeyrn inside with them. After calming himself with a few breaths, he faced Seona again. "My apologies—"

But she was not sitting back against the pillows any more. She was on her knees on the bedcovers directly in front of him. The height of the bed put them eye to eye.

Her lower lip slid free from the hold of her small, even teeth.

He stared as the rosy flesh turned even redder after the mild abuse. How beautiful her mouth was. How beautiful *she* was. She needed to put on more weight to be truly healthy, but even malnourished and disheveled from the morning's events, she stirred warmth in his core—in that place that only ever awoke when he indulged in fantasies of making the woman from his dream his lifemate.

She placed a slender hand along his cheek. The coolness of her touch thrilled him even through the coarse hairs of his beard. Her breasts, generously plump beneath her dressing gown, nearly brushed his chest. If he had taken time to put on armor today, he would have been deprived of the tingling awareness filling the space between them.

He cleared his throat. "My lady—" He stopped, unsure what he meant to say. He wanted to apologize for losing his temper with her. He should not have raised his voice. But he did not regret the sentiments he'd expressed. He would demand she answer for her actions. But the gradual swelling of his cock made it difficult to order his thoughts.

It was not like him to lack clarity of thought in the presence of a woman.

"You are magnificent when riled," Seona said. Her gaze dropped to his mouth. Then she leaned forward and kissed him.

All thought fled at the sensual press of her mouth on his. His body simply reacted, overwhelmed at having Seona act this way with him. His arms gathered her close. His hands roamed her head, her shoulders, her delicate face. His thumb stroked the paw print that perfectly matched the marking he'd seen in his dream.

Tender longing made him rub his mouth along hers. Back and forth, slowly. Their noses brushed. Their breath mingled. This was not the scripted kiss he opened with when he must bed a lady out of necessity, meant to turn both their thoughts to carnal activities so they could enjoy what was about to transpire.

This was sweetness in motion. This kiss burgeoned with a fullness of joy unlike anything he'd experienced with another woman. Seona was heaven in his arms. Pure, undiluted heaven.

Until he remembered himself. And he remembered Seona's hatred and betrayal.

With hands on her shoulders, he set her away from him. The chill of separating from her bordered on pain. He refused to pay it heed.

"It will not work," he said.

Her unfocused gaze came languidly back to attentiveness. "Hmm?" she said, touching her lips as though she could scarcely believe what they'd shared. An act, surely.

"I will not be seduced." He released her and took a step back.

Her body swayed forward, as if seeking to restore contact with his. He would not allow himself to be fooled.

"I know where you lived in your Highlands," he said. "What you did to survive. Your sister told me, hoping it would discourage me from—" He stopped.

He'd kept Seona in the chamber adjoining his, but he'd made no other attempt to inform her of his intentions. He'd not shared with her the fact she was promised to him by Danu in a sacred vision. He had determined not to burden her with such news while she hated him. Instead, he had resigned himself to slowly winning her trust and her heart. Knowing of her past did not dissuade him. Even if he did not love her the way he'd anticipated, he would still take her as his queen and bring new life into the world with her. This was Danu's plan. Seona's history with other men did not change the fact.

Seona frowned and sat back on her heels. Clearly, her body was fully mended. She showed no sign of pain or injury. The miracle of her life helped him keep a firm hold on his anger. He would be gentle with her.

"What I mean," he began more calmly, "Is that I know you were a prostitute. I say this not to insult you, but to inform you that your skill at seduction will not work on me."

She blinked wide eyes that held not an ounce of deceit. "Was I? How fascinating!" She spoke with unfocused eyes, as if to herself.

"You do not remember," he said, surprised. Or was she pretending this too, like she pretended her newfound affection toward him? Anya had told many tales over the dinner table of bending the truth to her purposes and using her wits to accomplish her will. She'd admitted, in general terms, to bending men to her will as well, and Magnus had understood what she'd left unsaid— that she had used her body to do so. She had also mentioned that she'd learned such things from Seona.

Seona looked away and said, "My memory—seems to elude me just now." Her brows drew together in an expression of frustration.

Concern drew him closer to the bed. Perhaps she was telling the truth. Perhaps this was a lingering effect of her fall. Studying her closely for subtle signs of injury, he said to Cadeyrn, "Find my physician."

Just then, Daly entered with Ruben, one of the servant lads who attended the women in the *Fiona Blath*. They carried a hipbath between them. Julian, a servant in Glendall, brought a bucket of steaming water, and Alexander came in with two.

"I sent a lad to fetch Giles already, Sire," Daly said as the lads poured the water. "I shall find out how soon he can arrive."

Seona clapped her hands. "A bath! Oh, how heavenly!" Seeming to forget her consternation, she stepped gracefully from the bed and tested the shallow water with her fingers. No, not tested. Played with. She patted the water and splashed it lightly against the wall of the basin. Favoring Daly with a smile, she said, "How delightful! I forgot how wonderful water is. The sound it makes. The way it sparkles." She laughed and beamed at Magnus. Then she dragged Ruben into a tight embrace. "My thanks. What a lovely treat you've brought me!"

With a panicked gaze Ruben sought Daly, who stared at the spectacle of a grateful, affectionate Seona. The head of household would not understand her words, since it was Magnus who held the translation stone, but judging by the shock on his face, he must be thinking the same thing as Magnus.

This was not the same Seona. The Seona who had enjoyed many baths in her time at Glendall, attended by Anya since she would not tolerate the presence of the servant lads. The Seona who refused to speak to anyone except her sister. The Seona who hated wolfkind one and all.

She released Ruben and wrapped Julian in her arms. Julian was quite a few years older than Ruben and of a height with her. Beneath his mop of black curls so like those of his brother, Riggs, his cheeks colored. "Pardon, my lady, but there's more water to bring up." He backed away from Seona and all but ran from the chamber with Ruben close behind.

"Precious," Seona said. "How I've missed the children."

"Daly," Magnus said. "Quickly. Summon Giles again. Tell him it's urgent." The royal physician would discover what ailed her. Magnus would have to wait to interview her about her alliance with Bilkes until he knew she was healthy and of sound mind.

Unfortunately, not knowing when Hyrk might strike again, time was of the essence.

§

DUFF WATCHED WITH amusement as an unladylike snort issued from the captive Seona. She reminded him greatly of her sister, Anya, whom Duff knew well, though she would not recognize him as Duff, Fae Lord of Darkness. If, however, he were to don his disguise as a mortal tinker who led a caravan of misfits, Anya would grudgingly acknowledge him as a friend, no doubt uttering her usual greeting, a curt "Gravois."

Danu's moonstone had led him to Anya, and just in time. If he'd arrived a day later, she might have died from her injuries, having fallen into a crevasse in her native Highlands. He was quickly learning that Seona was like her prickly and tenacious sister in many ways.

Glaring at his shadow through the bars, from the flawlessly beautiful face of his immortal friend, Seona spat, "What kind of fool would take a *hoor* for a wife?"

From his time with Anya, he'd known both sisters had served in a "bawdy house." But Seona had disappeared from her post. As

Gravois, he had helped Anya search for her sister. In the course of their travels, they'd visited establishments of pleasure across the Highlands and Lowlands, but no sign of Seona had been found. He now knew why—because she'd been in Bantus's dungeon.

In answering her, he chose his words carefully. "One who has much to gain from such a union. And one who can provide much in return."

"What can you possibly have to gain?" The question lacked venom. He had piqued her interest. "I have naught to offer. Even if I had a single possession to my name before coming to this place, I would have no means of laying hands on it. I suspect I am—dead." Her voice was small now. Frightened.

"Perhaps you should be," he said, sympathy tightening his chest. "But if that were the case, you would not be here in this physical place speaking with me. For I am very much alive. And I am very much a man in want of what you can provide."

She didn't know it, but she held within her Danu's power, or at least what remained of it after she had created her moonstone, which would still be more power than a mortal could fathom. She would have no idea how to wield such power. In fact, if he managed to free her, she could be a danger, not only to herself, but to others. She could destroy entire realms in a fit of rage or sorrow or even joy.

If Seona agreed to wed him, that power would be his every bit as much as it was hers. He could use it to control her, to teach her. Once she'd learned, they could wield it together.

How he longed to get his hands on that power!

Not only could he break free from this fucking curse, but he could also challenge the one who had cursed him. The Fae King Arawn. What remained of Danu's power would make them equals. Duff would stand a chance at defeating him. Then *he* could rule the Fae.

Instead of ruling with twin fists of power and fear, he would lead his people with fairness and affection. He would surround himself with those few friends who had never abandoned him, despite his being cursed to dwell in darkness. His court would be a place of loyalty and love, and the Fae would be stronger for it.

Of course, there was the problem of Danu. She would probably want her power back. That is, if she'd survived whatever Hyrk had done to Seona's mortal body. She was his friend, after all. He could not simply steal her power from her.

But it was not he who had caused this switch. Whatever magic had done it, *that* was the source of the theft. Not him. He merely sought to help Seona manage the power she'd been unwittingly saddled with. And to help himself in the process, of course.

He would deal with Danu when the time came. For now, he had enough on his hands. If Anya had taught him anything, it was that a suspicious Scotswoman was hard to win over. But once won, she would make a formidable ally.

"What I can provide," she said flatly, recalling him to their tête-à-tête. "You mean tupping. I can provide a warm cunny. Is that your game?"

Images and sensations from long ago accompanied her words. Danu's lithe body beneath him, her lips parted around a moan of pleasure, ecstasy racing through him as he embraced the carnal dance.

They were memories. And desires for the future. Only it wasn't his friend he wanted to take his pleasure with. It was this wary, defiant human locked in her body.

"Yes," he said, because Seona would understand such desires and because it was the truth. Just not the whole truth. "I have been without a woman a long time." Truth again. And again not the whole truth.

"If I agree, you'll free me?"

"That is my intention, yes, love. But you should know my plan may not work."

"If it doesna, you'll no be gaining access to my body."

"That goes without saying."

He waited while she considered his offer. A minute passed. Then two.

"What are you?" she asked. "Are you some wretched troll with pustules on his cock?"

It was his turn to snort. Arawn, in his jealousy, had cursed Duff so that no being, mortal or immortal, could look on his perfect face and physique ever again. And this woman compared him to a troll. "Do I sound like a wretched troll, love?"

She made a noise like a harrumph. He'd heard Anya make that noise when she was not impressed with something he had said. It brought a smile to his lips. "How am I to ken what a troll sounds like?"

His smile broadened. "I am no troll, dear. I am Fae, what your people would call the fair folk." He saw no reason to keep it from her. In fact, he suspected a little honesty would go a long way with this woman.

"Y—you are Fae?" Her voice trembled with awe. "Your kind are immortal. Tricksters. What would ye want with a mortal like me?"

"Aye, love. I am a trickster. An immortal. I will not pretend with you. I have reasons for wanting to wed you that go beyond the carnal. But make no mistake. I do want your body. I will have your body. I also swear to protect your body and provide for you for all time." She had the power to provide for herself, but she didn't know that yet. She would understand the assurances of safety and provision. He knew this because he'd known Anya and the kinds of things she had valued. "You will not regret becoming my wife. This I vow. And, you should know, love, my cock is quite free from pustules. In fact, once you become acquainted with it I think you'll rather enjoy it."

"Cocky bastard, you are, aye? Ye make a bonny speech, but ye ken I am a used up *hoor*. I am worthless."

He hated that word with fierce passion. "You are not worthless. No one is worthless. Each life has value. Without exception." If he accomplished nothing else by marrying her, he would prove to this woman her own worth.

"Very well," she said wearily. "Broken, then. No one of sound mind should want me, never mind one of the fair folk. Your kind are credited with otherworldly beauty and great power, no? Do you nay have a fairy lass, lovely and magical, to take as your wife?"

"No Fae woman will have me. I am cursed, shamed at the whims of our king." Most marriages among his people occurred as part of the eternal battle for position. Once, he'd been a prime target for both men and women aspiring to the king's court. He'd taken liberal advantage of the fact. But ever since Arawn's curse marked him as the lowest of the low, he'd had no status to offer. How quickly his pool of bedmates had dwindled then. Without his looks, without his position in Arawn's court, he'd been called worthless for centuries by his fellow immortals.

So he'd found worth in the mortal realm. Danu's moonstone had provided the means—the disguise of an eccentric tinker. No immortal would consider Bastien Gravois as anything other than a mortal meddler with an interest in outcasts rejected by their own. Like him. The disguise had given him a way out of the darkness right under Arawn's nose, and the self-absorbed king had never even noticed.

"Cursed?" she asked.

"I am chained to the darkness. It imprisons me as surely as these bars imprison you. No being can lay eyes on me, for darkness is my infallible, eternal cloak."

During a moment of silence, he thought she wouldn't respond. Or that she would respond with mockery. But she said quite soberly, "Peas in a pod, we are, aye? What did you do to earn such a curse?" She did not mock him. She did not judge him. This more than anything else revealed that despite her trials, a streak of compassion colored her soul.

"I seduced the Fae king's concubine. He did not take his cuckolding with grace."

"Men never do. Does that mean you were once a courtier to the Fae king?"

"Yes. Long ago."

"Before the darkness," she said thoughtfully.

"Yes."

Seona fell quiet. She would be considering his proposal. He gave her the time she needed, knowing full well she would agree. The possibility of freedom would outweigh her wariness.

"I suppose we'll be tupping with the lantern off, then," she said at long last.

He grinned. "If I have my way, love, we'll honeymoon on the brilliant shores of Faerie." With her power flowing through him, Arawn's curse would be nothing but a few millennia of memories. "Now, tell me how you managed to slip away from King Magnus." Someone had to have helped her. He would find out whom and then he would be one step closer to finding the missing Hyrk and freeing his bride-to-be.

Chapter 7

Danu took feminine pleasure in Magnus fixing himself at her side while he issued commands to men who came and went from the bedchamber. His concern—clearly the result of the fall Seona had taken—rolled off him in palpable waves. But even more pleasing than the concern of a king was the joy in her heart at the sight of the children.

She couldn't take her eyes off them. Three, ranging in age from perhaps thirteen to nineteen, brought bucket after bucket of steaming water for her bath. Every thought that ran through their heads showed on their expressive faces as they stole glances at her and at Magnus. Large eyes and rosy cheeks gave away their curiosity as they divided their attention between their task and their audience—except for one blond-haired lad, who carefully avoided looking in her direction or Magnus's.

These children were among the youngest wolfkind alive. Of all the luxury around her—the ornate furnishings, the warm room, the scent of perfume in the bathwater—being in the presence of these rare little ones was what she treasured most.

It grieved her to recall Hyrk's gloating over the thinning numbers of her people, especially the females. She'd been tempted not to believe him, but the proof was in the one power remaining to her in captivity. The burst of sheer joy in her breast accompanying a new birth occurred with pitiful infrequency compared to the pang signifying a wolfkind death.

Now that she was here, not merely able to observe her people but to move among them as a fellow mortal, she longed to witness their numbers for herself. She wished to learn how they'd changed in the centuries she'd been imprisoned. She wanted to see their homes, their trades, their feasts and celebrations, their way of worshipping her.

That was not all she wanted. The heat of Magnus, so close to her side and yet not touching her, sent carnal craving spinning like a water spout within her. Broad shouldered and golden maned, he stood with feet planted like a warrior charged with protecting her. His sharp eyes missed nothing as he commanded his servants, guards, and one gray-haired man in armor, whom she suspected was his war chieftain.

Magnus should have appeared out of his element, a warrior king amidst enameled furnishings, lavish silks, and delicate fragrances. A man with his authority should direct his men from a room smelling of armor polish and lined with racks of weapons. But he appeared every bit at ease amidst this feminine luxury as in a war room.

She couldn't help remembering the kiss they'd shared. The moment of bliss had been as thrilling as it was ill-advised. She hadn't been able to help herself. It seemed Magnus had been unable to help himself as well, at least at first. Then something had made him draw back. *I will not be seduced,* he had said.

Words meant to discourage her had instead filled her with a sense of challenge. *We shall see about that,* she'd thought until he'd intrigued her by mentioning Seona's past. The poor human had gone from being a prostitute in the human realm to an abused captive in this realm. Danu drew trails with her fingers in the heated water as she wondered again what had become of Seona's soul. Might the woman be captive again, this time in Hyrk's dungeon?

Duff! Duff would know. He'd been there with her. If only she could summon him. As a goddess, summoning a Fae was as simple as speaking his name with intent. Even her moonstone had been able to do it once she'd tossed it from Hyrk's cell. Lacking power, she would not be able to summon him now, but if she could find her moonstone, she could do it. If she found her moonstone, she could restore herself to her deity, but that would accomplish nothing but putting her back in her cell. No. What she needed now was information. She must find her stone and use it to summon Duff. But first, she would treasure the gift the children had brought her and take her first bath in two thousand years.

Magnus left her side, ushering one of his knights toward the open door. She took the opportunity to shed the silk robe he had provided her to cover her torn sleeping gown. The slide of the smooth fabric over her equally smooth shoulders and arms brought her newly-revived carnal awareness to the fore.

As Magnus gestured and conversed with his knight, his powerful back bunched and flexed beneath the fine linen of his shirt. His thickly-muscled thighs pushed at the pleats of his kilt. All his shapes and movements wove a spell of desire around her. Her body, borrowed and foreign, began to respond. Tingles of need circled like *faerieflies* in her midsection. Her thighs pressed together, capturing at their apex a trickle of moisture.

She frowned. It should not be so. Her love for her people had always been maternal in nature. They were her creation. Her charges. Some immortals chose to ignore differences in station and take moral lovers. She had always looked with disdain on those fools. Not only could such an arrangement cause harm to the mortal, but history proved no good ever came from such affairs.

This mortal body, however, did not care about possible consequences. It did not understand that she was a goddess infinitely high above the mortals surrounding her. It simply wanted, and the wanting churned like a storm with a charge built up over two thousand years.

Between the steam rising from the hipbath and the heat in her belly, she began to perspire. A brush of her hand over her brow brought away dirt and dried blood. Her aches and pains had disappeared, but the evidence of the fall remained in streaks of grime on her skin. She felt gritty and needy, and all the while, the water released its scented heat, beckoning her to step inside and enjoy it.

Without wasting another moment, she lifted the torn undergarment over her head.

At the door, Magnus spoke with his head of household. Daly stood just outside the chamber, only the sleeve of his blue livery visible. "Where has Alexander gone?" he asked. "Seona will have her bath while we wait for Giles."

The garment cleared her face and pulled free from her tangled hair.

Magnus gestured toward where she stood by the bath and glanced her way just as the silk fluttered from her fingertips to the floor. He'd been about to return his attention to Daly, who was saying something about fetching one of the lads, but instead, his gaze raked over her naked form. "Never mind," said Magnus. "I'll see to her bathing." Without another word, he closed the door on his servant.

It was just the two of them in the chamber now. The only sound came from the crackling of the fire next to the bath. And the rush of breath in her ears. And the pounding of blood through her veins.

Magnus faced her, tall and regal and fully clothed in a crimson kilt and a golden-hued shirt that paled in comparison to the whisky-rich glow of his irises. His gaze darkened to the color of hardened tree sap, making each drop of perspiration chill on her skin.

Never before had nakedness made her feel so—exposed. The sensation should have been unpleasant, especially in this strange body, but the pebbling of her flesh and the tightening of her nipples created a delicious tingling within her.

"How honored I am to have a king assist me in my bath," she found herself saying in a voice that carried deep, silken notes of craving. Even though there were a dozen reasons not to initiate more touching between them, she extended her hand, shamelessly expecting service like the goddess she was.

Magnus stalked toward her, stopping close enough for her to breathe in his scent of winter forest and black tea. Circling her like a predator, he took her hand in a firm grasp.

Sure and warm, his hold anchored her as she lifted one foot and then the other to step into the copper basin. Creamy heat enveloped her calves and licked over the tops of her knees. The warm floor of the hipbath welcomed her as she sank into the water up to her neck.

Heavens, it's been so long! A moan parted her lips at the grand sensation.

Magnus released her hand and rolled up his shirtsleeves. Her eyes must have been starving for the sight of manly flesh, because her gaze caressed the tanned, muscled lines of his arms. Up and down. She looked and looked. And lusted.

I am not in my goddess form, she reasoned. *In this mortal body, my passion would pose no risk to him.*

Magnus plucked a pitcher from a dressing table. "I meant what I said earlier." His hardened voice pushed at her haze of desire, but it did not quell the temptation to flirt with him. "I will not be lulled into letting my guard down with you. You'll not get what you're after." He dunked the pitcher and motioned for her to lean forward.

She complied, quite liking taking orders from this man. "What is it you think I'm after?" Warm water sluiced her head like a halo of comfort.

"It is no secret." Lathered fingers went to work gently massaging her scalp. Between Magnus's touch and his deep voice, she found herself slipping into relaxation. "You've made your desire plain from the moment I brought you out of Saroc. You long to return to your human realm. You so despise me and my people that you risked death today." His voice tightened at the end, his words clipped and precise.

Seona wanted to return to her human realm. Seona had not tolerated the presence of this majestic man. But these things were not true of *her*. In fact, quite the opposite. She wished to remain here and learn the secrets of what had transpired today. She wished to restore herself to her deity and then to her people, to be their goddess once more. She wished to destroy Hyrk. More than anything, she wished to explore these long-dormant feelings with her king.

The pain of rejection cloaked Magnus, and still, he was gentle with her, washing her neck with careful strokes. She did not like him being in pain. She was annoyed with Seona for the way she had treated him. The woman must have been daft or blind not to see what a fine companion Magnus would make for even the loftiest of mortals.

Seona was in pain too, said her heart. *Perhaps she is still in pain if she is locked in the place where I should be.*

Danu wished for a solution to Seona's suffering if, in fact, the woman still suffered. She wished for a solution to Magnus's pain. She could not help Seona at the present. But Magnus was another story. He was here and warm and hurting, and she could provide comfort.

"Perhaps I have changed my mind," she said.

His hands paused in their washing. She turned to look at him, finding weariness and resignation written in fine lines around his eyes.

"You do not believe me." She turned to kneel in the water, putting her face to face with the squatting king who bathed her like a servant. Her upper body chilled as droplets made crystalline rivers over her breasts. She touched his face. "You have known little comfort of late," she surmised. "I would like to give you comfort."

He cocked a doubtful eyebrow. He still didn't believe.

Mortals provided skepticism freely and faith sparingly, especially those who had known much sorrow.

"Will you not accept comfort from me when you so clearly need it?" she said, taking his face in her hands. His beard cushioned her palms with masculine warmth.

He relaxed into her hold but only for a moment. Straightening away from her touch, he said, "In the last months I have learned to question everything. Nothing is the way it seems. Not my allies, not my counselors, not my friends. Not even you. Your newfound acceptance of me, despite what I wish—" He smiled sadly. "Is not what it seems." Cupping her shoulders, he turned her back into the bath.

With a huff of frustration, she plopped back down. Her desire sifted away, leaving a nugget of regret. She regretted that she would have no answer to her carnal need. She regretted that she couldn't reveal to Magnus who she truly was. She regretted that Magnus would not accept the solace she offered. She regretted that he was so scarred by how Seona had treated him that she could not inquire about the insults he had just mentioned. His allies, counselors, and friends had all betrayed him. How alone he must feel! Here she was longing to share his burdens, but he had no trust left to give.

The tangled situation was enough to make her body tense up.

"There it is," Magnus said. "How you really feel. You cannot bear my touch."

"No!" She whirled to face him. "You misunderstand."

A knock sounded at the door, followed by Daly's muffled voice. "Sire, Giles has arrived. Shall I show him in now?"

Magnus stood and dried his hands on a folded linen. "Not quite yet, Daly." He strode to the door. When he stepped outside and closed it behind him, all opportunity to ease his pain disappeared.

Chapter 8

"GOOD AFTERNOON, GILES." Magnus greeted his personal physician outside the Orange Blossom chamber.

Under the watch of Daly and two guards, he clasped wrists with the man who had seen to his health since he was a babe in his mother's arms. Giles's fingers gripped with less strength than Magnus remembered from their last meeting, but the light in his blue eyes shone as brightly as ever. "Thank you for coming. How is Esmerelda?"

Being separated from Seona put him on edge, but his keen ears told him she hadn't moved from the bath. At the first sign of her doing so, he would sweep back in. He would not be fooled by her docile act. She would not lull him into allowing her to escape Glendall a second time.

"She is well. She is well." Giles said with a nod of his head. "Danu bless you for asking. How may I serve you, Your Majesty? Daly said something about lady Seona taking a fall."

Quietly, lest Seona overhear, he relayed what he and Riggs had witnessed. "It was a miracle, Giles," he finished. "I would swear it before Danu's altar. Her wounds were healed before our eyes, but her mind—I'm afraid she is not the same. I will not take the outward appearance of her good health for granted. You must determine if she carries injuries beyond what the eye can see, and if so, tell me how to mend them."

Giles nodded while he listened, his cloud-gray eyebrows sinking ever lower. It pleased Magnus that his physician seemed to understand the gravity of the situation, but then, of course he would. Giles had seen every sort of injury and ailment and had trained a dozen apprentices in their identification and treatment.

Magnus reentered the room with Giles on his heels. Seona peered over the edge of the bath, her expression open and curious. He would swear there was not an ounce of guile in her, but he had learned better than to trust appearances.

"Lady Seona, you remember Giles, my royal physician," he said by way of introduction, then he braced for her resistance.

But she did not resist as she had every other time Giles had visited since her rescue. Instead, her mouth tipped in a polite smile. "Greetings, Physician Giles," she said in a formal but cordial tone. "I suppose you should like me out of the bath." She rose from the water, exhibiting her form as any proud wolfkind woman would under the circumstances. Rivulets sluiced over her hairless breasts, around the hourglass shape of her waist and hips, into the triangle of dewy curls at the juncture of her thighs, down her slender legs. Regally, she held out her hand for a linen.

Magnus nearly tripped over his own feet in his haste to provide one. But instead of handing it off to her, he could not help but step near and drape it around her shoulders.

With a sideways glance and a pinch of color in her cheeks, she accepted his offering, clutching the linen before her. She also accepted his hand to steady her as she stepped from the bath.

Like twin caterpillars, Giles's eyebrows shot up. He had seen Seona before, having treated all the women rescued from Saroc, but he had never seen her like this—agreeable and in the same room as Magnus. "Lady Seona, it is good to see you again." He bowed at the waist.

Magnus reminded himself to translate. Seona did not wear the translation stone. He did. Therefore she could only communicate with him. "Giles says it is good to see you again, my lady."

She blinked at him. "Of course he did. There is nothing wrong with my hearing."

He stared at her. She had understood Giles. How could that be? Had she somehow learned their tongue while in Saroc and hid it from him all this time?

If Giles was shocked at Seona speaking their language, he did not comment on it. Instead, he began flipping latches on his case with gnarled but steady hands. "Take your time drying yourself while I set up my table."

Snapping sounds issued from the case as the physician unfolded the legs and lifted the lid to reveal his tidy rows of physician's tools. All the while, he kept his gaze averted out of respect for Seona's privacy.

Still unsettled by Seona's ability to communicate with Giles, Magnus did not show the same respect. Nor did she seem to expect it. Bare feet leaving pools on the hearth, she took her time rubbing the linen over her body. Stretching gracefully and bending lithely, she glided the linen over her skin until it was dry as lily petals.

When she finished, she let the linen fall to the hearth.

Legions of Larnian warriors could not force his gaze from her shamelessly displayed form. She was smaller than the typical wolfkind female, almost juvenile in size. But from the hair covering her nether lips to her full breasts to the knowing look in her eyes as she held his gaze, she was all woman.

Her lips appeared soft as she smiled sweetly at him, and he realized he'd thought they were hard and thin. Really, it had always been her expression that was hard and thin when he'd been near. When she was relaxed, her face radiated gentle, regal beauty.

"Have you a dressing gown for me?" she said, a twinkle in her eye.

"Hm. Should be one around here somewhere," he said, backing toward the armoire so he did not lose out on a single moment of looking upon her like this. "Daly and the lads would be much swifter at dressing you. I'm afraid you shall have to settle for the bumbling aid of a novice servant." By Danu, what had gotten into him? He was flirting with her. With Seona. If Anya found out, she'd no doubt attempt to "snatch his cods and have them for supper."

Even more remarkable was the fact Seona did not appear put off by his flirting. To the contrary, her gaze darkened with interest. Tendrils of dark walnut wove a tapestry of damp hair over her shoulder. She gathered the tendrils and squeezed. Droplets pattered to the stone at her feet. "Something tells me you are not a novice at all things where bedchambers are concerned." Flinging her hair behind her, she pursed her lips in a coy smile.

He nearly swallowed his tongue and forgot what he'd been doing. Ah. The armoire. Barely glancing within, he chose a lavender dressing gown and robe and brought them to Seona.

Still smiling, she stretched her arms up and over her head, allowing Magnus to sheath her in the silken gown. After the hem fluttered to her toes, she extended one arm for the sleeve of the robe.

He accommodated her, first sliding a sleeve up one arm then holding the other while she shrugged into the garment. Serving her like this made his midsection warm pleasantly. If only her acceptance of him were genuine!

"The settee should do," Giles said, giving Magnus a start—he'd forgotten they were not alone. The physician had his table open and ready in front of the settee. "Have a seat, if you would, dear lady. When you are quite ready."

Seona obliged, stepping lightly to where Giles waited.

Magnus couldn't take his eyes off her. Had she always been so graceful in her movements? Despite her occupying the room adjoining his, he had rarely enjoyed access to her. Between Anya's protectiveness and Seona's refusal to admit anyone save her sister, he had only laid eyes on her a handful of times, never when she was up and about. She had lived beside him for two moons but she was a stranger. A lovely, intriguing stranger.

Now that she seemed amenable to his presence, he intended to spend more time with her. Much more. He would use her newfound tolerance of him to his advantage so he could discover whatever new plot she had devised. Perhaps he could even soften her, make her see what a good mate he would be. Then she would forget her attempts to escape. She would see that no future she could create for herself would ever be as fulfilling as one at his side as his queen and the mother of his heir.

But her health came first.

After taking her seat, Seona grasped both of Giles's hands. "Thank you for coming to ensure my wellbeing. I shall assist you in any way you wish."

Over his half-moon spectacles, Giles blinked at her.

Magnus held in a chuckle.

When Giles began his examination, Magnus moved a small distance away. He did not want to distract either physician or patient. Aside from a few brisk touches, which Seona accepted with grace, Giles kept his investigation to questions.

"What is the last thing you remember before waking upon the king's mount?" the physician asked, peering over his spectacles.

Seona's gaze darted to Magnus. Several long moments passed before she answered, "Nothing relevant to this time and place. All of my memories are from…far away."

Interesting. It seemed Seona intended to avoid questioning about her involvement with Bilkes. Clever lady, pretending not to remember the events leading up to her fall. A smile tugged at his lips. The resemblance between Seona and Anya had never been more apparent. It seemed both sisters were skilled at manipulation.

"No memories of Glendall?" Giles pressed. "Your time in this chamber? Our previous meetings?"

"No."

Magnus stifled a sniff of humor. How far would she take this charade?

Apparently, he had not stifled his reaction in full. Giles regarded him over his spectacles, and he did not appear amused. Returning his attention to Seona, he said, "Do you remember Saroc, lady? Your time in the dungeon there?"

The question was a blow to his gut and wiped away all trace of amusement. *He* remembered Saroc. He remembered the soul-twisting agony that had driven him to his knees when he'd found a dozen human women living in deplorable conditions, when he'd learned the horrors they'd suffered. With great effort, he shoved the memory of that day aside and focused on Seona in the here and now.

She cocked her head, reminding him of a curious bird. "No. I have no recollection of that." Her gaze seemed to turn inward. "It must have been horrible."

Magnus had the distinct impression she was imagining the horrors the other women had suffered, as if she had heard of Bantus's atrocities rather than experienced them as one of his victims.

Her manner was so utterly without guile and so unexpected, considering the shell of a woman she'd been upon her rescue, that Magnus questioned his initial supposition. What if she wasn't pretending? What if she truly could not remember?

"What about before Saroc? Do you remember your home in the human realm? Your family?"

"I am afraid not. I wish I could be more helpful."

Since Magnus had known Seona, he had never heard of her attempting to be helpful to anyone, even Anya, who often left her sister's chamber in a foul temper, grumbling about 'the ungrateful, infuriating wench.'"

"Do not trouble yourself, lady," Giles said with a pat of her hands. "Simply continue to answer to the best of your ability, and you will help me plenty. Now, tell me about your sister. Do you remember Anya?"

"Anya," she said. "My sister." Her face lit with wonder.

Magnus held his breath for her answer. Surely if she was pretending, she would draw the line here. Knowing Anya lived in Glendall, that she would be interacting with her, she would not attempt to convince them she did not know her sister.

"I know *of* her," she said, her tone measured and careful. "I know of the good she has done, her slaying of the vile Bantus. But I do not remember her. I…do not know her as my sister."

Seona puzzled him. She had deliberately chosen each word of her response. He would swear to it before the high priest. She was either being incredibly honest or incredibly daft in denying any memory of Anya. The dark-haired Highland sisters who had come to Glendall were many things, but daft was not one of them.

He was convinced. Seona was telling the truth as far as she knew it. No one could pretend so convincingly for so long and deny a relationship with the one person they'd previously trusted.

Come to think of it, Seona's speech supported her answers. Anya spoke with a pleasing, rolling burr and a vocabulary that often made those around her blush. Shouldn't Seona sound like Anya? Have the same rolling burr? Use the same bawdy vocabulary?

He studied Giles, trying to guess at what the physician made of the interview.

But Giles's face gave nothing away. "I see." The physician asked several more questions about people and events Seona should easily recall—her childhood, her mother and father, the home she'd lived in, chores and duties she had carried out.

Each answer proved Seona lacked specific memories. She possessed only the most general knowledge of who she was and where she had come from. Her responses seemed like facts she had learned about some other individual rather than memories of personal experiences.

Giles thanked her for her time and cooperation. After packing up his case, he walked with Magnus to the door, where two guards met them.

Magnus posted one guard inside to watch Seona. With one hand, he took Giles's elbow, and with the other, he carried the case as he led the elderly physician down the corridor, out of earshot of the remaining guard. The physician moved slowly. Magnus had to force himself not to rush the man, so eager was he to question him.

At last they stopped under a sconce and bent their heads together. "Tell me what you make of her condition." The words tumbled free, urgent and more than a little anxious. With a drop of his stomach, he was a young man of twenty-five again. His mother was ill and in bed, and he was demanding Giles tell him what was the matter with her.

Please, Danu, do not let Seona's condition be fatal. I cannot lose her like I lost my mother.

"As far as I can tell, it is a defect of the memory, Your Majesty." Giles removed his spectacles and held them by a temple piece. The familiar mannerism only enhanced Magnus's anxiety. He'd done the same thing when telling Magnus that his mother's seizures would only continue to grow worse and that they would claim her life within the year.

But that was then and this was now. It was not his mother being examined, but the woman Danu had promised to him.

He scrutinized Giles. "Defect of the memory, you say. She might be pretending." He doubted it, but he had to suggest the theory if for no other reason than to have his trusted physician rule it out. "She did escape Glendall with a convicted felon. This memory defect might be a ruse to avoid questioning."

Giles frowned. "No. I do not think that is the case, Your Majesty. Her speech. It is different than before."

"She spoke to you before?" He'd thought she had refused to speak with anyone save Anya.

"No. Not with me. But within my hearing, yes. I overheard her shouting to Lady Anya that she 'wouldna be poked and prodded by a numb-pricked auld fool.'" At this, he cracked a rare smile before sobering again. "No. I believe her memory loss is genuine and that it is so severe it has affected every aspect of her personality."

So he had been correct in guessing her speech would have been like Anya's.

Giles went on. "Lady Seona has lost all sense of her own identity, including all personal memories prior to her fall. However, she appears to have retained her worldly memories, those functions of the mind that provide an understanding of how things work and how she should interact with the world. A very serious condition, indeed."

That was the second time Giles had used the word *serious*. "Will it worsen? Will her memory ever return? Tell me all."

"I can only guess, unfortunately." Giles replaced his spectacles. "The good news is that there is no sign of trauma to the head. Her physical healing appears complete. Remarkable, considering what you told me of her fall." He inclined his head, acknowledging the miracle.

Magnus took heart. Seona was not injured. She suffered no physical consequences of the fall. *Thank You, Danu!*

"It is unlikely her memory loss will worsen," Giles went on to say. "In fact, it is a good sign that she was able to tell me all that has transpired since her fall. This means she can create new memories. As to whether she will regain those memories she lost—" Sucking in a breath between his teeth, he rocked back on his heels. "That is uncertain. I have never encountered such a condition in a woman, let alone a human woman."

Magnus recalled the detailed medical reports Giles and his two most experienced apprentices had written about the twelve rescued women from Saroc. Malnourishment and trauma of the mind had featured prominently in each report, but there had been no mention of memory loss.

"Of the men I've seen with memory loss, some regained their memories once their injuries had healed. Others were not so lucky." He peered over his spectacles, his expression grave. "I am afraid there is no telling when—or whether—she might regain her lost sense of self."

Magnus let the physician's assessment sink in. Seona might never again be…Seona. This should pain him, for it was like a death in a way. Without her memories, she was not whole. She was only a shadow of herself.

But this new Seona did not feel like a shadow. The woman in the chamber down the corridor radiated vibrancy and life. She marveled at the simplest things, like tinkling bathwater. She found joy in the presence of children. Her reactions to things he took for granted made him see the world through the eyes of innocence. And, heavens, her kiss was nourishment for his moonsoul. Her embrace lightened the burden of ruling a dying people, made him forget how little sleep he'd had of late. She made him feel whole and alive as no other creature on Danu's green Earth ever had, most especially not the Seona she had been.

Perhaps it was perverse of him, but in Giles's diagnosis, he found relief. Not only was Seona physically healthy, but she had no recollection of the horrors she had suffered in Larna. Furthermore, she no longer loathed him. For the first time since learning of her existence, he had a chance to spend time with her. To woo her. Perhaps to entice her to feel for him the depth of love he'd felt for her since laying eyes on her in the canyon.

Best of all, he no longer needed to worry she was playing him for a fool. Giles's diagnosis confirmed it. She was not pretending to be something she was not in order to lure him into trusting her. She was not planning to run from him again. Her guilelessness was no act. It was simply *her,* the way she would have been, perhaps, without the suffering she'd endured in Larna. Perhaps even without the hard, uncertain life Anya had described from the human realm.

Seona's memory loss might actually be a blessing in disguise. Perhaps this was Danu's way of protecting her from all she'd suffered in the past. And her way of making a path forward for his courtship of her.

With new hope in his heart, he thanked Giles and strode back to Seona's chamber. "Summon Daly for me," he told the guard at the door. "The lady and I will be attending Temple this afternoon." He intended to thank Danu properly for this miracle within a miracle. And spend quality time with a Seona who not only tolerated his presence but seemed to find some pleasure in it.

But first, he was going to kiss the woman senseless, this time without pulling back out of suspicion. This time, he would show her what he felt for her, and nothing was going to stop him.

Chapter 9

"WHY IN BLOODY damnation did you nay tell me what happened to my sister?" No sooner had Magnus lain his hand upon the door latch than Anya's shouts rang in the corridor.

So much for nothing stopping him. Grinding his teeth, he faced the irate little human barreling toward him. "Lady Anya, how good to see you."

He'd barely gotten the words out when she launched into another tirade. "Good to see me my red *arse!* You good for nothing son of a—"

"Anya!" Riggs's bellow preceded him as caught up to her and swept her behind him. "Your Majesty," he said breathlessly, as though he'd been running full out. "Forgive her. She is distraught over Lady Seona."

"Distraught? Dis-*traught?*" Anya pounded Riggs with her fists in an attempt to escape the arm that pinned her behind him. "I'll show you distraught, you overgrown boar! 'Tis Seona who ought to be distraught after being thrown from a bloody cliff and living to tell the tale!"

The guard outside Seona's chamber put his body between Magnus and the arguing lifemates. At the same time the door cracked open.

"Sire," said the guard he'd posted inside. "Do you need me?"

"No. Stay with Lady Seona."

With a nod the guard sealed the door. The sound of the lock tumbling satisfied him. At least Seona was safe from this commotion.

During his exchange with the guard, Anya and Riggs had come toe to toe. "—not good for our baby," Riggs was saying.

"I'll tell you what's good for our *bairn*," Anya spat. "And that's for me to see. My. Sister!"

Anya was right. He loved Seona, truly and dearly, but Anya did as well. His plans to spend time alone with her would have to wait, because Anya had as much claim to her time as he did. He would see the sisters reunited as soon as possible. But not yet.

Before he could address Anya, his war chieftain, Cathal, strode toward them. "Sire, I heard a commotion. Is all well? We've been waiting in the solar for the conference you promised. We have information about the prisoner Bilkes."

Ah, yes. Bilkes. So many things required his immediate attention. There was also the matter of Hyrk. There was no telling where the vile being was or when he would strike again.

"And there's another thing!" Anya rounded on him. "When were you intending to inform me that good for nothing messenger had escaped? And absconded with Seona?"

His temper could bear no more. "Enough!"

Instantly, the corridor fell silent.

Anya blinked at him with startled eyes. Cathal assumed a stance of respectful attention beside the door guard. Riggs's jaw clenched.

"You will remember to whom you are speaking, Lady Anya," he said as he pinned his shoulders back. "And you will refrain from shouting at the top of your lungs about the miracle your lifemate and I witnessed this day."

Anya opened her mouth, no doubt to protest. He cut her off with a slice of his hand. "Unless you have an apology on your tongue for raising your voice to me, you will hold it in check. I am yet gathering information about today's events. I understand your desire to reunite with Lady Seona. You will have your time with her. For now, be assured Giles has found her to be in perfect *physical* health."

He was not surprised Anya cocked her head at his emphasis on the word physical. The little human's intuition would yank them all off course if he allowed it. Before she could give voice to the myriad questions in her eyes, he began issuing commands.

"Riggs, you will escort Lady Anya to my solar and wait for me there." He turned to Cathal. "I will meet you there as well, but first summon Maedoc and Clem." The captain of his knights and the head of his royal council must be included. "You will tell me all you have discovered, and we will discuss what must be done."

Cathal bowed his head in acknowledgement and departed.

"Daly," he greeted his head servant as he approached with his ever-efficient gait. "Have refreshments brought to the solar. Lady Anya and Lady Seona will require their midday meal."

"Of course, Sire." Daly followed in Cathal's wake.

Anya was not so quick to be dismissed. "You'll bring Seona to your solar? You'll allow me to see her?"

"Of course, Lady Anya. I have told you as much. Your lifemate is correct." Riggs seemed to have forgotten their argument. He held her against his side with a possessive arm. Magnus met the knight's eyes with a meaningful look before returning his attention to Anya. "I have not forgotten the treasure you carry, dear lady." Her womb held the first child conceived in nearly twelve years. He would be not only heartless but a witless fool to allow her stress to continue.

Anya placed a hand over her still-flat abdomen. Indeed, their people's latest blessing was still new and at its most fragile. Riggs settled his hand over hers and gazed lovingly at her.

"I would not have you fret for Lady Seona a moment longer," Magnus assured her. "All your inquiries will be addressed, and you will have your time with her. But be warned. I shall deal with the threat to my kingdom before all else." Because he knew Anya was not one to be convinced easily, he took a step closer and grasped her shoulder in an affectionate hold. "At your request, I remained patient where your sister was concerned. Now you will do the same for me. Yes?"

Anya thinned her lips but managed to say, "Aye, Your Highness."

"Thank you, Sire," Riggs said, and he guided Anya toward the solar.

Hoping Anya would not become a distraction during the impending meeting, he returned to the Orange Blossom chamber. Too long had he been separated from Seona. His chest felt tight, and only laying eyes on her again could loosen the sensation.

If he hadn't already decided she would remain by his side for all that must take place today, the empty feeling her absence caused would have sealed it. He needed her with him. Not only that, but he wanted her with him with a desperation he could scarcely comprehend.

Anya's request that he give Seona time and space had affronted him, but only because it grated to have his actions dictated by another. Not because he longed to bask in Seona's nearness and shower her with affection as he did now.

That was not all he longed for. This new Seona might have no memories, but she possessed intelligence and curiosity in abundance. He had not forgotten the question she'd asked during their return to the castle this morning. She'd wanted to know what dangers they faced. Beneath her wonder at experiencing everything as if for the first time, she had the desire and courage to face what needed facing. He longed to encourage those queenly qualities by including her, especially when she, herself, would be one of the subjects of discussion.

If he was honest, he also coveted her admiration. He wished for her to witness the command he wielded. He wanted to impress her with his ability to rule justly and act swiftly. Never before had he experienced the desire to be observed by another whilst conducting kingdom affairs.

Marveling at these new feelings, he entered the chamber and sent his guard back to his post outside. Pulling the door closed, he searched for Seona. Warmth like sunlight replaced the empty ache in his chest when he found her before the armoire, fingering the fine gowns within. Her lavender dressing gown shimmered in the light of the ornate sconces. The silken fabric highlighted the too-sharp angle of her hip. Even thinner than she ought to be, she stole his breath with her beauty. From her crown of walnut waves to the creamy length of her legs to her grace as she lifted a sleeve to test its softness against her cheek, she beckoned to everything male in him.

He stalked to her, humming appreciatively in his throat. Stopping a breath away from her back, he said, "Do they please you, my lady?"

He'd commissioned the gowns shortly after her rescue, but she had yet to wear a single one, refusing them, according to Anya, as "the trappings of those vile wolf people." She did not seem to find them distasteful now.

"They are exquisite," she said, confirming his suspicion.

"As is the one they were created for." He dared to kiss her silk-clad shoulder, a brief, almost chaste brushing of his lips.

She did not protest. Rather, she turned her head just enough that he could glimpse the coy smile dimpling her cheek.

How had he not noticed before just how alluring she was? He drew in a deep breath, filling his lungs with the freshly-washed scent of her. Lavender, orange blossoms, and vanilla danced in his senses with a hint of female musk. Intoxicating.

"May I recommend the forest green?" He reached past her to lower the dress in question from its place. The act pressed him snug into her so her rounded backside cradled his swelling cock. *Yes, lady. Feel what I have for you, if you'll only accept it, accept me. Goddess, accept me!*

"You may," she said, easing backward to mold herself even tighter to him. The motion put delightful pressure on his length as it thickened and hardened. "But who shall dress me? I see no servants near at hand."

The gown filled both his hands. Turning it just so, he held it against her, one hand supporting the ruffled collar near her throat, the other flattening the *V* of the garment's waist to her flat stomach. "Hm. Daly was up a moment ago, but I sent him to see to your midday meal." He could not help edging his hips forward. "And I have not seen any of the servant pups since your bath."

"Pity," she cooed, letting her head fall back on his shoulder. "It seems I shall have to remain in my dressing gown." She turned in his arms, making him wish he was not holding an elaborate gown so he could crush her to his chest. "Or wear nothing at all." She lowered her lashes. When they lifted to reveal her eyes, unmistakable hunger shone forth.

By Danu! She was tempting him! And according to what he'd learned from Giles, her motivation was pure. With her memories lost, she had no reason to mislead him in this.

Caring not one whit for the gown, he closed his arms around her slender form, garment and all. She felt delicate held to him like this, but so right. Their bodies were a perfect fit for one another.

Pin pricks of pleasure cascaded over every inch of him. His body hadn't sung like this for a woman in—he couldn't remember how long. Perhaps never. The rustling of abused fabric only heightened his arousal. If only there were time to stoke that pleasure higher, to stoke hers as well! How he longed to show her what it would be like to become his mate! He would ensure that if her memory returned she would be bound to him by the knowledge of how well he could please her. She would be unable to reject him again.

"I would enjoy nothing more, my lady, than to spend the afternoon appreciating your natural, radiant beauty. But I am afraid we have an appointment, you and I." Regret was a blade to his gut.

Tonight, he vowed. He would show her tonight. And by the moon, nothing—and no one—would stop him.

"An appointment?" The hunger in her eyes gave way to excitement. "With whom?"

He was right to assume she would want to be included. Her bright curiosity confirmed it.

"With my advisory council, my war chieftain, my priest, and," he stroked a thumb over the paw print on her cheek. "Your sister."

He watched for any sign of recognition on her lovely face, but there was none. Only innocent interest. "You speak of Anya."

He nodded, annoyed he would have to release her in order to dress her. *But to see her nude again...*

"Well, I cannot meet my sister in a dressing gown." Apparently, she was thinking the same thing. One delicate eyebrow arched, and a grin pursed her lips. It was a wholly un-innocent expression.

"No, you cannot," he agreed.

"What are we to do then?" Her voice dipped into husky tones that belonged wrapped in silken bed linens and luxurious furs.

His face lowered to hers. The act of breathing the same air felt natural, even necessary. "I shall have to take on the role of lady's servant, I suppose. Though you deserve one much more experienced than I."

She raised her face, bringing their mouths within a hair's breadth. "As you've said. And as I've said, I expect you shall make up for it with your experience in other matters of the bedchamber."

He could not form words, so powerful was his wanting of her. Instead, a feral growl ripped from his throat. Dropping the gown, he seized her head with both hands and descended on her like the raving beast she roused in him.

§

TWO THOUSAND YEARS. That was how long it had been since Danu had been blessed with a lover's kiss. There were so many questions she had, so many things she must learn in order to thwart Hyrk, but the sensations roaring through her new mortal body eclipsed all else.

All that mattered was the king possessing her with his kiss and the passion sparking between them.

Intimacy. How she craved it after so many lonely years in cold and darkness! What a treasure it was to be wanted like this and to want in return!

She'd created her precious wolfkind to require companionship. They could not thrive alone. Neither could she. Though she could not die, loneliness had diminished her these past centuries. Pieces of her moonsoul had shriveled and curled in on themselves like fallen leaves. No single kiss, no matter how perfect, could replenish those desiccated pieces of her. But the intensity of Magnus's affection for her—and hers for him—gave her hope.

She drank of Magnus's kiss. He took her mouth savagely, as if his very existence depended upon this connection with her. His hold on her shouted possession, his fists clenching the silk of her dressing robe. *He'll ruin the fabric,* she thought with delight.

She returned his ferocity with her own. Her hands clutched at his back, fingers like talons. Her tongue tangled with his, each vying for dominance. The battle was delicious. They would both prevail in the end.

Lust smothered all other cares. It shone like a hedonistic star. *Take pleasure. Enjoy. Thrive.*

Kissing was no longer enough. Her mortal body thrummed with need so potent it would not be denied. Unbidden, mewls of desperation escaped her.

Magnus received them and gave them back in fierce, private growls. Their sounds mingled in their open mouths. The vibrations drove her lust higher.

Memory failed her. She could not recall a time when she'd needed anything so intensely.

"Take me," she commanded between kisses. She pushed away from Magnus to tear the dressing gown off her burning body. Her sex throbbed, and only this man could sate her.

Magnus's chest heaved with his quickened breath. His irises had shrunk to sharp halos of golden light. His pupils expanded to drown her in their warm, welcoming depths. "Nothing would please me more." His fists clenched and unclenched at his sides. "But there is much to be done, and I will not be rushed when I take you the first time." Pain etched his strong features. His desire was more than apparent, and yet he denied her.

She stared, dumbfounded. He was telling her no. He needed her as badly as she needed him. She was a goddess, and had commanded him to quench the flames licking at both their bodies. And he denied her.

She should be furious. But she was not. In fact, admiration took the fire under her flesh and changed it into something she could live with. Because he spoke true. There *was* much to be done. He was wise to understand that his kingdom was in jeopardy. In denying what they both burned for, he was putting his people first. She understood this. He was taking his duty seriously.

As she had failed to do that day with Lachlan and Jilken. She had wagered with Hyrk and reduced the mortal ruler of her people to no more than a horse in a footrace. Guilt overwhelmed her. How inadequate she was as a goddess! Her father must be so disappointed in her.

"Shh, no, my lady." Magnus cupped her cheek and kissed sweetly at the corner of her mouth, which she realized was pursed in displeasure—aimed squarely at herself. She had so much to make amends for. She'd left her people defenseless while she wasted centuries upon centuries in her enemy's dungeon.

"It has been so long," she said, despondent over her failure. Her once thriving people faced extinction because of her foolishness. It was a wonder this king still had faith in her. She certainly didn't deserve it.

Her self-loathing turned to determination. She *would* make amends. She would destroy Hyrk once and for all and shower blessing after blessing upon her people. She had two thousand years of wrongs to right. Only then could she bear to face her father again.

Strong arms folded around her. Magnus's bearded chin rested atop her head. His warmth strengthened her resolve. She was not alone in this fight. Magnus knew of Hyrk, though she had yet to determine how much he knew. Together, they would overcome the vile demigod. She vowed it in her heart.

"It will have to be even longer, I am afraid," he said, unaware of the battle she'd begun mentally preparing for. "But do not despair. Tonight, I will give you all you seek. And then some." A cocksure grin dimpled his bearded cheek as he set her away from him and recovered the dropped gown.

He thought she'd said, "so long" in relation to having a man in her bed. And he attempted to reassure her. He cared that she suffered the effects of unsated lust. However misguided, his caring caused a tingle of something new and tender to bloom deep inside. The sensation was small but so precious, so novel. She longed to experience it again and again.

"Now, sweet lady, I shall attempt to dress you without ravishing you. Think you I can accomplish such a feat?"

She shivered, but not from cold. In fact, between the heat of the fire and the warmth from Magnus's body, the cold from Hyrk's dungeon was well and truly banished. Her skin pebbled under the golden gaze raking over her. Her nipples hardened to stony points. With nothing more than his voice and that gaze of his, Magnus had rekindled her lust.

But that would wait. Until tonight—she would hold him to his promise. But for now, if she was to become the goddess she had failed for so long to be, she needed to learn all she could about her present-day people and the threat Hyrk posed to them.

Above all else, she must find her moonstone. Only then could she return to her true form and leave this fragile, mortal body. Only then could she wield the power she would need to slay her enemy once and for all.

"I think you can," she answered as Magnus began to swath her in filigreed fabric and lace. "I am beginning to believe you can accomplish anything you set your mind to." And so could she, even in this temporary mortal body.

Chapter 10

A COUNCIL MEETING was no mundane event at Glendall, Danu
observed. Once Magnus had her clothed in a winter gown of
sumptuous embroidered silk and draped in a luxurious cloak of
mottled boar hide, he'd ordered Daly to summon a lady's servant
to brush and style her hair. While they waited for a servant to
come, Magnus submitted to Daly's hurried grooming and donned a
crimson sash which fastened at his throat with a broach fashioned
from gold and rubies. The fine piece depicted a roaring lion with a
book beneath one paw and a full moon resting in the palm of the
other.

When no servant lad appeared, Daly took on the task of seeing
to her hair. He sat her on a stool before a bronze mirror, brushed
out the tangles, and twisted sections into piles that formed a
delicate crown. The whole time, he muttered about the servant lads
becoming spoiled.

Finished with her, Daly draped a cloak around Magnus's
shoulders. The inky black set off the crimson in his war kilt,
making him look both commanding and dangerous.

"Are you ready, my lady?" her king purred. The heat in his
eyes proved he hadn't forgotten his promise about this evening. If
only he were asking whether she were ready for *that*. She would
launch herself into his arms and command him to take her to his
bed that very moment. But he was only referring to the council
meeting they were now late for.

She shivered at the promise in his gaze, but her voice was steady when she said, "I am."

"Come, then." He crooked his arm in an invitation she accepted. They strode together to a nearby room with a large fireplace and a grouping of comfortable looking chairs and couches at the far end. Closer to the entry, a rectangular table dominated the space. This part of the castle had not existed in Lachlan's time, but she recognized the chamber as an extension of Magnus's bedchamber. This would be where he took his meals, relaxed, and, as was happening now, where he held private meetings.

As Magnus led her into the chamber, the five men she counted around the table stood and saluted their king with fists over their hearts. Three of them sat along one side, and each man wore different styles of clothing.

The largest had broad shoulders and a gray beard. His weathered face had seen many years, and his dark eyes had seen many battles. A war kilt made a slash across his barrel chest. The wool was fastened over his heart with a broach similar to Magnus's but depicting a lion standing as if locked in battle with a silver crescent moon. While she had not recognized Magnus's symbol, this one she remembered from the time of Lachlan. The warrior was a Knight of the Crescent moon, one of the king's personal guard. It pleased her to see this tradition had stood the test of time.

Beside the knight stood a slim man in what she assumed were civilian clothes. A silken jacket covered a tunic with a high, lacy collar. The man's gray-streaked hair was tied back, emphasizing his high cheekbones and pointed ears. His beard was darker than his hair and trimmed into a tidy *vee*.

Next was a willowy man in brown robes. He bore no facial hair, and the hair atop his head was shorn close to the scalp in the style of priests. He wore spectacles that failed to sit perfectly straight on his nose. In his hands, he held a rumpled head covering, removed, no doubt, out of respect when the king had entered.

On the table's other side were two men and one woman. The first man was an older warrior with gray hair. He lacked the symbol that would have marked him as a knight. He must be the head of Magnus's army.

The second man possessed such significant height and breadth that the chair he had risen from appeared like child's furniture in his shadow. His hair tumbled over his shoulders in dark curls, and he wore the kilt and broach of the Knights of the Crescent Moon. His dark brown eyes followed her as Magnus drew to a stop at the head of the table. She had seen this knight before. He was one of the riders who had escorted her and Magnus to Glendall.

Between the two men sat a petite woman whose gaze had sought Danu's since the moment she'd entered the room. She wore a gown much like the one Magnus had dressed her in and had her chestnut waves pinned up into pretty loops atop her head. Scars like claw marks slashed across her cheek.

Instantly, Danu knew the woman was not wolfkind. Her smaller bone structure and dainty mouth were the fabled features of humans. Danu had never spent time with humans, but she'd heard many tales, some flattering to the mortal race, most not. This was Anya. Seona's sister.

Lines of worry creased Anya's forehead. Her eyes, similar in color to those of the warrior beside her, were liquid with concern. Her pinched mouth appeared to be reining in a hundred questions. The warrior took her hand and whispered something in her shell-shaped ear. Whatever he said seemed to relieve some of her anxiety.

Danu had looked forward to meeting Anya, the human who had slain King Bantus, but now that she stood in the same room as the small warrioress, she felt something she had rarely before experienced. Nervousness. Her stomach clenched and swooned as if she were soaring above the landscape and had taken a sudden dive.

She was glad for the distraction when Magnus drew an empty chair from the side of the table and placed it next to his at the head. "You will sit by my side," he said, easing her down.

"Thank you, Your Highness." She may have been imprisoned for the last two millennia, but she remembered her courtly manners.

The men around the table looked on, expressions ranging from surprise to disbelief.

Anya's gaze sharpened. A shrewd expression eclipsed her worry, and Danu received the impression that Anya did not miss much. Danu would have to be careful around her. With Hyrk on the loose, it was imperative the demigod remain ignorant of her whereabouts. If Anya guessed something was amiss, she could ruin everything, including Danu's plan to discover what, exactly, had happened to Seona.

"At ease," Magnus said in his clear, commanding voice.

Those around the table resumed their seats.

Magnus did not sit. Rather, he remained standing behind his chair, which was elaborately carved where the others were plain. "Ladies and gentlemen, Marann is under attack."

He'd already had the attention of everyone around the table, but this statement honed that attention to a sword's point. Her chest puffed with pride that her king commanded a room with such confidence.

"Not from Larnian invaders. Not from outlaws or bandits. Not from within, due to political infighting." At this, he cut a glance to the smartly-dressed man, who arched an eyebrow in response. "Our new enemy is like nothing we have faced before." Giving those in attendance a chance to soak in this dire news, he arranged himself in his chair, his posture impeccable.

"As most of you know by now, Lady Seona absconded from Glendall this morning—by all accounts—of her free will." He placed a reassuring hand on her shoulder, as if he expected this declaration to upset her.

Danu joined the others in giving Magnus her rapt attention, so eager was she to learn what had led to Seona's fall from a cliff.

All eyes were on her as Magnus continued, except for Anya's. The human woman fixed her gaze on Magnus's hand, where it remained on her shoulder.

"Unfortunately, she is unable to give testimony as to the events leading up to her flight, having suffered memory loss after a head injury. What we do know is—"

Anya gasped, interrupting Magnus. Leaning forward as if she would crawl across the table to get to him, she cried, "You told me she was unharmed! You lied! Seona, how do ye fare? Tell me all that has happened."

Danu tensed, glad for the large body of the dark-haired knight between her and Anya. She had no answers. She honestly didn't know how Seona fared. For all she knew, the human could have passed through the veil and be lost to the afterlife. As for the rest, Danu hadn't been in this body during the events Magnus described. She was as curious for the answers as Anya.

"Lady Seona has seen Giles," Magnus said. His glare carried a world of warning, but Anya did not appear cowed. "She has been declared healthy and hale with the exception of her memory. Now, I will not be interrupted again, Lady Anya. Your presence at this meeting is not required. Understand?"

Anya returned the king's glare but nodded. The knight by her side closed his eyes and shook his head.

"As I was saying, we know the prisoner Bilkes was an accomplice."

"Bloody degenerate mutt," Anya muttered. With a start, she seemed to remember herself. "My apologies, Your Majesty."

Somehow, she managed to look sheepish and petulant at the same time.

Magnus's mouth quirked. He gave no other indication he had been interrupted. "How and when Seona made contact with Bilkes we must discover. I will not abide vulnerabilities in the security of our ladies or in the keeping of our prisoners. Maedoc—" He addressed the elder of the two knights. "This is your top priority."

The knight nodded. "Yes, Sire."

"Assaph." Magnus directed his gaze down the table to the priest, who jumped at hearing his name. "Your testimony is that Seona and Bilkes trespassed into your apartment before dawn, stole a key, and removed an item from the strong room. Correct?"

Assaph drew himself to his feet, hands twisting his head covering. "Y-yes, Your Majesty." Behind his spectacles, his eyes gleamed with an earnest desire to be helpful. Danu found herself liking him a great deal. Pinning his shoulders back, he seemed to steel himself. "The—ah—item you mention was the gemstone Lord Ari used to cross the veil to the human realm."

At the mention of a gemstone, Danu leaned forward in her seat, but Assaph was not speaking of her moonstone. Rather, he referred to Hyrk's relic. It seemed like years ago that Duff had told her about it, when in reality, scarcely half a day had passed.

A cloud passed over Magnus's face as he said, "Ari betrayed the crown. He lost his lordly title along with his life."

"S—Sorry, Your Majesty," Assaph said, but Magnus waved away the apology and spoke over him.

"The gemstone was also used to hasten the rescue of the human women found in Castle Blackstone." He motioned to Assaph. "Thanks to you." The priest's cheeks colored. "Had you not secured Danu's blessing of the stone, we would never have risked using it to create a passage between Blackstone and Glendall."

Blessed? How interesting! She had been in no position to grant her people blessings. Here was more evidence suggesting some other power was at work in her realm. She must learn more.

"Therefore," continued Magnus. "We know that the gemstone can be used for good or ill." He looked to Assaph for confirmation.

The priest nodded. "It seems so, Your Majesty."

"The question is: why did Bilkes and Seona's seek it out?"

"Seona intended to use it to return to our home," Anya said. "To Scotia, in the human realm." Her intelligent eyes turned to Danu, her expression guarded.

"That explains Seona's motivation, yes," Magnus said, rising from his chair. He began pacing from the head of the table to the fireplace and back. "But what would a condemned prisoner want with a magical gemstone? He had already escaped from Glendall's dungeon. Did he hope to go with Seona to her human realm, where we know there is a woman for every man?"

Several heads nodded. This motivation was plausible, probable, even, considering the state of the wolfkind population.

"This seemed likely to me as well," Magnus said. "Until I spoke with Bilkes this morning at Lachlan's Promontory."

He let silence reign for several heartbeats. At last, he braced his palms on the table. His arm was so near, Danu could smell his fresh scent of forest and leather. She closed her eyes to breathe it in, but only for a moment. She must not let herself become distracted. Magnus was about to relate the events leading up to Seona's fall. If she listened carefully, she might determine what had happened to the human.

"The testimony I am about to give does not leave this room." Magnus met the eyes of each man and woman at the table, including her.

She couldn't help wetting her lips in anticipation.

Magnus's gaze dropped to her mouth. With a muffled growl, he shook his head and returned his attention to the room at large.

He expelled a breath that seemed to weigh a thousand stone and said, "Bilkes is dead. I killed him." Judging by the grim line his mouth made, he took no pleasure in the fact.

A feather could have been heard alighting on the tabletop, so quiet was the solar.

"But it was not Bilkes," Magnus said, piquing her curiosity. "At least, not entirely." He glanced at Assaph before continuing. "It is my belief that the prisoner was possessed. Tell me. Have you heard of such a thing, Assaph?"

Assaph's eyes widened. Slowly, he nodded. "I have heard of possession, Your Majesty. But I have never seen it with my own eyes."

"Neither had I, until today." Magnus resumed his pacing. "I believe the possessing entity was none other than the god Hyrk. The same god who held my cousin in his thrall and whose power was used to bring the human women here from their realm. Assaph," he said, coming to a stop. "We will conference today at the temple. I shall give you my detailed testimony, as will my knights Cadeyrn and Riggs, who witnessed everything. If you find our reports reliable and you feel led by Danu, you will verify the event and record it in the *Archives*. For now, suffice it to say I am certain I spoke with this Hyrk, and *not* the prisoner Bilkes. I believe it was not Bilkes who sought the gemstone, but Hyrk."

That snake! Every muscle in Danu's body tensed. To think Hyrk had possessed one of *her* wolfkind! He would pay. Oh, she would enjoy making him pay.

Assaph sank into his chair, his face ashen. "Oh, King, to think you came so close to wickedness." He was speaking quietly to himself, shaking his head.

Each face around the table reflected the seriousness of what Magnus had just reported. It pleased Danu to see that these mortals understood how rare it was for them to play a role in a battle between deities. Thanks to Hyrk's brazen interference, history was being made in the wolfkind realm. History was being written here at this very table. The outcome of the battle begun two thousand years ago would determine whether her people lived or died.

She would not fail them. She would not let Hyrk win.

Hatred created a second heartbeat in her chest. Her enemy had meddled in the affairs of her people long enough. It was time to put him in his place.

"Assaph." Magnus's tone was gentle. "I am quite hale. No harm done. But I need to learn everything I can about Hyrk."

Assaph wrung his hands. "But—but, Your Majesty, my research has uncovered no record of such a deity." He spoke as if this was not the first time Magnus had desired to learn about her enemy.

"I know," Magnus said, soothingly. "Fear not. I know that you have found nothing in the *Archives* about a god by that name, but perhaps—"

Danu huffed a bitter laugh at hearing Hyrk called a god. "That is because he is not a deity at all," she scoffed. "But a mere demigod seeking to steal my realm."

The entire chamber seemed to suck in a breath.

Danu's stomach dropped. She might be a goddess, but that did not make her infallible. She had forgotten her goal to remain inconspicuous. Seona would not be an authority on deities and demigods. She had said too much.

Magnus stilled. He studied her in silence for moments that stretched into an eternity. At last, he spread his arms and smiled, addressing the room as if she had not spoken. "This Hyrk—in Bilkes's body—had possession of the gemstone. But when he threw—" He swallowed and started again. "I looked on as Seona snatched it from him. Ultimately, it was lost to the canyon."

Danu relaxed as her slip faded into the past. She sat up straighter, listening as Magnus handed her the answer she sought. Seona had touched Hyrk's relic, which had been blessed in her name. That could explain how Danu had come to be in Seona's body. And it likely meant Seona was locked in Hyrk's dungeon in her place.

Worry made her hands clench into fists. No mortal could survive the cold power of those bars. But wait. Seona would no longer be mortal. She would be…a goddess.

"When I killed Bilkes, Hyrk left his body," Magnus was saying.

Danu forced herself to pay attention. She must repair this swapping of bodies, and to do so, she must learn all she could. She gathered Hyrk had not succeeded in reclaiming his relic. This was good news. But he would not stop trying. He must not be allowed to get his hands on it a second time. With his power restored and hers unavailable to her, her people would be sitting quail. So would she.

"That means he could be anywhere." Magnus said. Again, he locked gazes with each person in the solar. "Inside of anyone," he said as his eyes met hers.

She stirred, uncomfortable with his attention, though she couldn't place the reason.

Magnus stood tall, returning his attention to the whole table. "He will no doubt continue to seek out the gemstone. If he succeeds, there is no telling how much power he will wield or what he will do with it. What is clear—" He traded a significant look with the knight he had addressed as Riggs. "Is that he hates Danu and intends to destroy her creation." He pounded a fist on the tabletop. "We must prevent this at all costs."

Murmurs of agreement sounded around the table. The mood in the solar shifted. Action was imminent. Danu bristled with eagerness to act, even as a strange heaviness began to pull at her eyelids.

"Assaph, we will conference in the temple in one hour," Magnus decreed. "I must learn all I can about Hyrk." At Assaph's panicked look, he added—"I know you found nothing in the *Archives,* but I would like you to search your library of poems for any mention of this demigod."

Assaph's brows rose in surprise, but he nodded. "Yes, Sire."

"Riggs." Magnus addressed the younger of the two knights, the one with his arm around Anya. "You will gather as many men as you need and search for the gemstone in the canyon. You saw where she—" He cleared his throat. "Where *it* fell. Bring several pups with you. They have more recent practice with hide-and-seek." He smiled warmly, the expression dimpling his bearded cheek, before sobering. "Look as long as you have to. Tonight's moon shall be nearly full. It will light your way. The gemstone shall be returned to Assaph's care by the rising of the sun. I have spoken."

"My king has spoken, and it shall be done," Riggs said with a fist over his heart.

Danu watched the room clear. She wished to know whether her assumption was correct, that Seona was in her place in Hyrk's dungeon. She needed to speak with Duff. He'd been there when she had been thrust into Seona's body. He would know if Seona had been thrust into hers. But how would she summon him? She had no power in this mortal body.

Huffing with annoyance, she cursed her lack of power. Never before had she felt helpless. Not even as a child, because she could always ask for whatever she desired, and her father would grant it. Here, there was no one she could ask for help regarding what had happened to her and Seona. Adding to her dismay, her eyelids continued to feel heavy. Her stomach groaned painfully—and audibly, judging by the glances of those closest to her.

"Lady Seona," Magnus said quietly. "Is all well?"

She forced her features to calm. "Well enough," she answered vaguely. She did not wish to tell lies. Small deficits in morality paved the way for larger ones, and soon, a good heart could be blackened with selfishness. She would guard her identity and perform her investigations with as little deception as possible. Absently, she rubbed her stomach and tried to blink away the heavy feeling in her eyelids.

"She needs a meal," Anya said, locking eyes with Danu. "And rest. 'Tis plain she is hungry and weary. I'll see to her."

Danu stiffened, not only because having Anya "see to her" was the last thing she wanted, but because she had never before experienced hunger or tiredness. As a goddess, she ate food not because she required it but because she desired it. She spent time in bed for carnal reasons, but never to close her eyes and sleep the way mortals did.

Magnus said, "*I* will see to her. You may spend time with your sister once she is well fed and well rested."

Danu relaxed. She would not have to face the fierce little human yet.

Magnus dismissed the others and escorted her to the room he referred to as the Orange Blossom chamber. Once Daly had brought a heaping tray of culinary delights, Magnus left her with six guards, two outside her chamber and four inside. He promised to return after he had spoken with his priest.

Only after she had eaten and lain down upon the soft bed did it occur to her that Magnus's manner with her had been much more reserved than before the meeting. Was it because he had so many concerns demanding his attention, or was it something else?

Before she could develop theories or figure a way to contact Duff, her eyes closed, and she was lost to mortal slumber.

Chapter 11

"Your Majesty, a word." Daly stepped into Magnus's path, his face drawn with worry.

"It will have to wait, Daly." His head of household was late bringing the midday meal he'd requested for Anya and Seona. This was not at all like Daly, and suggested all was not well for his trusted servant. But he had no time for household matters. He must conference with Assaph immediately.

Leaving Daly sputtering in the east-wing corridor, he made a beeline for the eastern entrance, which led across Glendall's terrace to the temple. Already, he'd been waylaid by Nathan, an elderly council member, who had heard rumors about the morning's events. If he had no time for his head of household, he certainly had no time for rumors. However, he could not risk offending his council. He had forced himself to pause long enough to politely refer the man to the council head, Clem, who had been present at the meeting.

If Magnus missed his betraying cousin at all, it was at times like these, when his schedule felt strained to the breaking point. It was Ari who used to intercept questions and assist Daly when he had matters to discuss. It was Ari who would smooth ruffled feathers in the council and distill the day's events into a manageable list of tasks before bringing them to Magnus's attention.

He would have to appoint a new second, and soon. But he did not relish the time it would take to consider candidates. Or the inevitable uncertainty. So many men—and even some of the women—had proven themselves disloyal of late that he doubted he would ever trust again.

The absence of a reliable second, like so many other issues, would have to wait until he could resolve this latest crisis. Treachery was afoot, and every minute he was away from Seona was an opportunity Hyrk might use to strike again. He must find Assaph and share his recent suspicion before he convinced himself it was too daft to mention.

With the doors to the terrace tantalizingly near, he picked up his pace. One of his guards rushed ahead to open the door. Magnus was just about to barrel through when something caught on his sleeve.

"Ye'd think the hounds of hell were after you the way yer rushin' about!" Anya lunged for him and made a fist in his shirtsleeve. Her grip, surprisingly strong for her tiny size, effectively stopped him in his tracks.

He glared at Cadeyrn, the knight serving as one half of his guard this afternoon. It was his job to keep anyone from laying hands on the king of Marann.

Cadeyrn looked helplessly between Anya and Magnus, and Magnus had difficulty faulting him. There was a ferocity about the little human that struck fear into the hearts of most men, regardless of their size or training. Then there was the lifemate scent surrounding her, reminding every other man that she was not to be handled for any reason by anyone save Riggs. Of all the citizens in Chroina, Anya was the only one who could come so near without his guards intercepting her first.

Leave it to her to do so when he had urgent business. "What do you want?" he barked, perhaps more tersely than was required.

"*Och!* Ye have me fair puckled chasin' after ye, and *that's* the greeting ye choose?" It was then he noticed that she had the hand not curled in his sleeve pressed to her side. Quick breaths made her shoulders heave, and sweat had broken over her brow.

She should not be straining herself thus. It could harm the precious jewel she carried in her womb.

How callous he'd been!

His urgency lifted, and only concern for his subject—and friend—remained. "Sit, Lady Anya." He crowded her toward a bench upholstered in the gilt fabric his mother had filled Glendall with when Magnus had been a pup. "Where is Riggs? Shouldn't he be minding you?"

She refused to be pressed onto the bench, using her grip on his arm to remain standing. "Minding me?" Her chin tucked, and her eyes widened murderously. She seemed recovered from her efforts to chase him down. "I need no minding! And do ye no' recall? You sent him to find that bloody gemstone. And find it he will."

"My apologies, my lady." Anya was the only being he ever uttered apology to. She was also one of the only people who dared challenge him when he had offended her, a quality he quite admired when it did not consume him with annoyance.

Finally releasing him, she waved away his apology. "No time for that nonsense. I ken how busy you are. I doubt yer coursin' through the keep like a runner at the games for yer good health. I wouldna trouble you for somat that wasna of utmost import." She glanced at his guard, shifting on her feet. "Magnus." Her tone went still and serious. "That woman—she is no' my sister."

Anya's brow creased. All the bravado she normally cloaked herself with slipped away, and what was left gave him pause. Anya was well and truly concerned.

As was he.

Choosing his words carefully, he said, "I told you. She has lost her memory. Of course she would not seem like herself."

She jerked her head in fierce denial. "No. 'Tis no' memories she lacks but *herself*."

His skin prickled. He was not alone in his suspicions. "Explain."

Anya wrung her hands. "I ken my sister. E'en after all she's been through in Larna, she was still Seona. Now—" She expelled a breath of frustration. "She's all wrong. Her voice. Her manner. Her expressions. All of it. E'en if she has no memory of who she is, she should yet speak like herself. She should yet move like herself. 'Tis as if another person has taken up her body like a living doll. I dinnae like it, Magnus. Somat is wrong. *Where* is Seona?"

That was a very good question. One he planned to discuss with Assaph.

"Come." He offered his arm, bracing himself to endure her lifemate scent. Slowly, he was growing used to it, but he would never enjoy close proximity to the little human, not when the constant reminder of her union with Riggs battered his senses.

Understanding lit her face as she accepted his arm. "You ken it already. You believe me."

He nodded. "Yes." The word was half growl. Something had happened to Seona this morning, and he had a terrible feeling it was not the miracle he had assumed it to be. More like a curse. "I hope I am wrong."

Crossing the terrace at Anya's pace slowed him, but he didn't mind. Anya's sharp mind would be an asset, especially where Seona was concerned.

"Where is Travis?" he asked to make conversation as they walked. The pup was tasked with seeing to Anya's needs, a role he had taken even more seriously since Anya announced her pregnancy. It was rare to see her without her little shadow at her heels.

Anya wore special shoes to compensate for her severe limp, but long bouts of walking seemed to pain her nonetheless. Between labored breaths, she said, "I havena seen him since this morn, but I suspect he went with Riggs to search for that gemstone."

Yes. Magnus had instructed Riggs to take some pups to help in the search. He paused to finger a winter-bare rosebush, giving Anya a moment to rest. When they finally reached the temple, he guided Anya into Assaph's study, leaving his guard in the sanctuary. This time, she accepted the seat he provided her, a wooden chair across the slanted desk used for reading and writing. Scrolls and loose sheets of parchment covered the surface. The parchment on top held hastily-scrawled words in drying ink.

Assaph hurried to find a second chair for Magnus, but he was too busy pacing to use it.

"Tell me you have found something useful about Hyrk," he demanded. While Assaph rifled through sheets of parchment, Magnus paused in his pacing long enough to study the man. The collar of his robe listed to one side, as if he'd hastily loosened it with a finger. His spectacles sat crookedly on his nose, and ink stained his fingertips. Scarcely an hour had passed since the meeting, giving Assaph precious little time to scour the library. "If you please, Assaph," he amended.

A quick smile gave him a glimpse of the highly educated friend with whom he'd studied and spent untold hours discussing the marvels of their goddess. "You know most everything I do, Your Majesty." Assaph remained standing, as did Magnus. For once Anya remained quiet. She leaned forward in her chair, eyes boring into poor Assaph as if she could discern the answers before he spoke them aloud. "Last moon, we learned that Hyrk is a god. At least, that is the term Ari used when calling upon him. As you know, I found no mention of this name in the Temple *Archives*. But I had been looking for a deity."

Magnus nodded. Impatience vibrated through him, but he forced himself not to show it. Assaph had experienced quite enough strain today without him adding to it. "Go on," he encouraged.

"This afternoon in your solar, Lady Seona suggested Hyrk is not a god but a *demi*-god." He emphasized the *demi*. "I had never heard the term in relation to deities, but Lady Seona's words reminded me of a poem from *Abiding in Her Grace*." He reached beneath his desk and lifted out a heavy tome. As he opened it to a marked page, his eyes glowed with excitement. "Wouldn't you know, Sire, the poem mentions a being I believe to be Hyrk. Here." Finding a sheet of parchment with writing on it, he said, "I took the liberty of transcribing the passage if you wish to take it with you."

Magnus took the parchment and followed along as the priest read aloud from the tome.

Her people are her first love.
She holds them closer to her heart than a lover.
Her creation is her lifemate.
Nothing created or eternal,
Mortal or immortal,
Not the most transcendent of the Fae,
Not even the raven-haired courtier to the queen herself,
The one known as Darkness,
Not the most magnificent of the lower gods,
Not even her spurned suitor spawned from the goddess Rachelle,
The one known as Viehyrken the Red
Nothing and no one,
Not even godhood itself
Shall separate her from her lifemate.

Magnus closed his eyes and let his awareness expand with love for his goddess. "I treasure this passage," he told Assaph. It was one of the pieces that had shored him up when he had lost his father at the age of twelve. Nothing filled him with peace like dwelling on the love of Danu for her creation. "Her lifemate is her people. All of us. The poem claims no power in heaven or on Earth can keep her from us." Sorrow filled him. "But Tanisten is wrong. She has not been with us in a long time."

"'Tis lovely," Anya said. "Even if it is wrong."

"*Wrong* is rather harsh," Assaph said to Magnus. "Perhaps her blessing is not with us now, but I take heart in the words of this passage. In the end, Danu will be one with her lifemate." He turned to Anya. "These are the words of the poet Tanisten, scribed over six hundred years ago. I find it remarkable that they describe a 'lower god' with a name remarkably similar to Hyrk's. And 'the Red' may refer to his gemstone. I believe we can learn from this passage that Danu will be victorious in the end, that Hyrk will be defeated."

"But not before he's worked plenty of mischief, I'd wager," Anya said. "The poem said he was a spurned suitor." Anya leveled a serious look at Magnus. "I have been spurned in love before, and 'tis no' a nice feeling. I doona consider myself wicked, but I have done some wicked things believing them justified by my pain. If a human with respect for her Lord and God can sink to such depths, what might a spurned demigod do?"

"The prospects are dire, indeed," Assaph said.

"Perhaps," Magnus said. "But Tanisten was a poet, not a priest. We should take care when interpreting writings that are not part of the *Archives.*"

"I agree," Assaph said.

"Care to enlighten me, o' learned ones? What does it matter if the passage isna 'of the *Archives*?'" She intoned the phrase in a passable imitation of Magnus's voice.

Assaph straightened his spectacles. "Every word in the *Temple Archives,* from the story of how Danu created the world to the records of visits she would pay to the rulers of Eire in times of old, has been verified by high priests of the temple as originating with Danu, herself. Though written by the hands of men, they are her words, and they are utterly without fault. This—" Assaph laid a reverent hand on the tome. "Is *Abiding in Her Grace,* the collected works of the great poets, twenty-one monks spanning the last thousand years." Assaph gazed lovingly at the volume before a wistful sigh escaped his lips.

At Anya's raised eyebrow, Magnus explained, "*Abiding* is the closest thing we of this century have to recent revelation from Danu."

"Don't forget the vision the goddess gave you," Assaph said.

"And the vision," Magnus agreed with a warm feeling of pride. "But in the last two thousand years, there have been no additions to the *Temple Archives.*"

"Every word we have from Danu herself is two millennia old," Assaph said. "Preserved faithfully by temple priests and monks. But no revelations have been verified since ancient times."

"Why?" Anya asked. Her simple question made Magnus wish there were a simple answer.

"Some think Danu has revoked her blessing," Assaph said. "Others—"

"Since the time of Jilken," Anya interrupted, bouncing in her chair like a student with an answer. "The Larnian king used dark magic to breed his warriors with wolves, aye?"

Magnus nodded, surprised she knew this dark chapter of their history.

"Riggs told me," she said, and her eyes reflected pride in her lifemate. "He told me bairns who werena fierce enough were discarded like refuse, and that some believe Jilken's acts caused Danu to cease her blessing of wolfkind."

"Yes," said Magnus. "The birth rate of females began decreasing around Jilken and Lachlan's time. That is also when our priests stopped receiving revelations from Danu."

Anya peered thoughtfully at Assaph. "Ye said 'some think.' That means no' everyone believes in the curse."

Assaph held up a finger. "Ah-ha. Yes. You are absolutely correct, Lady Anya. *Some* believe we are under a curse. Others, like me, wonder if perhaps something happened to separate Danu from her creation."

"But the poem," Anya said.

"Is not of the *Temple Archives*," Magnus said, and Assaph nodded his agreement, though with some hesitation.

Anya's brow furrowed. "What could possibly happen to a goddess to keep her from her creation?"

"Nothing," Magnus said. "It is merely a poem."

Assaph spread his hands. "We do not know, my lady. But my whole ministry, I've believed that Danu did not choose to curse us, that something or someone caused her to be separated from us against her will."

Magnus quelled an impulse to shake his head. This was an argument he and Assaph had long debated. He must not have succeeded in disguising what he thought of Assaph's theory, because the priest smiled ruefully at him.

"I know, I know, Sire. We have always disagreed on this. I have no proof or revelation to support my assumption. It is more of a gut feeling."

"A wise Scotswoman trusts her gut," Anya said with a decisive nod.

Magnus said, "If Danu has been forcibly separated from us, then how could I have received a verified prophecy from her? How is it we have the Translation Stone? How is it we have Anya and the babe growing inside her? These are clearly blessings from Danu." He motioned to Anya and did not miss how she sat taller in her chair. "Besides, we need more than 'gut feelings' to fight Hyrk. He has made us a target, and I have no doubt he will strike again. We must be prepared."

Assaph sighed. "On this, we most definitely agree. Unfortunately, we have little more to guide us than this single poem written six-hundred years ago." Assaph had done precisely what Magnus had asked of him. He ought to be grateful. Instead, he had even more questions.

"It's not good enough." Magnus pounded his fist on the writing table. How he wished there were more information on Hyrk. On his motives, his tactics. "Wait." Memory lit like a flame. Hyrk's words filled his mind, accompanied by the sight of that eerie light burning from Bilkes's eyes and the gemstone clutched in a dirt-streaked hand.

"How quaint that you think your goddess has any power to aid you. It is I you ought pray to. It is I who shall soon rule your entire world. And your precious Danu shall be my servant for all time."

"I remember." He wheeled to face Assaph. "This morning, when I encountered Hyrk, he was clearly possessing the prisoner. He held the gemstone, and his eyes glowed red." Magnus had been so furious at Hyrk's manhandling of Seona he had barely paid heed to the words falling from Bilkes's lips. It was a miracle he remembered them at all. He relayed them to Assaph with urgency. "He spoke about ruling us. He said Danu would be his servant for all time." All day, he'd been seeking knowledge about Hyrk, and as it happened, he held it within himself.

"Good. Good." Excitement came over Assaph, his fingers drummed at the air as he talked. "So we know what he wants. To rule us. To make Danu his servant. And he must need the gemstone to accomplish these things, or else why would he have stolen it? This helps, Sire. Do you recall anything more?"

Magnus let himself fall into the memory. He relived the terror he'd felt for Seona, the fear at realizing he faced a wicked immortal, the sharp wound to his pride when Seona had wished for death over being returned into his care. "He mentioned Ari and Bantus. It seems he is furious with me for his loss of those two men."

"He was using them," Assaph said. "And now he doesn't have them anymore."

"He said he wanted me to suffer, and that's when—" Magnus broke off, remembering the woman sitting close by.

"The stone went over the cliff," Assaph finished for him, tactful as always.

"And my sister," Anya said. "Dinnae censure your words wi' me. I ken she isna right. 'Tis why I'm here, no?"

"Yes," Magnus confirmed. "In fact, that is why I am here, as well, Assaph. I suspect there may be more to Lady Seona's state than mere loss of memory."

He'd been over every interaction he'd had with her since her fall—nay, even before her fall. In the split second it took Hyrk to toss her over the cliff, she had managed to grab the jagged gemstone from his hand, but when he'd gotten to her down in the canyon bed, the stone had been missing, perhaps hidden on her person. No doubt, the stone's power was to thank for the miraculous healing of her broken and bloodied body.

Then, during the ride back to Glendall, her first words to him had been, *"What have you done, you sly mongrel?"* She had also demanded, *"Tell me what you know of Hyrk, mortal—Magnus."* He had pretended not to notice the slip, but notice he had.

Then there was her wonder at every aspect of life in Glendall, exaggerated, no doubt, as part of an act. And, of course, her blurted declaration during the meeting, revealing knowledge of Hyrk's status as a demigod.

The facts all pointed to a single, dreadful conclusion.

"'Tis no' memory she's lacking," Anya said. "That woman isna my sister."

Assaph's eyebrows climbed his forehead. He looked from Anya to Magnus.

"I agree with Lady Anya's assessment," Magnus said. "I need you to tell me how to test whether Hyrk might have taken up possession of Lady Seona."

Chapter 12

"Danu, love. Wakie, wakie." A familiar voice tugged at her ears. She longed to respond, but her body felt heavy. Her eyes were hot and swollen. They refused to open.

"Go away." All she wanted was to sink deeper into the embrace of mortal slumber.

"Ah, love. Don't be like that. Come. Join me." Duff. The voice belonged to Duff. She liked Duff, but she did not feel like waking.

"Too tired."

"I have information for you." The sing-songy voice encouraged her to blink a few times. She had been wanting to speak with Duff, she remembered. "Information about Hyrk."

That did it. She forced her eyes open. They wanted to close again, but she dug her knuckles into them until the sensation passed. Was it always so difficult for mortals to rouse from slumber? How awful for them.

She expected to see the inside of what Magnus had called the Orange Blossom chamber. Enameled walls lined with tapestries should have welcomed her along with gilt furniture, the sweet scents of citrus and flowers, and guards protecting her in her sleep. Instead, she opened her eyes to a field of magenta and periwinkle wildflowers. On the horizon, the sun cast a golden light over the landscape. It hung like an ornament, too large and almost too beautiful to behold. A gentle, perfumed breeze tickled the flowers, sending waves through them, like an ocean tide.

"There she is." Affection sweetened Duff's voice like honey through tea. He sat beside her amidst the flowers wearing the traditional silvery robes of the Fae court. He was resplendent with his shining black hair, skin of smoothest ivory, and lips that beckoned endless nipping and nuzzling. Not that she desired those things from Duff any longer. It was Magnus who stirred her longing now. And his kingdom was in danger from Hyrk. "I was worried about you," Duff said. "Are you well, love?"

She thought about the question and answered with some surprise, "I am." Despite the many questions plaguing her as she'd fallen asleep, a strange peace had settled over her. Her limbs were languid, her mood happy. It was this place doing it to her. "Where are we? How did you take me away from Glendall? Magnus had guards watching me."

"Do not fear, love. You are still there, sound asleep. This is the realm of dreams."

"I'm dreaming?" Heavens. She had walked through the dreams of mortals countless times, but since she required no sleep as a goddess, she had never dreamt. "How strange."

"It feels much like waking, no?" Duff watched the brilliant orb. It had moved not a single inch since she'd opened her eyes.

"Yes. Only different. I feel…at peace."

His eyebrows lifted, and he studied her. "Interesting."

A laugh bubbled from her. "You sound surprised. Should I not enjoy a few moments' peace?"

"No one deserves peace more than you." He gazed at her with sober intent. "It is interesting because your mood in this realm reflects what is in your heart." He brushed his hand over the tops of nearby flowers. Against his skin, the petals whispered and danced. "In dreams, mortals' hearts are set free."

"But I am not mortal." She said it without ire. It was simply truth, and she was sharing it with Duff.

"Ah, but you are. And guess who is now a goddess?"

"Seona," she said without hesitation.

Duff nodded, confirming her suspicion. She now knew for sure where Seona had gone.

"So, she is in Hyrk's dungeon."

"Unfortunately."

"No. Not unfortunately. If we had not traded places, she would be dead. At least she lives."

Duff grasped her hand. "And you? How is it you are not dead? You took the fall for her, yes?"

She shuddered at the memory. "I did. But I was healed. By whose power, I do not know, but I am grateful for it." She laced their fingers together. "It is good to see you as yourself, friend. I have missed you."

Duff smiled warmly at her. His eyes twinkled with affection. Not lust. Only affection. "I have missed you, as well." His lips quirked playfully. "How is Magnus?"

Her cheeks warmed. She remained silent.

"I see he is well," Duff said on a quiet laugh. Sighing, he became serious. "I should not tarry. Seona was loath to see me go. She is very afraid. I came to tell you what I've learned from her."

She sat up straighter. "Tell me." She craved knowledge of how Seona had ended up in Hyrk's clutches. Knowledge of how to rescue the human. And how to put herself back in her true form.

"It started with a boy," he began. He reclined on an elbow with one knee bent. Between his finger and thumb, he twirled the stem of a plucked flower. "A blond-haired pup. Seona felt alone in the king's home. She had her sister, but even Anya kept trying to convince her to love the very beings she hated—and with good reason after what that filth, Bantus, did to her." Rage flashed like lightning in Duff's eyes. He cared for the mortal.

Now *that* was interesting. She was careful not to reveal that she'd noticed his feelings as he went on.

"The boy sympathized with her plight and made no secret of his disgust with Magnus—a king like the one who abused her. He offered her a way out. A way back to her home, but to get it, she had to tolerate the presence of wolfkind man."

"The prisoner," she said, remembering the meeting in Magnus's solar. "And the way out must have been Hyrk's relic."

"Very good, love. Seona and the prisoner found common ground. They both coveted freedom. Together, they raided the temple and took the gemstone."

Her molars ground against each other with her anger. *Her* temple had been desecrated by a pair of thieves consumed with self-interest. "I can guess what happened the moment they got ahold of it."

Duff's eyes darkened. "Hyrk entered the prisoner. Seona remembers it happening. They had been on horseback, racing away from Chroina. One moment, the prisoner had been holding her to him as they rode, making promises of how he would protect her and serve her in her realm. The next moment, he drew the horse to a stop at the edge of a canyon and yanked her off. He treated her roughly, and his voice had changed. His eyes glowed red."

"She must have been terrified," Danu said. Her anger gave way to sympathy. The human had been searching for freedom, but what she found instead was the imprisonment that Danu deserved.

"Soon after, Magnus appeared," Duff said. "He and Hyrk argued. Hyrk said he wanted to make Magnus suffer. Then he threw Seona from the cliff." His gaze went distant. "Grabbing his gemstone and trying to use it is the last thing she remembers."

Danu blinked. "Really? She tried to use it as she fell? That was cunning of her."

"She's a cunning woman. It didn't work, though."

"She ended up in an immortal's dungeon instead of in her realm. What a shock that must have been."

"It was a shock, all right," Duff said. "For all three of us."

"Indeed." Now Danu knew the events leading up to the fall. But she still didn't understand whose power had made them trade places and healed her after the fall. Not Duff's. He had been talking with her in Hyrk's dungeon at the time. Not hers. She'd had no magic to use while imprisoned. Not Hyrk's. He would never have worked magic to help her in any way, and according to Seona's memory, he'd wanted her to die so Magnus would suffer.

"How in all the realms did this happen?" She stood and began pacing. The flowers made a soft cushion beneath her sandaled feet. "Seona's wish was to return to her realm. Why did the magic involve me?"

Duff shrugged, as if the origin of the magic was of no concern. "I have learned that magic is not predictable. I think—I think it is sentient. It has motives that we can only guess at."

"That's ridiculous." She stopped her pacing and frowned at her friend, who remained seated amidst the flowers as if he hadn't a care in the world. "Magic originates from immortals with sentience. It does not act on its own."

"If you say so. Either way, it doesn't change the circumstances. Magic has occurred. Now it is our move."

She frowned. "You make it sound like a game. Is that all my fate is to you? Is that all Seona's fate is to you?"

Duff shot to his feet. "Of course not. Just because I choose not to obsess about magical origins doesn't mean I don't care what becomes of her. Or you."

She hadn't missed how he put Seona first. Despite their disagreement, it warmed her heart to see her friend riled up over a woman.

"You care for her."

Duff's head jerked. Surprised eyes met hers. "You guessed?"

She huffed a petite laugh. "It was not that difficult."

"You care for Magnus," he said with a tug to her hair.

"Ouch! Stop that. Are we children now? Teasing each other about romantic fancies?"

His laughter was a delight. The joyous sound sent visible ripples through the flowers.

She couldn't help joining him. But her mirth only lasted a moment. "What are we to do, Duff? Seona has been caught up in a battle of immortals. After all her suffering, she should not have to face imprisonment. We must find a way to trade places again."

Duff blinked at her as if she'd lost her mind. "Trade places? You would put yourself back in Hyrk's clutches to free a mortal? A human?"

She stiffened. "Of course I would. She may not be wolfkind, but I refuse to let Hyrk punish her in my stead. He has no right to her."

"He has no right to you!" Duff's vehemence flattened stems in every direction.

When the echo stopped and the flowers recovered, she said, "You are wrong. I was foolish enough to bargain with him. I played his game, and he won. My imprisonment is my own fault. The sorry state of my realm is my own fault." She stared at her feet and noticed a bud striving to bloom. Its petals were just beginning to separate. Inside the tight furl, stamens peeked out like butterflies trying to push free from cocoons.

"Oh, *boo-hoo,*" Duff said. He pretended to knuckle tears from his eyes. "Poor Danu, she made a mistake and now she deserves to suffer for all eternity." He threw his hands in the air and paced on long, graceful legs. "Her entire creation deserves to die because a bad demigod tricked her. Is that the legacy you want to leave your people? That their mistakes are unforgivable? That they should bear their suffering with dignity instead of fighting to fix what needs fixing?" Under his feet, flowers crumpled, but only momentarily before springing upright again.

So shocked was she at his anger it took her a moment to untangle all he'd said. When she did, rage pushed her to stand toe to toe with him. "How dare you mock me?"

"I'll mock you all I want when you're being ridiculous."

Nearby flowers cinched up their petals, as if to protect themselves from the shouting. Danu was not accustomed to the lesser stature of her new body. Duff towered over her where once, they had been of similar height. The difference fueled her ire even more.

"Ridiculous?" she hurled at him "I'm being honest! It should be me in Hyrk's blasted cell. Not her."

"And I suppose it should be Seona by the side of your King Magnus."

No! "Yes." Only her heart didn't believe that. Not for one second.

Duff's satisfied smirk made her ball her fists.

"I've admitted I feel for Seona," he said. "It is time you admit you feel for your king."

Damn him. Her shoulders rounded, and her fists loosened. "So what if I do. Maybe you're right. Maybe I don't deserve Hyrk's prison. But Seona deserves it much less. I must take her place. I must."

"People only say things twice when they are trying to convince themselves." His tone gentled. "Neither of you deserves what Hyrk has wrought."

"But one of us must suffer it." It had to be her. She must return to her true form. Even if it meant leaving Magnus.

A fierce ache stabbed through her center at the thought.

She didn't want to leave her mortal realm so soon. She'd only just arrived. There was still so much she wanted to experience. She wanted more time to enjoy the children. She wanted to attend balls and celebrations. She wanted to peruse the library Magnus kept at

Glendall. Most of all, her body burned for more of Magnus's embrace. More of his kisses. More of *him*.

But this could not be. It was not *meant* to be.

Sadness overwhelmed her. She buried her face in her hands. Tears fell between her fingers.

Strong arms circled her. "Let it out, love. Let it all out. Losing your deity cannot be easy. But since when do you bend to a fate another has chosen for you?" He held her away by her shoulders and sought out her gaze. "Cry your tears, then stand and fight like the warrior wolfwomen of old. The ones who defended their young and guarded their borders. The ones we used to cheer on in battle." He stroked her back, and she leaned into his soothing.

A hiccup escaped her. "But I have no power to lend anymore."

"So what? Hyrk is not much better off. He lost his most powerful followers. As far as I know, he lost his relic to the canyon." He bent to pluck a blooming lilac. "What I am certain of is that a simple trading of places is not the solution we must seek. Do you agree?"

She met his gaze. Heavens, he was a beautiful man, all perfect angles and irresistible charm. Seona was a lucky woman to be the focus of that charm. Or she *would* be if they could find a way to free her. "Yes." She nodded, resolute. "I want freedom. For her and for me."

Duff poked the stem into her hair, adorning her with the fragrant bloom. "Happy endings all around. I quite like those."

"All right. How shall we accomplish this?"

"We defeat Hyrk."

"Easier said than done. He's immortal." And she was not. Not any longer.

"Allow me to count the ways a demigod can be defeated." He held up a perfectly manicured finger. "Lose all his followers." Another finger rose to meet the first. "Have his relic destroyed." A third finger. But Duff paused. "Hmm. All right. There are only two ways. But that's better than none."

Danu smiled. "That's better than none."

§

"WHAT ARE YE planning to do, Magnus?" Anya walked at his side, her limp barely noticeable. But she had accepted the support of the arm he offered, so he understood she was disguising her pain.

He was still learning how to handle the human women. In some ways, they were much more proud than the sybaritic ladies of wolfkind, like when Anya pretended her legs didn't pain her. In some ways, they were far more humble, like when Anya had given him the Translation Stone so he could communicate with the rescued women. He had hoped to employ every last bit of his learning in wooing Seona, but now he did not even know if the woman asleep in the Orange Blossom chamber *was* Seona. Or if she was a woman at all.

Keeping his pace slow, he said, "I will do precisely as Assaph suggested and bring her to the temple." If Seona was possessed by Hyrk, as he feared, her behavior would change upon entering the temple. She would show signs of discomfort or anger. No amount of acting could disguise the hatred in the heart of Danu's enemy. He would be compelled to show himself as the wicked demon he was.

When Hyrk revealed his true nature, Assaph would be ready with a blessed vial of holy oil and a caged rat—a fitting receptacle for Hyrk's spirit—no, too good of a receptacle. The poor rat didn't deserve Hyrk, but if Magnus's suspicion was correct, the small beast's impending burning could save them all. Magnus would not rest until it was done.

He only wished he knew what this would mean for Seona. If she were, in fact, possessed by a wicked demigod, what state would she be in upon becoming herself again? Would she shove him away as she had in the past? Try to escape again, racing toward death as an alternative to spending one more minute in his care?

"I'm coming with you," Anya said. "You need me," she added, no doubt anticipating his refusal.

"What I need is for you to take some rest, Lady Anya. It has been a long day. You have been taxing yourself." The future of his people rested in her womb. He would have her chained to her bed for the baby's safety if not for the certainty she would hurt herself trying to escape. Unlike many wolfkind women, Anya was not one to remain abed and expect service.

Of course, Anya argued. "I willna sit by and watch you do everything yourself when 'tis clear *you* need more rest than I."

Perhaps she was correct, but such was the price of leadership. He had learned to live with his exhaustion. His kingdom could not afford to lose the precious gem Anya carried. He would not be swayed on this. "You will rest," he said. "If you do not give me your word, I will post guards at your door to ensure you sleep through the night."

Her lips flattened. "You need every man you've got. You canna spare any for looking after a thorn in yer side."

He sighed, weary of arguing with her. "You are not a thorn, Anya. You have been most helpful. You are always most helpful. But you absolutely must help me in this moment by ensuring you and the child you carry rest well. Then wake and eat well. This privilege Danu has blessed you with is not to be taken for granted." He took both her hands in his. "Even if you don't agree with me, I ask this of you. Rest. Eat. And rejoin me in the morning. I will tell you all that happens tonight, I swear. Now, do I have your word you will rest?"

"Curse you," she muttered. "Fine. Ye have my word. I shall rest."

"All night."

"*Och*, for the love of haggis. Aye. I shall rest the whole night."

"Thank you, my lady." He kissed the back of her hand and left her at the doors of Glendall.

Squaring his shoulders, he marched to his residential wing. He had a date with a demon.

Chapter 13

OUTSIDE THE ORANGE Blossom chamber, Magnus conferred with the guards watching over Seona. According to them, she had slept soundly and made not a peep the entire time he'd been gone. Relief filled him to know Hyrk had attempted no evil while he'd been with Assaph. Perhaps the entity was resting. Perhaps he was biding his time.

Soon, his time would be up and his wicked influence would be ended once and for all. Magnus would make sure of it.

Quietly, he slipped into the chamber and exchanged quiet greetings with the guards inside. On the bed, Seona lay covered in lush fabrics and furs. Creeping closer, he took in the innocent way she slept, cheek pillowed on one hand, her other tucked under a silken pillow. Her hair fanned over the pillow, revealing one rounded ear. Without his telling it to, his hand reached toward her, finger poised to stroke the delicate curve so like a seashell. Horrified at himself, he dropped his hand to his side.

It was as if he'd forgotten for a moment who and what she was. Still, the sight of her vulnerable in sleep made his breath catch. A deep longing to protect her filled his chest, vital as air.

But it is not her. These feelings cannot be trusted.

"Time to wake, Lady Seona," he said none too gently.

She stirred. Her eyelids fluttered, and her full lips parted in a yawn. "Hmmmm?" A feline stretch had her gracefully sprawled beneath the blankets. When she blinked open her eyes and smiled up at him, his heart squeezed. Of course, he ignored the sensation. "How long did I sleep?"

"A few hours." He strove for a natural tone, not wishing to give away his intentions. "I hope you feel up to a short walk. I have something to show you."

Excitement lit her eyes. "Yes!" She pushed herself up, and her creamy breasts plumped beneath her dressing gown. Perhaps this was an attempt by Hyrk to seduce him into letting down his guard. "I would love to walk with you. Will you help me dress?"

"No." He cleared his throat. "I'll send for Daly." He strode to the door and commanded one of his men to summon Daly and a lad to help Seona dress. When he faced her again, he found her helping herself to a cup of water from the pitcher on the bureau. The dressing gown skimmed over her slender figure, displaying feminine curves that tempted him toward arousal. As she drank, her delicate throat moved with her swallows. He did not let himself become mesmerized or entertain the desire to feather tender kisses over that throat.

Finished with her water, she placed the cup beside the pitcher and reached for a hairbrush with refined movements. "Did you learn anything about Hyrk while I slept?" she asked, her voice casual.

For a moment, he imagined her as his queen. This would be her dressing chamber, but the bed would go unused—they would sleep together in his chamber every night. For the rest of their lives. While they readied themselves each morning, she would discuss kingdom matters with him, just as she was doing now.

When he didn't respond quickly enough, she added, "You were hoping to learn more about our enemy from Assaph, yes? And your knight—was it Maedoc?—was to determine how the prisoner escaped—Oh!" She froze with the bristles half-way down a lock of hair. Whirling to face him, she said in a rush, "A boy helped the prisoner. A blond boy."

He sucked in a breath, surprised at her seeming certainty a mere breath after inquiring about what he'd learned. Perhaps Hyrk intended to mislead him.

"Tell me how you know this," he challenged.

"Seona remembered—I mean, *I* remembered." She averted her gaze and continued brushing her hair. "It was a boy," she continued smoothly, but he had not missed the slip. "A blond boy who convinced—me—to steal the stone. And I believe he helped the prisoner escape as well."

Inadvertently, she had referred to herself as *Seona.* What more confirmation did he need that she was not a *she* at all, but the vile Hyrk?

"You say a blond boy convinced you. Tell me more. Now that you remember." He doubted the tale was true, considering the source, but he would listen and investigate nonetheless. Perhaps Hyrk's misinformation would reveal something useful.

But at that moment, Daly arrived. "You sent for me, Sire?" He wrung his hands. His normally tidy gray hair was disheveled as if he'd been rushing about. Unfortunately, Magnus had no time to inquire after Daly's state.

"Fetch a lad to help Seona dress. And bring her a meal, please." To Seona, he said, "I will investigate what you've told me and return shortly. Do not dally. We will leave at once upon my return."

Leaving Daly sputtering, he hastened from the chamber and made his way to the dungeon. There were precisely two blond-haired pups in the whole of Chroina: Travis, the youngest of their race, and his elder brother by seven years, Alexander. The presence of either of Diana's boys in the dungeon would be noticed. A few simple questions would clear up the matter, and he knew just where to begin.

One of his guards pulled open the door to the dungeon and held it while Magnus strode into the central chamber. Four labyrinthine wings branched out from the circular room, and it was here where the prison guards met and kept their records. With Chroina's population so low, two of the wings were long abandoned, or so Magnus had thought.

Two moons ago, he had discovered that a far end of one wing had been in use. Accessing the space through a disused corridor, members of the Breeding First party had furnished the cells and used them to further their aims—aims that directly opposed the traditionalist values of the crown.

Magnus, like generations of kings before him, strongly believed that the sires of children should be documented. The *Temple Archives* taught that bloodline was an essential part of a moonsoul's identity. Therefore, even though multiple bedmates were a necessity for their women, the law stated that only one bedmate could be taken per breeding season. The breeding lottery ensured every male had an equal chance of siring a child each season, and careful records were kept to ensure Danu's teachings were followed. Breeding First had betrayed the crown, and Danu, by allowing women of the party to secretly take as many bedmates as they desired in the effort to breed.

That wing of the dungeon was now filled in with rock and debris. Magnus had ensured it would never be used again. The women caught participating in Breeding First's plot were under house arrest in the *Fiona Blath,* and the men now resided in the dungeon, where they would never again experience the honor of a lady's company.

The central chamber's desk and shelves of records looked in order. The unoccupied wings had their doors sealed shut. The other two stood open. Beyond one, a guard made his rounds, his back disappearing around a corner as he paced away from the central chamber.

Sitting at one of the desks was the aged warden, who had served since before Magnus's reign. He looked up from where he hastily scrawled on a sheet of parchment. "Sire!" The man shot from his chair and saluted. "About the escape this morning—I am looking into the matter. I offer my sincerest apologies—"

"At ease, Frederick. Cooperate with Maedoc on his investigation. That is all I ask of you. We will get to the bottom of this."

Frederick sagged with visible relief that Magnus was not irate with him. "Of course, Sire. I'll do anything. How may I be of service to you this evening?"

Was it evening already? The time flew past too swiftly. He must make haste here and return to Seona. Every minute he delayed was an opportunity for Hyrk to wreak havoc.

"I shall be interviewing prisoners. I will not need your assistance at this time. Carry on with your task."

He left the warden and entered the east wing first. Here, prisoners were permitted the luxury of a private room and a bed for sleeping. Visitors could come during certain hours. There were precisely two individuals in the wing currently, both here because of their high rank and because Magnus had a soft spot for them both.

The cell closest to the central chamber contained his former war chieftain, Neil. When Magnus strode past his cell and saw the man napping in a rough-hewn chair, the pain of his betrayal stung afresh. Neil had faithfully served him and his father before him. He had led a merciless campaign against Larna twenty years past in which all the remaining Larnian women were rescued from their sadistic king. Neil was uncle to his newest Knight of the Crescent Moon, Riggs, and had been renowned for his ruthless and cunning war tactics. Forevermore, he would only be known as a traitor. To the crown and to the human women Ari had brought over from their realm. Neil had stood by and done nothing—*nothing*—when Ari handed those poor women over to Bantus in exchange for the use of Larna's army in an attempted coup.

Passing Neil's cell, he continued on to an isolated cell at the center of the wing and found who he was looking for. "Lady Diana," he greeted.

"Your Majesty!" Sinuous as a snake, she rose from the chair where she had been reading a thin volume. "You've come to visit! I knew you would. You've missed me, haven't you?" Curling her crimson-tipped fingers around the bars, she put on the airs of a demure maid, batting her lashes at him. She took full advantage of the low cut of her gown, one of only three simple garments she had been permitted to keep, pressing her lightly-furred breasts between her wrists, where they mounded up as if in invitation.

He was immune to the effect, knowing now that Diana was every bit the snake she moved like. She had been Ari's accomplice in every step of his treachery. Her goal had been to sit on the smaller of the two thrones in the great hall, the queen's throne. And she had done everything in her power to see Ari sit the other, including sending Anya through a magic portal to Bantus's dungeon when the human had gotten in the way of their plot.

His stomach curdled at the memory of having Diana in his bed. He'd taken every lady of breeding age to bed at one time or another—Diana more than most because of her proven fertility. She had four sons. One woman, Riggs's mother Hilda, had three sons. The rest were fortunate to have one or two. Sadly, many of the women had never birthed a child. And time was running out for them.

Ignoring Diana's flirting, he said, "I've come to inquire after your sons."

"How lovely! Would you care to come inside and sit? I'm afraid I have no tea to offer and no servant to wait on you. Though if you saw fit to move my residence back to the *Fiona Blath,* I could offer you *much* more hospitality." Her emphasis on the word *much* left no doubt as to which type of hospitality she would like to offer.

Once, Diana was the prize of the breeding lottery. Not only did she take a lottery winner to her bed every season, but she had met Ari and countless other men in the ruined wing of the dungeon in a bid to get all the seed she could. At the moment, she was banished from the lottery, having so recently shared her bed with any number of men. If she grew with child, the precious jewel would of course be welcome, but the true father would never be known. If she did not, she would be permitted to take part in the lottery again, this time under close guard. One man per season, and he must come here, to the dungeon, to breed with her.

"You will remain here, where I can keep close watch on you."

She preened, misunderstanding him. "Of course, Your Majesty. I am happy to be of service to my king anyplace he desires."

"I've not come for your *service*," he said with no small amount of disgust. "Tell me of your last visit with Travis. When was it?"

She blinked. When she realized he had not come here to bed her, she rolled her eyes. Hardness came over her smooth features, making her look every day of her eighty-three years. At her temples, white hairs lightened her golden hair. She was the youngest woman alive in the world, and her hair was now graced with the evidence of age. She had ten or fifteen years left to breed—a frighteningly short time. If not for the child growing in Anya's womb, he would struggle not to despair.

Releasing the bars, she put her hands on her hips and said, "Travis doesn't come to see me anymore. I hear that awful human won't let him." She pushed out her lower lip, as if she expected him to intervene on her behalf.

He doubted Anya kept Travis from seeing his mother. If Travis wasn't visiting, that was his business. Perhaps, when Magnus saw the lad, he would encourage him to bid her good day now and again. Diana was a wicked woman, but as Danu taught them, bloodlines were important. Family was important.

"And Alexander. Tell me when he was last here."

She shrugged an elegant shoulder. "I haven't seen him in a while. Maybe two weeks. I hear he's very busy at the *Fiona Blath*. He brings me news from the common house when he finds the time. It seems without me to intervene, there are catfights aplenty. The serving lads get caught up in them, the poor things. If you sent me back, I could have order restored in no time."

Magnus held back his snort. He made it a point to inquire daily after the affairs of the ladies. According to his reports, there was practically no bickering amongst the women anymore. Hilda, Riggs's mother, had settled into the role of highest lady, and in Diana's absence, harmony had taken the place of the constant infighting.

Ignoring Diana's attempt to change the topic, he continued his line of questioning. "When Alexander was last here, did he speak to anyone besides you?"

"How would I know?" she asked with a hand poised to draw his gaze to her chest.

Magnus looked her dead in the eye. "You would know because you are close with Alexander. He would have told you if he intended to visit other prisoners."

She sighed airily. "Ah, but he is growing up, the strapping lad. He no longer tells his mother everything. Independent, that one. Are you certain you do not wish to rest for a few moments? I have not had a visitor in a long time."

He didn't deign to answer her question. Turning on his heel, he left and ignored her calls behind him. He'd gotten the answer he'd expected. Neither Travis or Alexander had been in the dungeon in at least two weeks. This was nothing but a distraction by Hyrk.

On his way out of the east wing, a rough voice broke the silence. "Sire." It was a voice he knew well.

He was already past Neil's cell, and considered not stopping. However, he and Neil had shared many victories, many drinks, and many laughs. As a boy, Magnus had looked up to the older man.

When Neil had trained him as a warrior, he had striven to please the craggy chieftain. He could not simply walk past.

He turned and approached Neil's cell. "Make it quick," he said. He had to get Seona to the temple as soon as possible. Daly was likely done dressing her by now.

"I won't keep you," Neil said. He didn't bother rising from his chair. He still slumped as if he'd only recently woken from his nap. "But you should know she's lying." He lifted his chin in the direction of Diana's cell. "Xander was here two days ago and again early this morning. He helped that shite Bilkes get out."

Magnus stiffened. The thought Neil could be lying slid through his mind, but it did not stick. Neil had betrayed him, true, but he had always taken matters of security seriously.

"Why are you just telling me this now?" He should have heard of this as soon as it happened.

"No one asked," he said. "Lax security. Lax investigation. Your soldiers and guards are getting soft. They're easily tempted away from their duties."

Magnus gripped the bars. Neil made it sound like vulnerabilities abounded. If this was the case, why had Maedoc not informed him? He'd sent the head of his Knights to the dungeon this morning to assess how Bilkes had escaped and just now realized he hadn't reported back. "Did you tell Maedoc today?"

"Haven't seen Maedoc."

Magnus frowned. Neil might have been asleep when Maedoc came to investigate.

A guard rounded a corner and paced toward them. Magnus stopped him and asked after Maedoc.

"Haven't seen him today, Sire," the guard replied.

"Told you," Neil said.

The guard saluted and continued his rounds.

It seemed every time Magnus turned a corner some new problem demanded his attention. He must add to the ever-growing list Maedoc's absence from the dungeon when Magnus had commanded him to investigate a prisoner's escape.

"And don't bother with that lad." Neil interrupted his thoughts. He lifted his chin in the direction of the guard. "He wasn't here this morning. Just came on shift a few hours ago. It was Henders that was on duty. *Only* Henders. There's usually two guards patrolling overnight, but I never saw a second guard. And when I heard the door to Bilkes's cell open, Henders was getting a pole job from that bitch down there." He jerked his thumb down the corridor toward Diana's cell.

"You heard Bilkes escape? And you did nothing?" Anger made his face hot. Did Neil's betrayal continue even now? He'd confessed in time to warn Magnus of Breeding First's coup, showing he had some loyalty left in him. It was part of why his cell was in this wing and not the other. He'd thought Neil would at least speak up if he saw a prisoner escaping.

"How did I know it was an escape?" Neil growled, glaring from beneath his heavy brow. "He might have been summoned to trial or taken for a medical exam. There are any number of reasons a guard would open his cell." Beneath his prison tunic, he shrugged a meaty shoulder. "I only put the pieces together after I'd heard about Bilkes. He's dead, now, aye?"

Neil's explanation made sense, but Magnus would not fully trust any testimony coming from him. He would have to summon Maedoc and determine whether he had been in the dungeon today to investigate how Bilkes had escaped, and if he had not, Magnus must discover the reason. It was not in the knight's character to disobey a command.

Absently, he confirmed that Bilkes was, in fact, dead, but his mind roiled with all Neil had told him. If everything was true, it meant Diana had managed to betray him from her prison cell. This represented a clear rift in Glendall's security. He would not stand for it.

"So Diana was in it," he said, stroking his beard in thought.

"Aye," Neil said. "My guess is when Xander slipped in before dawn, he let her know it was time to seduce Henders. Henders, the ball-sac, didn't take much convincing to lift his kilt. When he was busy is when I heard the cell door." He jerked his thumb over his shoulder, indicating the back wall of his cell. Bilkes's cell in the other wing must have abutted his; Magnus would confirm this. Fine cracks visible in the stone would allow sounds to pass through.

Yes. The scenario was possible. But it wasn't enough to bring charges against Henders or Diana. He would instruct Maedoc to find witnesses—that was, if the knight could be found.

"Killian." Magnus addressed one of his escort. "Inform Frederick that Henders is not permitted back on duty until further notice."

"Yes, Sire." Killian hurried toward the central chamber.

"You're stretched too thin," Neil said, his voice close. While Magnus had been speaking with Killian, Neil had approached the bars. "You look weary. It's no good, Magnus. You can't do it all, son. You need a new second."

He bristled at Neil calling him son, like old times. "You'll call me Sire," he said. "You lost the right to address me by any other name when you betrayed me."

Color rose in Neil's cheeks, above his gray-streaked beard. "I did what I did for the good of our people. That bitch down there and your snake of a cousin were in it for themselves. I only wanted our women to have more births. Breeding First seemed to have the way of it." His eyes glinted with conviction a moment before they dimmed. "I was wrong. I know better now. What those human women suffered—shite." His voice broke, and Magnus was surprised to see moisture at the corners of his eyes.

Neil looked away to hide his emotion. "Whatever's happening," he said, "You must send them back to their homeland.

As long as they remain here, they'll be in danger. Bantus is gone, aye, but there are still Larnians who will stop at nothing to get their hands on women. Hell, there are Maranners who will stop at nothing to get their hands on them—look at Bilkes, for Danu's sake." He shook his head in an agitated jerk.

"I know," Magnus conceded. "It is one of my top priorities. But there are other things that take precedence." Like ending Hyrk's existence. And finding the gemstone that would open a door to the human realm.

Neil leveled a gaze at him. "You need a second, *Sire.*" He emphasized the title with a quirk of his mouth. "And you need him yesterday."

Of all Neil had said today, this was the truest. If only there were a man he could trust beyond all doubt, a man of wit and strategy, of patience and strength. A man loyal not just to him but to Danu as well.

Of course! He knew a man like that. Why hadn't he seen it before?

With quick steps, he left the dungeon. Perhaps by the time he and Assaph had dealt with Hyrk, Riggs would have returned from hunting for the lost gemstone.

Chapter 14

"YOU HAVE QUITE an escort, Your Majesty." As Magnus walked with Seona across the terrace, her voice pulled him from his spinning thoughts. The smooth alto tone of it soothed him even though he knew she was not herself.

His skin should be crawling to have her gloved hand tucked in the crook of his arm. His senses should rebel at the sound of her voice, the scent of her perfumed skin, and the sight of her clothed to perfection in a forest-green winter gown. She was possessed by an entity that desired his destruction. He should find her abominable.

But nothing about her offended him. Having her on his arm felt *good.* It felt right.

He'd been too long without a bedmate. The impatient fire in his loins was to blame for his lapse in good judgment. He would ignore the way his body leaned toward hers, the way it longed to dominate hers until she lay replete beneath him. He *must* ignore it. He must focus on freeing Seona from Hyrk's hold.

"Do you take eight men with you everywhere?" The question was asked innocently, but surely, this was Hyrk's way of assessing the security at Glendall.

"I take as many guards as I deem necessary," he answered vaguely. "We're almost there."

"Where are we going?" As they neared the temple, she looked in every direction, marveling at the towers of the castle, the winter-bare rose bushes, the ornamental trees, the fountain, the soaring spire of the temple topped with a crescent moon. She treated each sight as something novel and wondrous, but it was merely a mask. Hyrk lurked behind it, scanning Magnus's home for signs of weakness.

"It is a surprise," he said as they neared the temple's entrance. The entrance facing Glendall's grand courtyard was more beautiful by far. Adorned with marble sculptures of winged Fae and golden ornaments depicting the moon in all its phases, the main entrance clearly marked the building as a place of worship. But from this side, only simple columns of stone and a door of aged timbers greeted them. Let Hyrk wonder where they were. All the better for surprising him into slipping up and revealing himself once they were inside.

Two of their escort pulled open the door. "Cover the entrances," he commanded them quietly. They obeyed without question, accustomed to waiting outside while he sought privacy and refuge in the presence of his goddess. In this case, he desired privacy because he did not wish for news of Seona's predicament to spread before he could compose a statement for distribution by the proper channels.

Once inside the temple, he tuned all his senses to the woman on his arm. He searched for any sign of discomfort, but Seona made not the slightest flinch as they stepped within the holy house of Danu.

"Sire," Assaph greeted. He had been waiting for them, as they had planned. "Lady Seona." He bowed his covered head. Looking above the lenses of his spectacles, he said, "It is my honor to welcome you to Chroina's First Temple of Danu."

Seona gasped, but it was not a sound of pain. She withdrew her hand from Magnus's arm and clapped. Joy shone from her face as clearly as when the pups had brought her bathwater earlier.

Curious. This was not the reaction he had expected.

From Assaph's raised eyebrows, Magnus guessed he had not expected the reaction either.

It was possible Hyrk found delight in the prospect of wreaking havoc here in Danu's holy house. If that was what the entity intended, he would be sorely disappointed.

"I have heard of your temple," Seona said, eyes bright and curious as she turned in a slow circle to take in the modest alcove. She came to a stop facing the arched entry to the sanctuary and smiled softly. Rocking up on the balls of her feet, she seemed eager to explore, but a darting of her eyes back to Magnus showed some hesitation.

Ah. She wished to enter but she could not. Because Hyrk's evil prevented her.

"You have treasured the temple, as have all the kings of your line," she said to Magnus, her eyes locking with his. Something passed between them. He must be mistaken, because he had an impression of gratitude filling her countenance. To Assaph, she said, "And you have devoted your life to my—to the service of Danu." She clasped both his hands in hers. Her lips parted as if she would say more, but then she clamped them shut.

Again, he and Assaph exchanged a look.

Releasing Assaph's hands, Seona sailed into the sanctuary, uninhibited as a freshly-released bird.

No expense had been spared in building and maintaining the temple. The central structure dated back a thousand years and was made of eight towering, interlocking arches. Over the years, marble, gems, silver, and gold had been used to enhance the stone for dazzling effect. When the sun shone through the tall east- and west-facing windows, the sanctuary gleamed with beauty for Danu's glory. A large window of stained glass featuring a scene from the *Temple Archives* let in the southern light from above the pulpit, where Assaph would read the scriptures on the morning of each full-moon.

Seona walked the length of the sanctuary, her face tilted to take in the windows and arches. Fingers encased in supple boar skin skimmed the worn armrests of the benches. Her slippered feet stepped soundlessly over the marble of the central aisle.

Magnus watched from where he and Assaph stood, still in the entry alcove. "What do you make of her reaction?" he asked the priest in a whisper.

Assaph only shook his head. He seemed as perplexed as Magnus.

At the altar, where the citizens of Chroina had taken communion for centuries, Seona came to a stop. Her head tipped back, and she gazed up at the stained glass.

The hues of sunset made the scene glow like a giant lantern. In the window, Lachlan, an ancient king of Eire stood on a shelf of rock overlooking a canyon bursting with color. He raised both hands to the heavens in worship of Danu, who was shown as a blinding figure cloaked in glory, floating above the scene like the sun. Around Lachlan, his Knights of the Crescent Moon formed a protective ring, and behind them were worshippers on their knees with their hands lifted in praise. Danu's blessing shone around them like an aura.

Artists had also rendered this scene in expensive inks and stains in the *Temple Archives,* and given it the name *Lachlan's Last Communion.* It was said that Lachlan was so favored by Danu that she appeared to him at the famous shelf of rock—Lachlan's Promontory. Sadly, shortly after this communion was said to have taken place, Danu's blessing disappeared from the face of the Earth. No more revelations were recorded in the *Archives,* leaving Danu's followers no explanation. Priests and scholars had proposed theory after theory as to exactly why Danu's blessing had been replaced with a curse on the births of females, but no two students of the *Archives* agreed in full. Not even Magnus and Assaph.

Magnus assumed the curse had something to do with Jilken, Lachlan's brother, whom Lachlan defeated in battle. Allowed to live despite his defeat, Jilken was exiled to the west, where he created the kingdom of Larna. He summoned dark magic to breed wolfkind with wolves, the goal to create an army of the fiercest warriors to ever walk the Earth. This perversion of Danu's creation was reason enough, in Magnus's mind, for her to curse them. But all hope was not lost. His dream vision promised Danu's blessing would return. Magnus and Seona would birth an heir that would begin a new era for their people. He'd seen it clear as day. He believed it with all his heart. This was to be his legacy.

But before that could happen, he needed to deal with Hyrk.

He saw only Seona's back from this angle. It wasn't good enough. He needed to witness what secrets her face revealed as she gazed up at the scene of Danu and Lachlan.

Quietly, he made his way toward the altar. As step after silent step led him toward the place where he knelt each morning in prayer, he planned what he would say. He would invite her to worship with him, and then he would utter words of devotion to Danu and watch Hyrk reveal himself. With a glance back at the alcove, he assured himself Assaph was ready.

The priest nodded. In his hands was a cage covered with a cloth.

When Magnus was a single step from Seona, he scented something that brought him up short. Salted tears.

The unmistakable weight of sorrow rounded her shoulders. Nearly inaudible breaths hitched in and out, sending tremors over her. The lady wept freely. This was most unexpected.

He had been prepared to witness hatred pouring from her eyes. Or disgust curling her lip. He had not expected tears. Nor had he expected to feel an overwhelming urge to wipe them away and comfort her with kisses.

"My lady." He had not meant to speak. The words simply came forth, quiet and strained because her apparent pain caused him pain as well.

Her shoulders jumped, and she sniffed. Trembling fingers swiped tears from her averted face. He had startled her, and she attempted to compose herself discreetly. These simple acts suggested her emotions were genuine.

This morning, at the very place depicted above them, hatred had glowed from the red eyes of a possessed Bilkes. The evil entity possessing the prisoner would not show such vulnerability, not in Magnus's presence, and especially not here in the temple of the goddess he'd scorned with such venom. Perhaps he had made a mistake in thinking Hyrk controlled her.

But he could not be certain. Nothing was certain where Seona was concerned. Even if she was not possessed, she still was not herself. Whether the change in her was due to memory loss, deception, or interference from a wicked entity, the truth of the matter was that Seona was different than she had been. She was a mystery, and the need to solve her plagued him to his core.

"I remember that day," Seona said, interrupting his thoughts. Her voice held strength even as it carried strains of sorrow.

His hand twitched with the need to rest on her shoulder, to comfort her, but he kept it at his side. He did not trust his body's urges. He would not trust them until he was certain Seona was Seona.

Following her gaze to the stained glass, he tried to see the scene through new eyes. Seona must be remembering her altercation with Bilkes, her fall. Perhaps Giles had been right all along and she simply suffered from memory loss. Her tears might be a sign that her memory was returning, and with it her terrible experience in Larna.

The prospect of her remembering herself made a stone of dread settle in his gut. Regardless of *why* she had been different, he cherished the new Seona. He did not wish to hasten the return of the old one.

Nevertheless, he would help her remember. "It was only this morning. Though it feels like much more time has passed."

The corner of her soft lips twitched. "Much more, indeed," she said, eyeing him with a speculative glint in her eye.

He could not help standing straighter and jutting his chin forward. He did not know why she studied him so, but whatever the reason, let her see the strength and confidence in him.

Out of the corner of his eye, he saw her lips purse with pleasure.

She finds me pleasing. The sure knowledge puffed him up like a lad with his first boar-kill.

He nodded at the window. "The scene we see here is an artist's rendition of King Lachlan's last communion with Danu." Under her scrutiny, he felt compelled to demonstrate his respect for their traditions and his love for their goddess. A feeling of rightness filled him as he told the ancient tale. "It occurred two thousand years ago and was the last time Danu appeared to us. After this day—" He motioned toward the glass. "Danu gave us no more revelations. Our numbers began declining. There were fewer and fewer female births until—well, today our hope rests on the wombs of only a handful of women."

He had not meant to tell her so much of their dark history, but now that he had started, he could not seem to stop. As he spoke, he kept his gaze on the window, but every other sense was tuned to Seona's reactions. He felt more than saw her tilt her head as she listened intently.

"Some think Danu did not curse us intentionally, but rather she was taken from us. Forcibly." Her shoulders stiffened as he gave voice to Assaph's theory. Why the theological debate spilled from his lips, he could not guess, but Seona's attention, focused on him like a moonbeam, encouraged him to continue.

"I do not believe such," he said. "For the *Temple Archives* tell us of Danu's power, her steadfast devotion to her creation. I do not believe there is any power in existence that could overcome a goddess filled with love."

Nothing and no one,
Not even godhood itself
Shall separate her from her lifemate

The words from Tanisten's poem popped into his mind, even though he had dismissed the writings as irrelevant. Was Danu trying to tell him something? Could she be leading him in this moment?

He felt Seona's gaze soften. Turning to face her, he found fresh tears shimmering in her eyes.

"You are correct." Her voice was softer than a whisper, almost as if she spoke without meaning to. It entranced him. "No power can overcome a goddess. But she can fall victim to her own foolishness."

The Translation Stone grew warm against his chest. A frisson of awareness passed over him. Suddenly, Seona's transformation—the miracle of her mended body, her changed speech, her wonder at every small detail of life, her tears at the altar—it all made sense. Profound, miraculous sense.

"Can it be?" His voice sounded like he was in a cave. It echoed in his ears.

Desperation and fear collided in Seona's eyes as she held his gaze. But it was not Seona looking back at him.

It was Danu.

Chapter 15

MAY THE WORDS of the goddess echo through the generations: To be known—deeply known—is the highest, most blessed intimacy.

Words that Danu had given her people long before her imprisonment echoed in her mind as Magnus looked at her, genuinely looked at her.

For the first time since inhabiting this mortal form, she allowed a witness to her lowly state. Here at the marble altar where generations of wolfkind had worshipped her, she could no more hide her true self from Magnus than she could wave her hand and return to her immortal form.

He knows.

Panic fluttered behind her breastbone. But there was something else there, too. Relief.

The only other person who knew what had happened to her and Seona was Duff. While she appreciated her friend, he was not the one she craved intimacy with.

Magnus knows.

The relief swelled and filled all her corners and spaces. It felt so *good* to be completely known.

Until her king dropped to his knees. "My Goddess," he whispered, and he prostrated himself before her, forehead to the marble floor.

No, no, no.

This was not what she wanted. She didn't need him awestruck. She needed him strong, so she could take shelter from this strangeness in his arms. Besides, if he worshipped her like this, Hyrk would discover her. No, this would not do.

"Get up," she hissed. "Quickly."

But Assaph's voice trampled over hers. "Sire!" He dashed to Magnus's side and fell to his knees. In his haste his head covering fell off and spun to the floor. "What have you done to him?" he snarled at her.

"Nothing!" she answered before she bent to tug on Magnus's arm. "Please get up. Do not do this. You'll put me in danger."

"Don't touch him, you vile monster!" Assaph made a grab for her hand, but Magnus caught his wrist before he could make contact.

"Do not touch her." At last, her words seemed to have gotten through to Magnus. From his knees, he said, "She is not Hyrk."

Hyrk? Was that why Magnus had been acting strangely? Since the meeting in his solar, he had been reserved with her. The passion she'd tasted in his kisses had bled away and left coldness in its place. Indignation puffed her up at being mistaken for that wicked bastard.

"Of course I'm not," she said hotly. "But if you remain on your knees, he will most certainly discover me." She spoke in a rush, needing to convince Magnus as soon as possible. It was unfortunate that Assaph was there, because her identity must remain secret. The more people who knew, the more danger she would be in. But it couldn't be helped.

At her insistent tugging, Magnus finally came to his feet.

Assaph looked back and forth between them, waiting for an explanation. His confusion might have been comical under other circumstances.

"I am not myself," she confessed. "Something I cannot explain has happened to me and to Seona, and it must be put right. In this mortal form, I am practically helpless. If Hyrk finds me, I'm as good as dead."

"Where is Seona?" Magnus said.

At the same time, Assaph said, "If you're not Hyrk, then who are you?"

"She is Danu," Magnus said, gaze still locked on hers. Truth be told, she could not look away, either. Now that he knew who she truly was, she longed to share everything with him.

A thump dragged her attention to the floor. Assaph lay there, feet splayed and sticking out from the hem of his robe. He had fainted.

"Oh dear," she said.

She and Magnus dove to his side.

"Assaph!" Magnus patted his cheek.

"What can I do?" she asked.

"Water. He needs water." Magnus blinked. He turned mortified eyes to her. "My apologies, my—Goddess. I'll fetch it." He started to stand, but she stopped him by curling her fingers in his sleeve.

"Tell me where it is. I'll fetch it." She would not let him treat her like one who must be waited on hand and foot. She was a goddess, yes, but she was also a woman quite able to undertake necessary actions.

He stared a moment. As if coming to a decision, he nodded. "Assaph's apartment is through there. You should find an ewer by his pallet." He pointed behind him, toward a closed door. She hurried to fetch some water.

Assaph's apartment was dim, with only a bit of gloaming light coming in through a window, but she found his pallet, and the ewer on a nearby table, easily enough. She scooped up some water with a tin cup and jogged back to the sanctuary. As Magnus took it from her, she felt herself smiling at the irony of a goddess serving in her own temple.

"My thanks," he said. With a powerful arm, he lifted Assaph's head and tipped a dribble of water over the priest's lips. "Wake up, Assaph. Come on."

Assaph's tongue darted out to catch the drops. Behind his spectacles, he blinked awake.

"There he is," Magnus said. "You had a bit of a shock, friend. Take a few moments to rest. Here. Drink." He held the cup so Assaph could sip from it.

"My thanks," the priest said. He peered from Magnus to her, and his eyes widened.

"Yes," she said. "I am Danu." She softened the news with a smile. "I do not understand why I've come to be in this mortal body, but once you are feeling quite well, I am happy to discuss my predicament with you. Perhaps you may have a way to help me."

"Help *you?*" Assaph went pale.

"Yes. Help me. I am…unaccustomed to being powerless."

"You are not powerless," Magnus said. "You fetched water for Assaph." His lips quirked, and she remembered being in his arms earlier. She remembered his kiss.

Her cheeks warmed. Assaph might have difficulty adjusting to her presence, but Magnus, it seemed, was able to take it in stride. "Perhaps not powerless by mortal standards," she allowed with a quirk of her own lips. Now that they had dispelled the idiotic notion of her being Hyrk, she hoped they could return to the flirting and touching she had enjoyed so much.

Assaph cleared his throat.

Though, perhaps not this very moment. She and Magnus had been leaning toward each other across the priest, still prone on the floor. With a start, they both jumped back.

A thrill went through her at the thought of entertaining carnal thoughts in the temple, as if she were some mortal fantasizing about her would-be lover while she ought to be worshipping. She nearly chuckled, but managed to hold it back.

"Here," Magnus said, offering the priest his hand.

Assaph clasped it and stood. Immediately, he bowed his head and began to kneel before her.

While his faith and respect touched her, she could not allow anyone to make displays of honor. Hyrk could never know how vulnerable she'd become. "No. Do not kneel." She rushed to urge him upright.

"She does not wish for Hyrk to know where she is," Magnus said. "We must pretend she is still Seona. Is that right, my Goddess?"

"That is correct. But do not call me Goddess. *My lady* will do, or—" She did not wish to be called by another's name, but she supposed it was the safest option. "*Seona.*"

Assaph's eyebrows climbed his forehead. "How is this possible? What are we to do?"

"Come." With a hand on Assaph's shoulder, Magnus guided the priest to a room beside his apartment. "Let us sit and discuss this where there are no windows. It would not do to be overheard or spied upon." His sober face comforted her. In seeking a more private forum, he proved her secret was safe with him.

Assaph's study bloomed with light as the priest lit a lamp with shaking hands. His color was returning little by little.

Magnus drew a simple wooden chair to her, and she accepted his hand as he helped her sit.

"My thanks," she said.

He shook his head. A rueful light twinkled in his eye. "I cannot believe I thought you were Hyrk."

She arched an eyebrow. "Neither can I." He blanched, but she pulled his face close with a fist in his shirt. "I will think of many interesting ways for you to make it up to me." She let her desire for him show in her gaze, in her voice.

Color kissed his cheekbones. His eyes darkened to the color of aged whiskey. "My Goddess," he whispered, completely ignoring her earlier directive. But she forgave him in light of the reverence shining from his face. She craved his reverence, but not here in the temple. In his bed he could worship her all he wanted. And she would worship him with every ounce of her being.

Magnus grazed her cheek with the backs of his fingers. Carnal promise laced the caress, and she blessed the stars he was not so awestruck that he could not see her for the woman she was. She resolved to hold him to his promise. Straightening away from her, he moved a second chair into the space directly beside hers. He sat and commanded Assaph to do so as well.

Still wide-eyed, Assaph took the seat behind his slanted table. Tomes of all shapes and sizes made stacks on shelves all around the small room. Sheets of parchment covered the sloping surface of his desk, and inkwells in various states of fullness lined the top, each in a carved slot designed for the purpose. She imagined priests studying her words in this room for centuries and let her appreciation for each and every one of them wash over her. Her people had created a grand temple for her, and even though she had not been able to hear their prayers, they still worshipped her, still studied her ways.

In the sanctuary, she had run her fingers over the worn arms of wooden benches. Generations of wolfkind had come to this very place to be near her. She mourned for every prayer that had gone unanswered, for every priest who had devoted their life to an absentee goddess, for every woman who had knelt at the altar and prayed for a child to grow in her womb only to be disappointed season after season, for every man who had no mate to complete him.

She became aware of a warm presence at her side. Magnus.

For some reason, her sorrow lifted. She still ached with sadness all the way to her bones, but the ache no longer threatened to crush her, body, mind, and soul. With Magnus beside her, she could bear her regret.

His presence allowed her to mourn all that had been lost. All the years. All the people. And to look past the mourning to what could be—what would be once they set everything right.

"I suppose I should start when it all went wrong," she said.

Both men leaned forward.

In her mind, she went back in time. Way back.

§

NOW THAT MAGNUS understood who dwelled in Seona's body, his new attraction to her made sense. It was not Seona who inspired his affection. It was the goddess he had worshipped since his earliest days. Perhaps it was wrong to feel this way for the mother of their race, but he could not deny those feelings. And she did not dismiss them. Quite the opposite. She welcomed them.

But he could not dwell on his desire. Instead, he must find a way to help her return to her heavenly form, where she belonged and where she could bless them. Not to mention, they still had Hyrk to deal with, and no idea where he was or what he planned.

Magnus angled his chair so he could see Danu fully. She sat primly, with her hands clasped in her lap. Wearing Seona's form, she was more beautiful than any other woman he had ever seen, including Seona. Eyes like tawny beads reflected the light of Assaph's lamp with honest vulnerability where before this miraculous trading of places, Seona's eyes had always been hard and guarded. Now her cheeks glowed with rosy life, where before, bitterness had made them sunken and gray. Even the paw-print brand on her cheek held a new sort of beauty. It had been meant as a mark of a wicked man's ownership, but to Magnus, it reminded him that this precious being belonged to all of them. She belonged to wolfkind.

He watched in fascination as her gaze turned inward.

"Long ago, in the realm of immortals," she began, "a selfish demigod pursued a goddess whose power and position he coveted. He aimed to bind her to him by Sacred Tradition, thus sharing in her power."

Her lip curled, and even that expression of disgust held beauty. "Knowing his nature, she rejected him swiftly and decisively. He retaliated by infiltrating her creation and tempting some of her followers away from her laws and worship."

She looked from one to the other of them. Magnus nodded his understanding and encouragement, and Danu accepted it with a brief, sad smile.

"In those days, a good and worthy emperor ruled the goddess's creation. He honored her and loved her, and his people followed his example. But his brother listened to the whisperings of the rejected demigod. For years, the brothers feuded over which deity their people should worship, until one day, their enmity came to a head."

Some of what she said was familiar to Magnus. She spoke of Lachlan and Jilken. The ancient story told of Jilken's attempts to dethrone Lachlan, a long-ago echo of what Ari had attempted.

"Without the mortals realizing," Danu said, "the demigod suggested a wager. He vowed upon his relic of power to leave the goddess's creation in peace if her mortal slew his in the inevitable forthcoming battle. But if his emerged the victor and became ruler, she would become the demigod's bride.

"Sure of herself and of her faithful mortal, she agreed, laughing all the while at the demigod's stupidity. Her mortal, the elder brother, was taller, stronger, wiser, and even more handsome than his brother. He would never lose a battle between them. To her, it seemed an easy way to purge her creation of the demigod once and for all."

Danu sighed, and the sound was one of regret. "What she did not count on was the mercy of the elder brother nor the treachery of the younger. The two battled, but not to the death, as she'd assumed. The elder brother emerged the victor, but rather than take the life of his brother, he banished him and his followers and allowed them to become their own kingdom.

"The battle had ended in a virtual draw. The outcome did nothing to resolve the wager. The demigod continued to meddle in the goddess's realm, and the goddess refused to submit to his demands.

"Determined to have the goddess as his bride, the demigod tired of this non-resolution. After years of peace, he convinced his champion to invite his brother and his court to a feast on the pretense of celebrating their thriving kingdoms. But the feast was a trap. At the demigod's urging, the younger brother poisoned the elder and attempted to take the throne as emperor of all.

"The elder brother's followers were strong. They fought their way free of the younger brother's army, and their fallen king's firstborn son took the throne. The kingdoms were once again at odds."

Magnus remembered studying that war. Jilken had managed to escape the wrath of Marann's army and remained king of Larna for another fifty years.

Danu went on. "Though a tenuous peace eventually returned in the mortal realm, in the immortal realm, the damage had been done." She stared at her hands, which twisted in her lap. "The demigod gloated at the murder of the goddess's champion. He attempted to force her into becoming his bride, claiming his mortal had taken the life of hers, and was therefore the ultimate victor.

"She refused him, but the Way of All Things chose to subject her to the demigod. She had bargained with him, and she must submit to the agreed-upon terms." Her hands began trembling.

Magnus swept them up in his.

Danu met his eyes.

He struggled to make sense of how she could be the goddess who created them and yet appear so vulnerable. His heart ached at the thought of her being forced to submit to her enemy.

"What happened?" he asked gently.

She took a steadying breath. "Because the demigod had used trickery to win the bargain, the goddess was given a choice. She could honor her word and become the demigod's bride or she could go to his dungeon, where he could not harm her physically but would be her keeper for all time. She chose her enemy's dungeon over his bed."

Dread dug a burrow in his chest. "You speak of Lachlan and Jilken. The battle, when Lachlan was killed, occurred two thousand years ago."

"Yes." Eyes downcast, Danu confirmed his suspicion.

"You've been locked away by your enemy for two thousand years," he said.

Her silence was answer enough.

The human women rescued from Larna had been in Bantus's dungeon for months, some of them, like Seona, a full year. But this woman had been imprisoned for centuries upon centuries. Magnus could not fathom that kind of time.

"By the moon," Assaph whispered.

Magnus met the priest's eyes. All along, Assaph's theory that Danu's blessing had been forcibly taken from them had been correct. To think, the immortal goddess had been rendered powerless. He could hardly conceive of it.

He turned to Danu and dragged her into his arms. He could not help himself. This precious being deserved comfort after what she'd endured. "Never again," he said. "Never again will you be subject to that wicked *thing*. I vow it."

She sniffed, and he realized she wept into his shirt. When she pulled away, he did not want to let her go, but he forced himself to.

He would never trap her someplace she did not want to be. She would never regret confiding in him.

Danu sat up tall, eyes swollen but otherwise composed. "I am free at last, but Seona is not. She is in my place. I have heard it confirmed by a friend who is able to steal into Hyrk's dungeon. Something must be done to help her."

Magnus frowned. She had not been in contact with anyone but him. He had hardly left her side. "When did you see this friend? Who is he?" Was that jealousy ripping through him?

She smiled and laid a lily-cool hand along his beard. "Calm yourself. His name is Duff, and he is of the Fae. He is a friend and an ally. Even now, he abides with Seona, comforting her. He came to me in a dream while I rested today. Without him, I would not know what had happened to her. He is the one who told me about the blond-haired boy."

The nap she had taken under the watch of six guards. She had spoken to one of the Fae while she'd been sleeping. That was how she'd known about Alexander. Her information had helped Magnus learn how Bilkes had escaped. Perhaps there was more where that had come from. "I wish to meet this 'friend and ally.'"

"I have no way of summoning him," Danu said. "But if I see him again, I will tell him of your request."

"Extraordinary," Assaph said. "A faerie in our midst." His brows drew together. "You said he comforts Seona? How does she fare?"

Magnus was angry with himself that he had not thought to ask.

"She is afraid," Danu said. "Hyrk's dungeon is not a nice place. But the bars that confine her also protect her from Hyrk's power. He cannot harm her beyond taunting her; that is, if he returns there. Duff has not seen him since our swapping places."

"We must discover Hyrk's whereabouts," Magnus said. "He desires my downfall and the destruction of Marann." He pounded his fist on the arm of the chair. "I will not allow it."

"But how can we find him?" Assaph said. "And when we find him, how will we fight him?"

Danu said, "As a demigod, Hyrk is not innately powerful, as is a full deity. But he can gain power by stealing worship from other gods or goddesses. He will seek followers, like this prisoner who escaped. Ask yourself which of your people have a mindset like the prisoner, and you will know where to begin looking. As for fighting him—" She gripped the arms of her chair. "There are only two ways to destroy a demigod. Take away every last one of his followers or destroy his relic of power. Hyrk's relic is a red gemstone. Destroy it utterly, and he will be rendered powerless. But a relic is not an easy thing to destroy. It is said no mortal weapon can harm one."

Magnus stood and began pacing. At this very moment, Riggs was searching for the red gemstone. Perhaps he had found it by now and was returning to Glendall. "Then how do we destroy it?"

"Only an act of pure faith can destroy a relic," she said.

"What does that mean?" Assaph asked. "Could it be a song of worship? A sacrifice made?"

Her eyebrows slanted. "I'm afraid I do not know. I have never heard of a relic actually being destroyed."

Assaph rose from his desk. "I will begin researching immediately. Unless you require me, Sire."

"Go," Magnus said. "We need all the information we can gather." He intended to scour the shelves of Glendall's library. Perhaps he would begin with Tanisten's poetry.

Assaph shuffled from the study, bidding them goodnight.

"We will find a way," Magnus promised Danu. "And once Hyrk is destroyed, we will return you to where you belong. I will not rest until it is done."

Danu's eyes dimmed. Perhaps she doubted him. He was only mortal, after all. But he was also a king, and he had an army at his command.

"Do not fret, my lady." He tugged her to her feet. "I will set everything right. You will sit your heavenly throne again and have the worship you deserve."

A shuddering breath parted her lips. "If I am to have only a little while in this mortal body, then I would like to be worshipped somewhere other than this temple." The darkening of her gaze as she licked her lips was unmistakable.

"As you desire." He would sooner die than disappoint his goddess.

Chapter 16

DANU CLUNG TO Magnus's hand. Pace swift, he led her to Glendall, but they did not enter through the same grand entrance they'd used on their way to the temple. Rather, he took her to a sunken alcove with a narrow door that looked as though it hadn't been used in ages. He took a key from his sporran and turned it in the lock. No sound emitted from the tumblers, indicating someone kept it well oiled.

"Two of you remain here," Magnus commanded his guards. "Four of you take up posts outside my chamber and the Orange Blossom suite. The rest of you are dismissed. Rest and be ready for duty at first light." She was pleased to see him value his guards' rest. Truly, this king impressed her in many ways.

There was one more way she hoped to be impressed. When his gaze fell hot and dark on her, she shivered with anticipation.

"We are not to be disturbed for any reason," he told his men.

A chorus of "Yes, Sire" sounded, and Magnus whisked her through the door.

They were in a passage with a ceiling so low, he had to bend so as not to catch cobwebs in his golden mane. His pace did not slow.

"A secret passage," she surmised, as their steps stirred up dust.

"You deserve corridors lined with choirs and scattered with rose petals. But you get this instead, because I fear I'll behead any man who tries to speak to me right now."

She smiled to know he wanted her so badly he refused to risk interruption. Then she felt her smile dim. If they passed through

Glendall's proper doors and passages, Magnus would certainly be accosted by a number of individuals needing his guidance. Her king carried an entire kingdom on his shoulders, and from what she observed, he had no one with which to share the load.

Tonight, she would help him forget his responsibilities. And he would help her forget the cold loneliness of Hyrk's dungeon. She squeezed his hand tighter. "I do not mind darkness and cobwebs," she assured him. "I have known much worse."

At her admission, he stopped suddenly and scooped her to him. In the pitch blackness, his hands seized her face, and his lips descended on hers. Shocks of desire heated her through as his mouth took hers in a desperate kiss.

Once they were both breathless, he pressed his forehead to hers. "I regret every minute of captivity you've suffered. If I could do anything to erase it—*anything*—I would do it in a heartbeat."

"You can," she said, fists curled in his shirt. She let her hips cant forward. The difference in their heights put her pelvis quite a bit lower than his, but he understood her meaning nevertheless.

The rumble in his chest sounded like an earthquake in the narrow passage.

At once, they were moving again. A set of worn stone steps led them up and up until level ground met her feet. Magnus knew this path well, for he always told her when to expect a change in footing. She didn't stumble once, but if she had, he would have caught her. She knew this instinctively, just like she knew he would fall on her the moment they were in his chamber.

Finally, *finally,* golden light pierced the darkness as Magnus dragged open a heavy door. He lifted a tapestry and held it as she passed beneath his arm. Once he had secured the door behind them, he let the tapestry fall into place, hiding the door.

The room burned with sunset hues thanks to a fire a servant must tend every hour. The soft light revealed a sturdy bed with four posts and a pair of tall armoires with a decidedly more masculine look than the enameled furniture in the Orange Blossom chamber. This must be Magnus's bedchamber.

He didn't give her time to get her bearings. Before she could take in the whole chamber, he swept her into his arms and lifted her against his chest. In three strides, he had her on the bed.

She sank into a mountain of furs. Surrounded by their softness, and Magnus's hardness as he crawled over her, she felt delicate and protected. And *so* needy.

An oil lamp beside the bed cast a wavering glow over them. His eyes reflected the flame, golden irises glinting with hunger. Magnus was a large man, taller than most and cut lean with muscle. On all fours, he seemed impossibly large, impossibly powerful, a beast about to fall on a fresh kill. But he didn't pounce. Not yet.

Instead, he cupped her face in tender, battle-hardened hands. "I have need of you, Goddess."

"Yes," was all she could say. This king had her tongue tied. But her hands knew what to do. Already, they were clawing his shirt from his belt.

"No," he said, gathering her hands and pinning them above her head.

She sucked in a startled breath. She had always been the aggressor with her lovers. But she had also always been the more powerful in any pairing. She was not the more powerful here. This man, this wolfkind male, could easily overpower her small human form. For the first time, the thought of being overpowered thrilled her. It heightened her arousal near to the point of pain.

"You will not lift a finger," Magnus said. "I will show you what it means to be worshipped."

Her head sank into the bed furs. Free. She felt free.

"Make me soar," she commanded.

"As you desire." Holding her wrists with one hand, he lowered his body along the length of hers. His delicious weight pressed her more firmly into the bed. She was surrounded by him, his heavy, muscled body, his heady scent, his fiery gaze.

Pressing her down from wrists to ankles, he began a tender assault on her mouth. He nipped, nuzzled, and licked, but ages passed before he accepted the invitation of her parted lips. When he did, oh, when he did, she melted.

His tongue slid like heated silk along hers.

She remembered the sensations of kissing, the anticipation of carnal fulfilment. But her memories paled in comparison to the joy filling her now.

As she lay beneath her king, every inch of her body tingled. All thoughts of her people and her duties faded. Her entire physical and mental being focused on the man above her. The man loving her lips and tongue, her jaw, her neck—*oh, her neck—yessss*. She was more sensitive there than she remembered. Could it be this different body possessed different secrets?

His kissing and sucking left a trail of warm spice along her skin and seemed to connect to her very core. How strange! How delightful!

Magnus sat up tall above her. His stomach and chest rippled as he drew his shirt over his head. A shake of his mane set his hair to rights, but she hardly noticed for the leagues of pure muscle at her disposal. Magnus's torso tapered from broad, tanned shoulders to the belt wrapping his narrow waist. Pectorals like rocky plateaus bore a coat of silky, dark blond hair. The pattern of growth tempted her fingers to play, the hairs making tantalizing whorls around dark, small nipples.

Should she move her hands from where he'd pinned them? He no longer held her there, but his command had been clear. She was not to lift a finger. Oh, how she enjoyed obeying commands from her king.

She decided to continue obeying. Keeping her wrists above her head, she let her gaze do the caressing. Moving up his abdomen and chest, her gaze caught on a chain of gold making a line across his throat. How odd. The *vee* of his collar had displayed his throat all day. There had been no chain visible there before.

While she watched, mesmerized by the play of his muscles, Magnus reached behind his head. With nimble fingers, he drew a pendant over one shoulder and forward. The chain was a necklace, which must have been set askew when he'd removed his shirt.

The pendant, now set to rights and enclosed in his fist, hung just low enough to be obscured when he wore a shirt. That explained why she hadn't noticed it before.

Thoughts of what else could be hidden beneath his shirt made her mouth water. Love bites, marks from her fingernails. Oh, yes. She desired to mark him—her carnal thoughts came to an abrupt halt as Magnus dropped his hand from the pendant.

There, gleaming between his perfect pectorals, lay her moonstone.

The vessel for the portion of her power that sustained her people. The object created from her hair in her darkest hour so Hyrk could never take control of her precious wolfkind. The treasure she had entrusted to Duff.

"Easy, love. I have not lost it. I gave it away."

Before she could learn more, she and Seona had swapped bodies. Upon discovering herself in her mortal realm, she'd determined to find her moonstone. Reuniting with it was the only way she might restore herself to her true form. But she'd since forgotten all about it. Because she was in no hurry to return to her true form—and Hyrk's dungeon.

Now, here it was, facing her boldly. It had been beneath her nose the whole time.

I'm not ready to go back.

Not only to Hyrk's dungeon, but to her goddess form. She did not wish to leave Magnus so soon. She did not wish to leave her people. She felt like she had only just rediscovered them.

Magnus unclasped the necklace. "I have been meaning to give this to you. It is a very special amethyst." Chain open, ends in his hands, he gazed over it at her. "It allows the one wearing it to speak and understand any tongue."

It could do much more than that, but perhaps not in mortal hands. She refrained from saying so.

"I have been using it to speak with the human women rescued from Larna," he went on. "But I've known it belonged to you from the moment I laid eyes on it."

He had? How?

Her confusion must have shown on her face, because he said, "I dreamt of you." His face held tender reverence. "I thought the dream was of Seona, but it was you. And in that dream, you were wearing this."

While she lay frozen with apprehension, he leaned down and fastened the chain around her neck. The cool stone rested smooth and heavy in the valley between her corset-plumped breasts.

Magnus scooped her to him and kissed her.

Would this be their last kiss? Was she about to be dropped back into her true form? Of course not. She was being ridiculous. Just because her moonstone was in her possession didn't mean she had to use its magic. She was in control. She could use it to return to her true form when it pleased her.

It did not please her to go just yet. Not while Magnus's mouth moved like a confident conqueror over hers. Not when they were so close to the intimacy she'd been craving.

She welcomed his affections, at ease for the moment, despite the nagging knowledge that every moment she tarried here, Seona suffered in Hyrk's dungeon.

Just a little longer.

She would do the right thing, but first, she required more of her king.

"Open for me, now," Magnus encouraged.

She eagerly obeyed. She would absorb as much of his affection as she could before returning to her prison. Opening to him, she dove into the kiss. She clung to Magnus with every ounce of strength this mortal body possessed.

"Take me," she commanded.

"Gladly, my goddess." He began slipping silk buttons from their delicate plackets, working down from her neckline, one fastening at a time. He was taking too long.

Shoving his hands away, she grabbed both edges of the parting fabric and tore it. Used to wielding more strength, it took her two tries before the sound of shredding fabric filled the room. Buttons pattered like raindrops to the floor.

Next was the corset, tied with ribbons that Magnus undid with an expert swipe of fingers. The moment her breasts were bared to him, they ached for his touch, for his tongue.

With the dread of Hyrk's dungeon nipping at her heels, she dragged Magnus's head to where she wanted him.

He came more than willingly. Breathing hot over her nipples, he murmured, "I have been waiting so long to taste these." He mouthed one breast and then the other. "So long."

Eyes closed, he chose one and latched on, laving and sucking, humming.

Sudden delight made her back arch, an act which pressed her breast even more securely into Magnus's mouth. Oh, this was heavenly. It had been so long for her as well. She'd nearly forgotten how satisfying these preludes to intimacy could be. She needed more.

"More. Now." She clawed at his kilt, dragging the wool up his thighs, reaching for the one part of him that could bring her ultimate satisfaction.

But he scooted back, putting himself out of reach. "My impatient goddess." Stripping her ruined gown from her body, he grinned a predator's grin. "Fear not. You shall have what you seek.

But I have many more pleasures in store for you tonight. Beginning with this.”

Once she lay needy and naked on his bed, he lowered his face between her legs and began to tease her most sensitive place with long, firm caresses of his tongue.

Oh. Oh!

She forgot why she was so impatient for his cock. This waiting was more than tolerable. This waiting was—men's voices sounded outside the chamber.

She stiffened, but Magnus only chuckled against her sex. “Fear not, my divine lady. We shall not be interrupted.”

The voices intensified, matching the rising of her pleasure at her king's mastery. Magnus did not slow in his attentions, and she chose to trust him.

“Yes, my king. *Oh, yes.*” Her breath came heavy and quick. Within moments, her pleasure crested a shattering peak. She cried out at the overwhelming wonder.

The chamber door burst open, and a guard came in, face red as a pomegranate.

Her king became a beast. “I said no interruptions,” he growled, her pleasure dripping from his beard.

“Sire, I would not interrupt, but—but—”

“Get *out!*” Magnus yelled.

“Sire, I cannot. It's the children. They're missing.”

Magnus's lean body went taut as a bowstring. The guard had his full attention. “Which children?”

“A—all of them, Sire.”

Chapter 17

THE FIRE IN Magnus's veins turned to ice. Time seemed to slow as his guard's words penetrated his fog of lust. With steady hands that belied his rising panic, he covered his goddess with a bed fur.

"Tell me again what you said," he commanded, as he rose from bed.

Behind his guard was a middle-aged man, who had served in his army faithfully for decades. Brant stood tall and said, clear as day, "He speaks true, Sire. The children are missing. No one has seen any of them in hours. None can be found. They are gone. Every last one."

All the children. Gone. Unthinkable. "Impossible. The children are adored by all, seen by all. Have you been to the classrooms? Have you inquired with Hatrick? Connoly? The tutors may be instructing the children in sum at the moment."

Even as he said it, he realized how daft it was. There were twenty-eight precious ones under the age of twenty—still young enough to serve and required to take lessons. The younger ones took different lessons than the older ones. Having different schedules and chores, the lot would have no reason to be in the same place at the same time.

"Yes Sire," Brant said. "We've been—"

"Of course we've been to the tutors." Brant's answer was flattened under the rolling barrel of Cathal's growl. Magnus's war chieftain shouldered through the door.

His personal guards peered into the chamber after Cathal. Each face bore the same worry gripping his heart. This was no misunderstanding.

"That was where we started, Sire," Cathal said. "The children didn't show up for their lessons, and only a few performed their chores this morning. We've been all over Glendall and the grounds, and we've searched all of Chroina. Every last man and trainee is actively searching as we speak. We didn't come to you until we were certain."

"The trainees are searching? They're all accounted for?" Magnus asked. Between the ages of twenty and twenty-five, one hundred and thirteen adolescents trained in the king's army. While not considered full-grown men, they were mature enough to wield weapons of war and learn to fight.

"They're fine," Cathal said. "It's just the young ones."

He could hardly comprehend what he was hearing. How could twenty-eight children disappear without a trace?

A cool hand came to rest on his bicep.

He glanced down to find Danu by his side, concern making sloping hills of her delicate eyebrows. The bed fur wrapped her from the neck down, obscuring her beautiful body from the eyes of his men. Good thing, since he would have hated to slay so many for ogling what was his.

It seemed not only natural but necessary to pull her close to his side as he addressed Cathal. "This is why Maedoc didn't interview the prisoners this morning as I commanded," he surmised.

"Aye, Sire." Cathal's face was a roiling storm. "I enlisted his help in the search. This was more important than Bilkes. Been looking for the pups all day, and I can confirm. The children are gone. Disappeared. All twenty-eight of them. None have been seen since this morning."

"Three of the children brought me a bath this morning," Danu said. "Where and exactly when were the others last seen? Some serve in the ladies' residence, yes?"

Magnus's chest filled with pride, even in this dire circumstance. How queenly his goddess was! Like a true ruler, she focused on the disaster at hand. He wished he could keep her, but she belonged on her throne above them all. One thing was certain, however. No one would take her from him before he showed her the worship she deserved—the worship she craved. Sadly, it would not be tonight.

Cathal blinked as if just realizing Danu was there. To him, she would simply be Seona. Shock showed in the lift of his brow, whether at her sudden interest in wolfkind affairs or at her state of dress, Magnus could not guess.

Cathal nodded at Danu but addressed Magnus. "Daly last saw the Glendall pups after they finished with your lady's bath. They exited the castle through the bailey. Daly called for them to finish their morning chores, but they didn't stop. He assumed they didn't hear and were headed to the *Fiona Blath* to serve the ladies there. He thought naught of it and returned to his duties."

Magnus remembered the three Danu referred to. Julian, Ruben, and Alexander, the latter of which had been seen in the dungeon before Bilkes's escape. "Alexander, again," he said. At Cathal's confused look, he apprised the war chieftain of the conversation he'd had with Neil in the dungeon.

"We need to interview Diana," Cathal surmised. "She'll know if her third-born's been up to something suspicious."

"Not interview," Magnus said, recalling how she lied to protect Alexander this morning. "Interrogate."

Magnus saw red as he stormed to the dungeon with Cathal. He'd left his personal guard to watch over Danu. They were to protect her with their lives. No one was to be admitted to his chambers until his return. Which would be soon. He had no doubt Diana would talk, considering what he had in mind for her.

While they navigated Glendall's passageways, he learned all he could about the search for the children.

"Have you given the children's scents to the wolves?" he asked Cathal.

"Aye. We gave them clothing from several—all different ages. Each group of wolves tracked the scents to the same place. Brawhaven." Magnus's memory supplied Chroina's stone and mortar schoolhouse. Now abandoned, the two-story structure had once been as grand as the *Fiona Blath*. In his grandfather's time, the best instructors from all over Marann taught the city's children at the prestigious institute for learning. By his father's reign, most of the building's classrooms had been converted to housing for the instructors, since they were no longer needed for lessons, so low had the population dropped. "The schoolyard is where the wolves lost the scents." Magnus pictured the grassy yard with its swings and roundabouts, pole ball circles, and hop-square grids. "It's like someone reached down and plucked them off the face of the Earth."

Magnus felt the blood drain from his face. He knew of only one way a group of people could vanish like Cathal described. Hyrk's gemstone.

He exchanged a dark look with his war chieftain. "Have you seen Riggs?" Had it been only this morning Magnus had sent the knight to search for the lost gemstone? It felt like days had passed, but in truth, it had been merely hours.

Cathal nodded. "He came back a little after dark. No luck finding that stone. Now he's leading a group of civilians. They're canvassing the east quadrant of the city."

If the stone had been at the bottom of the canyon, Riggs would have found it. Magnus had a sick feeling the stone had been found by someone else, and that someone had used it to move the children somewhere. The question was, who had found it, and where were they now? He could only pray Hyrk was not directly involved.

"We need some idea where to search for the children." His gut told him they wouldn't be found in Chroina. Perhaps not even Marann. "Have their quarters searched. Especially Alexander's." Remembering Danu's suggestion that they look for people who sympathized with Ari and Bantus, he added, "Look for any sign of Breeding First paraphernalia."

"Yes, Sire." Cathal left him at the entrance to the dungeon. It was the first time he'd been alone in a long time.

Weariness hung around his neck like a jougs-stone. And there was no rest in sight.

He didn't deserve rest. Not when he had let this happen.

The youngest among them held service positions of honor, but the goal of such positions was so much more than the satisfactory completion of chores. He desired to teach the children humility through service. Furthermore, Glendall and the *Fiona Blath* were the two most secure places in Chroina. Serving in the king's home and the ladies' common house kept them safe and close at hand. Magnus was supposed to be watching them, caring for them.

And still, they'd been taken.

The fault lay squarely on him, but there was no time for self-flagellation. He must find them. Whatever it took, he *would* find them. And there was a certain prisoner who would help, whether she wanted to or not.

Simmering with rage, Magnus stormed through the dungeon until he reached the east wing. "Where are they?" he bellowed as he passed cell after cell. Near the middle of the block, he turned and pinned a wide-eyed Diana with his gaze. "Where. Are. They."

Hand at her chest, she said, "Where are whom, Magnus?"

"You'll call me Sire, like everyone else," he growled, "And you know damn well I'm talking about the children. You'll tell me where they are, and you'll tell me *now!*" His shout echoed off the stone.

Diana feigned a look of shock. He repressed the urge to wring her neck. "Which children?" She sounded confused, the manipulative actress.

"Do not pretend you know nothing of this. You're always involved when conspiracies are afoot. Where. Are. The. Children!"

She backed up to the wall of the cell. "Magnus—Sire, I truly have no idea what you are talking about."

"No more lies, woman. I know you saw Alexander this morning. I know you were in on Bilkes's escape. You'll be in on this too. If I have to ask again, you'll lose your hand, just like Ari."

She paled. Her slender throat moved with a swallow. "Sire, if I can help, I truly will. Please, tell me which children you mean. Is Alexander among them?"

She continued to pretend ignorance. Magnus roared with rage. "Guards, take her to the interrogation room."

They did not hesitate in obeying his order. The cell was opened, and two pairs of hands dragged a struggling Diana toward the dungeon's entrance. One of the abandoned wings led to the room where Magnus had begun Ari's interrogation by chopping off his right hand then commanding him to confess to the coup lest he lose the other.

"Magnus!" Diana sounded genuinely terrified. Good. He didn't plan to actually harm her, but he needed her to believe he would. "Sire! If I knew what you were on about, I would tell you. Truly!"

"Sire." Neil called out to them as they passed his cell.

He paused while the guards continued to the interrogation room. "What is it?" he asked shortly.

"What's this about? Children are missing? Which ones?" Neil asked.

Magnus wiped a hand over his face. By the moon, he needed rest. "All of them. Every last one. Disappeared without a trace from the schoolyard."

His former war chieftain paled. After a moment's shock, he stroked his beard and said, "No such thing as without a trace."

Magnus nodded. "That's why I need Diana to confess what she knows."

"Well, don't go cutting off anything that won't grow back. I think she's telling the truth this time."

"How do you know?"

"Don't know. But for all her selfish ambition, she's devoted to Alexander. If he's in danger, she'll help all she can." Neil's words cooled his head.

He pinched the bridge of his nose. "You were right," he confessed. "I cannot do it all alone." Nodding with decision, he met the dark eyes of his former war chieftain. "Help bring the children home, and I'll give you your freedom."

Neil jerked his head back, as if he'd been punched. "Tell me you're smarter than this. I can't be your new second. I'm a fucking traitor."

Magnus huffed. "Do not worry. That honor will go to your nephew. But you're a good tracker, and an even better strategist. I fear there's a battle to come, the likes of which we've never fought before. I'll need you standing with me. Can I count on you?"

Neil drew himself up to his full height, nearly half a head taller than Magnus. With a steady hand, he made a fist over his heart. "Aye, Sire. You can count on me."

§

TRAVIS HUGGED HIMSELF as his brother issued orders. Bitter cold blanketed the great hall of the abandoned fortress Alexander had claimed as their headquarters. He might have mentioned they were going to northern Larna's Black Mountains—a misleading name, since the range was always covered with snow. They were all dressed for the mild, wet winters they were used to in Marann, but none of them had been prepared for this bone-chilling, finger-numbing cold.

"Blue party," Alexander said, his voice ringing off the black stone of the great hall. "You're on fire detail. Red party, you're hunting. Find us some dinner. Green party, you're on cleaning detail. Sweep this place out and drag down whatever furniture you can find. Seal up the windows with tapestries. Until the weather warms, we'll huddle in here for eating and sleeping. Yellow party, scout the area and familiarize yourself with the grounds. Bring in snow for melting, then search the fortress for usable supplies. You have your orders. Let's go!" He clapped his hands and joined the oldest boys with the red party.

Travis huffed warm air over his icy hands and set off to find the kitchen, and a broom. Being in the youngest cohort, the green detail, he was happy to remain indoors and carry out familiar chores. He would pretend to cooperate for now and use the time to plan his next move.

It hadn't been difficult for Alexander to convince every last child to meet at the abandoned school yard for a meeting this morning. Many of them, Alexander included, had abandoned their duties to do so. Then, showing he'd inherited Ari's talent for public speaking, Alexander had spouted propaganda that turned Travis's stomach but seemed to energize the other children.

The kitchen was a garbage-strewn, frost-covered room with a hearth at one end and a butcher block in the center. At least he thought that's what it was. At the moment, it looked like a mound of frost topped with dented pots and pans. Shuffling through inches of snow, blown in from the window and open door, he started digging through piles of stiffly-frozen rags, broken utensils, and dried leaves. There had to be a broom in here somewhere. Though a shovel might prove more useful.

While he searched, his mind replayed the scene from a few hours ago.

"Every one of us has spent our youth serving the ladies," Alexander shouted from his elevated position on a climbing tower. "But will we ever get a chance to breed with them? No! By the time the youngest of you are old enough, there won't be any ladies left still able to breed."

Looking around, Travis saw the other children nodding in agreement. He counted. All twenty-eight pups under the age of twenty were present.

"What about Anya?" an older boy named Linas hollered.

"What about her?" Alexander scoffed. "She's not one of us. Her get won't be pure wolfkind. It'll be smaller. Weaker. Shorter-lived. And how do we know it'll be female?"

Travis was not surprised to hear Alexander taking up his father's torch for Breeding First, but this purity nonsense came as a shock. Sure, Travis had heard grumblings about Anya not being wolfkind—especially from his mother, but most were pleased there was a pregnant lady among them. Most wanted their people to live on, mixed blood or not.

He had not known Alexander cared one way or the other. But then, he didn't spend much time with his brother, not when there was so much to do between his lessons and seeing to Anya's needs.

"Are we content to trust our future to a race we know next to nothing about? To a king who worships an archaic goddess? If Danu exists today, where is she?" He motioned and looked around himself, as if inviting Danu to make herself known. The action struck Travis as blasphemous, but no one else seemed bothered. "Where is her blessing? What kinds of fools continue to rely on a deity that shows no interest in them?"

"If we want to survive, we must carve our own path. We must take matters into our own hands."

Nods and murmurs of approval filled the schoolyard.

"No more will we serve those who deny us a future! No more will we accept the lies our elders tell us."

"What lies?" Ruben asked.

Alexander met the eyes of each child as he answered. "We have been told over and over again that the only females in existence are here in Chroina. Yet just two moons ago, twelve new females were found in Larna."

"Human females," someone scoffed.

"The point is," Alexander said, "King and council were wrong. The point is there are more females out there, and they can be ours for the taking. If we're brave enough. If we work together."

"What females?" Craiden asked. His scruffy face twisted with skepticism. He was the second oldest among them, his twentieth birthday only weeks away.

Alexander paced to the end the platform where Craiden stood, feet planted and arms folded. "There are females in Larna," he said with a toothy smile that made the hackles on Travis's neck rise. "And they're ripe for breeding."

"Boar-shit," Craiden spat.

"I can prove it," Alexander said. "All you have to do is come with me on a short journey, and you'll see. Our elders don't want us to know that there are females to be had. They think they're lesser because they're Larnian. But I say they're a far sight better than human *women. They're Larnian, yeah, but they're one-hundred-percent wolfkind. They're part of us. They carry the same blood as us in their veins, and they've been hidden from us all our lives!"*

"How do you know this?" Ruben's measured voice cut through the rising grumbles. Though not the oldest, the others always seemed to look to him as their leader.

"I know because I've had my ear to the ground. I pay attention. I read between the lines. And—" Alexander paced while he spoke, but stopped dead center to make eye contact with the children on the outskirts of the group. "Because I've seen them."

A collective gasp lifted on the cool breeze.

Alexander spread his arms like Travis had seen their father do. "We have the opportunity today, right now, to make a stand. To say to the council, to say to Magnus 'We Will Not Walk Calmly into Extinction!' We may be young. We may be overlooked. But if we work together, we can Change. The. World!"

Cheers soared into the sky. The other children were soaking up Alexander's rhetoric. One voice Travis recognized as belonging to Julian, Riggs's youngest brother, said, "What's your plan, Xander?"

Alexander grinned. Holding his fist high over his head, he opened his fingers. Between his forefinger and thumb was the gemstone that had been stolen from the temple that morning. "We take a little journey, friends. We show our elders that they cannot overlook us anymore. And we claim what's ours!"

Beneath a pile of straw and broken jugs, Travis's frozen hand met a wooden handle. Shifting debris aside, he found not a broom, but a pitchfork. "Good enough," he muttered. Taking the tool to the great hall, he started to make a plan. He had to get back to Marann and tell King Magnus where the children were. And that they had the red gemstone.

The only problem was the journey. The Black Mountains were on Larna's northwest coast. Chroina was the crown jewel of Marann's eastern harbor. The entire island of Eire stretched between. In the most pleasant weather, the journey would take two weeks on foot. Here it was the dead of winter, and Travis had no experience cutting a trail through wilderness.

Then there were the tales he and the other children liked to frighten each other with. Of course, they were all make-believe, but Travis couldn't help his wariness at the thought of passing through the Larnian forests. It was said the mutant wolves rejected from Jilken's breeding experiments roamed there, monstrous, murderous, and fertile enough to have maintained their numbers all these years.

He sank the tines of the pitchfork into a pile of bracken and garbage and began pushing it toward the nearest door.

I can't do it alone. It's too far. Too dangerous.

But he must. Otherwise, Magnus would have no idea where to look for them. The whole of Chroina was likely already turned inside-out with every able-bodied man searching for them.

I could try to take the gemstone from Alexander.

And likely be discovered.

Digging the pitchfork into a new pile, he tried not to let hopelessness sink as deeply as the cold had. *Danu,* he cried from his heart, *please help me.*

Chapter 18

"Took you bloody long enough," was the greeting Duff received when he made his presence known to Seona after visiting Danu in her dream. "For a man wanting to wed one lass, you're spending a fair amount of time with another."

Earlier, he'd explained what he knew about her and Danu swapping bodies, a fact she'd accepted with the predictability of a woman who had known precious little luxury in her life.

"I'm a goddess," she said, running her hands over her body. "How powerful am I?"

"You have no power whatsoever," he said honestly, because Hyrk's bars made it so. Though technically, if she were free, she would be quite powerful indeed. Certainly more powerful than him. But he was a trickster, after all, and tangling the truth came as easily to him as breathing. "Long ago, Danu created a relic to hide her power from Hyrk." He did not specify the relic contained only the portion of her power that sustained the wolfkind people. "She gave it to me, and I saw it safely to the mortal realm, where Hyrk will never find it."

"So the power that is rightfully mine is in a—a relic? What is a bloody relic?"

He clucked his tongue at his power-hungry bride-to-be. "A relic is an embodiment of an immortal's power. You've touched one. Remember the red gemstone?"

The dungeon's shadows did not prevent him from seeing her face grow deathly pale. "Aye. I remember."

"That, love, is Hyrk's relic. Danu's relic is what allowed your sister to communicate with Riggs when she arrived in the wolfkind realm. It is what allows King Magnus to communicate with you and the other women from your realm."

"I thought you said Danu gave the relic to you. How did my sister get her hands on it?"

"I gave it to her. I sensed she would need it, and I was correct. I'm often correct, you'll find. And you can trust me on this: the power within Danu's relic belongs to Danu. What 'rightfully' belongs to you is death, my dear, since Hyrk threw you from a cliff." She sucked in a breath, but he did not temper his rebuke. This woman needed a man with a strong hand to lead her on the right path. He was that man. "You'll remember what's rightfully yours when you speak of the goddess in whose body you dwell. But—" He softened his voice. "Once we are wed, you'll have all that is mine, and I will have all that is yours. What power we find ourselves with, we will use together. For our good and for the good of others." That was every bit the truth, and he meant it with all his heart.

Seona had grumbled but eventually agreed that if she was suddenly granted a goddess's power, she wouldn't know the first thing to do with it. That was when Duff had sensed his magic calling him to his friend's dream. Heeding the summons, he'd told Danu about the blond boy who'd helped Seona and Bilkes escape. Now he had returned to Seona and was eager to resume their conversation.

Reclining in a shadow as comfortably as the sharp rocks would allow, he said, "Tell me, love. Why do you hate wolfkind so much? There has to be more than what you suffered at the hands of that shite-bastard Bantus."

"More than that? Are you mad?" Her furious screech echoed off the dungeon walls. "Was that nay enough?"

He regretted the implication of what he'd said. He hadn't meant it like that. "My apologies. What you suffered was horrible. Despicable. Unforgivable. What I meant was that you are a smart woman. You know that one evil man does not make an entire race of people evil."

She was quiet for so long he thought she wouldn't answer, but at last, she spoke. "'Twas more than one man." Her voice slid over the stones, sad and wet with tears. "I was shared." She sniffed.

Duff was glad Bantus was dead. He only wished his death had been more painful. An eternity of agony wouldn't be punishment enough for what he'd done to this woman—and the others. "You'll never be harmed like that again. I vow it." His vision pulsed red with fury. He almost forgot the question that had started this line of conversation.

Until Seona said, "You are correct. 'Twas more than the violence in Larna that makes me hate them all." She wiped her tears away, and her gaze turned hard as ice. "You think I dinnae understand there are groups of those wolfmen? Two opposing clans. Anya has explained it to me more times than I can bear to recall. The Larnians are the ones who held us. Who—who abused us. But she acts like the Maranners wear robes of white and bloody halos atop their shaggy heads."

She scoffed. "That moldering bastard Ari was a Maranner. A sweet-talking, finely-dressed Maranner who lied as smoothly as the devil when he put on a snakeskin. And like that simpering idiot Eve, I bit right into his apple. Promised I'd be consort to a king if I came with him. Promised me riches, power. And I was fool enough to believe it.

"And then there is Magnus." She bit out the king's name as if it were a thorn in her tongue. "He had in his possession the very magical gem Ari used to bring us women over. Used the bloody thing to send us across leagues of mountains and lakes and forests as easily as a lass steps from one cobblestone to another. But does he use it to send us home, where we long to be most of all? No." Her fists clenched. "He locks it in his bloody temple and says no one can use it. That was why I went along with that prisoner. I wanted to go home." A tinge of sadness softened her ire.

She looked toward his shadow. He longed for her to be able to see him, the real him. If she could, she would see that he felt for her. He cared about her trials. He hated that she'd been deceived and abused, tortured.

Face resolute, she said, "The Larnians arena the only wicked ones. They're all wicked no matter what side of their bloody island they live on. And dinnae suppose I think the men of my kind are good and pure. They're wicked too. Every last one of them. Men. Are. Wicked. You're wicked, too." Her pointing finger was slightly off from aiming directly at him, and it made him smile sadly. "But at least you pretend to want goodness." Her shoulders slumped. "All I wanted was to go home, where I understand the wickedness. Where I ken how to live with it."

His heart cracked for this broken beauty. "Sweet darling," he said, but he did not have a chance to continue. His spine straightened with the unmistakable knowledge that Hyrk had entered his residence. "Shite. He's coming."

He stood as tall as his shadow would allow. "You must pretend to be Danu," he whispered. "Do not speak no matter what, or he'll know something is amiss. Act furious, act proud, but do not speak. I must hide, but I will be close. I swear I will not leave you."

"Why should I protect the goddess who created that awful race of beasts?" She had no love for wolfkind or Danu, but at least she followed his example and kept her voice low.

"Because I'm begging you to. Because I want the chance to show you goodness." He wanted to say more, but they were out of time. Hyrk was nearly upon them. "Please," he said before melting into the smallest shadow at the back of the dungeon.

Hyrk pivoted at the foot of the stairs, cape flashing its blood-red lining, and strode to the cell. He wore a gruesome grin and carried himself with the air of a conquering king. "Have you missed me?" he asked in his slimy, haughty voice.

Duff held his breath. *Say nothing, love. For the love of all the realms, say nothing.*

His prickly beauty folded her arms over her chest, lifted her chin and looked away, as if Hyrk's presence was inconsequential.

That's my brave girl.

"Are you certain you wish to ignore me? After all, this will be your last chance to speak with anyone." He studied his fingernails, looking as though he had not a care in the world. "You see, I'm on the cusp of victory. These bars are about to close around you. Once that happens, there will be no escape. Ever. You'll be mine for all eternity."

Seona kept her gaze averted, but her flaring nostrils showed her fear. He prayed Hyrk didn't catch on that she was someone other than Danu.

"Your precious Maranners are even greater fools than I thought," Hyrk went on. "You see, they have ignored their most precious asset. Their children. So that is where I have focused my efforts. And wouldn't you know? It's working." The demigod sounded slightly unhinged.

"It wasn't even difficult. All I needed was to convince one of them, and give him my relic. The boy took care of the rest!" He clapped his hands with delight. "Would you like to know how I convinced him?"

Shite. Hyrk had once again given his relic to a mortal. Which boy had he singled out? Duff ought to warn Danu that another of Hyrk's plots was afoot.

Seona remained silent while Hyrk continued to crow.

"I sympathized with him. That's always step one. Step two is to dangle a carrot."

The maniac sounded like he was reciting from the Handbook of Evil. If Duff weren't so worried, he would give the haughty, little slug a piece of his mind. At least Seona was playing her part perfectly.

"Do you know what carrot I dangled, love?"

Duff cringed. Seona was *his* to call *love*, not Hyrk's.

"You see, the children are all under the age at which their society considers them fully-mature. But do you know when one of your mongrels can begin breeding? At age sixteen."

Duff's blood ran cold. He had a sickening feeling he knew where this was going.

"And do you know what young men talk about when they're old enough to have a cockstand but too young to join the breeding lottery? They talk about fucking. Some of them even fuck each other. You can imagine their eagerness when my Alexander told them there were females ripe for breeding in Larna."

Seona's hands curled into fists. He could only imagine what images these words were calling up in her memory.

"No, no, it's not what you think." Hyrk rushed to answer a question no one had asked. "I'm through bringing humans over. Those bitches served their purpose well, but the females I have in mind this time are even better. Wilder. You see, the females I intend the children to breed with are the mutts living in the mountains and caves since Jilken's experiments." He laughed, and the sound was too high-pitched. "They're the rejects from the magic I gave the Larnian king all those years ago! But you know what they say: one man's trash is another man's treasure. It so happens that the deformities these beings were rejected for make them so much more than Jilken ever imagined. More than I imagined. And I have them in my pocket.

"See how perfect it is? How it all comes together? The new wolfkind will be more vicious and powerful than you ever intended them to be. And that's not even the best part." He bounced on his toes like a delighted toddler. "The best part is that I am gaining power every minute. Didn't you know, love? There is no force in all the realms as powerful as the faith of a child. Soon, I will be strong enough to raze Chroina to the ground, beginning with Glendall. The world will be repopulated with our new wolfkind, and they will be all *mine*. Unless."

He paused and scented the air. A wicked smile curved his lips.

Duff inhaled. A sweet, metallic smell tickled his nose. Drops of blood dripped from Seona's shaking fist. She had cut her palms with her fingernails, but she remained silent, likely as frozen with horror as Duff was, hearing this evil spew forth.

"Unless—" Hyrk sounded pleased with himself, as if the victory had already been won. "You fulfill your obligation and marry me."

Seona made a choked noise.

Duff's body coiled with the need to rush to her, to tell her it was just words. Hyrk was trying to get a reaction from her. He was painting Danu's worst nightmare in bold strokes of lie upon lie. At least, Duff hoped they were lies.

He should go to Danu and inform her and Magnus of these ravings, but he did not know if he could bring himself to leave Seona here alone.

"I'm *wai-ting*," Hyrk sang out. "Give me your answer, love. This is your last chance. And I do mean *last*."

Wide eyed and trembling, his brave beauty shook her head from side to side.

"Have it your way," Hyrk sneered. "You are dead to me now, and your people are now my people." With a whirl of his cape, he stormed from the dungeon. At the top of the stone steps, the heavy door thudded shut.

They were alone again.

Duff waited until he could no longer feel Hyrk's presence before sliding as close as he could to Seona's cell. "By the immortal realms, love, you were magnificent." Seona jumped at his voice. "You did wonderfully. I would kiss you if I could pass through the bars." Her posture softened. She searched his shadow with tear-filled eyes.

"That *thing* is pure wickedness," she said, wiping at the wetness on her cheeks. "He's the one who took us all to be—to be—" She took a shuddering inhale, as if she was just understanding that Ari had been manipulated by Hyrk.

"Easy, love. He can't harm you." How he wanted to reach through the bars and comfort her, cold-iron be damned! But the space between the bars was so narrow, he would be lucky to fit a hand through.

"He said I would be locked in here for all time," She said on a hiccup. "Can he accomplish such a thing?"

"I won't allow it," he vowed.

"Can he do what he said—about the children?" Her eyes focused inward, as if she were deep in thought. Perhaps she was remembering the children she'd encountered in Glendall. Perhaps she thought of Alexander wielding the same gemstone his father, Ari, had, making way for Hyrk's evil. Did she regret playing into Hyrk's hands, giving him the opportunity to steal back his relic?

"I don't know," he answered honestly. "He may have been saying those things because they would enrage Danu. She loves her creation. If anything would get her to crack, it would be the threat of perverting her wolfkind."

Seona was quiet a long time. Finally, she said, "You must go to them."

"To whom, my brave beauty?"

She snorted. "I'm no' brave. You must go to *them*. To your goddess and to Magnus. You must warn them. If what that vile thing said is true, they need to ken it all."

He shook his head, even though she wouldn't be able to see. "I won't leave you." He couldn't. Not after the taunting she'd just endured.

"You must. My sister is in danger. You heard what he said. He plans to destroy Chroina." Her shoulders rounded, but her voice was steel when she said, "You'll go, and you willna fash over me. I deserve to be alone. The blame is mine. That bloody lunatic would never have laid hands on his relic if I hadn't believed his lies. You must see him stopped."

He sighed. She was right. "All right, love. I'll go."

She nodded, even as her chin trembled. She was in Danu's body, but her expressions, her movements, her speech was all Seona. And he was falling in love with her.

He slid into a large shadow at the base of a jagged boulder. Putting his shoulder into it, he shoved the boulder toward the cell.

Seona screamed. "What's happening?"

"It's just me," Duff said as the boulder met the cold-iron bars, casting a swath of shadow into the cell. "I'll go. But not without leaving you with the only gift I can." Keeping to the shadow, he angled his hand and slid it between the bars. "Come to me, love. Feel me. I'm here." As his skin met the cold-iron, he hissed with pain. The substance was potentially lethal to the Fae if wielded against them as a weapon. A wound caused by cold-iron was the one thing they could not heal from with ease. He gritted his teeth against the pain. "Let me touch you."

She stepped into the shadow and lifted her hand. When her fingers met his, she gasped. "You're warm."

He chuckled. "As warm as you are." Turning his hand, he grasped hers gently. The cold-iron branded his wrist, but he ignored it.

She closed her hand around his, leaned forward, and pressed a kiss to his fingertips.

He sucked in a breath. "I wanted to leave you with a warm touch in this cold place, but you have given me a gift instead."

She released his hand and took a step back. "Save your pretty words for those shores of Faerie you told me of."

He would prove to her that a man could be good, and that a woman who trusted a man could know happiness. Or he would die trying.

Chapter 19

Danu paced Magnus's bedchamber, fist secure around her moonstone. She ought to be rejoicing at having it back, and in a way, she was, but worry eclipsed her joy.

The children were missing.

They were the hope of her people. Without them and without her restored to her deity so she could bless them, wolfkind would perish.

Her pacing brought her to the window. A tapestry covered the opening to keep in the warmth. She lifted the corner to judge the time. Beyond Glendall's manicured, frost-covered grounds, a faint blue glow on the horizon meant dawn was near. Magnus had been gone all night.

She wished she could be at his side, but when she'd offered to go with him, he'd reminded her that everyone thought she was Seona. It would raise too many questions if she fixed herself at his side after shunning him for so long.

Still, she craved the knowledge of all he'd learned. She wished to soothe him and to discuss with him this dark turn of events.

She squeezed her moonstone. Indecision pulled at her.

I could restore myself right now. In a heartbeat, I could be Danu Goddess of Wolfkind once more.

But she would have no power with which to bless her people. She would be locked in Hyrk's dungeon, and Seona would be here in the bedchamber of *her* king, wearing *her* moonstone.

Unthinkable. Not only would the human woman have no idea how to handle Hyrk, but she would offer no support to Magnus.

Magnus needed support. He needed counsel. He needed *her*.

She could not leave. Not yet. She must see Hyrk defeated first, and despite this fragile, mortal body, her current circumstance put her in a better position to fight than when she'd been locked behind enchanted bars.

That settled, she turned her mind to the children's disappearance. Only Hyrk could be behind something so devastating, so there was no question of *who*. But *why* would he strike at the children? Why not go after the human women? Or the wolfkind women? Why not attack Magnus, Anya, or Riggs, the mortals who had thwarted his plan by killing his most powerful followers?

They needed information. And she knew just the Fae who could get it for them.

Focusing on her moonstone, she pictured Duff's face. "Fae Lord of Darkness," she said quietly, so as not to draw the attention of the guards outside. "Cursed by Arwan, Shadow Walker, Mischief Maker, by my power and for the good of wolfkind, I summon you to me now."

She waited for her relic to warm in her hand as her power rose to meet its maker. And she waited. And she waited.

Nothing happened. Duff's familiar voice did not call to her from the shadows, and shadows there were aplenty since the fire was down to glowing embers and all but one candle had sputtered and died.

She repeated the incantation. Still, the chamber remained empty save for her.

Her moonstone did not warm in her hand. It held her power— she knew it did, because Magnus had told her how it granted the holder the ability to understand any tongue. He had used it to speak with the rescued human women. Anya had relied on it as her only means of communication when she had first come to this realm.

Mortals, of course, could not access the true power the relic contained—an infinite galaxy of miracles within a tiny, inconspicuous housing. But power was known to bleed from relics. This was why, when in mortal hands, they could produce magical effects, like translation, or the opening of portals.

Of course!

She was mortal. At least temporarily. Her moonstone did not recognize her. It did not answer her because it did not sense the origin of its power within her human body. It was Seona who wore the cloak of deity the moonstone answered to. Not her.

Before she could fully consider the implications, the door to the chamber opened. Two guards strode in, and behind them was one weary-looking king.

"Magnus." Without thought, she ran to him and threw herself into his waiting arms.

"My love," he said, and he embraced her with such strength she forgot about her failure to summon Duff. Once he had set her on her feet again, he took her face in his hands and kissed her. Slowly at first. Then fiercely. "I've missed you," he said, whisky-gold eyes ablaze in a face wearing the stress of the night.

"And I you," she said honestly. "You need rest, my king." She would prefer to carry on where they had left off earlier, or even to discuss all he'd learned while he'd been away. But exhaustion etched lines into his handsome face. It shadowed his eyes and dimmed the air of virility she found so irresistible.

"There is no time for rest. I've only come to freshen up. We'll break our fast in the solar with my advisors. I trust you slept well, dear lady?"

She frowned at his insistence on breaking his fast when he had not slept a wink. "Of course I didn't sleep. I was worried sick for the children. And for you."

His whole face softened. He tucked her nose to his neck and held her there, their bodies pressed together so they shared their warmth. "You do not need to worry for me. I have spent many sleepless nights in service to my people."

"You should not have to," she said, arms tight around him. He felt strong and wonderful. Her fingers delighted in exploring his lean waist and muscled back, his broad warrior's shoulders. Even unwashed, he smelled divine. Like earth and man and leather and—and like sex. The scent of her new body's arousal clung to him. Her face heated with remembrance even as pride filled her that she had managed to mark her man.

"In a perfect world, I would not have to." He spoke into her hair. His body relaxed in her hold, as if being with her brought him respite from his troubles. "But our world has not been perfect in a very long time." He sighed, and guilt pricked her heart.

"It's my fault," she whispered. "I let myself be fooled by that—that—"

"Hush, now." He petted her head and back. His roaming hands soothed her guilt. "We all look back on mistakes and see how we could have avoided them. But none of us—not even a goddess, I'd wager—can go back in time. We must learn from our mistakes."

"Goddesses should not make mistakes."

"Kings should not make mistakes. But we do. All the time." He smiled sadly. "Let's put it right together."

Her heart lifted with hope. Magnus almost made it sound like everything could be fixed. The children found, her deity restored, wolfkind flourishing once more. His quiet, humble confidence turned despair into possibility.

"How?" She was not accustomed to asking questions. Usually, she was the one with the answers.

"I do not know." He held her securely. "We need to find the children, but we have no clues, no idea where to begin our search." He led her to the ewer and removed his shirt while explaining that the children seemed to have disappeared as a group from the schoolyard.

They shared a look that said they both understood what that meant.

"Hyrk's relic has been found," she said.

Magnus nodded as he poured water from the ewer. She loved watching him move about in nothing but his kilt, the way his muscles bunched and slid beneath his bronzed skin. "But by whom?" he said.

Before he could wash himself, Danu took up the cloth, soaked it in the cool water, and wrung it out. Never before had she thought to serve a lover, but it seemed natural to run the cloth over her king's sculpted chest and ridged abdomen. Oh, if she only had the time to claw her fingers through all that decadent hair. The coat of dark blond hair covering his chest tempted her like nothing else. But they were discussing Hyrk's stone.

Forcing her mind to the problem at hand, she said, "Tell me all you remember from yesterday morning." Had it only been a full day since she'd become mortal? It felt as though much more time had passed.

Magnus recounted his confrontation with Hyrk and Seona's fall while Danu washed his strong shoulders. Lifting his arms, she cleansed the soft hair growing there. At the mention of a hawk flying overhead, she froze.

"The hawk," he said, no doubt noticing her stillness. "Could one like him take the form of a wild bird?"

"No. But he could slip into the mind of one as he did with the prisoner. He could control it for a time."

"A hawk could swoop down and snatch a gemstone from a woman's hand."

She nodded. Dread filled her at the thought of Hyrk being in possession of his relic. And now that very relic had likely been used to transport the children somewhere.

She finished washing Magnus's torso. His luxurious coat glistened with moisture. He looked utterly delectable. Despite the grave circumstances, her mortal body heated at the sight of her virile king. She let the cloth fall to the floor and gave in to the impulse to dry him with her tongue.

"My lady," he sighed, gently hugging her head while she lapped at him.

He tasted of salt and clean skin. He smelled like black tea and winter forests. Beneath her roaming fingertips, he felt like heaven. If only they had the luxury of time. There was so much of him yet to explore. So much of *her* new body to explore. She had experienced a brief pinnacle of pleasure as a mortal and craved so much more. She wanted to give Magnus so much more.

But it was not meant to be. Hyrk was on the move, and they had to act. She forced herself to back away.

"Don't stop now. It was just getting good." The masculine voice did not come from Magnus. She recognized that voice.

Magnus spun to face the shadow of the privy screen. A dagger had appeared in his hand, drawn so quickly from its sheath, she had barely caught the movement.

"Show yourself!" he commanded.

The door to the chamber flew open. "Sire? Is all well?" A guard stood at the ready, axe raised at his side.

Danu stepped in front of Magnus. "False alarm. Merely the wind moving the tapestry." She motioned toward the covered window.

"Sire?" The guard was not going to accept a dismissal from anyone but his king.

She reached behind her and caught Magnus's wrist, trying to convey that he must trust her.

"We are fine, Holt," Magnus said in a clipped voice that showed he would trust her but he was not happy about it. "Perhaps I am prone to overreacting this morning."

Holt sheathed his axe. "Understandable, Sire." He gave a curt nod then closed the door as he returned to his post.

"Explain," Magnus growled. At the same time, he made a quick movement so he was the one clutching her wrist instead of the other way around. With a twist much like a dance step, he put himself between her and the privy screen. He had not returned his weapon to its sheath.

"Magnus," Danu said, soothing his tense back with strokes of her hand. "May I present Duff, Fae Lord of Darkness." Stepping to Magnus's side, she peered into the shadow Duff had chosen. "Duff, it is my pleasure to introduce you to Magnus, King of Marann, Emperor of Eire."

"At last, we meet." Duff's voice issued from the triangular patch of darkness. "I would greet you properly with a bow and a kiss, but I am chained to darkness, cursed by the Fae King Arwan."

Magnus still had a firm hold on her wrist. She rolled her eyes and twisted free. "Duff is no threat," she said. "He is on our side." To the shadow, she said, "Did you feel me summon you?"

Magnus cut a glance at her, but his attention remained fixed on the shadow. "You're the one who brought information of Alexander freeing the prisoner. You're the one who visited Danu in her dream." For the last part, his voice dropped to a near growl.

"I am," Duff said breezily. "And if it pleases the king, I have more information."

"Why do you wish to help us?"

Danu elbowed him in the ribs. "He's a friend."

"No Fae offers aid to a mortal without exacting a price."

Danu snorted.

Duff said, "My price is this."

She stiffened, not expecting her friend to trade information for his own gain. She had thought they were beyond that.

"Once Hyrk is defeated, the human women are to be returned to their homes. Immediately and with escorts to protect them."

She felt tension pour off Magnus. He gritted his teeth. "I don't trust that gemstone. I've used it, yes, but I cannot abide exposing those innocents to dark magic any more than necessary. It's unpredictable. I cannot agree to your terms."

Duff made a dismissive noise. "If we defeat Hyrk, you won't need to rely on his relic to send the women home. Trust their wellbeing to me, and I will see it done."

"Never."

Danu stood on her toes to kiss her protective king's cheek. "You can trust him," she said. "He is not like the Fae you've heard about in magical tales."

"She's right," Duff said. "I'm much more handsome."

Danu ignored his quip. "Is this what Seona wants?"

At the mention of the human's name, Magnus's shoulders relaxed.

"It is. And I would see it done because I love her."

Danu felt her mouth fall open in surprise. Then her heart warmed. Duff in love. That was something she never imagined to see with her own eyes. "My, my," she said. "The human has you charmed."

"You mean I have her charmed," the Fae said, sounding affronted. "Do we have a deal?"

"The humans are in my custody," Magnus said. "I cannot simply hand them over to one of the Fae, no matter how well-meaning."

"Which is why you'll send escorts," Duff said. "I'll take one at a time and see them back to where—and when—they wish to go. Your escorts will ensure their safety. I shall provide the magic. Upon my return each time, you'll receive a full report from your men."

Danu wondered how Duff planned to accomplish such magic, considering how limited he was under Arwan's curse. But she trusted him completely. She squeezed Magnus's arm, hoping to reassure him.

Her king bent his head to her. "You're certain he is trustworthy?"

"Yes," she said. "I truly believe he wants what's best for those women. And if he says he can do it, he can do it."

"All right," Magnus said. "You help us defeat Hyrk, and I vow to allow the women to return to their homes. With one exception."

Danu held her breath. Did Magnus have an attachment to one of the human women?

He tucked her tight against his side. "Seona must remain. She is to be mother to my heir."

Oh. He meant her. Or rather Seona. Her stomach curled in on itself. Magnus was holding *her,* but he still planned to impregnate *Seona* with his heir.

She felt Duff's eyes on her and squirmed under his perusal.

"Seona's fate will be decided by Seona," Duff said at last. "That is my final offer. Take it or leave it."

Magnus huffed a breath out his nose. What was going through his mind? Was he even now planning how he might tempt Seona to remain with him once they were returned to their rightful bodies?

"I accept," her king said. He sheathed his dagger. "Now tell us all you know."

§

TRAVIS RUBBED HIS hands together, willing warmth into his stiff fingers. At last, enough wood had been gathered to keep one of the two fireplaces in the great hall lit. Along with the other pups assigned to cleaning the great hall, he'd found several moth-eaten tapestries folded in dusty chests above stairs. Using sticks from the kindling pile, they'd created frames for the fabric and arranged the makeshift screens to create a small room around the fire. Despite the holes in the tapestries, the area retained the fire's warmth. They would not freeze in the night, at least.

A commotion in the kitchen caused some of the pups to get up and shift the screens for a better view. The older boys had returned from hunting. They carried the cleaned carcasses of a small boar and three foxes.

Travis jumped up to help prepare for dinner. Amidst the debris in the great hall, they'd found one serviceable table and righted it. No tableware had been found, so pots and pans from the kitchen would serve to hold portions for each of them. There were no goblets to drink from, but the deep snow outside would be simple enough to melt. Travis chose a large pot from the pile of supplies and took it outside to fill with the frozen white powder.

During dinner, Alexander positioned himself at the head of the table with Marcus and Boone on either side of him. Looking like a stick between two boulders, he carried himself like a king. The blond hair Travis shared with his brother may as well have been a crown upon his head.

"Good work today, men," Alexander said, motioning with a boar leg. Travis rolled his eyes. The age of manhood was twenty-five. The eldest among them was Marcus, who would be twenty in a few days and able to enter training. Even *he* was five years from adulthood. "We need to make this place suitable for female company, so eat, rest well, and tomorrow, we begin setting this keep to rights."

The older boys, clustered toward the head of the table, began jostling each other and wagging their eyebrows. How could they be so daft? There *were* no females. Either Alexander was lying—though to what end, Travis couldn't imagine—or he believed his own claims. Travis recalled the red gemstone and wondered if perhaps the same mania that had caused his father to betray Magnus was now beginning to fester inside Alexander.

Whatever Alexander's aims, Travis had to find a way to reach King Magnus. The whole of Chroina was no doubt looking for them this very moment. They wouldn't rest until each pup was found. Since Travis knew his king wouldn't rest, he determined to do the same.

I'll escape tonight, when the others are sleeping.

He had thought it through while cleaning all day. The fastest way to get to King Magnus was to steal the gemstone from Alexander. If Travis pretended to go to sleep near his brother, he might have a chance. The thought of actually using the stone made his stomach churn, but it must be done. He couldn't risk a journey on foot this time of year. Nor could he bear the idea of taking weeks to reach Marann when the journey could be as short as a single step.

A single step, and he could be back by Anya's side, back at the chores and lessons he loved so much, back where his heart was.

The screens were around the fire again, and musty hay had been brought in from a collapsed structure that must have been the stables. They would sleep in a group to keep warm. This would make slipping the stone from Alexander's pocket easier.

The younger pups were lying down to sleep while the older ones sat around with cups of warmed water, talking quietly. Travis would be expected to fall asleep with the younger lads. Not wanting to draw attention, he curled up next to Ruben and Nolan. He was exhausted and cold, but he refused to sleep. Instead, he watched Alexander move from lad to lad, talking privately with them. He spoke to Ruben now, who had been one of the more outspoken skeptics during his speech at the schoolyard.

Travis had seen Ari do this a hundred times. His father would bend the ear of a council member, a governor, or a captain in the army. Travis had watched as the faces of powerful men changed. Skepticism would turn to caution, then to acceptance. Ari had been a master at convincing others to his way of thinking. It looked like Travis had not been the only one watching.

Finally, Alexander came to the fire. He nudged Julian with his boot and told him to give up his pallet. The younger lad did so without question.

Travis motioned him over. "Here. We'll keep each other warm."

Julian nodded his appreciation and lay down with his back to Travis's. In a moment, he was snoring again.

He longed to ask the other lad what he thought of all this, but he dared not with so many ears around. He could not risk standing out in any way. He had one chance to steal that gemstone. If he failed, all would be lost.

Dim orange light flickered over the few lads still talking. As the closest one to the fire, Alexander was easiest to see. Only a few sleeping bodies separated them. It was just a matter of time.

Yawning, Alexander stretched out and appeared ready to sleep. Before closing his eyes, he motioned his two overgrown lackeys to him. Travis's heart sank as the two older boys sprawled out on either side of his brother. To get to Alexander, he would have to climb over at least one of them.

There was no help for it. He had to do it.

Biding his time, he watched the fire grow dim. No one roused to fuel it. He was certain if Alexander were still awake, he would command someone to add some logs. Beside his brother, Marcus snored loudly. Boon's back was to him. It rose and fell with slow, deep breaths.

It was now or never.

Moving slowly, he rose to a crouch then paused to listen for anyone stirring. He heard nothing but snores and Julian's customary sleep-muttering. Placing each step carefully between his sleeping companions, he made it to Marcus's feet.

His heart pounded so loudly, he feared the sound of it would wake his brother or his guards. *Slow,* he commanded the pumping organ. *Easy,* he told his lungs.

He began a painfully slow crawl over Marcus's legs, planting one hand in the hay beside Alexander.

A great, rumbling fart came from Marcus, making Travis freeze. He held his breath, waiting to see if the older boy would stir. He didn't.

Travis began breathing again and nearly fainted from the stench. Eyes watering, he inched his fingers to the lip of Alexander's trousers pocket, the one he'd seen him slip the stone into.

In the smallest imaginable increments, Travis's finger slipped into his brother's pocket. He felt the warmth from Alexander's hip. A little farther, a little farther. Watching Alexander for any sign of stirring, he searched for a hard, jagged shape.

Danu, help me.

A little farther. A little farther. There! He only had to dip in a little more until he could secure his hands around it.

Alexander's eyes flew open.

For a heart-stopping moment, Travis could have sworn his irises glowed red.

He whipped his hand from his brother's pocket, but too slowly.

Alexander grabbed his wrist. "What have we here?" his brother said. "A traitor to the new kingdom? Marcus," he said sharply. "Boone. Get up. My little brother needs a lesson in loyalty."

Travis's heart sank. He'd lost his only chance. What would happen to him now?

He didn't have to wait long. With Alexander trailing behind, Marcus and Boone dragged him outside by his coat collar.

A few of the other boys had woken and stumbled out after them. "What's going on?" Travis recognized Ruben's voice.

"Caught little Travis trying to take my gemstone, that's what," Alexander said. "Now he's going to learn what happens when someone thinks to usurp my position. Marcus, hold him. Boone. Teach him a lesson."

Travis twisted in Marcus's cruel grip until he could see Ruben. "I wasn't. I didn't mean to." He didn't know what he was saying, only that he didn't want to be taught any kind of lesson by the ham-fisted Boone.

Ruben's brow furrowed with concern, but when the blows started falling, he did nothing to intervene. Boone's fists connected with his face, his stomach, his ribs. He didn't know how long the beating went on, only that it was long enough for nearly every pup to come out of the keep to see what the trouble was.

When it was over, Alexander said, "Everyone. Go back to bed. Traitors get to sleep out in the cold." He followed the words with a kick to Travis's side that made him cry out. "You better pray the cold finishes you, little brother. Because I hear these mountains are filled with caves, and those caves are filled with the rejects from Jilken's breeding experiments." He laughed a wicked laugh. "Give my greetings to the monsters."

Through swollen eyes, Travis watched everyone pass through the fortress's large doors. The meager light spilling onto the snow disappeared with a thud as the doors closed.

He was in darkness. His mouth bled freely. His face felt like mush, and his body felt like he'd been run over by a dozen merchant carts.

What a fool he'd been for thinking he could be a hero! He wasn't brave like King Magnus or strong like Riggs. He was the smallest of them. The weakest. And now, if he managed not to freeze to death, he would be eaten by the animals of the forest. Or the monsters.

He curled into a ball and shivered. He ought to crawl around the keep to the stables. The structure was as broken as he was, but it would offer some protection from the elements.

Yes. He ought to crawl. But he was so cold. And tired.

He didn't want to move.

Minutes passed. Or it might have been hours. The cold took on life around him. It seemed to press at him, nudging him. Wait. It wasn't the cold. It was a wet nose.

He whimpered.

The sounds of paws crunching in snow filled him with terror.

A warm tongue licked a line across his cheek.

"P-p-p-please don't eat-t-t-t m-m-me." He raised his arms over his face, protecting himself as best he could.

The jaws of what had to be an enormous wolf closed over his arm at the elbow.

He screamed, expecting the teeth to slice through him.

But they didn't. As if his elbow were a handle, the wolf dragged him through the snow, away from the keep.

Travis kicked his legs, but they didn't work right. He was so cold his body wasn't following the commands he gave it.

I'm going to die tonight.

It was his last thought before the cold overtook him.

Chapter 20

MAGNUS PAUSED IN tossing grain bags into a provisions cart long enough to take off his cloak. The winter air chilled his skin, but hard work heated him from the inside, making the added layer unnecessary. The cloak would prove essential, however, since he was about to lead his army into the mountains of northern Larna.

The walls of the bailey echoed with hurried shouts, rattling cart wheels, clomping horse hooves, and the clangs of armor and weapons being loaded. The music of war.

A few hours earlier, while the sun had risen over Chroina, Danu's Fae acquaintance, Duff, had recounted Hyrk's gloating. Not only did the demigod confirm Magnus's worst fears—that the children had fallen prey to Hyrk's evil—but he also unwittingly revealed where the children were. The demigod had mentioned mountains and caves, and the rejects from Jilken's breeding experiments. Magnus knew those caves. And there happened to be a fortress jutting up from a hillside near the western entrances.

The fortress was two day's ride far from Eire's western shores, and the now abandoned city of Saroc, from which Larna's kings had ruled. In the war twenty years ago, spies like Riggs and his father had mapped the caves and discovered they ran directly through Mammoth, the largest of Larna's mountains.

Ever the cunning strategist, Neil had used those maps to outwit the Larnians on their own turf. The cowards of Bantus's army had so feared the supposed monsters descended from long-ago breeding experiments that they avoided Mammoth and her caves at all cost. However, Marann's army had discovered no living thing in the caves. Signs of ancient habitation littered the mountain's belly, but there had been no wolves, no monsters, nothing in those caves larger than a beetle.

Marann's spies and soldiers had won the war because the caves had provided shelter and hiding places near the fighting. They would use the caves again, this time to find their children, cure them of whatever Hyrk had done to them, and bring them home.

"Think the caves will be like we left them, Sire?" Riggs came up alongside him, clapping him on the back.

Back in the war, Riggs had been an axe-man in Marann's army. Since Magnus had led the cavalry, they had not crossed paths until two moons ago, when Magnus had received a report that a lone Maranner was travelling with a stolen woman. Of course, the woman in question, Anya, had been rescued, not stolen, a fact that came to light after no small amount of misunderstanding—and, perhaps, jealousy on Magnus's part. Now, Riggs was one of his trusted Knights of the Crescent Moon. In a few moments, he would be more.

Magnus nodded. "I think the caves will be as empty of monsters and useful to us as ever."

Riggs grinned and hefted a water barrel onto his shoulder. A moment before he turned to stride to the water cart, his gaze darted past Magnus's shoulder. The grin died, leaving icy anger in its place.

A deep voice said in Magnus's ear, "All is ready, Sire." He recognized that voice as belonging to Neil, Riggs's uncle. Neil had stood by and done nothing when Ari had sent Riggs and then Riggs's lifemate, Anya, through Hyrk's portal to be tortured by Bantus. While Magnus had not fully forgiven his former war chieftain, he suspected he was closer to it than Riggs.

Magnus regarded Neil coolly. He would not let him forget he was free strictly out of necessity. "Very well. And the *Fiona Blath?*"

"My men and I will protect it with our lives."

Magnus knew it was the truth. Neil had betrayed him not long ago, but something seemed to have changed within the former war chieftain. Perhaps his stay in the dungeon had given him perspective. Whatever the reason, Magnus trusted him to protect the women while he led his army to Larna. Even if Neil's loyalty to him—and his nephew—was suspect, no one could ever accuse him of lacking loyalty to Marann or her precious ladies.

Since the *Fiona Blath* housed more than just Marann's ladies, but also the human women rescued from Larna, Magnus had designated a quarter of his army to remain. He would not leave Chroina vulnerable while he rode to liberate the children from Hyrk's spell. Neil was now Lieutenant over the Chroina contingent, and Magnus had faith he was leaving the city in capable hands.

The sun was high in the sky. Soon it would begin its descent to the horizon. They must be going. But one more thing needed to be done.

Magnus found his new war chieftain, Cathal, and relayed Neil's message that the great hall was ready. A little celebration would lighten their burden before they left Chroina. Their warriors deserved a brief meal and a fond send-off.

Content with the state of the supply carts, Magnus ducked into the castle. Short on time and hands, his servants had been instructed to prepare only the most rudimentary of feasts. As he strode into the great hall, the scents of spiced meat and fresh bread suggested they'd done well considering the circumstances. Instead of children dashing about to fill goblets with beer, older servants did the work. They bowed to Magnus as he stepped upon the dais.

Above his throne was a portrait of him. Above the smaller throne, there was a portrait as well, but the second one was covered with a curtain. Magnus had longed for the day when the curtain could be opened, and Seona's image would declare her position as his queen. Since finding Danu, Magnus no longer wished to have Seona sit the smaller throne. He wished it could be Danu. But she had her own throne to return to, and it was not here on Earth.

He spared the thrones only a glance as he made his way to where his head of council stood speaking with a council member. Clem greeted him with a bow and a wrist clasp. He had Magnus's crown waiting for him, and Magnus bent his head so Clem could place it over his sweat-dampened mane.

Chroina's governor, a rotund man with a gray beard noticed them and ambled over.

"Kell," Magnus greeted, clasping the governor's hand. "How fares Lady Nan?"

"She is well, Your Majesty." Kell bowed. When he straightened, his eyes were sober. "You'll be leaving soon, then?"

"After the feast," Magnus confirmed. They would ride through the afternoon and stop only for a few hours in the night to rest the horses before continuing on. They must reach the entrance to the caves as soon as possible. Who knew what evil Hyrk was convincing the children of? All Magnus knew was that Hyrk cloaked himself with the faith of Marann's precious youth, hoping to become powerful once more. From conversing with the demigod at Lachlan's Promontory yesterday, he knew Hyrk hated everything Marann stood for. He hated Magnus. Danu help them if he succeeded in turning the children to his evil whims.

Clem and Kell took up positions to Magnus's left. Servants threw open the doors to the great hall, and guests began streaming in. Gentlemen and ladies entered alongside axe-men, cavalry men, and archers. Each lady, dressed in bright silks and lace, floated like a flower in a sea of red kilts and dark cloaks. The guests were mingling and smiling as they found seats at the tables, but tension kept their speech quiet and their smiles brief.

A few of the human women were also in attendance, and Magnus's heart lightened to see them gathered around Riggs's mother, Hilda, who had become like a leader to the women of the *Fiona Blath* in Diana's absence. The human women appeared well. Whole. Beautiful.

But there was one human form in particular Magnus could not wait to lay eyes on. The one inhabited by Danu.

As if his thoughts had summoned her, a pair of guards escorted her through a side door. With them was Josiah, the aged servant whom Daly relied on above all others. At seeing Danu, Magnus's chest relaxed. He had not realized how tense he'd been without his goddess until she came to his side and wound an arm around him.

"Where is Daly?" Magnus asked Josiah, a clean-shaven man with spectacles. "Has he had any rest?"

"Aye, Sire. He refused to go to bed last night, but he's fallen asleep in the kitchen, and we're all tiptoeing around him so he doesn't wake."

Magnus would command his head of household be moved to his bedchamber so he could be more comfortable, but he doubted it could be done without waking him. If Daly woke, he would get back to work.

"Good," he said. "Let him rest. Make sure all the servants get at least four hours of sleep each night. You're in charge of schedules. All unnecessary tasks are hereby suspended until the children are returned. See that only meals, fires, and necessary chores are addressed."

"Yes, Sire." Josiah bowed and hurried away.

Danu touched his elbow, and warmth spread through him. "You are a fine king," she said.

Sweet surprise washed over him like summer rain. How often did a man receive praise from a goddess? He was blessed among wolfkind. He was blessed among mortals everywhere. His divine lady's words gave him the strength to carry on.

"I've missed you," he told her, and he wrapped her in his arms and kissed her soundly.

Her arms circled his neck, and her lips moved under his, appreciative, receptive, impossibly addictive. How her kisses soothed him!

"And I you," she said with a radiant smile. "This is new." She touched a graceful finger to the bejeweled crown atop his head, which he only donned for royal functions such as this.

The room quieted. It took him a moment to realize why. Everyone knew Seona despised him, so her sudden, apparent acceptance of him would be unexpected. Perhaps even alarming. Pinning her to his side, he rearranged his features into a reassuring smile.

Be confident, and they will be confident. Appear unruffled, and they will be unruffled. Expect victory, and they will expect victory.

How he missed his father! It should be him wearing this crown and leading this charge against the enemy. At least Magnus still had the former king's words of wisdom.

In this moment, he could imagine his father saying, "The woman at your side will one day be their queen—at least in body. You must begin acclimating them to her."

If only it could always be Danu in the lovely body at his side. If they succeeded in Larna and destroyed Hyrk, Danu would be restored to her rightful place, and it would be Seona at his side. This would likely be the only time his people would witness him and Seona trading smiles and kisses.

Pain twisted his heart at the impending loss. He could not afford the feeling. Shoving it aside, he pulled himself upright and took on a stance befitting a king.

Once the great hall was filled, Clem announced, "Esteemed ladies and men of Marann, I present His Majesty King Magnus,

Emperor of Eire." With a flourish, he bowed low and gestured to Magnus.

He cleared his throat. True, the introduction had changed since the slaying of Bantus and Marann's conquering of Larna, but it was not complete. He caught Clem's startled gaze and nodded toward Danu.

Clem straightened hurriedly. "A—and—" he said, "Lady Seona, Sister of Anya."

Still not a complete introduction, but the closest they could get without endangering Danu by revealing her whereabouts. Magnus stepped forward with his goddess anchored at his side. She stood as tall and regal as he, and pride filled him from toe to crown.

Polite applause filled the hall. He spoke into the clapping, setting a tone of efficiency for the feast. "You have heard, I am sure, that we are at war."

At this blunt statement the hall fell silent.

"A war unlike any we have fought before. In the past, we have fought battles with fists, axes, swords, and arrows. Today, we face an enemy not of flesh and blood but of spirit. We face evil incarnate, and that evil has hold of our children." He paused, letting his words float softly to the floor in the deathly silence.

"With Danu on our side, we have seized victory before, and we will seize it now. We will rescue our children and defeat evil-doers and evil-makers alike. Good will prevail." He squeezed Danu, seeking to encourage her as well as his people—their people.

His soldiers shouted in agreement, and the guests cheered, but he sensed the restraint in it, the hesitancy to believe all would be well. Truly, it had been many years since all had been well. Even if they reclaimed their children, they would still be on the verge of extinction. No rousing speech could change that.

He cut the half-hearted cheers short. "There will be time for celebration," he promised. "But we must ride this day. Only a fool indulges in meat and wine whilst an enemy fortifies his position.

Maranners are not fools!" he shouted to a round of applause and cheers a little more enthusiastic than the first. "Maranners are brave! Maranners are strong! Maranners are cunning! Maranners will win the day!" With each shout, his audience supplied more enthusiasm until he could almost believe they held hope for their future.

With morale as buoyant as he could expect, he gazed down at Danu and kissed her forehead. She returned his gaze with cautious happiness that touched his soul.

The crowd settled into murmurs.

He spoke into the noise. "It has been two moons since our last battle." The crowd fell silent. "In that battle, Lady Anya—" He motioned to the intrepid human, who sat at the high table in a position of honor. At her narrowed eyes, he realized he hadn't yet informed her of his discovery that Danu and Seona had traded places. Did she suspect as he had that Seona might be possessed by Hyrk? He owed her the truth and promised himself he would tell her privately as soon as he was able. He cleared his throat. "Lady Anya and her lifemate, Riggs—" He nodded at his friend, who had a protective arm around his lifemate. "Secured our victory by slaying our enemy, King Bantus." Cheers went up, but he pressed on. "We were victorious, but at great expense, for through that victory, traitors were revealed."

The cheers died. An uncomfortable silence prickled at the skin of his forearms.

Danu hugged his side, reminding him that he was not alone.

"My second in command, the man who would have sat the throne upon my death, proved himself a liar. A traitor not only to the throne but to Marann. To all of you." He made eye contact with the noblemen who had been associates of Ari's, letting them know he was aware of their participation in Ari's plot, even if he had no proof.

It pleased him when they shifted in their seats.

"Let me be perfectly clear," he said. "Our kingdom was founded on the principles gifted to us by our beloved goddess." He pulled Danu even tighter against him and met her surprised eyes as she gazed up at him. Holding her gaze, he addressed the room. "In the Teachings of Danu, it is clearly written that bloodlines are the bedrock of community. Any man or woman engaging in activities contrary to our breeding laws will find themselves in the company of Diana and the others now residing beneath our feet."

He let the silence reign. Those who had spurned the lottery and paired one woman with many men in a single breeding season were traitors to Danu. He met the eyes of each unofficial traitor until they dropped their gazes to their laps. It did not take long.

"Promises made by those who oppose our laws are as substantial as dandelion fluff. Not only do such promises scatter when the wind blows, but where they land, weeds take root. Such weeds will be ripped out and stored where they will never see the light of day."

"My strong king," Danu whispered as she hugged his waist. He was only strong because she was here with him. He did not know if he would be this same king once she left him.

"With my cousin gone, there is an empty seat at my council table." Many faces around the hall showed relief at the change in subject. "We gather this afternoon not just to send off our soldiers with luck and goodwill but to appoint a new council member. It has been suggested—by more than one person—" He caught Anya's eye and looked around for Neil but did not see the former war chieftain. "That I am in need of a helper. A new second." Around the room, several council members showed their agreement with enthusiastic nods. "I would ask Riggs, Son of Hilda, Lifemate of Anya, and Knight of the Crescent Moon, to rise and come forward."

Riggs had just taken a sip of beer and promptly choked on it. Anya slapped his back and nudged him until he stood from his seat.

The big man's legs looked shaky as he climbed the steps. As always, when he was in Magnus's vicinity, he rounded his shoulders in an attempt to deemphasize his height. How many times would Magnus have to tell him not to do that?

"Do you accept your new position as second to the king of Marann?" he asked. "As aid and helper to the throne and as ruler should death come for me?"

Riggs's bearded mouth opened and closed. He looked like a fish gasping for air.

Magnus felt his lips twitch in a smile, but he kept his expression serious. "It is a simple question, friend. Answer 'I do,' or 'I do not.'"

Riggs swallowed audibly. Finally, he gathered himself and said clearly, "I do, Sire."

"Then kneel."

Riggs took a knee, bowing his shaggy head.

Magnus drew his dagger and touched it to Riggs's right shoulder then his left. Then he used it to cut a lock from Riggs's hair from the base of his bowed head. Holding the blade and the lock of hair aloft, he said, "With this sacrifice, you take on a heavy mantle. Rise and stand by my side."

Riggs shook his head, as if he couldn't quite believe what was happening, but he obeyed.

With Riggs on his right, and Danu on his left, he said, "Esteemed ladies and men of Marann, Women of the human realm, I present to you Riggs, Second to Magnus, Keeper of the Throne of Marann until such time as Danu—" Sadness clogged his throat. He cleared it and pressed on. "Until such time as Danu blesses me with an heir." He could not fathom Seona allowing him to plant his seed in her womb. He had lost the only opportunity he had to do so last night. Because of Hyrk.

The crowd erupted in applause. Around the perimeter of the room, soldiers hollered their congratulations. Riggs had earned their respect not just through defeating Bantus with the help of his small lifemate, but through his quiet humility and spirit of service.

The celebration was bittersweet, but Magnus did not let his sadness show. Forcing a smile, he clapped Riggs on the back and sent the blushing man to his seat.

Anya locked eyes with him and nodded her approval, but when she cut her eyes to Danu, Magnus knew her patience was at an end. With that look, she demanded an explanation.

Magnus spread his arms. "Everyone, eat. Drink. Be merry. Send off your warriors with gladness in their hearts." A small group of fiddlers and bards began playing, and the feast was underway.

Clem and Kell went to their seats at the ends of the high table while Magnus offered his arm to Danu. "I would like nothing more than to steal a few private moments with you," he murmured into her hair while he pulled out her chair, an ornately carved seat that echoed the style of the smaller throne. He took his own elaborate seat, but angled it so he could be as close to his lady as possible.

"But you cannot," Danu finished for him. Her sad smile meant she understood. He must be here to encourage his troops, to comfort his people. This was not a time for him to hide away and seek his own comfort.

He pressed his forehead to hers, creating a bubble of solitude around them. Speaking softly, just to her, he said, "Never have I wished to know the future more than I do in this moment. Whether I have the strength and cunning to best an immortal. Whether I can save the children. Save my people." Pain lanced his chest as her hand clasped his tightly. "Whether I will lay eyes on you again." He cupped her cheek. "You as you are now." Mortal. With him not just in spirit but in body. She seemed so *right* to him like this. It felt to him as though Seona had always been destined to give up her body for Danu, so *he* could have his goddess in every way imaginable. So *they* could bring an heir into the world and change the fate of wolfkind together.

But an Earthly throne was an insult to a goddess. She deserved so much more than he could ever give her.

Danu's eyes, tawny and bright, filled with unshed tears. "Your victory means our separation," she said. Knowing she was right, his heart ached. "I hate this. I'm not ready." Her fingers threaded through his. Her knuckles blanched white.

He was not ready, either. But Hyrk had moved against them, and he must respond. They did not have the luxury of time. Rulers rarely did.

"I want you here with me always," he confessed. "But Marann needs you restored to your rightful place." In fact, the whole world needed her restored. Once, there had been kingdoms spread over the face of the Earth. No more. Only Marann remained. He was convinced they had been honored thus because of all kingdoms, they had always remained true to Danu's teachings. And they always would. But the world needed life again. Only with Danu in her rightful place would the entire realm bloom the way it was meant to.

"I know." Her breath fanned over his beard as they breathed the same air. "I only wish we'd had more time."

"Eternity wouldn't be enough time." His lips found her forehead. He kissed her there, letting the touch linger. He had hoped to bed her and plant his seed in her womb while she dwelled in Seona's body, had even believed this had been his fate all along. He had been so near to doing so last night when his guard had burst in with the news of the children. Now the opportunity was lost. Duty demanded he act swiftly to locate their lost progeny and slay the one who had dared to take them.

During their conference with Duff, Magnus had learned that the cell Danu had been confined to, the one now holding Seona, took its strength from Hyrk's power. Once Hyrk was defeated, the cell would fail. Seona would be free, and she would possess the power of a goddess.

Since such power would be dangerous in the hands of one not accustomed to it, Duff would immediately transport Seona to Glendall and Danu. *"She will have to utter the incantation to restore my power," Danu had said to Duff. "Can you ensure her cooperation?"*

"I vow to you the circle of your power will be completed," Duff had said, and Danu had nodded with resolve.

And so their course had been set. Hyrk would be defeated, and Danu would be restored to her full power. They would be forever separated, and he would have to woo Seona for the good of his people while Danu looked on from her heavenly throne.

Speaking of Seona, Magnus commanded Riggs to trade seats with Anya so she would be at his side. She wasted no time beginning to question him the moment she was seated, but he silenced her.

"I apologize, Lady Anya."

That made her snap her mouth shut. She narrowed her eyes, an expression he was well-acquainted with. "For what?" she asked suspiciously.

"I should have sent word to you last night as soon as Assaph and I discovered the true whereabouts of your sister."

Anya's eyes went round and worried. "You ken where Seona is? Tell me." She grasped his arm and tugged.

"Be easy. She is well. Or, I suppose, as well as she can be under the circumstances." He cut a glance to Riggs, content to find him deep in conversation with Maedoc. While patting Anya's hand, he quietly explained that during Seona's fall from Lachlan's

Promontory, she had been holding Hyrk's gemstone. "Somehow, the stone's power sent her soul into his dungeon in the low realm."

Anya's eyes widened. "Hyrk's dungeon!" Despite her obvious shock, she kept to whispers, following his lead.

"Yes. Into the body of one whom I have only just learned has been imprisoned there for centuries. And that one is now inside the body of your sister."

"Not Hyrk, then," Anya surmised, glancing around him at Danu. "I figured as much when I saw you stealing a moment with Seona—or whomever." Her brow furrowed.

"Not Hyrk," he confirmed. "But Danu."

Anya dragged in a sharp breath.

Danu patiently watched their exchange. At Magnus's revelation, she graced Anya with a reassuring smile.

Anya gaped. It was the first time Magnus had ever seen the little human speechless.

"It is an honor to meet you, Anya, Lifemate of Riggs, slayer of Bantus," Danu said.

Anya blinked. She smoothed her hands over the silk of her gown in her lap, apparently gathering herself from the shock. "You—" She cleared her throat. "You are a goddess?"

"I am," Danu said. "But we must keep this a secret. In this form, I am defenseless against Hyrk. Do not fear. We have every intention of repairing this unexpected circumstance." As she said it, Magnus heard the sadness in her voice.

He took her hand and squeezed it.

Anya assessed Danu for a long moment then said, "Well, I suppose we'll have time to discuss all this when the men ride out."

"I look forward to it," Danu said, sounding as if she meant it.

The feast went on around them. Magnus fed Danu from his dagger, but he took no food for himself. His stomach was in no state to receive so much as a morsel, let alone a meal.

After a scant hour or celebration, Cathal gave the order for the cavalry to mount up. Magnus would ride at the front along with his Knights of the Crescent Moon.

With leaden feet, he escorted Seona to the bailey. Ladies embraced their sons and grandsons. Older men clapped their younger relatives on the backs. Magnus faced Danu for what was likely the last time. When he returned from Larna, she would have already been restored to where she belonged.

His throat felt thick. He did not know if he could speak. Never had a parting felt this significant. This final. Not even when he'd whispered his goodbyes to his parents on their deathbeds. A piece of his very soul would go with Danu, and he would never again be a whole man.

"Whatever happens," Danu said, bravely saving him from speaking first, "I will be with you, here." She placed her hand over his breastplate.

He wrapped both her small hands in his. What were her real hands like? What did she look like as a goddess? Did the statue in the temple do her justice? She must miss her heavenly body.

"I know you will," he said. He'd often wondered if the goddess had abandoned them, but he knew now that the lack of blessings had not been because she did not care. An evil demigod had tricked her and taken her from them. It was time to set their world to rights. He laid a hand over her heart, loving the warmth of her skin through the gown. "I go to fight for you, my goddess. I fight for what is right, and I will defeat your enemy. I will not fail you."

"I believe in you." A tear fell from each of her eyes.

He kissed the salty trails they left on her cheeks. He could say no more. If he tried, he would shed tears himself, and that would not be acceptable. Clearing his throat, he backed away from his beloved.

His horse waited for him. Mounting up, he mouthed the words, "I love you," to his lady, and he cantered out of the bailey to lead his men to war.

Chapter 21

TRAVIS WAS CONFUSED. He had been dragged away from the fortress, but somehow, he was back. He was looking into the great hall from the outside, as if crouched in one of the windows set high in the stone walls. Beneath him, the children were huddled in the room made from screens. They clutched cups of hot water and wiggled their toes in front of a freshly-stoked fire.

Alexander and his lackeys stood on a platform built from stacks of rubble overlaid with a broken tabletop. "We have more right to a voice in our future than any other Maranner, yet we have none. We are expected to keep the law, but we have no say in the laws being made. Here—" He made a sweeping gesture as if indicating the whole of Larna. "There are no laws save the ones we choose to make. There is no waiting to breed until a lad comes of age. Many of you are more than ready to begin sowing your seed, and our survival depends on you doing exactly that."

Some of the other lads nodded. Murmurs of agreement were like poison in Travis's ear. How could they accept Alexander's ideas so easily? Was it so simple to turn their backs on their mothers and fathers, on their instructors and the council members, on their kingdom and the laws that held it up?

"Where are the women you told us about, Xander?" Ruben spoke up. The older boy stood with his back to a screen, making room for the younger ones to be closest to the fire.

"Not far," Alexander said.

"Boar-shit," Craiden said. He stood near Ruben with his arms folded. "You said you've seen them. Show them to us or give us that stone so we can go back to Marann. At least we have plenty of food there."

Craiden could be a jerk, but Travis was glad to hear him challenge Alexander.

"That stone is dangerous," Ruben said. "We shouldn't be using it. Magnus had it locked in the temple for a reason."

"Don't be ridiculous," Alexander spat. "It's not dangerous. My sire used it countless times without harm." He pulled the stone from his pocket and waved it around, as if to demonstrate how safe it was to handle.

"Yeah, and look where it got him," Craiden said.

All eyes turned to Alexander, whose face twisted with rage. "There is one reason and one reason only my sire is dead. Magnus." He growled the name, making the hairs on Travis's neck stand on end. "If you want to see where loyalty to that Danu-whipped coward gets you, you have only to look outside. At the trail left in the snow when the wild beasts dragged my little brother away."

A soft growl issued from Travis's throat, and it sounded strangely animalistic. What Alexander had just said disturbed him, but not as much as the fact he was here, high up in the shadows of the hall, when he had been beaten and supposedly dragged away.

That confusion from earlier returned. What was happening to him? Why did he feel warm and protected and yet his vision insisted he was in a cold, dark place, eavesdropping on his brother? Why did it feel like gentle hands were washing his face with a damp rag and smoothing his hair off his brow?

"Ask yourselves this," Alexander went on. "Would you rather wait for a slim chance at breeding with Anya's get—*if* it happens to be a girl? Or would you rather have free access to this?" He held the gemstone aloft, and red light spiraled from it, coalescing into a flat oval, like one of the mirrors the ladies used to apply their cosmetics. The eerie light made Alexander's eyes glow crimson.

While Travis watched, skin crawling at the casual use of dark magic, an image took shape on the mirror-like surface. A lean, hooded figure stood by a tree. Snow covered the ground. In the distance, a small doe nosed at the snow, looking for roots to nibble. The figure silently raised a bow and let an arrow fly. It struck the doe in the neck. The animal took flight, arrow protruding, and the figure gave chase. The wind of the figure's speed caused the hood to fall away. Flowing flame-colored hair whipped out and streaked the air in the figure's wake. It was a young woman, fleet enough of foot to catch up to the wounded doe and slit its neck with a dagger.

The hall fell silent.

Alexander spoke into the silence. "She's out there. And there are more where she comes from. But before we can bring them here, we must make this place habitable, and we must arm ourselves well. Because once we have women here, word will spread. We must be strong enough to protect what's ours."

Travis heard himself growl again. The vision of the hall shifted. He had the sensation he was on four legs, turning from the scene below and dashing on silent feet down a crumbling set of stone stairs exposed to the elements. The vision faded, and he was in the dark.

No. Not the dark. Warm light pressed at his eyelids. The soft touch he'd felt before came again. "You saw it, didn't you?" said a kind voice.

He blinked his eyes open. His face and body ached, but he was warm. He seemed to be in a cavern of sorts, judging by the low, rocky ceiling. The scent of fresh hay and the comfort of thick blankets surrounded him. Beside him was a young woman with elfin features and white-blond hair. Her lips were the color of spring roses, and they covered teeth that held more bulk than that of human women like Anya and Seona. This young woman was wolfkind.

He blinked a few more times, certain he was dead and seeing a vision of an angel.

"Braeden's at the fortress," she said, wringing a cloth over a bowl of steaming water that smelled of garlic and astringent. She wore a loose-fitting tunic and doeskin leggings. "He let us see through his eyes, so we know what the enemy is planning."

Travis frowned, and it hurt his jaw. The things the girl said made no sense. No one could see through the eyes of another. Something hot tricked over his lip.

"Oh, there it goes again." She dabbed a dry cloth at his upper lip. "I just got your nose to stop bleeding, and now I've upset you, and it's going again. I'm sorry. What's your name? Mine's Nenna."

He licked his swollen lips, tasting traces of blood. "Travis," he answered. "Am I dead?" If he was, that would explain the magic of seeing through the eyes of another. Maybe angels could do that. "Are you an angel?"

She smiled, and her pale cheeks bloomed with color like the sky under a red sunset. "No, silly. You're very much alive, and I'm no angel." Her laugh was musical. Travis wanted to capture the sound in a jar and listen to it over and over again.

"You're too beautiful to be real," he blurted.

Her blush deepened. His tongue felt like it was tied in a knot.

"Well, I am real. But I can imagine my existence comes as a shock to you. My people have taken great pains to remain hidden here in the caves." Her eyes went distant, and her voice darkened. "Outsiders are cruel. All of them. But not you. I could sense it. That's why Vera let me bring you here."

Caves? Her people? Outsiders? His head hurt trying to make sense of it all. "Where is here?"

"Our home," Nenna said, simply. "This is my room."

He took in his surroundings more fully. The cavern had rough walls, but the floor was smooth with packed dirt. A small fire provided adequate heat. The smoke drifted through a wide crack in the stone. A rough-hewn cabinet with carved doors held a stone basin and a wooden pitcher. Besides the pallet, it was the only furniture in the space.

"It's nice," he said. And he meant it. He felt warm and safe, even though his body ached and his stomach growled.

Nenna beamed. She looked like she wanted to say more, but a shrill whistle sounded from a dark opening across the cavern. "Oh. That'll be Vera. She went hunting. Do you think you can rise, or shall I bring the food to you?"

Travis's curiosity overpowered his pain. He rolled to his hands and knees, testing his body. He had broken ribs that were very sore when he breathed, but someone had bound them for him. His face felt hot and puffy. The skin was tight with healing. "I can get up," he said, hoping it was true.

He got to his feet slowly, and Nenna rushed to his side. She slung one of his arms around her shoulders and performed the duties of a crutch. A very pretty crutch. She was taller than him and appeared to be around twenty. Not quite a woman, but no longer a girl. Not that he had any experience judging the ages of young females.

By the goddess. He was with a female! A young one! The realization struck him like a blast of joyous sunshine after a long storm. A female had her arm around his waist, was helping him hobble on bruised legs through Larnian caves.

"Who are you?" He shook his head. "I mean, who are your people? Are you Larnians?"

They entered a dark tunnel. It was short, and at the end was another glowing cavern. In this cavern, a larger fire flickered in a fireplace built with mortared stone. A chimney of black shale rose to the high ceiling. This cavern had many carved pieces of furniture, including a low bench that Nenna directed him toward.

A slender woman with fire-colored hair nodded at them as she hung a cloak on a rack of antlers from a large elk. He recognized her from the hall—from the mirror-like surface that had come from the gemstone. "We're the Remnant," the woman said, answering his question. Her face was not as open and friendly as Nenna's.

"We saw you in Braeden's communication," Nenna said. "Those boys used magic to watch you hunt. You found us a doe. Yum!" She bounced on her toes, jostling Travis and making him wince. "Oh, sorry. This is Vera. Vera, I learned his name. Our new friend is Travis."

Vera eyed him but said nothing. She passed into a tunnel and disappeared.

Nenna lowered Travis to the padded bench. "I'll go help her bring in the meat." She dashed into the tunnel on light feet, and Travis stared after her. As she disappeared into the darkness, he saw her pulling her arms into her tunic, as if to remove it. Blinking, he tried to make sense of everything.

The Remnant. What did that mean? Was he in the caves Alexander had mentioned—the caves where monsters lived? He didn't see any monsters. Only pretty women.

Heavens! Magnus needed to know about this! There really were women in Larna! Wolfkind women!

But how would he get to Magnus? Where was he? Still in Larna, for certain, since he'd been brought here by Nenna. She didn't seem strong enough to carry him far. His cheeks warmed at the thought of being in her arms, even if he'd been unconscious at the time.

A rustling in the tunnel made him look up. It sounded like growling, and like paws scrabbling over stone. The sounds grew louder, and made him tense. They were wolf sounds. Magnus kept tame wolves for tracking and hunting, but wild wolves were very dangerous. Especially Larnian wolves.

He looked around for something, anything, he might use to defend himself. There were tools by the fireplace, but he didn't think he could get his damaged body to them quickly enough.

He was out of time. A great white wolf emerged into the cavern, rear end jerking and front half lowered as if dragging something. When it came fully into the light, the wolf's cargo was revealed as a limp deer carcass.

Oh, no! Nenna had gone that way to help Vera bring in the meat. This wolf must have overtaken them.

"Nenna!" he cried, launching himself off the bench and toward the fireplace tools. His whole body ached, but he forced himself to grab up a heavy shovel for ashes. Spinning around, he brandished it at the wolf. "Back!"

He had to get past the thing to search for Nenna.

The wolf had dragged the doe to the middle of the room, where a stony depression in the floor bore claw marks. The carcass lay in the bowl-like depression. The wolf stood over it, but it wasn't falling on the fresh meat. Instead, it cocked its head at Travis, ears pricked in an expression of curiosity.

Travis didn't feel threatened by the wolf and suddenly felt silly for aiming a shovel at it.

Hoping his instinct was right and the wolf meant him no harm, he edged around it, careful not to make any sudden movements. When he got to the tunnel, he turned to run and find Nenna. Instead, he ran into a solid wall of russet fur. Another wolf!

He fell back on his bottom. Pain shot up his bruised back, and he cried out.

Suddenly, the white wolf was at his side, licking his face. No, wait. It wasn't the wolf. It was— "Nenna?" He blinked up at her worried face, which was exactly where the wolf's enormous head had been a moment ago.

"Travis, are you all right? Braeden! You need to be more careful! You nearly ran over our guest." She slipped her arms into the holes of the loose-fitting tunic she'd been wearing. Her leggings were nowhere to be seen.

"Sorry." A young man's voice sounded from inside the cavern.

Travis twisted around with some difficulty until he saw the source of the sound: a naked young man of a good height, but not yet filled out. Probably in his early twenties. Stubble shadowed his chin and cheeks, but he did not have a full beard yet.

Where had the russet wolf gone?

The boy went into the tunnel that led to Nenna's room. He returned a minute later wearing leggings and a tunic and carrying a carving hatchet. "Normally, we eat as wolves," he said as he lifted the hatchet and brought it down on the doe. "But Vera says that might frighten you." He rocked the blade free then set to sectioning choice cuts. "Here." He'd expertly hacked off a generous helping of hindquarter—Travis's favorite, and held it out.

Gingerly, Travis got to his feet. Nenna helped him toward what must be an eating pit. He'd read about eating pits in his history lessons. His ancestors used to gather all the fresh meat into a stone bowl set into the ground. The elders in the clan would gorge themselves first. Then the rest would eat by clan order. At the end, the bones would be collected by the poor and turned into tools that could be sold or traded.

"Thanks," Travis said, taking the hindquarter from Braeden. He tore into the meat and chewed. It was fresh and delicious. Not spiced or tenderized like the meat they prepared in the kitchen at Glendall, but warm and gamy. Refreshing.

Once he'd swallowed his first bite, Nenna and Braeden dug in. Clearly, they were a civilized bunch, not like the ancient wolfkind from his lessons.

"So, uh—you said you normally eat as wolves. Are you two—?" he wasn't sure how to finish the question. Were Nenna and

Braeden the two wolves he'd seen? Could they somehow be both wolfkind and wolf?

"We're the Remnant," Braeden said with relish. He widened his eyes and grinned, reminding Travis of the older boys when they would tell ghost stories to the younger ones.

Unfortunately, the word meant nothing to Travis, so he couldn't give Braeden the reaction he was fishing for.

"The cast-offs? From the time of King Jilken?" Braeden made it a question.

He must mean the breeding experiments from long ago. Travis nodded to show his understanding.

Braeden brightened. He rose to a crouch and gestured with his rib of venison. "We were the unlovely. The unwanted. We were not what the king was looking for. So he tossed us out of the keep, leaving us for dead in the wilderness."

As he told the tale, he moved with practiced steps around the pit. The crackling fire cast his shadow on the cavern wall. Slinging an arm around Travis's shoulders, he waved his venison as if using it to paint an image in the air before them.

"We were left to die. But some of us lived. Wild wolves rescued us and brought us to the caves. They raised us as their own. Now we are the Remnant. We are what's left. What was not intended, but what thrives in secret."

Travis stared in wonder. All this time, the Remnant had been living alongside them. And they could change into wolves! The strange ability must have come about through Jilken's use of magic to breed Larnians with wolves.

"And when *they* are all gone," Braeden said, "we will emerge. We will claim our birthright and rule over Larna. The despised, the abandoned, the ones discarded. We will become the rulers over all the land." Braeden lifted Vera's cloak off the rack and wrapped himself in it. He spun with a flourish, making the cloak swirl in a great arc. He swept up the shovel Travis had used as a weapon and held it like a scepter, looking quite royal save for his lack of beard.

Whoa. Not only did these people exist, but they had a plan for when the last of the Larnians died off. Struck dumb, Travis looked at Nenna.

She nodded and smiled, as if she took it for granted that Braeden's prediction would come true.

"Take off my cloak." Vera strode into the cavern. Stopping near the pit, she tossed a rumpled bit of leather to Nenna, who caught it neatly.

Nenna shook out the leather, which turned out to be her leggings. With total disregard for modesty, she thrust her legs into them and pulled them up, then returned to devouring her hindquarter.

Vera hung her bow and quiver on the rack, along with her newly reclaimed cloak, and used Braeden's hatchet to carve herself a shoulder. "I see Braeden has told you our history." She wore a smirk, but her gray eyes were somber. She appeared young, because there was no gray in her hair, but her eyes seemed ancient.

Travis nodded, a little afraid of Vera. He cleared his throat and said, "All this time, you were here and no one knew."

"Some knew," Vera said, sinking her teeth into fresh meat. She chewed then wiped the back of her hand across her mouth, leaving a grisly red smear. "From time to time, someone stumbles across us." She met Travis's eyes. "We don't give them the chance to share our secret."

Travis swallowed the lump in his throat. Magnus needed to know of the Remnant. But he had a feeling escaping these caves would be even more difficult than escaping Alexander and his lackeys.

Chapter 22

DANU STOOD IN the bailey until the last rider had passed through the gate. "I would like to watch them ride out of the city," she told Maedoc. Magnus had left her with eight guards. Maedoc, the captain of his Knights of the Crescent Moon, was in charge of her security. He alone knew her true identity, because Magnus deemed it wise. The others thought they were protecting Seona.

"Yes, my lady," Maedoc answered in his gruff way. "This way, if you please." Since Magnus had revealed her true identity to him, Maedoc had been practically tripping over himself to serve her. He led her to Magnus's solar and threw open a pair of great oak doors. A blast of cold, damp air surrounded her.

Stepping through the doors, she found herself on a stone balcony overlooking a courtyard bordered by fine buildings. Beyond was the main street of Chroina. Mounted soldiers and supply carts filled the road from edge to edge and stretched into the distance. She could not see the front of the party, where Magnus would be.

"The east gate is about a mile that way." Maedoc pointed in the direction of the party. She knew from talking with Magnus that one thousand men rode for Larna. The number represented three quarters of his fighting force. The final quarter remained in Chroina to guard its citizens, especially the ladies in the *Fiona Blath*.

She had learned that of wolfkind's population of just under six thousand, the vast majority were too old to serve in the army. In another hundred years, the population would be next to nothing. All the females, including Anya and Seona, would be gone. Their only hope for survival rested in Anya's womb.

A pang of loss struck her, not just that her people had been reduced to this while she'd been imprisoned, but also that the hope of her people would come through another woman. Duff's words from Hyrk's dungeon came back to her. *A human woman is said to have appeared to Magnus in a vision as the mother of his future heir.*

She'd dismissed this supposed vision, because she had been in no position to grant one. Perhaps she shouldn't have dismissed it so hastily. Magnus's vision seemed to be unfolding before her eyes. *Anya* was the human woman. Magnus had just made Riggs his second. That meant in the absence of a blood heir, Anya and Riggs's offspring would one day sit the throne of Marann.

She clutched her boar-skin cloak around her as she looked upon a city with nine vacant buildings for every occupied one. She was happy for Anya, happy for wolfkind that they had this precious hope. But she could not help feeling as though Marann's hope should come directly from Magnus.

He was a good king. A good man. Ruling was in his blood. He bore the mantle of leadership with grace, strength, and fairness. His line should go on. He deserved an heir to love and to raise, to teach as his father had taught him.

But for Magnus to have a blood heir, he would have to impregnate a female. Her fists clenched at the thought.

Beneath the cloak, her hands cupped her empty womb. She imagined her current body round with Magnus's child. She pictured him beaming over her protruding belly, pacing Glendall's corridors as a physician oversaw the birth, cradling his newborn child, eyes brimming with love.

It made her sick to imagine any other woman sharing those moments with *her* king. And that was without considering the coupling itself. If the thought of Seona carrying Magnus's child upset her, imagining Seona under him as his seed took root in her womb made fire pulse in her breast. Pain made her look down. Her fingernails had bitten half-moons into her palms.

It should be me. I am their Mother. I would be their mother again.

But she could not see a way.

The wintry air battered her skin as the last of Magnus's party disappeared from view. Her would-be lover rode for Larna with his army. The distance between her and Magnus felt like a rope pulling at her insides. Over the coming days, that distance would grow, until finally, with Magnus's victory, that distance would become infinite.

She would regain her deity, but lose her king. And any chance of participating in his vision.

I'm being selfish. What kind of goddess puts her own desires before the wellbeing of her people?

She would lose Magnus, true. But, restored to her throne, she would have the power to bless her precious wolfkind beyond measure. She would shower them with life and beauty and happiness for two thousand years to make up for the time she'd languished in prison. Then she would add another two thousand and another. She would gift her priests with new passages to pen in her *Archives*. She would ensure that Magnus's name would be revered for all time.

She must do what she could to help her king win this war. She might be powerless in this mortal body, but she wore something that held nearly unlimited power, if she could only access it. Her hand wrapped around her moonstone at her neck.

I need to see Anya.

She must discover what the human had done to get the moonstone to work for her. It had given her understanding of the wolfkind tongue, a great power indeed. Once she learned Anya's secret, she would speak to Assaph. The priest had blessed Hyrk's gemstone, allowing Magnus to use it. Perhaps a blessing would make her moonstone work for her.

Once she could wield its power, she could aid Magnus and his army. Her help might mean the difference between defeat and glorious victory.

Course set, she whirled around to demand that Anya be brought to her, but when she turned, it was to nearly plant her face in the broad, armored chest of Maedoc.

The knight steadied her with two massive hands on her shoulders. "Beg pardon, my lady. Didn't mean to make you start." He set her away from him with a rising of color to his bearded cheeks. He cleared his throat. "Lady Anya is here. You want to receive her?"

What perfect timing! "Yes, Maedoc. Send her in. Thank you."

Striding into the solar, she smoothed the velvet of her gown, the color like deep ocean waters under a full moon. Her stomach lifted with a strange sensation. Nerves? She was not accustomed to feeling nervous.

To one of the guards, she said, "If it is not too much trouble, would you ask that tea be sent up?" Without the children, Glendall was short-staffed. She did not want to burden anyone, but she would like to provide hospitality to Anya, especially since she planned to interview the human at length.

The guard left to pass along her request, and in through the open door came Anya.

The human wrung her hands as she approached the table where Magnus dined and met with his council. She was small in stature compared to wolfkind females, but similar in height to the human body Danu occupied. Waves of chestnut hair cascaded around delicate shoulders and made a soft waterfall over her forest-green gown. She, too, wore a cloak, as did most everyone since the children had disappeared and there were fewer attendants for the fires. Large eyes like polished tiger's eye gems displayed curiosity and concern.

How odd it must be for the human to face her sister's body knowing someone else dwelled within.

"Sister," she greeted, setting a tone of conspiracy for them. She rushed forward and took the human's hands. "I am glad you came."

Anya's eyes widened. Her hands trembled in Danu's grasp. She appeared uncertain how to proceed.

"Speak freely, my dear, but keep your voice soft." She spoke close to Anya's ear while kissing her cheek in greeting. "We must pretend I am Seona. Let us converse as secretive sisters, shall we?"

Anya nodded. Following Danu's example, she kept her voice low when she said, "I suppose I shouldna attempt to curtsy then, since I wouldna do so for Seona."

"Precisely." She smiled, pleased Anya caught on so quickly. She had a feeling this human was no stranger to secrets and plotting. "Come. Sit." Arm in arm, she led Anya to the far end of the table, where the guards would not overhear them. "We have much to discuss."

Anya came along with limping steps and took a seat. Behind her, two white-haired servants started a fire in the hearth. "Aye, we do, indeed."

Danu arranged herself in the chair beside Anya's. They sat close, as sisters might, heads bent for private conversation while the fire began warming their backs. "Congratulations on being with child." She let none of her earlier thoughts show on her face. "You must be elated."

Anya's hand went to her womb. A small smile played at the corner of her mouth. "Aye. 'Twas unexpected to say the least, but most welcome." Anya's wide eyes showed her nervousness, but the smile on her lips felt genuine.

"Unexpected?" she asked. "Did you not hope for a child when Riggs took you as his lifemate?"

Anya shook her head, her hair shifting on her shoulders. "*Och*, Riggs dinnae *take* me as his lifemate. At least no' wi' intention. It simply happened. As for being with child—I've never shown signs of it before. Figured I was broken."

Infertile, she meant. Interesting. Even more interesting that she and Riggs became bonded as lifemates while Danu had been imprisoned. The creation of a lifemate bond was a sacred blessing gifted to a deserving couple under the full moon. The couple would pray and ask to become lifemates, and Danu, if she felt so inclined, would grant the request. But for two thousand years, she had not been able to receive or answer prayers.

Oblivious to Danu's musings, Anya said, "Riggs showed me I'm no' broken. At least no' in any way that matters." Color infused her cheeks. "But I willna bore you gushing over my lifemate. Tell me. How does Seona fare?" Gone was the glow she wore when speaking of Riggs. Her hands twisted in her lap.

"She is as well as she can be," Danu answered, "Considering she dwells in Hyrk's dungeon. For a mortal, such a place would be deadly, but she is protected by my deity. And by Duff. He will ensure no harm befalls her."

"Duff?" Anya frowned.

Ah, yes. Anya did not know him as Duff. "You know him as a gypsy. Gravois, I believe, is the name he goes by in the mortal realm."

"Gravois! You ken of him?" She sat forward in her chair.

Danu smiled. "Yes. I know him. He's of the Fae. He spends most of his time in the mortal realms since the king of the Fae, Arwan, cursed him to dwell forever in darkness. Duff is chained to night and shadow, but he disguises himself as Gravois so he may circumvent the curse." At least he had done so when he possessed her moonstone. For the first time, it occurred to her just what Duff had sacrificed when he'd given the stone to Anya. She resolved to help her friend any way she could once she was restored to her throne.

Anya's mouth hung open while Danu spoke. She snapped it shut and thumped a small fist on the table. "I knew there was somat fishy about that tinker." At that moment, the guards admitted a servant with a tea tray. Oblivious to the interruption, Anya muttered, "So Gravois's a bloody faerie." Her eyes darted back and forth, as if she were slotting pieces into a mental puzzle.

The servant set the tray before them. If he thought it strange that the two human women were discussing the Fae, he showed no sign of it.

"Always surrounded by magic, that one," Anya said, reaching for the teapot. "I never saw him use it himself, but every tinker in his camp had somat magical about them. He told me once he was attracted to magic. I should have guessed he was a faerie. Magic-lovers, one and all, that lot." She nodded, as if she were an authority on the Fae.

Danu found herself liking this human who blurted whatever she thought and used her mind to solve problems.

"Attracted to magic," she mused while helping herself to a cup of tea. Steam swirled into the crisp air as she poured. "Yes. That describes Duff—and the Fae—perfectly. How did you come to meet him?"

Anya sipped. When she put her cup down, a faraway look came into her eyes. "I had chosen a path of wickedness, and it led me to take a terrible fall." A wry smile twisted her full lips. "A legacy of daughters who fall from high places. 'Tis what Fergus left behind." She raised her cup and sipped again, leaving Danu confused about this Fergus. "'Tis where Gravois found me," Anya went on. "At the bottom of a crevasse. He took me to his camp, and his fellows helped mend my legs. As soon as I was hale enough, he sent me on my way. Gave me some speech about destiny that I dinnae understand until only recently. And without my kenning it, he slipped a bloody magical stone into my dress. 'Twas as though he knew I would need its power of translation. And need it I did. Would have been lost without it."

Something in her relaxed at hearing Anya mention the moonstone. She untied her cloak so Anya could see she wore it around her neck. "This stone is one of the things I wish to discuss with you."

Anya's gaze fell to the moonstone. She did not look surprised to find it in Danu's possession. "So, he gave it to you, then. I wondered when he would. 'Tis in the painting, after all."

"Painting?"

"He hasna shown it to you? *Och,* but he wouldna, would he? At least, he wouldna have shown it to Seona, lest he frighten her senseless."

Danu blinked. She had no idea what Anya was talking about. "Shown me what?"

"Come." Anya stood briskly. A wince pulled her face taut, but she did not slow her movements. "Take a walk wi' me."

Excited to explore more of Glendall, she left the solar with Anya. Her excitement fizzled when they reached their destination. Surrounded by her guards and Anya's, they entered a place she'd already seen: the great hall.

Gone were the tables and benches where the guests had been seated. Servants swept and mopped. Anya led the way to the dais.

Curious, Danu followed.

Magnus's throne sat in a position of prominence. Behind it, a large portrait of her king hung on the wall. The artist had captured him in the moment of victory following a hunt. A great mottled boar lay at his feet, and a fearsome spear glinted from his gloved hand.

Anya circled around the throne, and for the first time, Danu noticed a smaller throne set back from the other. She had not seen it at the feast, perhaps because Magnus's advisors had been lined up in front of it.

Without ado, Anya pulled on a golden cord of braided rope. A curtain parted, and a second portrait was revealed. This one was smaller than Magnus's, and the subject was a female. A human female, judging by her delicate build. In fact, the female looked somewhat like Anya, though there were subtle differences. The figure in the portrait was more slender. Her hair and eyes were both a lighter shade of brown than Anya's. And on her cheek was a purple paw print.

Danu gasped. Her hand went to her cheek, fingers playing over the scar there. "It's her—me."

"Seona," Anya said. "Aye. The artist painted it as Magnus described his dream vision. When I first met him, he thought *I* was the woman in the portrait. Because of this." She turned her head, giving Danu an opportunity to see her scars up close. They looked like claw marks dug in her flesh from cheekbone to jaw. Had she gotten them falling from the high place she had mentioned in the solar? Anya faced the portrait again. Her fingers trailed over the carved frame. "He supposed mayhap the dream erred by showing him a paw print instead of claw marks." She huffed with wry humor. "The moment I saw this, I knew it was Seona. 'Tis her perfect image."

The likeness was remarkable. It looked exactly like the face staring back at Danu from the polished bronze mirror in the Orange Blossom chamber. Sure enough, the woman in the portrait wore the moonstone. But what captured her attention and refused to let it go was the bundle in the woman's arms. A baby, fair of skin and blond of hair. Chubby fingers and pink cheeks looked so real they sparked to life a fierce longing in her womb.

The baby had fair hair. Unlike Anya and Riggs. The child in the portrait could only be Magnus's blood heir.

Her eyes wandered to the portrait of Magnus. His mane of gold surrounded him as regally as any crown. Her human heart pounded fiercely. If Magnus truly had this vision, and if it prophesied the future, he would one day be blessed with a blood heir. And the smaller portrait seemed to imply that Seona would be the mother.

"Will I get her back?" Anya asked.

Danu dragged her gaze from Magnus's portrait to find Anya touching the image of her sister.

"I believe so," she said. "Once Magnus defeats Hyrk, the cell holding Seona will be no more. Only then can we return to our true bodies. Duff will ensure she is brought to where I am the very moment the cell fails."

Anya watched with hopeful eyes. She nodded once with purpose. "Good. Marann needs you where you belong."

Anya was right. But for some reason, hearing the words left her feeling oddly unsettled.

For a while, they studied the portraits in silence. At last, Anya said, "I canna imagine Seona allowing Magnus close enough to bring this image to life. Nor can I imagine Magnus doing aught to force the matter."

"Of course, he would not force the matter," Danu said, perhaps more harshly than necessary.

Anya's eyebrows shot up. Then her eyes danced, and her lips quirked. "Which leaves me to wonder how this *bairn* will come to be." Danu fought the urge to squirm under Anya's assessing gaze.

"How should I know? I didn't give this vision. I was in Hyrk's dungeon." She shouldn't speak so frankly where there were ears to hear and mouths to relate her whereabouts to Hyrk, but something about this little human put her on edge. She did not hold as much control over her emotions as she would like. Still, she looked around them. The guards were alert, but far enough away not to hear their every word. The servants cleaning the great hall worked diligently, paying them no heed.

"Someone gave it," Anya said. "Magnus told the vision to his priest, who confirmed it as more than an ordinary dream."

Could Anya be right? Could some other immortal have blessed a king in *her* realm with a vision? She couldn't imagine any other immortal bothering with a realm they had no stake in. Except, perhaps Hyrk, but it wouldn't be him. He seemed determined to prevent the vision rendered here in flawless brushstrokes.

Duff was benevolent enough for a Fae to offer some hope to her people in her absence, but she doubted he could have pulled off a vision. The Fae were attracted to magic, true, but their innate magic was limited to sifting place and time and using glamour to appear any which way they desired. To her knowledge, the Fae had no power to meddle with the inner workings of mortal minds.

The vision had to be a mistake. "Mortals often mistake the ordinary for the divine," she said, though in her heart, she didn't quite believe that both Magnus and Assaph would make such a mistake.

Anya studied her a moment before gazing up at the painting. "So the portrait is rubbish, then? Pity. It brings Magnus hope. It'll pain him to know 'tis naught but nonsense."

"I did not say it was nonsense," Danu snapped. The idea of Magnus losing hope threatened deep sadness. She knew what it was like to lose hope. "Besides, we have more pressing things to worry about."

"*Och,* I suppose you're right." Anya sounded weary all of a sudden. "You're to rule in Magnus's stead, and I'm to oversee the running of the keep." She spoke of the duties Magnus had left them in his absence.

Danu waved a hand. "Not those things." Perhaps the portrait was rubbish, as Anya so bluntly stated. But if any chance existed for Magnus to know the joy of an heir, one thing was certain: He must defeat Hyrk. And she was determined to help any way she could. She met Anya's questioning eyes. "We must plan how to help our men."

Excitement lit Anya's features. "What do you have in mind?"

Danu tapped her moonstone. "You know this as the Translation Stone, but in reality, it is much more than that."

Anya smiled broadly. "I've been wondering about that." She grabbed Danu's hand. "Come to my chamber. There is only one way in and out, so the guards willna need to be inside with us. We'll be able to speak freely."

"Lead the way."

Chapter 23

"Here, try this one."

Danu plucked a ball of white cheese off a serving platter and popped it in her mouth. Her palate danced with the herbs and fragrant oil drizzled over the mild, creamy bite. "Mmm. That's wonderful."

Anya licked her lips and settled her hands over her belly. She was only just starting to show physical effects of being pregnant. If Danu hadn't already known she carried a child, she would have guessed not from the size of her stomach but from the amount of food she'd just consumed.

On the way to Anya's chamber, they'd stopped in the kitchen, where servants kept a healthy supply of Anya's favorite dishes. They'd each carried a platter up to the north tower and had been stuffing themselves on spiced, cooked meats, roasted vegetation, and succulent cheeses. Watered-down beer was Anya's preference over wine, which she hadn't found palatable since learning of her pregnancy. Danu sipped a fruity red wine that made her lips tingle pleasantly.

They were alone in the chamber Anya shared with Riggs. It was a generously-sized room with a single window too narrow for a person to fit through. A large bed surrounded by curtains made a private, warm retreat for the lifemates. At the moment, however, it served as a den for two conspiring women.

Two bed warmers kept the space within the curtains cozy, and small trays provided a home for their soiled tableware. Anya lounged on pillows, and Danu reclined on a decadent bed fur. The pleasant company almost took the edge off how badly she missed Magnus.

"I canna imagine Seona as a goddess," Anya said. "What do you look like? Help me picture her. I've only seen the statues in the temple, but none of them feel like a real woman to me. I've always been that way—unable to look at a sculpture and see it as in life."

Danu could look any way she wanted, but she chose to describe her truest form, the one she had been created with and always reverted to. "It was no mistake that I made wolfkind to have Fae characteristics. I am slender and comely, as the Fae. My hair is gold, my skin sun-kissed."

"You sound lovely, indeed." Anya's voice was wistful, as if she were imagining her sister in the body Danu had just described. "She'll be back here with me when we defeat Hyrk, you say?"

Danu nodded. "At least, that is the plan. Duff has a role to play, and so will your sister. Although Magnus's role will be the most difficult." Her lover must defeat Hyrk. "If everyone plays their part, this should all be over before long." It might be selfish of her, but she indulged in a fantasy of remaining in this form so she could spend a mortal lifespan loving her king.

"What will become of you, then?" Anya frowned.

Danu's chest warmed at the worry on Anya's face. She'd had the worship of mortals for millennia, but she had precious few friends. "With Hyrk destroyed, his prison will be no more. I'll be restored to my true form and free to rule my people again." She tried to sound happy about this prospect—and she was. But a thread of sadness pulled taut within her, like that string connecting her and Magnus. She sighed and rubbed the spot over her breastbone, where the string felt tightest.

"And the children will be home," Anya said.

Danu latched onto Anya's words as a distraction from the discomfort in her chest. "Those poor dears."

"'Tis one matter to have Riggs away. I dinnae like it, but I ken he's strong and he will return to me. Travis is another matter, altogether." She wrung her hands in her lap. "He's the youngest and smallest of them. And the most loyal to Magnus. I'm worrit for him."

"He is your servant, yes?"

Anya nodded. "But more than that. He was the first to make me feel at home here in Glendall. He's like—" She cupped her womb. "He's like a son to me now, and I willna rest until I have him home again."

"We shall have him back," Danu said. "And the other children, as well as our men." Realizing what she'd just admitted to, she cleared her throat. "You mentioned you have been wondering about this." She lifted her moonstone and watched it wink in the lantern light. "Tell me your thoughts." Anya struck her as a canny woman. Danu hoped they could rub their two minds together and come up with some way to help Magnus and his army, even if they could not be with them.

Anya smiled wryly, seeing through Danu's abrupt change of topic, but she did not comment on it. Sitting forward, she took on a mien of planning and preparation. A whole new energy seemed to fill her at the prospect of solving a problem.

"I've been thinking," Anya said with a tap to her temple, "and I dinnae think the stone is limited to translation. You see, when I first came to this realm, I was helpless and in the wilderness. Those bloody Larnians found me, and their plans for me were barbaric. Riggs rescued me, and I wonder if some magic didn't ensure I would come to be in that very place at that very time for a reason. If I had come to any other location, I wouldna have met Riggs or overheard those boil-assed degenerates discussing Bantus's harem. And that isna the only time I suspect that stone nudged my fate.

"See, I had it with me when I escaped the Larnian commander who took me from Riggs, and when Riggs and I came together the first time. Riggs made me his pledgemate that night, but somat more happened."

"You became lifemates," Danu said, wondering not for the first time how such a union had occurred while she'd been in prison.

Anya nodded. "You were locked up, so you couldna have done it for us. It must have been the stone." Anya looked at it pointedly. "And when that bloody bastard Ari sent me through to Larna to face Bantus, I had the stone in my hand the whole time. I dinnae ken how to stab a man, but somehow I was able to grab a blade and stick it in just right. And Riggs was able to tear a great bolt from the beam he was chained to, allowing him to slay Bantus. My mate is strong, but I doona ken if he could perform such a feat a second time. 'Twas somat more than his own strength," she said with a decisive nod. "Mayhap 'twas Faerie magic, the kind you said Gravois's attracted to. The stone came from him, after all."

Danu listened to all the miracles that had occurred near her moonstone. With each one, her gladness built. She had not been present to aid her people, but her moonstone had brought them aid in her stead.

"Not Faerie magic," she said. "But the power of a goddess." At Anya's surprised look, she said, "This stone is *my* relic. I made it early in my imprisonment and sent it to the mortal realm with Duff to keep it out of Hyrk's hands." She rubbed the stone between her fingers, wishing she could make it work. Even if she wasn't ready to return to her immortal form, she would like to use it to work miracles the likes of which Anya described. "If Hyrk was to keep me imprisoned for all time, I wanted a piece of my power to remain where it might do my people some good. I call it my moonstone."

"Your moonstone," Anya repeated. One corner of her mouth lifted. "So I'm no' mad to suspect magic has been lending us aid all along?"

Danu chuckled. "No. You're not mad. In fact, it seems to me you're quite astute."

Anya's cheeks took on a rosy hue. "Well, you accomplished what you meant to by sending your moonstone away with Gravois. Somehow, he knew where I would be going. He slipped it in my pocket without my knowledge, and look at all the magic it worked for the good of wolfkind. Half the time, I forgot I carried it, but it was there all the time, helping us." Anya sat up straighter. "Now that you have it back, you can wield its power!" she said as if she'd just realized what good luck they'd stumbled across. "You can make it help our men!"

"I wish you were right." Danu let the stone fall to her chest. "It does not recognize me. I fear the only one who can truly wield its power now is Seona."

"Because she's in your body." Anya's eyes darted to and fro in thought. "*Och,* but it worked for me and for Riggs. Even Magnus uses it to speak with the human women. Mayhap 'tis aiding now and we dinnae even ken it."

"Perhaps," Danu said slowly, tapping her chin. "Perhaps my moonstone cannot be *commanded* by mortals. Perhaps its magic simply happens when it is needed, almost as if it is sentient."

"I have learned that magic is not predictable. I think—I think it is sentient. It has motives that we can only guess at." Duff's words from her dream came to mind.

"Sentient? What are you haverin' about?"

"Sentient," Danu repeated. At Anya's questioning look, she said, "Thinks for itself. Duff said he thought my moonstone was sentient." Anya wasn't the only one to experience miracles while holding her moonstone. "He had my moonstone for centuries. It provided him the means to circumvent Arwan's curse. It bonded you and Riggs. It provided rescue for you in Larna. It allowed Magnus to speak with the human women. What if its magic gives the one possessing it whatever they desire most?"

Anya shook her head, chestnut locks dancing on her shoulders. "No. I could speak with Riggs before I even knew the stone was in my pocket. I dinnae desire to speak with him. I simply could—before I even realized we spoke different tongues."

"Then it provides what is needed. The one thing that is needed most." Excitement teased up and down her spine. This line of thought would take them in the right direction. She was certain of it.

"Like kenning the wolfkind tongue for me," Anya puzzled out. "And wi' Riggs, if we hadna been lifemates when Magnus met us on the plain, I fear he would have claimed me then and there. He was so certain I was his promised lady that he wouldna listen to either of us. Only the lifemate scent gave him pause. Even then, he had a pledgemate contract drawn up that very night. He merely included Riggs in the contract."

Heat flashed over Danu's face, there and gone, at the thought of Magnus claiming Anya. But the jealousy did not distract her from the fact Anya was right. Somehow, her magic within the moonstone had known what was needed most. Away from her, her power acted in her interest, in her people's interest, of its own accord.

A frisson of fear felt like ice water in her stomach. It was her power, and yet somehow more than just her power, since it acted independently of her. Still, she had some understanding of its nature now, and its goals seemed in line with her character. Perhaps she and Anya could use the stone if they approached it with this new understanding.

"What is it we need most right now?" The moment Danu voiced the question, she thought of Magnus. She craved the feeling of his arms around her. She wanted to finish what they'd begun in his chamber last night before they'd received news of the children. She needed to know he was safe from danger. But she was being selfish. "Not merely what the two of us need, but what wolfkind needs."

"Victory in Larna," Anya said. "You said it yourself. You and Seona being back where you belong hinges on Magnus besting Hyrk. What we need is victory for our men."

"Yes." She nodded. Anya was right. She closed her hand around the stone and pictured Magnus and his army finding the children swiftly, besting Hyrk, and returning home as victors. She could not help imagining herself being here to greet her king. She would hold him and kiss him and take him to bed so they could finish what they had started last night. Of course, the last part was what she needed, not wolfkind. But still, she could not help herself.

"Who goes there?" A booming voice sounded directly outside the bed curtains. One of their guards must have come into the chamber without them hearing.

Anya went stiff at Danu's side. Her eyes rounded.

"Maedoc?" Danu said. "Is that you? Is all well?"

A large hand whipped open the curtain at the foot of the bed. The hand did not belong to Maedoc. It belonged to Riggs.

Shock filled his dark eyes. Then rage. "What in the name of the moon have you done?" he shouted at Anya. "What is our bed doing in the middle of the Larnian mountains?"

Fat flakes of snow blew around Riggs's head. Beyond his massive form was the animal-hide flap of a tent. The flap opened, and Magnus appeared silhouetted against the lamp-lit interior. At once, his face filled with shock and something that looked suspiciously like relief.

Both men crowded before the parted curtain, looking wild, shocked, and, at least in Magnus's case, extremely appealing.

Magnus's mouth opened and closed, but he seemed unable to form words.

"Explain," Riggs said, fierce eyes pinning Anya.

"Dinnae fash at me," Anya said. "'Twas her doing." She pointed at Danu.

Chapter 24

TRAVIS HAULED A bucket of water from the spring to the section of caves where Vera, Nenna, and Braeden lived. For five days, he'd been resting and healing. He was more than ready to finally contribute. Sitting still had never been one of his strengths.

"Are you feeling all right?" Nenna asked. Ahead of him, she hauled two bucketfuls. A yoke braced them across shoulders he would have thought too slender for such a load. The passageway was so dark he could barely make out her form. But he heard her just fine. He would venture into the darkest of places if it meant hearing her sweet voice.

"Fine," he said, cheerfully. "Feels nice to do work. I could have carried two, you know." He wanted Nenna to find him strong and capable.

"Perhaps." Her voice sounded playful, as always. "But we have six more trips to make. I didn't want to tire you out on the first one."

He laughed with her, liking the tinkling sound of her happiness.

Back in the manor, as Nenna and Braeden called their rooms, he and Nenna poured their buckets into a barrel before setting out for more. At first, the darkness within the caves had felt claustrophobic, but he was beginning to grow used to it. His feet were learning the dips and rises of the well-worn paths between caverns.

The caves were located within a large mountain in northern Larna, he'd learned. The fortress Alexander and the other children had claimed was a quarter-day's walk, though Braeden bragged he could run it as a wolf in a single hour. There were twenty-five or so of the Remnant living in the caves, but they kept to themselves in small packs, like the one Nenna, Braeden, and Vera made.

Travis had tried many times to learn how old Nenna was, but she always playfully redirected the conversation. Even though they seemed to think he was one of them now, they still kept many secrets. He intended to learn as much as he could before making a run for Marann.

"Bread, here! Get your fresh, wholesome bread!" Braeden's voice echoed through the tunnel. He sounded very far away.

"Oh, yum!" Nenna said. "Let's hurry. We'll finish this trip then have lunch before we finish collecting the water."

Once they'd emptied their second load of water into the barrel, they sat around the pit. Braeden tore off large chunks of warm bread and handed one to each of them. Travis thanked him and tore into it, hungry from the work he and Nenna had done.

"Is Vera hunting?" he asked.

"Patrolling," Braeden said.

Travis had learned Vera was the provider and protector of their little pack. Braeden did some patrolling, but Vera didn't like for him to leave the caves by daylight. He was too reckless and might be seen, she claimed. Nenna was forbidden to leave the caves, not that she allowed that to stop her. She'd found Travis, after all, which explained why Vera had acted so crossly with them for a few days.

"Why don't you talk to the other packs?" Travis asked as he devoured his bread.

"We do, sometimes," Braeden said. "But most of them aren't very social." His eyes darted away.

Travis had a feeling he wasn't sharing everything. Of course, this only heightened his curiosity. "Are your caves connected to theirs? How many are female?"

"Braeden." Vera's voice punched through the cavern. She had a knack for appearing when Travis started asking questions. "It's almost nightfall. Finish up then do your rounds at the fortress."

"Yes!" Braeden got to his feet and shoved the last chunk of bread into his mouth. While he chewed, he dashed from the cavern, already stripping off his clothes.

"Wait for dark!" Vera shouted after him. There was no response. Shaking her head, she came to the pit and took some bread. "You got the water?" she asked Nenna.

"We're in the middle of it." Nenna dipped a tin cup into the barrel and sipped from their fresh, cold haul. "Travis is helping."

Vera eyed him.

He straightened his shoulders and attempted to appear very useful.

"See that you finish soon. It's almost dark."

On their way to the spring for their third trip, Travis asked Nenna, "Why do we have to finish before nightfall?"

"Today's our day to use the spring. Each of the packs has a set day to collect water. If we come on a day that's not ours, we get in trouble."

"What if you run out before your day?"

"Then we have to go to the river and risk being seen."

Travis frowned. "By Larnians?"

"Outsiders, yes."

Up ahead, the dim light of the spring cavern highlighted the arched shape of the entry. Far above the cold-water spring was a great crevasse allowing in light from the outside world. Now and again, a sprinkling of snow would float down to the water. Travis wondered if the crevasse was accessible from the mountainside. With a shiver, he wondered if a person might fall in as easily as the snow seemed to.

"I don't think there are many Larnians left," he said, trying not to imagine skeletons at the bottom of the spring. He and Nenna stepped up to the rocky lip and filled their buckets. The water was slightly cloudy and greenish-blue in color. Their buckets stirred up sediment, but even when the water was still, he could not see to the bottom.

"You're right," Nenna said. "There aren't many. But as long as there are outsiders, we bide our time here in the caves." The Remnant seemed to hate the Larnians for discarding them, Vera most of all. While he didn't blame them, he couldn't understand wanting absolutely no contact with the outside world.

"When they're all gone, you'll come out? What'll happen then? Where will your people go?"

"Wherever we want. All our years of waiting will be worthwhile, because we'll have the whole of Eire all to ourselves."

She was wrong. She seemed to think of all "outsiders" as the same, but they weren't. The Larnians were dying out, having no women left to carry on their lines. But in Marann, there was still hope. Anya was with child. If she had a girl, Marann would go on. Sure, they would dwindle to a low number—Travis hated to think about that—but they would go on as a people. In a few centuries, they would have Chroina populated again. King Magnus and his mother before him had built up an enormous library of volumes ensuring all trades could be relearned and no knowledge would be lost. Even Riggs had a volume in the library on tanning. He had written it with his father, and all the children had read it since Riggs had become a hero so recently.

He didn't inform Nenna that she was wrong. Not only did he not want to disappoint her, but Marann's hope felt private to him in a way he couldn't quite place. Nenna, Vera, and Braeden were kind enough, but their secrecy inspired him to keep secrets himself. He did not know their true motivations and didn't wish to reveal too much about his people.

Instead of correcting Nenna, he said, "It won't be worthwhile to you. Or Braeden or Vera. You'll be old when the rest of us are gone."

"No, we won't," Nenna said. She hefted her yoke onto her shoulders. "No more questions," she said with a grin and a wink. "We've got to hurry or Vera will have a fit."

What did she mean by *No, we won't*? Did she plan to outlive him by many years? And why must she be so maddening? She answered questions up to the point where his curiosity piqued, and then she closed herself off.

"Fine," Travis said. "I won't ask you anything. But I have a lot to say." Even though he was starting to breathe heavy from the exertion of lugging the water, he kept talking. He wanted Nenna and the Remnant to understand at least one thing about them. "All outsiders are not the same. You know, my people, Maranners—we're not like the Larnians. There's a reason we're two kingdoms. Our ruler, King Magnus, he's good, not like King Bantus."

"Maybe that's so," Nenna said, the darkness swallowing her form. "But even good men fear what they don't understand. You know what we are." She meant they were rejects from breeding experiments. "If anyone finds out about us, they'll be afraid. When people are afraid, they are dangerous."

"I'm not afraid of you. Why should the other Maranners be? I'm telling you, King Magnus wouldn't harm any of you. He would welcome you. You could leave the caves right now and travel to Marann, and you would be protected."

Nenna stopped walking. "You're wrong. You were afraid at first, when you saw what we can do, how we can change. Besides—" Her tone turned uncharacteristically dark. "I'm no fool. And neither is Vera." She set down her buckets and half turned to him. "We've seen what outsiders have done to some of the wild wolves. Even to some of us when we've been caught unawares." Her voice became quiet and distant, as if she were remembering scenes from long ago. "They do such horrible things because there are no women left." Silence throbbed around them. So the Remnant knew. They understood why wolfkind was dying out. "You think your king would protect us, and maybe you're right. Maybe he would, but only because he would want us to breed for your precious Maranners. I'm no one's breeder." She spat the final word and yanked up her yoke so hard Travis heard some of the water slosh from her buckets.

He stood stunned at her sudden vehemence while she marched away down the tunnel.

"No. More. Questions," she said.

He followed, but a strange heat unsettled his stomach. He'd made Nenna angry, and he didn't like that. But he'd learned something valuable. The Remnant didn't remain hidden purely because they hated the Larnians for discarding them. They feared what would happen to them if they emerged.

While he and Nenna finished collecting water, he thought about what she'd said. Would Magnus force them to breed? Would he insist their females become part of the breeding lottery? Travis hated to think so, but when the survival of wolfkind was at stake, their king just might resort to force. Maybe it wasn't so strange that the Remnant hid themselves away. Maybe it was wise of them.

But what would happen when they learned that Marann still had hope, that they weren't as far gone as the Larnians? Would they be content to remain hidden then? Or would they grow impatient and decide to act? Could the Remnant be a threat to Marann? Nenna had told him that within this mountain, there lived twenty-five of the Remnant. What if there were more living in other mountains?

Travis's thoughts came to an abrupt halt as one of Braeden's visions opened up in his mind. The sensation was strange, but Travis was growing accustomed to it. With Nenna's instruction, he had learned to see the vision in one part of his mind and still be aware of his surroundings. With his physical eyes, he saw the warm glow of the manor as they entered with the haul of water. With his mind's eye, he saw that Braeden had reached the fortress. Like the previous nights, he perched on a stone landing looking down on the great hall.

For a band of fewer than thirty children, his cohort had worked wonders. The hall glowed with light. Both fires burned high, and torches lit the walls. Tapestries hung in the open windows high above the hall. A great boar roasted over one of the fires.

Cots were lined up near the fires, but there seemed no more need to have a section cordoned off. Firewood was stacked all along the edges of the hall, and there appeared to be a supply to last several days. Travis knew that more would be added each day as the older boys cut down trees.

Looking through Braeden's wolf-eyes, Travis counted twenty-five children. That meant only two were missing from the great hall, not including him, of course. Perhaps they were out gathering supplies or snow to melt for water. He put them out of his mind.

The boys feasted around two long tables that had been mended. There was laughter and light conversation. The mood was far brighter than in those first days before Travis had been exiled. It saddened him to see the children so content away from their parents, their instructors, their city, and their king. Had they no loyalty?

He was reminded of the reason for their mutiny when Alexander stepped up on the dais they'd erected at the front of the hall. They had even repaired a huge throne that had likely served the governor of this fortress at one time. Alexander was wise not to sit on it, since the ornate chair would only exaggerate his adolescent form.

"Men! Well done today!" Conversation stopped. "Give yourselves a round of applause. Each and every one of you has worked his fingers to the bone to make this place comfortable." He clapped his hands, and the other children followed suit, jostling each other good-naturedly. His chest ached to see their smiles, but he could well understand the satisfaction of a job well done. It should be Mr. Daly praising them for their work, though. Not Alexander.

"Every day, we're making progress!" Alexander spoke into the fading applause. "We have stored meat, plenty of wood and water, and a clean, warm home. Most importantly, we have three chambers furnished for our female companions. I do believe, gentlemen, that it is time to invite the women to join us."

The older boys hooted and cheered. Travis felt sick to his stomach. The sounds they were making and the lecherous looks on their faces meant they were hoping to act as full-grown men. They were talking about finding Vera and Nenna as if they were no more than bodies to be had, to be bred.

"Linas," Alexander called out.

The lanky nineteen-year-old stood from a table. "Here, Xander."

"Is the lottery ready?"

"It is," Linas said.

"Then we're ready."

"Ready for what?" one of the older boys called out. "How will you find the women, Xander?"

"And what will we do with them once we find them?" Another called out. "What if they don't want anything to do with us?"

"Listen here," Alexander barked out. "None of us in this room is under any delusion. These are desperate times. Magnus has allowed our people to come to this. Never forget that *all* of this is his fault. If we are to go on, if we are to be strong—not weakened by human blood—it is up to us."

The hall seemed to breathe with a palpable silence. Every round face below demonstrated understanding of the gravity of their situation.

Alexander paced the dais like an experienced orator. Never had he so reminded Travis of their father. "When we first meet the women, we will present gifts. The handmade things each of you have been working on in your spare time, the jewelry and clothing we've scavenged. We will provide them with food. We will show them how strong and capable we are. But I'm afraid we cannot allow them the luxury of choice. They must remain with us, and they must submit to our lottery."

He met eyes all around the tables, as if challenging anyone to argue. No one did, though several of the children looked down at their laps.

"In Marann, men purchase lottery tickets. A single ticket is drawn for each fertile lady, and the pair takes the entire season to try and breed." His face twisted with disgust. "This practice is archaic and is the reason there are so few of us here in this hall."

He spread his arms wide. "Here, in New Larna, the lottery will work differently. On the day of each full moon, games will be held. Swordsmanship, archery, chopping, climbing, hand-to-hand combat, you name it. We'll choose a different game each moon and spend the month training for that skill. Every man eighteen years of age or older will play, but all may train. This will ensure we keep in shape, you see.

"The winner of the game will draw the first ticket, the runner-up the next ticket, third-place the next, and so on. On the ticket will be the name of a woman in our custody. There may only be one at first, but we'll find more. We'll continue to make repairs and furnish our keep until we have room for as many females as we can find.

"There are twelve of us eighteen or older. That means twelve tickets will be drawn. If there is only one woman in the lottery, the tickets will simply reveal the order in which she is to be bedded by all twelve men within the season. If there are more women, their names will be distributed evenly over the tickets."

Travis was pulled from the vision by the sound of Nenna's voice. "That pompous little snake! Can you believe what he's saying?"

She was talking to Vera, who returned Nenna's fierce look. Vera shook her head, not in denial but seemingly in resignation. Resignation to what, though?

The vision drew his attention once more.

"Linas is lottery head," Alexander said. "He's documenting all this." Travis noted Linas bent over a sheet of paper, scrawling hastily. "When he is finished, I will stamp it into law. New Larna will be a kingdom of lawfulness. We will organize ourselves as time goes on, but I will be your governor. Anyone have a problem with that?"

He scanned the hall with sharp eyes. No one said anything.

Alexander clasped his hands behind his back. A smile lit his face. "Congratulations, gentlemen. We are now a new kingdom. A better kingdom. One with hope for survival!" Lifting his fists in the air, he shouted, "Welcome to New Larna!"

The other children applauded. The older boys hooted and hollered.

"How will we find the women?" one boy shouted as the cheers died down.

"We will not have to find them," Alexander said, a smug grin on his face. "They will come to us." His eyes darted up to where Braeden perched.

Travis's heart stopped in his chest as he—or rather Braeden—made eye contact with Alexander. Braeden's vision shifted as he made a run for the crumbling stone steps, but it was too late. A net fell around him. Rock-weights made it impossible to scrabble out from underneath.

The two missing boys appeared from behind the crumbling side of the fortress. One held a sword at the ready while the other poked a pole collar through the net. The loop from the pole collar spread around the vision as it went over Braeden's head, and the vision faded away.

"No! Braeden!" Nenna cried. "Vera, we have to get him!" She threw off her tunic and leggings. Bending forward, she changed into her other form—a majestic white wolf.

"Nenna," Vera said sharply. "Do not be impatient. You and I coming to his rescue is precisely what they want. I have a better idea." She put on her cloak and took from the chest not the bow and quiver she used for hunting, but a fierce-looking crossbow. "Stay here, both of you. I'll handle this."

Nenna jumped in front of Vera, blocking her way into the tunnels.

"I'm *not* going alone," Vera said, as if Nenna had made a vocal protest. "Yes, *them*. And when we reach the fortress, those foolish infants will wish they'd stayed in their precious Marann." Vera shoved past Nenna and strode into the tunnel. As the darkness swallowed her, she called back, "Don't let him out of your sight."

Nenna wheeled on Travis, blue eyes blazing and teeth bared. He decided against an escape attempt, not wishing to have his throat torn out.

Chapter 25

"Sire, is everything—what in the name of moon?" Cadeyrn's voice spurred Magnus into action.

He could not stand out here in the cold gaping at his beloved and her mischievous companion when at any moment, more of his men might witness this—this—he wasn't sure what this was, only that something magical had occurred. Whether debacle or miracle remained to be seen. All he knew for certain was that Anya and Danu were hundreds of leagues from safety.

"Get my other knights," Magnus commanded Cadeyrn. "Guard this area from view. You two." He fixed Anya and Danu in his sights. "In my tent. Please," he added, remembering one half of this pair was a goddess.

Anya scrambled off the bed and Riggs lifted the tent flap for her.

Danu followed, stepping gracefully onto the packed snow. When she looked up at him, she wore a radiant smile. Her eyes danced with delight. All at once, his chest filled with joy and ire.

How could the women look so unperturbed when he'd spent the last several days and nights worried sick about them? A runner had caught up to their party three days prior and informed him that Ladies Anya and Seona had disappeared without a trace from Anya and Riggs's tower chamber. Their disappearance had occurred only a few hours after he'd led his army out of the city. All of Chroina had been searching for them. Despite daily runners bringing news from the city, he had received no hint of their whereabouts.

A bubbling laugh parted Danu's lips as she went up on her toes to kiss his cheek. "I can hardly believe it," she said. "It worked!" Clapping her hands, she ducked under Riggs's arm into the tent. He was left outside in the bitter cold, wondering what she was talking about.

The great bed, which had been a fixture at Glendall from his grandparents' time, had appeared out of nowhere between his royal tent and the rocky rise sheltering their camp from the worst of the mountain weather. Thank the moon his portable dwelling shielded the bed from the view of the camp. He did not wish to explain a magical event to his men without first understanding it.

Cadeyrn came around the tent with spare sheets of canvas. More of Magnus's knights followed. They set to work constructing a second tent behind the royal tent. Content to let his knights conceal the bed, he went inside to question the women.

Riggs, Anya, and Danu stood around the bowl-lamp set on the floor. The fire made their shadows reach across the canvas in every direction. Bed furs large enough for a single man stretched the length of one side, and a collapsible table covered with maps took over the other. His clothing and armor were kept in a chest that currently served as a tray for a half-drunk cup of strong black tea.

He rounded the lamp and dragged Danu into his arms. He would question her for certain, but at the moment, he absolutely required her lips beneath his. Wasting no time, he descended on her. Mouth touched mouth, breath met breath. She tasted of cooked meats, herb-encrusted cheese, and rich wine as if she had just dined at Glendall only moments ago. He delved inside, taking the intense flavors into himself, spearing her with a part of him the only way he could at present.

She welcomed his invasion with a moan. Her tongue caressed his, and she clung to him. Had their near week of separation worn her down as much as it had him? Never before had he felt sick for home while away for battle. But this time, every step his steed took away from Chroina had increased his agitation until he could barely think for lack of his goddess in his arms.

Holding her tightly to him, he kissed her and kissed her some more until he was panting with a need that could not be indulged while questions must be answered. From the sighs and rustling of fabrics rubbing together, he gathered Riggs was greeting Anya much the same way, but he didn't spare them a glance.

Trailing kisses along Danu's jaw, he said, "I have been so worried. Where have you been? I'd feared—" He cut himself off, not wanting to voice his deepest fear, that she had somehow been forced back to Hyrk's dungeon and he would never see her again. Overwhelmed with relief, he scooped her to him as tightly as possible and cupped her head beneath his chin.

"I'm all right, love," she said soothingly as she clung to him.

He set her away only far enough that he could take her delicate face in his hands and peer into her eyes. She appeared well rested and well fed.

"Tell me all that has happened since I left Chroina," he said, eager to know if she had been hurt or captive or under any kind of distress. "Omit nothing."

She lifted his hand and kissed his palm. "Anya and I talked," she said. "She showed me a very interesting portrait." A dimple appeared in her check beside her smile. Leave it to Anya to do what he had feared to do himself. He shook his head ruefully as she continued. "We had supper in her chamber, and we conspired over my moonstone. You can see the results of that for yourself." She spread her arms and again appeared delighted.

He waited for her to fill in the events of the days between, but she only frowned.

She stepped into his arms and peered up at him. "My darling king, I can understand your relief at being together unexpectedly, but why such concern? And why are you making camp tonight? I thought you would stop only briefly to rest the horses in your haste to reach Larna."

"'Tis been nearly a week?" screeched Anya, drawing both their gazes across the tent.

Between Danu's question and Anya's surprise, he made the connection. To the women, inexplicably, not much time had passed. That would explain why they smelled of Glendall's warmth and wine.

He watched Riggs place a protective hand over Anya's abdomen. "Calm yourself," he cooed to her. "This excitement can't be good for our little one."

Trusting his knight to see to Anya, he said to Danu, "I led my army out of the city five days ago. This is our third time making camp. We're at the foot of the mountains Duff described. Tomorrow, we'll be hiking to the caves and using them to cut through Mammoth to the fortress. Where have you been all this time? I received word days ago that you and Anya disappeared from the north tower." He couldn't stop smoothing his hands over her head and face, reassuring himself of her wellbeing.

Her lovely eyes widened as she gained understanding. "No wonder you appeared so worried. To my mind, you left Chroina only hours ago. I watched you go from your solar. Then Anya and I took a walk through Glendall and had supper up in her chamber. We puzzled out that my moonstone may just have a mind of its own, and suddenly we were here, bed and all." She huffed a chuckle that was equal parts nervous and pleased.

He closed his eyes at the sensation of her small hands smoothing over his cheeks and brow. Neither of them seemed to possess the ability to stop touching the other.

"Mind of its own, hmm?" He slid his fingers beneath her moonstone, loving the feel of her warm skin, and lifted it for his scrutiny. "Looks like it can do more than translate for the one wearing it." In its amethyst depths, he saw nothing he hadn't seen before. Returning it to its resting place, he added, "Unless the one wearing it is a goddess, perhaps."

A look of guilt passed over Danu's features.

"What is it, my beauty?"

"I never had a chance to tell you," she began, brows sloping as she tapped the necklace. "This gemstone, it belongs to me."

"Of course it does. I gave it to you." He'd recognized the gemstone the moment he'd seen it in Anya's hand on that grassy plain. It felt like years ago he'd met the human woman and her lifemate. But it had been only two moons. Even though he had yet to learn of Seona's existence, he had instantly known the stone belonged to the woman from his vision.

Danu shook her head, shiny, walnut waves tickling her shoulders. "No. I mean, yes, you did. But even before that, it was mine." She lifted the stone, cradling it in her palm. "I made it in my prison and placed within it the portion of my power that sustains wolfkind. If Hyrk succeeded in sealing me within the cell, I did not want my power to be cut off from my people for all time."

Magnus's eyes widened. He cupped both his hands around hers, making a secure cave for the object. The gemstone was much more valuable than he'd realized. Its magic was not arbitrary. It came from Danu herself.

"You made this?" From their hands, the stone winked at him.

She nodded. "It pained me to separate myself from my people, but I could not risk the consequences if Hyrk bested me." She sighed heavily. "I gave it to Duff to look after in the mortal realm. He is an expert at hiding, so I knew he would keep it safe from Hyrk. I've since learned that Duff gave it to Anya shortly before she came to this realm. I think it has worked subtle magic to help wolfkind or perhaps to find its way back to me."

She opened her hand, and Magnus loosened his hold on the stone. They both gazed at it.

"For being its creator, I understand precious little about it," she said, frowning. "I had heard of relics, but had never made one before. I know this, though. Only this stone can return me to my true form."

Panic made his spine straight as a rod.

"Do not worry," she said with a sad smile. "I am not able to command its power in this mortal body, and even if I could, it is not in wolfkind's best interest for me to leave you just yet." Her gaze went distant, and fear lodged in his heart. They both knew she would have to leave at some point. Wolfkind needed her to rule over them, as she had done in ages past. But he could not stomach the thought of her leaving. Not yet.

He caught the reflection of his furrowed brow in the stone's gleaming surface. "If you cannot command it, then how is it you and Anya are here? It altered time and place. Are you saying it did so of its own accord?"

"Partly, yes." Excitement lit her eyes. She squeezed his hands as she went on. "Anya and I agree it has likely accomplished far more than translation. It was with her and Riggs when they defeated King Bantus in Larna, and Anya claims that was not the only time Riggs showed remarkable strength in defending her."

Magnus realized the truth of it. The stone—Danu's moonstone—had been present through all of Anya and Riggs's adventures.

"It seemed there were several miracles that brought the two of them safe to Glendall," Danu said. "It has also helped the wearer communicate when necessary. We wondered if perhaps its magic provides what is needed most at a given time." She smiled brightly. "We began considering what you and your army needed most. We wondered if we might somehow direct the moonstone to help you." His heart warmed at the thought of his goddess wishing to aid him. "We agreed what you needed most was to have victory in Larna. Then, all of a sudden, we were here." Her laughter brought joy to his heart. And her explanation of what she and Anya had been up to pleased him more than he could say.

Scooping her to his chest, he said, "You were correct. Our people need my victory in the coming battle. But do you know what I need most of all?"

She peered into his eyes, her irises darkened with what he knew to be lust. He knew it because he felt it too. The air around them was charged with it, and he could not resist its pull much longer.

"What?" she asked breathlessly.

"You. In my bedfurs." He lowered his lips to hers, and their mouths melded together as if they'd been made for this kiss, this moment.

"Sire." Riggs cleared his throat, and Magnus contemplated murder. Would they never enjoy an intimate moment without interruption?

He glared at his second.

Riggs held Anya close against him, his body a protective shield of flesh and bone around her. Anya's cheeks were flushed, and her lips looked like they'd been properly ravaged. She met his eyes with a bemused smile.

"What are we to do?" Riggs said. "Do we inform the men? Send a party back to Chroina with the women?" As he voiced the question, his hold on Anya visibly tightened. Magnus understood how he felt. Having Danu in his arms again felt like breathing after days of longing for air. He could not bear to let her go after being without her so long.

"I do not wish to leave you," Danu said, echoing his thoughts.

"The gemstone brought us here," Anya said. "If you bring us back, it'll only send us again."

Riggs looked on Anya with affection but also deep concern. "For what purpose? We may be going to battle against a demigod.

This is no place for women." He turned pleading eyes to Magnus. "They should go back, Sire."

Magnus quirked a brow. "Are you attempting to command your king, knight?"

Riggs paled. "No, Sire. Of course not."

"He's only worrit for me," Anya told Magnus. "Dinnae fash, love. I'll be fine," she said to Riggs. She patted his cheek, standing on her toes to do so. "I'm here with a goddess, and around her neck is the gemstone that brought you and I together and kept us safe through all manner of trials. All will be well. The magic has a purpose in it, even if we canna see it."

"A goddess?" Riggs said. He frowned at Magnus, giving the impression he feared his lifemate had gone mad.

"Yes," Magnus confirmed. "A goddess." He kissed Danu's forehead and met his second's confused gaze. "It happened when Seona fell. Somehow, they traded bodies, and now Seona is in Hyrk's dungeon while Danu is here. With us."

Riggs's mouth hung open. Anya nudged it shut with a finger.

"You knew?" Riggs asked.

"Only just," Anya said. "Magnus told me at the feast."

Riggs stared at Danu a moment, then he strode to her and dropped to his knees. "My goddess."

Magnus's chest filled with pride. He had done well to make this man his second. He put a hand on Riggs's shoulder. "Outside this tent, you must treat her like you would Seona."

"I am completely without my power," Danu said. She held out a hand to Riggs, who stared wide-eyed at it before taking it like her skin was made from fine crystal. Danu urged him to rise. "I cannot afford for Hyrk to learn of this."

"Not completely without power," Anya said. "Look where we are."

"Perhaps, not completely," Danu admitted. "But I still do not understand exactly what power I have, and I would not want Seona's body endangered."

"I will keep your secret, Goddess," Riggs said reverently. Still holding her hand, he lifted it and kissed it. The gesture was so obviously one of worship that Magnus felt no jealousy. Only pride in his knight.

"I agree with Anya," Magnus said. "The women shall remain here. If magic brought them, I trust there is a purpose in it. Riggs, gather the other knights and tell them the women have been found. Let them know magic brought them here, but keep Danu's identity a secret. We march in the morning, as planned, but a century of men will remain with the women here at camp. Once we have cleared a safe passage through the caves, the century will move the women there. They'll be safe in the caves while we continue on to the fortress. We'll collect them when we return as victors, with our children in tow."

"Yes, Sire." Riggs made to leave, but Magnus stopped him with a hand on his shoulder.

"You and Anya shall sleep in your own bed tonight. You'll have privacy away from the others there."

A lopsided smile lit Riggs's features. "My thanks, Sire."

"And we," he said to Danu as Riggs departed, "Shall have privacy as well." This time, he would ensure they were not interrupted. Perhaps the moonstone would help, because there was absolutely nothing he needed more than to finally bed his goddess. "Long awaited privacy."

Chapter 26

DANU CRAVED MAGNUS with a ferocity she had never known for any other lover. His promised privacy could not come too soon. Unfortunately, they must wait, for Anya was still with them while Riggs ran his errands.

The lamp on the floor gave light, but it did precious little to dispel the cold. She and Anya had left their cloaks behind in Glendall, so it was with gratitude she accepted the heavy fur Magnus draped over her shoulders as he led her to the maps. He placed a fur around Anya as well and graced her with a kiss on the cheek. "I am glad you are well," he said before returning to Danu's side.

Arm snug around her waist, he bent over the maps and pointed out their location. The map showed a range of mountains covering the northern third of Larna. Their camp was in the foothills of a mountain called Mammoth, named, Magnus informed her, for the way its rounded back called to mind the four-footed, tusked beasts that roamed the northern lands across the Eastern Sea. On the other side of the mountain the map showed the fortress, where they suspected the children had gone based on Duff's information.

How strange it was, looking at her creation from this perspective. She'd woven this landscape together eons ago and filled it with creatures great and small before introducing her precious wolfkind to the realm. She'd walked these mountains as their maker and caretaker, appreciating their wild beauty and bothered by not an ounce of fear. Looking at maps, however, made her feel small.

No longer could she view her entire realm as though from above. Her human eyes and mind could examine only one aspect of her creation at a time. With the map, she could view a large area, but only in sketched lines that hardly did justice to the grandeur they were perched amidst. Furthermore, she could not affect any of it. She could not warm the weather to speed their journey or push up obstacles to hinder the enemy. A sense of powerlessness left her chilled, and she pressed against Magnus's warm side.

Her king was mortal as well, but there was nothing weak about him. Like her now, he could not view his kingdom from above. He could address only one problem at a time. But he did not grow overwhelmed. He simply did his best. How she admired him! How his quiet competence strengthened her spirit!

Her king slid a second map from underneath the first. This one showed the interior of the mountain, which was riddled with a complex system of connecting caves, like the tunnels formed by her hard-working ants.

"Years ago, the caves were mapped out," he explained. "The Larnians fear them. They claim the surviving rejects from Jilken's breeding experiments live there and that they are fierce and territorial. But our spies searched the caves thoroughly and found them completely abandoned. Thanks to these passages, we were able to push into Saroc from the north as well as from the east. If not for these maps, our victory might not have been so easily secured."

Danu recalled Hyrk's fury when Magnus's army had defeated Bantus's two decades ago. He'd stormed into the dungeon shouting about Magnus stealing Larna's women and ruining everything. His anger had not lasted long, however, before he began crowing about a new plan, the one that had recently been foiled by Magnus,

Anya, and Riggs. That was one thing Magnus must understand about Hyrk. He never gave up.

She followed his finger as it traced a route through the mountain from one side to the other. "That is the way you will go tomorrow?" she asked.

"Yes. And here is where you and Anya will remain." He touched a place near the center of the mountain. It was a small cavern not far from a larger one marked, *Spring of all Seasons.* "The spring will serve as our temporary base. Medics will be ready to receive any wounded, though I'm hoping for a quick and painless recovery of the children."

Danu doubted any plan where Hyrk was concerned would come off quickly and without pain. She darted a look to Anya and found her brow furrowed. Her friend feared the same.

"So," Anya said. "You suppose the children will come willingly when you march up to the fortress?" Doubt laced her voice.

"Of course," Magnus said. "They are Maranners. They do not belong in Larna."

Danu petted his beard, feeling all at once tender toward him and quite annoyed at his optimism. "Have you forgotten, my king, that they came here of their own free will?"

His lips pulled into a frown. "We do not know that."

She smiled gently to soften the fact she was questioning him. "We would do well to assume it. There were no signs of a struggle at the schoolyard, were there?"

"No. There were not," he admitted, his brow creased in thought.

"Hyrk is a master at deception. He will have poisoned them against you." She desperately needed him to understand about Hyrk. They could not underestimate him. "Unless you want a fight on your hands, you must consider how you shall win back their loyalty."

"No one will raise a sword to any child," he vowed. "My men will not fight."

"Then you will lose some of your men," she stated. Magnus frowned, but she pressed on. "You must prepare for the children to resist. They have been here a week now, having the means to return home but choosing not to do so."

His eyes darted over the map, not seeing it, she ascertained, but rather turning over her words in thought. Lines bracketed his eyes and his mouth, making him appear weary. When had he last slept?

At last, he said, "How can I plan what to say to them when I do not know the lies Hyrk may have told them?"

"That I do not know. Let us rest for tonight. Perhaps the answers will come to you while you sleep."

Magnus raised a doubtful eyebrow.

"*Och,* I would listen to her if I were you," Anya said. "You need rest if you're to lead your men out tomorrow."

Magnus scowled at the map. "I'll rest when the children have been found."

"Stubborn man," Anya muttered.

Riggs came into the tent. "Everything has been seen to," he told Magnus as he tucked Anya against his side. "Unless you need anything else, I would very much like to retire with my lifemate."

Magnus nodded absently, eyes roving over the map with the sharp focus of a falcon. "Go on. Rest well."

Finally, they were alone. But Magnus seemed to have forgotten his earlier promise. His furrowed brow and darting eyes meant his mind was busy. He did not appear remotely interested in the privacy they found themselves in possession of. She did not blame him. Her king had much on his mind.

Still, Anya was right. Magnus needed rest, and Danu knew just how to lure him away from his maps.

Going to the furs, she began removing her clothing. Once she was nude, she said, "I am cold, Magnus. Come make me warm."

His body did not shift, but his head turned, as if to glance her way between bouts of stringent concentration. When he caught sight of her, everything about him stilled.

His shoulders straightened. His eyes took on the dark hunger of a predator. Then he was stalking toward her, maps forgotten.

Inwardly, she smiled.

"What happened to the fur I gave you?" His voice slid over her skin like warm velvet.

It lay on the bed with the others, and she knelt on it, legs slightly spread. "I seem to have lost it."

His gaze fell to her sex, then caressed up her stomach to her breasts. His pupils expanded. "You are chilled."

Her stomach tightened pleasantly when he licked his lips, as if he planned to warm her stiff nipples with his mouth.

She cupped her breasts. They were larger and heavier than the ones she was used to. The nipples were a shade lighter, a rosy peach that reminded her of cloudberries just shy of ripening. "Will you share your warmth with me?"

Suddenly, he was on the furs with her. His hands gripped her hips, and his mouth was on her right breast. Before he'd latched onto her with the heat of a forge, he'd gasped, "Always."

Her arms encircled his head, fingers combing through locks the color of rain-drenched wheat. His hair was slick against his head with natural oils and the weight of the helm he wore while riding. Beneath her fingertips, his scalp was warm and reassuring. He rumbled appreciatively at her petting, the vibration tickling her nipple.

Then he pulled on her, taking her flesh deeper into his hot mouth.

She gasped. Carnal heat lanced through her. She couldn't decide whether these sensations were completely novel or if it had been so long she'd simply forgotten what it was like to be in such harmony with a lover. One thing she knew for certain was that she *needed* her king this night.

Releasing his head, her hands traversed his neck and chest, snagging and loosening shirt laces on their journey to his belt. Slowly, she unclothed him, a challenge considering the nearly-debilitating pleasure he bestowed.

So focused was her king on laving one breast and then the other that she had to fist her hand in his hair and tug him away to lift his tunic over his head. The moment the fabric cleared his head he was back, lunging like a ravenous newborn desperate for milk.

"So smooth," he muttered, the words garbled because of his mouthful. "Hairless. Cool. *Mmmm.*" He treated her like a delicacy. And to him, this human body would be. It made her proud to be utterly unique compared to other lovers he'd taken.

"So sweet," he whispered, and he inched down her body. His hands parted her legs, making his destination clear. She spread for him, anticipating a repeat of the sensations from the night before. Before the interruption that had set Magnus and his men on a course for war.

I will give him this respite, and I will take my pleasure. Then I can return to my true form without regret.

She committed memory for each decadent swipe of his tongue and each resulting dart of ecstasy. Seona, if she was wise, would be the recipient of these sensations from tomorrow forward. But tonight, Magnus was hers. His pleasure was hers to bestow. She would not leave him wanting.

Entwining her fingers in his hair, she attempted to tug him upward. She longed to join with him, to at last provide a heated home for his erect cock. She'd longed to sate him since their interlude last night, when she'd reached her peak and had not been able to reciprocate. But her king did not wish to cooperate.

He grunted a denial, pushed her legs wider and intensified his efforts.

Her head pressed back into the furs. Pleasurable heat built like a fire devouring kindling and beginning to lick at heavy logs.

Oh, his licking! His sucking at her sensitive pearl. His probing into her depths with his tongue.

Oh. Ohhhh. Just there!

The fire swelled, searing every inch of her like a glorious explosion.

The furs beneath her felt like a floating cloud as she came down from the height her lover had so sweetly sent her to. Stars danced in her vision when she opened her eyes. Her body lay limp, legs splayed ungracefully.

Magnus moved over her, lifted one of her legs around his hip, and entered her.

Golden gaze reverent on hers, he slid home in her ready sex. She welcomed him with arms around his shoulders and fingers clinging to his back.

The fullness of their joining was more than the coming together of body with body. Rather, she felt wrapped with a sense of completion that penetrated her heart, mind, and spirit. This mortal man somehow filled up places within her she hadn't known were empty.

As if sensing her joy, her moonstone warmed between her heaving chest and his. Together, they moved not to chase pleasure but in obedience to a primal urge. Their bodies mated, and they looked into each other's eyes. She would remember what she witnessed in those golden depths for all eternity.

He loves me.

Her body danced with her king's, and she crested once more, this time with a deep, resounding burst of ecstasy. Her cry mingled with his shout of completion, but the waves of pleasure did not recede. Their lovemaking continued as did the joy of their mutual pinnacle. The fullness he caused inside her swelled as if he'd somehow grown larger within her. The carnal peak went on and on, blinding her, deafening her, obliterating all thought except one: *Mine.*

When their bodies at last settled into the furs, still joined, sweaty, and spent, Magnus gathered her close and kissed her over and over again.

So intense had the pleasure been that sleep claimed her almost immediately. Before she succumbed, she managed to command her king to sleep as well. Whether he listened or not, she did not remain awake to see.

When morning sent muted light past the tent flaps, Danu was pleased to find Magnus at her side with soft snores sawing from his open mouth. "Good king," she praised in a whisper. He had needed rest, and it made her proud that she had helped him attain it.

Too soon, activity outside the tent roused him. The instant his eyes opened, they fixed on her. His sensual grin had her melting into his arms, heedless of the slickness coating her thighs. She welcomed his seed on her skin, luxuriated in it. Its presence meant he was so virile he had overflowed her channel. She greedily accepted his kiss and would have pushed for more if it was not clear his men were awake and arming themselves for battle.

Jangling gear and shouts to the ready made it impossible to deny that this moment was to be her last with her king.

Not enough time. I need more. So much more.

His brow furrowed as he stroked her cheek. "Do not fret, my beloved. I will return to you soon."

It was a pretty lie. He would return, but Seona would be in this body instead of her. Duff had given his word to see it done.

Of course, her return to her true form depended on Magnus besting Hyrk. In a corner of her selfish heart, she hoped Hyrk would not show himself, that Magnus and his men would find the children and convince them to come home without the demigod's interference.

But she knew Hyrk better than that. He wanted to rule her realm. He wanted her sealed in his dungeon. To accomplish his aim, he would persist until every last wolfkind soul true to her had perished. Or until he met his end.

"When I return," Magnus said, oblivious to her musings, "I will have the children with me." Determination lined his brow as he rose from bed and began dressing.

She stood to help, taking this last opportunity to appreciate his well-honed physique. Hands gliding over his shoulders, she smoothed the linen of his shirt and fastened the laces.

While she worked, he watched her with gentle eyes.

She loved how well he wore his age. He was a man late in his prime and at his peak of power. From his lean muscles to the white hairs dusting his temples to the fine lines around his eyes, experience and wisdom cloaked him.

"You are stunning," she said.

"Not nearly as stunning as you, My Goddess." Taking her hands, he kissed her fingertips. "You were right last night. I needed you."

She sighed, wishing to fall back with him on the bed furs. But it was time to let him go.

Clearing her throat, she said, "Hyrk will not let you simply walk away with the children. You know this, do you not?"

He nodded. "I am prepared to fight. He is powerful, but I have an army. We are well-prepared and will not return until he is destroyed."

"You must either convince every last child to hate him or you must destroy his relic."

"I will do both, to ensure he never harms you again," he said fiercely.

She could not help fearing for him. For his army. True, Hyrk was a single demigod, but he was smart and ruthless. He would have a plan, and she feared he would trick the children into helping. The children were the one thing he could use against Magnus and which Magnus could not harm.

An idea struck her. Her hands went to the back of her neck. "You'll take this," she said. "I believe it will provide precisely what you need precisely when you need it." She removed the necklace holding her moonstone and reached to fasten it around his neck.

He stopped her with a gentle hand. "No. It is yours. I gave it to you."

"And I am allowing you to borrow it."

"I cannot. You said this is your moonstone. Your power." His eyes were large and golden, concerned, loving, generous.

"Exactly, my love. I cannot go with you in any other way, not in this mortal body. You must take this. It will help you when you need it most." It would help him be strong and to see through Hyrk's plans. It would help him know what to say to the children.

A sigh came from his parted lips. His hand on her wrist loosened. He allowed her to finish fastening the necklace.

"Bring it back to me safe and sound." She did not make it a request. And she did not dwell on the fact that once she had it again, she and Seona would be together and they would be sent back to their true forms.

"Yes, My Goddess."

With a final kiss, he left the tent, and she curled in on herself. The sounds of boots crunching in snow meant Magnus and his army marched for the caves. She listened until she could hear them no more. Then she wept.

Chapter 27

AS MAGNUS HAD suspected, the caves were completely abandoned. Torchlight shone on barren rock walls as he led his army through Mammoth. Occasionally, they passed through a cavern with scattered remnants of past habitation, like old hay in moldering piles and broken animal-bone tools. Near midday, they reached the Spring of All Seasons, so named because no matter how cold the weather outside the caves, it remained unfrozen. They stopped to refill their canteens and marched on.

By mid-afternoon, they had emerged on the other side. The fortress lay but a few hours' walk away if they kept their pace swift. Horses would have sped them along, but the men would have lost that time coaxing the large warhorses through such narrow passages.

Each step through the snow-covered hills increased his agitation at being away from Danu. He'd thought finally bedding her would ease the clenching of his lungs at their separation, but their night together seemed only to have worsened it. How he loved her!

She was his goddess. She was his lover. If he had his way, she would be his pledgemate, and queen, his lifemate, his everything. But she was not his to keep. He would never constrain her as with a lifemate bond. Such a bond would cause her pain when she returned to her heavenly throne. She must never be bound again, not for any reason.

He would return to her a victor, having slain her enemy. Then he would let her go.

Their entire world depended on her speedy return to a place of power where she could bless them. With her reigning over them, more children would be born, a respectable number of females among them. His efforts to maintain a library of their history and occupations would be worthwhile. A new generation would grow and learn not directly from mentors as in the past but from their words and images, captured on paper with ink so their trades and discoveries would live on.

Until his dying breath he would lament the loss of his Danu in bodily form at his side, but he would carry on. He had many tasks to see to which would keep his grief at bay, such as ensuring their culture survived along with them. Training up a new king or queen, likely Riggs and Anya's firstborn, as his parents had trained him. Instilling a love for Danu in the next generation, beginning with the children Hyrk had deceived.

He had failed them in this, and in many other ways. His dream last night had shown him the error of his ways in excruciating detail. The moment he'd gathered Danu in his arms and lay down, the scene started. Whether it reflected reality or was simply the workings of his conscience, he did not know, but it played over and over in his mind as he led his men today. With each remembrance, it became easier and easier to understand why the children had followed Hyrk to Larna.

Three boys sat together at one end of a rough-hewn table. He recognized them easily as Ruben, Craiden, and Riggs's youngest brother, Julian. Each held a tin cup of steaming liquid that might have been tea, or perhaps simply hot water if they had no tea leaves at hand.

Behind the boys, flames leapt in a great fireplace. This was the main hall of the fortress he and his men sought. The long room was clean and appeared warm, but furniture was sparse. The boys' clothing was dirty and worn.

At another table, Alexander bent his head with a group of younger children, eyes alight with planning. Magnus recognized the gleam in his eyes. He'd witnessed it many times before in the eyes of the boy's father. It was the self-satisfied assurance of one who had yearned for position and recently attained it.

Focusing on the three older boys, who were closer to Magnus's vantage point, he listened to their hushed conversation.

"I don't like Alexander's plan," Ruben said, sipping from his cup. "He wants to lure the women here and force them to stay. He'll put them in his sham of a lottery regardless of their wishes. It's not right. That's not how ladies should be treated."

Women? What women? Not human women. He'd rescued them all last moon. And not Larnian females. They'd been taken out of Larna for their safety in the war twenty years past. Sadly, they had been so old and in such rough shape they had all gone to Danu's breast since then. Magnus knew for a fact there were no women in Larna, let alone healthy women of breeding age.

Craiden snorted. His scruffy, teenage face scrunched up. "Those females—if there's even more than the one we saw in that mirror thing—aren't ladies. They're Larnians. Rejected Larnians at that. If they're smart, they'll be grateful when we give them warm rooms instead of those caves they're living in, never mind the fine clothes we've scavenged." His scowl softened. "But I agree about the lottery shite. They might not be Maranner ladies, but I'm not about to go sticking my cock into someone who doesn't want it. That's no way to make our kind live on."

The other boys nodded while Magnus's mind reeled with all he'd just heard. He prayed his imagination was conjuring all this, but he feared the dream was like the one he'd had on the night of his coronation, that it was divine and given for a purpose. He held a sleeping goddess in his arms, after all, and her magic moonstone had brought her to him. Perhaps the stone was showing him all this.

Perhaps there were females in Larna. Craiden had mentioned caves. Not the caves his army was to pass through, surely, but perhaps there were caves his men had overlooked during their scouring of Larna after the war.

The presence of women would explain how Hyrk had gained the confidence of the children. They were young, but they understood the state of their world. The existence of females would prove too strong a lure to resist, at least for the older lads.

But what had Craiden meant by "rejected Larnians?" And what was this business about a lottery and taking women who were unwilling? These boys weren't old enough to enter Marann's breeding lottery. Only adults were permitted to purchase tickets.

Then again, he remembered being eighteen and nineteen, like many of these boys. He had been years from full adulthood, according to their traditions, but his cock hadn't known that. Like most other boys, he'd fantasized liberally about taking ladies to bed. Society said he must wait until the age of twenty-five, and he had, but he could have bred a female much earlier.

It seemed the children, led by Alexander, thought to do just that. They must intend to set up a lottery of their own in Larna with whatever females Hyrk had promised them.

He felt sick. Not only because this plan of theirs was a perversion of Marann's necessary lottery system, but because he had never once considered how heavy a burden these young men carried. The weight of their world rested on their slender shoulders, yet Magnus had never so much as discussed their futures with them.

Clearly, these young ones intended to be part of the solution to their population crisis.

The boys were silent for a time, each sipping his drink and seemingly lost in thought.

Julian said, "Someday, we'll be old, and there will be hardly any of us left. I think we ought to court these Larnian females slowly. Make friends with them first, see to their needs, offer protection. Once they trust us, we can explain that we'll all be done for if we don't find some way to come together in breeding." Magnus approved. Julian had a quiet wisdom about him like his brother.

"Yeah," Ruben said. "We're young. We've got time on our side, but Alexander's in some kind of rush. And he's got this spark in his eye I don't like."

"That's just Xander," Craiden said. "He's like his sire with his grand ideas and his ego. But you have a point about taking our time. If we force breeding on the females, what'll we tell our sons and daughters? How will we raise them up if their mothers hate us? Better to take our time and get them comfortable with us. Maybe start by finding out why they've been in hiding all this time."

The other boys nodded.

"Do you think the others are buying into it?" Julian asked.

The three boys glanced at the other table, where Alexander joked and talked with the younger pups.

"I don't know," Ruben said. "I know you two are of like mind with me, but I wouldn't risk talking to anyone else. Not unless they say something first."

"So what are we going to do?" Julian asked. "Are we going to keep sitting back and observing this madness, or are we going to do something about it?"

"For now, we wait and see," Ruben said. "We don't want to wind up like Travis."

The dream ended, leaving Magnus with a hundred questions, foremost of which was what had happened to Travis. So lost was he in thought he didn't hear Riggs come up alongside him. The big man had been leading the back centuries while Magnus led the front. But now that they were out of the caves, they could move as a unit instead of in the single-file formation forced by the narrow passages.

"So," Riggs said, sniffing the air. "It's true, then."

"What's true?" He focused ahead, picking out their trail by keeping an eye on the mountain to their left and the slope of the ground. Within the hour, they would intersect Black River Gorge. Despite the foreboding name, he anticipated a smooth crossing. The water would be shallow this time of year, and though steep banks cradled the river, men on foot could take them easily. Once on the eastern bank, the fortress would be in sight.

"You called on last night's full moon," Riggs said, a lopsided grin on his face. "Sire," he added.

"When it's just the two of us, you can leave off with that nonsense." He didn't expect his second to constantly refer to him by title, and had told him so many times before. "And what do you mean about the moon?"

Vaguely, he recalled it had been a full moon last night. If he weren't out here with his army, a lottery drawing would have been held, and winners would have greeted their new breeding partners in a celebration at Glendall. As it was, the drawing had to be delayed and would take place upon their triumphant return, providing reason for a double celebration.

Riggs's eyebrows drew down. "You mean, you didn't call on the moon? On…Danu's blessing?"

Magnus's mind was on the route they must take to the fortress and on the children. He had no time for riddles. "Say what you mean, knight." His patience grew short, especially since the only reason a man would call on Danu's blessing on a full moon was— He hitched in a breath.

"That's how it was for me and Anya," Riggs said, voice grave.

Magnus's heart leapt like a falcon eager to leave its cage. "Lifemates," Magnus said, but surely he was mistaking Riggs's meaning. He could not have made Danu his lifemate during their coupling last night. True, their finish had been the longest, most glorious finish of his entire life, and true the moon had been full, but he had sought no blessing, as men of old did when wishing to bind their moonsoul to that of another for all time. How could he, when their goddess's heavenly throne sat vacant? Danu was in no position to grant a lifemating. She was mortal.

But then, she had been in no position to grant Riggs's lifemating with Anya, either. That hadn't stopped it from happening.

His mind spun with hope and confusion. And dread.

"Was the end—" Riggs cleared his throat. "For us, the end was remarkable, at least according to Anya. I had nothing to compare it to."

Magnus cut a sharp look at his second. "How was it remarkable?"

"*Uh-hem.* Longer, I guess." He shook his head, the skin above his beard pink.

"Don't mince words with me. I want to know." He was desperate to know. He could not have made Danu his lifemate. The risks were too great to contemplate. What if he'd done it by accident and it bound her to him so she could not return to her true form? What if he'd unintentionally bound Seona's human body to him, and when she returned to it she hated him even more than she already did?

Riggs sighed. Looking around to make sure they were a respectable distance from the men behind, he said, "Being with Anya makes me blind with pleasure. Not just the first time. Every time. And my prick—it extends at the tip when I finish. I never knew it could do that." His entire face was red, but he pressed on, ever the obedient and loyal knight. "It feels like heaven. It's more than I ever felt on my own." He looked pointedly at Magnus to get his meaning across.

"I see." He spoke the words coolly, but inwardly a riot of emotions pummeled him. What Riggs described matched what he had experienced last night.

Magnus had bedded every woman alive without exception, at least the wolfkind women. As soon as he'd come of age, he'd done what his father had commanded. *You must bed them all, son. Keep records. Take as many to bed in a season as you can. Those you take will be kept separate from the lottery that moon. It is vitally important that we produce children, especially daughters. But it is ten-times more vital that you sire an heir. Promise me you will see it done.*

He had not known, when he'd made that promise, that it would be the last time he would speak to his father. The king's heart had failed the very next day, and Magnus had promptly been crowned the new king of Marann.

He'd been grieving his father bitterly when he'd begun taking ladies of breeding age to his bed, and he found much pleasure and comfort in the duty he had sworn himself to. But those experiences had paled in comparison to last night with his goddess. If bedding a woman was a goblet of fine wine, making love to Danu had been a storehouse full of barrels, a lifetime supply of heady drink to last through the ages and beyond.

He had assumed the extraordinary pleasure was a result of the deprivation he'd experienced the past two moons. Since Seona had been found, he had determined to trust his vision. He ceased all attempts to breed with the other women, being faithful to his future queen even though her behavior had done nothing to encourage his faithfulness.

All thoughts of siring an heir had vanished since he'd discovered Seona's body was home not to the human but to his beloved goddess. Breeding had been the furthest thing from his mind when he'd sunk inside her welcoming sheath last night and poured his love into her, thrust by decadent thrust.

By the moon, his cock was thickening just remembering it.

"It cannot be," he said firmly. For many reasons it could not be, even if his moonsoul craved to be bound with hers. Could a goddess even be bound to a mortal? There was nothing of the like in the Archives.

"I thought so, too," Riggs said. "But everyone smelled it on us." He referred to the distinct lifemate scent. On Anya, the scent repelled all males save her lifemate. On Riggs, it served as a constant reminder to the other men that he was blessed above all others. He alone among wolfkind males had the right to one special female, and she had a right to him. They were irrevocably bound in this life and beyond. "*You* smelled it on us," Riggs reminded him. "Now everyone smells it on you."

Magnus looked at him sharply. "What do you mean?"

"Just what I said." Riggs looked ahead as they walked, keeping a swift pace. "Your scent has changed. Everyone knows it. The men can't stop talking about it."

"Fuck."

He could think of nothing else to say. Nor did he have time to dwell on the implications of what his second was telling him. They were nearing the gorge, and the hairs on the back of his neck prickled. They were being watched.

Chapter 28

DANU LOWERED HERSELF to a rock, grateful for another rest. How weak this human body was! She could scarcely walk for an hour before becoming winded.

A water skin appeared before her, held out by the large hand of the commander in charge of their safety. Verden was a large, muscle-bound warrior with a gray beard and a bald head beneath his helm. "My thanks," she panted as she raised it to her lips.

Verden nodded before returning to the distance he and his men kept from her and Anya.

The water was cold and refreshing as she gulped it down. Not long ago, their party had stopped in a wide cavern lit with daylight, which shone through a gap in the rock overhead. A deep, blue cold-water spring took up the majority of the space, and it was from this water source the men had refilled their canteens. She and Anya had knelt by the pool and used their cupped hands to slake their thirst. Immediately, the men near them had moved to the other side of the pool, as if they did not want to risk coming into contact with them.

Another stretch of walking through tunnels had brought them to their current location, a barren cavern the size of a modest bedchamber with two tunnels providing access. Rough rock made up the walls, and the ceiling hung so low most of the men had to stoop. The space was empty except for a few boulders, two of which she and Anya sat upon.

She'd lost track of their winding path through the mountain long ago, but she gathered they'd arrived at the cavern Magnus had shown them on the map. The men had stowed some of their gear along the walls and had spread out through the connecting passageways, no doubt to guard her and Anya from every direction. It seemed they would stay here awhile. Not too long, she hoped, because having her king away caused a pang of longing in her chest.

Today, the pain of separation was even sharper than when Magnus had left with his army. The send-off from Chroina felt like only yesterday for her, but in reality, it had occurred six days ago. Her moonstone had brought her and Anya through space and time, and during their walk today, she had been trying to sort out the reason.

Perhaps Magnus needed the moonstone for the coming battle, and now that he had it, their purpose was complete. Or perhaps there was more to it.

Could it be that she and Anya were needed in Larna? Certainly not to join the army in marching to the fortress. Their fragile human bodies could scarcely withstand walking this far from their camp. They could not have trekked another half-day without slowing Magnus and his men. Furthermore, if they met Hyrk and a battle took place, they would surely come to harm. With Anya carrying the first child to be conceived in years, risking her life would be the height of foolishness.

Thirst slaked, Danu fastened the water skin. Only a few of the men, including Verden, remained inside the chamber. With their furrowed brows and the darting glances they shot toward her, they seemed on edge. The distance they kept made it easy for her to speak privately with Anya.

"The men are uncomfortable," she noted. "They do not like to come near me. Is it because Seona was so standoffish?"

Anya wiped her lips on the back of her wrist after a long drink from her water skin. "'Tis no' you." She stretched her legs out in front of her and aggressively kneaded one of them with a wince. "They dinnae like the lifemate scent on me. 'Tis like a mint candle to the gnats. My scent repels them."

Ah. The lifemate scent. She'd forgotten about that, likely because her human senses were not sharp enough to notice it. But there seemed more to the tension in the mens' shoulders than avoidance. They had kept their distance from her and Anya all morning, but here in the cavern, they seemed agitated in a way they had not been earlier.

Across the cavern, Verden held his helm under one arm while bending his head with some of his men. They kept their voices too low to be heard and peered around the cavern with narrowed eyes.

"Like a gaggle of hens they are," Anya muttered with a roll of her eyes. "You'd think they'd be accustomed to my scent by now." Clearly, Anya thought the men were speaking about them, but Danu was not so sure.

Her body craved rest, but a sense of unease made her loathe to close her eyes. She could not help feeling as if there were something obvious in front of her that she could not see. In her breast, there was an urge to leave this place. Perhaps the men felt it too and were on edge because they could not leave. Their king had commanded them to wait here for his return.

She gasped with realization. An unsettling feeling. A sense that she was missing something obvious. A desire to leave a place. It all made sense now. Someone had cast faerie glamour over this cavern.

"What is it?" Anya asked. "Are you well?"

Danu held up a staying hand for silence while she observed the men more carefully. As they came and went, they never crossed the cavern directly. They always kept to the perimeter, as if avoiding some obstacle. They sensed the glamour too, even if they were unaware of it.

"There is faerie glamour in this place," she whispered. As an afterthought, in the event Anya did not know the term, she added, "Like the guise Duff uses to hide from Arwan."

Anya stiffened. "Gravois is here?" she asked.

Danu shook her head. Duff had vowed to remain with Seona until Hyrk's cell failed. Glamours were not indefinite. Whoever had cast this glamour was nearby or had been not long ago. "Not him, but someone of the Fae."

Magnus had assured her the caves were long abandoned. What if he was wrong? *The Larnians fear them. They claim the surviving rejects from Jilken's breeding experiments live there.*

Not for the first time, Danu considered the offspring of Jilken's magical breeding experiments. She had been imprisoned, so she had not witnessed the abominable undertaking, but Hyrk had crowed about it.

"Darling, they are magnificent! You should see them. The prize pups are large and strong. Their bloodlust runs deep. Their jaws are powerful. Their hands can tear through rock. On the outside, they appear like your wolfkind, but on the inside, they are ravening wolves ready to tear apart their foes on my command.

"They are so much more than you intended, so much more powerful than your creation. More wolf-like. More Fae. And they can be ours. All you have to do is become my bride, and we will rule them as one."

"Never." She forced her voice not to reveal the rage boiling in her breast at this perversion of her creation.

Hyrk went on a tirade at her refusal, shaking the bars of her prison with his screeching. After composing himself, he said, "Have it your way. But know this. Not all those born of my magic and Jilken's obedience are prize pups. Those who come out of their mothers deformed or weak have been quickly and mercifully disposed of. If you bind yourself to me, no more pups will be discarded. All will be cared for. Continue to deny me and I will ensure those pups suffer before they die."

She had almost broken. It was not the fault of those children that Hyrk had manipulated their breeding. The thought of those innocents suffering had almost made her agree to Hyrk's demand. But if she had done so, she would have taken his wicked soul into herself. True, he would have taken her soul into himself as well. Perhaps her goodness would temper his evil. But perhaps his evil would snuff out her goodness. She could not take that chance, could not condemn her people to the rule of a joint deity whose nature she could not predict. Nor could she condemn herself to an eternity of intimate oneness with her enemy.

"As long as you treasure love, I will always be proud of you."

"I will, Papa. I will treasure love forever and ever."

Hyrk treasured wickedness and hatred. Union with him could not be her fate. It would not.

Still, her decision haunted her to this day. So many children had been harmed, abandoned, outright killed. Perhaps whoever had cast this glamour had descended from those times. They might be survivors of Hyrk's mania and cruelty—victims of her choice.

"Are we in danger?" Anya whispered. Her friend's arm wound through hers, a slight tremble in it.

"I do not think so. But whoever cast this glamour does not wish for us to take any special notice of this cavern." She studied the rocky wall, noting how her gaze jumped over certain places.

In her goddess form, she could easily identify glamour and decipher it to see what lay underneath. Apparently, she could sense it in human form, but could she see through it? She focused on one such place, a large boulder not far from where she sat. Her human eyes strained to look away, but she forced them to remain. The object was not a boulder. She insisted on seeing the truth, and suddenly, the image of the boulder wavered. It became a rough-hewn, wooden table with a cabinet beneath.

A thrill of success warmed her. Now to see if Anya could decipher the glamour as well. She instructed her friend to do as she had done. When Anya's grip on her arm tightened, she knew her friend saw the table.

"'Tis like Gravois' camp," Anya said with wonder. "Some things, and even some of the other tinkers, are not what they seem. They want the world to see them a certain way, and the magic makes it so."

"Yes." Danu let her gaze move past the table and continued to unlock glamour around the cavern. Beside her, Anya did the same.

A cold fireplace appeared where only rock had been. Black shale formed a chimney that rose to a hole someone had carved into the ceiling. The boulders they sat on became a wooden bench, lovingly engraved with the shapes of trees and plants. Folded cloth padded the wooden surface, and the moment Danu saw it, soft cushioning took the place of the hard surface. The center of the cavern became an eating pit set into the floor, explaining why the men avoided that space. On the wall was an elk's rack that might serve as a place to hang cloaks. A well-maintained, tidy home emerged where only moments ago an abandoned cavern had been.

Suddenly, Anya bolted from the bench. "Travis!" Limping wildly, she rounded the cave and squatted at the far end of the table.

The image wavered and the youngest boy alive came into view. Tears streaked his dirty face, and ropes bound his ankles, and presumably his hands behind his back. Another rope tied him to the table, and a rag had been stuffed in his mouth.

Instantly, Danu dashed to his side. Anya was already cutting at the ropes with a dagger pulled from her dress. Danu pulled the rag from between his chapped lips.

"You heard me!" he whimpered, looking between them. "It took you so long!" He shuddered and sniffled while Anya shifted his small body and sawed at the robes behind his back. "I was shouting and shouting, but you didn't know I was here. I was so frightened!"

"*Och,* love, we're here. We're here. You're safe now," Anya cooed. With Travis freed from his bonds, she gathered him to her chest and smoothed his straggly, blond hair.

Travis sobbed into her shoulder, and Danu could not stop herself from rubbing soothing circles on his back. Someone had tied up the youngest wolfkind and had not wanted him found. Anger darted through her. Like the warrior women of old, she craved blood. Whoever had done this would suffer.

"What in the name of the moon!" Verden clomped to where the three of them huddled together. "Travis? Where did you come from? What's the meaning of this?" he demanded, as if she and Anya had somehow brought him with them from Glendall.

Anya got to her feet and puffed up her chest, forcing Verden back. "Dinnae fash at him! He's been captive here and you did naught about it!" She poked her finger in Verden's chest. Tears ran down her cheeks.

Danu held Travis, and he clung to her, wide-eyed gaze darting between Anya and the commander. "The commander did nothing wrong," she said with a tug of Anya's skirts. "The cave is under a glamour," she said to Verden. "Someone doesn't want us to know they live here."

"The Remnant," Travis said. He sniffed bravely and clamored to his feet. He faced Verden. Fading bruises marred his pale cheeks. "They came from the breeding experiments, and they live here in the caves. They don't want us to know about them, and I think they've gone to the fortress with Vera to collect Braeden. You have to stop them. They'll hurt the other children."

Danu's head spun. She'd been right about who lived here. Worse, it seemed this Remnant was a threat to the children.

Ignoring Anya's ire, Verden knelt and took Travis by the shoulders. "Tell me everything."

Chapter 29

MAGNUS LED HIS army across a snowy plain. In the distance, the gorge was nothing but a black line drawn on the pure-white ground. Once they crossed the gorge and climbed the hill on the other side, they would be able to see the fortress.

In his mind, he rehearsed what he would say to the children. Apology first, then assurance that from now on, they would have a say in their futures. He would provide them opportunities to voice their fears and ideas. He would explain to them why certain laws existed, how the laws protected them all and honored Danu. No longer would they feel so powerless that they considered making an independent future for themselves apart from the safety of Chroina.

They would come home willingly once they understood.

Then he would speak with Danu. He did not know whether he owed her an apology for making her his lifemate or if she would celebrate their union. If she despised him for what he'd done, perhaps Assaph could undo it. If she rejoiced, perhaps they could find a way to be together now and again. After all, legend said she had visited Lachlan. It had happened at the very promontory where he had confronted Hyrk. Surely, if they were mated, she would set aside time to visit him.

He prayed she would forgive him and rejoice over what had been done. The thought of living out his life apart from her left him with a hollow sensation in his chest.

But matters of the heart must be put aside. Every sense he'd honed as a tracker and hunter told him they were being watched. Though he could spot no enemies hiding in the hills, he felt malice in the air. The sound of Hyrk's laughter as it had echoed through the canyon haunted his memory.

Beneath his armor, Danu's moonstone heated near to the point of pain. His entire body went on alert. "Be ready," he said to Riggs.

His second drew his axe, a fearsome-looking double-headed weapon large enough to split a boar in two. "Yes, Sire," the knight said, and he swept the hills with a wary gaze.

Suddenly, a vision came upon him.

Imposed over the bright winter hills was the great hall he'd seen in his dream last night. The double image disoriented him, and he staggered.

Riggs steadied him with a firm grip on his shoulder. "Sire? Are you well?"

"A vision," he said, but his voice faded from his hearing. The snow and trees around him faded, as did Riggs. He stood in the fire-lit hall of dark stone. The children were gathered near the end farthest from the twin doors, where a platform had been erected. They all gazed up at Alexander, who sat upon a throne with his arms spread in a gesture of grandeur. His eyes glowed red.

"Here they come," Alexander said. He grinned, and Magnus recognized the twisted expression. Hyrk was controlling the boy. Red gaze fixed on the heavy timber doors, he said, "Brace yourselves, children. You are about to witness true greatness."

The children murmured and shifted on their feet. Toward the front of the pack stood Ruben, Craiden, and Julian. The three older boys traded expressions of discomfort.

"My plan is working," Hyrk said. "They are all here." The evil laugh following the proclamation echoed in the hall as if it had come from all around.

"We have to stop this," Ruben said.

"He's mad," Craiden said.

"No," Julian said. "He's possessed."

The doors at the front of the hall burst open. Flurries of swirling snow circled a hooded figure in a black cloak. The children huddled together. Behind the figure were more than a dozen larger figures, each cloaked, their features hidden. But Magnus noticed wolf-like snouts protruding from many of the hoods.

"We've been waiting for you," Alexander said, his voice no longer Hyrk's. His eyes were the silvery-blue he'd inherited from Ari. "We found something of yours and have been keeping it safe for you. Ruben!" Alexander spotted Ruben and motioned him forward. "Go get her pet," he commanded. "So he may be returned safely to his owner."

Her? While Magnus watched, the foremost cloaked figure peeled back its hood. A waterfall of hair the bright color of autumn leaves fell around slender shoulders. A woman!

Ruben left the hall at a run, his two friends watching him go.

At the entrance, the woman narrowed her haunting silver eyes. The unique color reminded Magnus of Bantus's eyes.

"The wolf is not my pet," she bit out. "He's my brother." She flipped a corner of her cloak over her shoulder, revealing a crossbow hanging at her side. A quiver of short arrows hung from her hip. "You weren't keeping him safe for me. You held him prisoner to get me to come to you. Well. I'm here now." She raised the weapon and aimed it at Alexander.

Alexander held up his hands. If the news of the wolf being the woman's brother surprised him, he showed no sign of it. It certainly surprised Magnus. Alexander also showed no fear of the weapon. He smiled disarmingly. "Now, now. We are your new neighbors. We only wanted to introduce ourselves. Come in. Take off your cloaks and enjoy the fires. We are preparing dinner and have plenty to share—"

Ruben burst from a doorway behind the platform and ran to Alexander. Between panting breaths, he said, "The wolf's…gone…escaped…cage opened."

"What?" Finally, something had surprised Alexander. "What do you mean escaped? How can a wolf escape? Unless someone freed him." He glowered at Ruben, who held up his hands in a show of innocence.

"He's not a wolf," the woman said, her gaze hard as ice. "And you are not our neighbors. You are trespassers." Shifting her weapon, she let one of her arrows fly.

Heart in his throat, Magnus tried to run toward Alexander, but his body would not cooperate. All he could do was watch as the arrow hit its mark. Not Alexander, but Ruben.

At Alexander's side, Ruben lurched, wide-eyed. His hands clawed at his neck. Protruding from his throat was the arrow's brown fletching. Gaping silently, he stumbled to the floor.

The woman grinned and notched another arrow. She advanced on the children, her cohort following. Hoods peeled back one by one, revealing monstrous faces that appeared half wolf and half man. King Bantus had a face like that, the lower half more of a snout than a wolfkind mouth.

The whites of Alexander's eyes showed his fear. It seemed he had not expected violence. Foolish lad. "Come, now," he said in a wavering voice.

"Enough talking," the woman said. "We did not come for conversation. We came for blood."

"Draw arms!" Alexander shouted. "Protect your ruler!"

The children stared, wide-eyed as the monstrous beings closed around them.

"Fight!" Alexander shrieked.

Several children screamed.

Julian grabbed a tarnished sword from the pile near the fireplace. The weapon's size and weight required him to use both hands to wield it. Clearly, he had no idea how to fight, but Magnus admired his courage.

Alexander tried to run from the hall, but he didn't make it far.

Craiden grabbed him. "Stand and fight, you scabby coward! You got us into this, and you'll damn well help get us out."

Alexander jerked against Craiden's hold, and then sagged. A distant stare settled over his features, like he was listening to something no one else could hear.

Craiden tried to shove a sword into his hand, but it only fell to the floor.

Alexander nodded. "Of course," he muttered. He pulled something from his pocket and lifted his clasped hands over his head. A red glow emanated from his hands and shone through the hall. "I call on the powerful Hyrk, god of darkness! Take physical form and come to our aid!"

The hall went still for a moment as Alexander's voice echoed unnaturally.

The gemstone floated from his hands and spun in the air, casting shards of blood-red light around the hall. Then, with a whizzing sound, it sped through one of the windows high in the walls.

A bone-rattling screech cut through the hall, coming from outside. A shadow passed over the boys as something very large moved through the sky close to the hall.

Magnus turned to look out the windows. Blocking out the wintry clouds with its giant wingspan was a soaring dragon, the likes of which should only exist in legend. Reddish brown scales and crimson, slitted eyes flashed as, with the sound of wind in sails, the beast swooped low over the fortress then out of sight.

The vision cleared. Magnus gasped a lungful of cold air. "The children," he said to Riggs. "They're in danger." It hadn't been a dream. None of it had. He knew it with a certainty he couldn't explain.

Riggs and the other men who had gathered around him looked to the sky. "They're going to have to wait," Riggs said. "Because so are we."

An unholy roar cut through the winter air.

Magnus followed Riggs's gaze. The dragon from his vision flew toward them. It flapped its enormous, bat-like wings, once twice, three times as it came to a floating stop over the gorge. With a great bellow, it unleashed a plume of fire from its mouth.

"To arms!" he called, and he heard the command carried through the centuries. Sword drawn, he led the charge toward the beast.

§

"SOMAT IS HAPPENING." Seona's voice brought Duff out of deep thought. He had been trying not to worry about Danu, and failing miserably.

"What is it, love?" He sat up straight within the shadow of his boulder.

She rubbed her chest. "I feel queer, as if somat is pushing at me."

He frowned, not knowing what could cause such a sensation. He searched his memory for any conversation with Danu that might shed light on Seona's discomfort. With a start, he remembered something.

They had been making love once long ago, and during the carnal dance, she had exhaled sharply and shed a single tear. He'd thought he'd hurt her somehow, though he couldn't imagine what a

Fae could do to harm a goddess. It was more likely she'd hurt herself, since she'd been riding him like a glorious cavalrywoman, all flowing blond locks and bouncing tits.

He'd paused in his thrusting. "All right, love?"

She waved away his concern, though her mood had shifted. Her pace had been fast, as if she'd been sprinting in a race. But she slowed. Lowering herself into his arms, she breathed into his neck. "I've lost one," she whispered. "When my people die, their moonsouls return to me."

He knew how much she loved her people.

Stroking her hair back from her face, he kissed her. "I'm sorry, love."

"I'm used to it," she said, but their lovemaking continued more tenderly than before. Perhaps she was used to it, but it still affected her.

Returning to the present, he watched through the bars as Seona clutched her robes over her chest. Her brow furrowed with pain. Could it be she was feeling a moonsoul as it sought eternal rest? He wished he'd paid closer attention when Danu had mentioned the phenomenon. But then again, he'd had other things on his mind.

"I think you're feeling a wolfkind death. You're their goddess, now."

Wide eyes blinked at his shadow. Her brows lowered. "I doona like it. How do I make it cease?"

"I'm afraid I don't know. Perhaps, try letting it in?"

She grimaced. "*Och,* I doona want a dead soul inside me!"

"I doubt they remain there, love. Danu would have provided her mortals with a path to heaven. Perhaps she, herself—or rather now you—serve as the gateway."

She wrinkled her nose, the thought obviously distasteful to her. With a sigh, she folded her arms beneath her breasts. "Well." She tapped her foot. "How do I let the bloody thing in?"

Duff pinched the bridge of his nose. "Dearest. This is not a mosquito we are talking about. It is a soul. A soul *you* have charge over. Tell me you feel the weight of that. Tell me you have an ounce of compassion somewhere in that bruised heart of yours." He did not blame this woman for the wounds she'd suffered, but he'd be damned if he didn't challenge her when she let bitterness and selfishness rule her emotions.

"Compassion? You speak to me of compassion when I've been lied to and used by every man whose path I've crossed? How dare you scold me? You're no different from the rest!"

He shot to his feet within his shadow. Anger pulsed through him. "How dare I? How dare I? I dare because I'm not every man whose path you've crossed. I dare because I'm in love with you, you stubborn woman."

He snapped his mouth shut, surprised he'd admitted his feelings to her.

She stilled and stared at him. She opened her mouth to say something, but all that came out was a groan. She staggered, clutching at her chest. "*Och!* 'Tis growing worse. *Do* somat! Help me!" She fell to her knees on the jagged stone floor, and the scent of blood rose to meet him. She must have cut her knees on the rocks.

His fists clenched and unclenched. He almost grabbed the bars, but stopped himself at the last second. He still nursed wounds from his earlier encounter with the cold-iron and was in no rush to add more. All he could do was pace within his shadow and watch as his woman became increasingly more distressed.

"What is it, love? Tell me what's happening." Her pain filled him with a sense of urgency, yet he was helpless to give her aid. This was intolerable!

"I doona ken!" she gasped. "'Tis like before but stronger. So much stronger. Make it cease!"

Was that one soul becoming more insistent, or were more souls seeking the peace of the afterlife? Could it be that Magnus's army was battling Hyrk this very moment? He longed to go to the ream of wolfkind so he could know for sure, but he would not leave Seona. Not for anything.

"Hang on, love," he said uselessly. "Just hang on."

Chapter 30

FIRE RAINED DOWN on Magnus and his army.

The dragon—a living, breathing dragon like he'd read about as a pup in the legends—flapped its massive wings to hover over the gorge. Weak winter light gleamed off its scales, making it appear red one moment and gold the next. Its eyes glowed with blood-red light, and Magnus had the impression those eyes searched for *him.*

This was Hyrk. Somehow, Alexander's words had called him forth in this form.

Now great fountains of flame shot from the dragon's jaws and blanketed his army in sweeping arcs. His men lined up along the northern slope of the gorge, but the boiling hot air prevented them from descending to the river. The snow at their feet turned to slush. They could not cross, could not get to the children.

Magnus's arm tensed as he held his shield high against the fiery onslaught. His feet scuffed at the gorge's slope, sending mud and rock tumbling down the incline to the dark waters beneath. Every time he began side-stepping down toward the river to make a crossing, plumes of fire pushed him back up to the edge again.

All around him, his men were doing the same—advancing a foot, then retreating two feet. Despite their raised shields, some had been burned. At least a dozen fine soldiers lay in the melted snow with charred limbs. Groans of pain surrounded him. Worse, some of the men lay still. Too still.

Danu, help us.

Prayer came naturally to him, but he must remember that Danu could not help them, not at the moment. She was as mortal as the rest of them and even more fragile than most in her human body. There was no one to answer his prayer. He must be the one to provide victory for his men. For the children. For all wolfkind.

Still, he wasn't completely without his goddess. Against his chest, her moonstone lay cool and smooth. Feeling it there gave him strength. It had warned him of the dragon and showed him that the children needed him. It would not allow him to fail.

"We must reach the fortress!" he called out. "The children are in danger!"

He must end Hyrk as quickly as possible, but this was no ordinary foe. The airborne beast had the freedom to swiftly counteract every last man as they tried pushing into the gorge.

"Spread out along the edge and advance when you can!" But it seemed no matter how far his army stretched along the river's high bank, the dragon was able to fly to meet them and force them back.

He took in the battle and the landscape. His men crowded the northern edge of the gorge, fending off flames with their shields, and launching arrows when the flames subsided. The dragon's wings swept the air, keeping itself elevated. Most of his archers' projectiles bounced harmlessly off the beast, but a single arrow protruded from the milky scales covering its chest.

The dragon was beyond the reach of their swords, and their arrows were ineffective. As long as it breathed fire, they could not reach the fortress. How were they to defeat this enemy? Where was its vulnerability? It must have one.

Frustration made his heart pound. This stalemate was intolerable!

If they were defending Chroina against this foe, the city walls would have given them protection from the fire. They could have launched a net to capture or at least hinder the dragon enough to take the upper hand. But out here in Larna's wintery wilderness, the dragon had the clear advantage.

"The only ways to defeat a demigod are to take away his mortal worshippers or to destroy his relic." Duff's words echoed in his mind.

Taking away Hyrk's followers was impossible. He could not reach the children, and even if he could reach them and quickly convince them to abandon their ill-founded loyalty, there were likely more followers hiding in Marann.

That left the red gemstone, Hyrk's relic. If he could destroy it, the dragon would be no more. But last Magnus had seen the stone, it had been in Alexander's hands. He could not reach it while the dragon barred their path to the fortress. Wait. It had not been in Alexander's hand. It had flown out the window into the sky.

A stream of flame singed the air directly over him. He ducked behind his shield. Around him, his men did the same, but some of them bellowed with pain. Magnus's helm heated with the onslaught. Pain bit at his ears as the metal caused burns, but his shield protected him from the worst of the blast.

The jet of fire swept away, and he straightened. Danu's moonstone slipped free from his armor. Was it his imagination or did it gleam with inner light? Yes! It was glowing. Sparks like distant stars shone within the amethyst's depths, like a night sky alight with beauty.

Lowering his shield, he touched a finger to the stone, finding it warm. Not from the dragon's fire and not from his body. It was the heat of a rock that had baked in the sun all afternoon, and it filled him with hope.

Danu's power was alive within the stone. He sensed not only its presence but its intent. It beckoned him. It had a plan.

Focusing on the stone, he tilted it between finger and thumb. *Show me what must be done.*

As if the stone heard him, its inner light cast a shimmering beam out and away from him. He followed its path and watched it come to rest on the dragon's chest, directly where the single arrow protruded. Midway between the beating wings, where logic said the dragon's heart should be, the spot wavered with the moonstone's soft, lavender light. It was the only place an arrow had been able to lodge. With most of its shaft visible, however, the arrow hadn't penetrated deeply enough to cause harm. Still, the highlighted spot was vulnerable.

The moment he had the thought, the beam of light from Danu's moonstone faded. A faint red glow remained behind that thin milky skin. That glow was about the size of the red gemstone.

Hyrk's relic is *the dragon's heart.*

"A relic is not an easy thing to destroy. It is said no mortal weapon can harm one." Danu's words from Assaph's study came back to him. They cast doubt on what the moonstone had shown him. *"Only an act of pure faith can destroy a relic."*

Have faith.

How many times had his father given him that advice? How many times had he encouraged himself thus? But could he have faith when it mattered most?

He must. There was no other option.

He must believe that Danu's moonstone had shown him the answer.

Steeling himself, he moved through his men, shouting encouragements as he sought out his second. Riggs was not hard to spot, being one of the largest in his army. He stood over a pair of wounded men, shield up, ready to defend them from more fire.

"Riggs! Lead twenty men around to the east. See that jutting rock? I need you to draw the dragon's attention beyond it." Far down the gorge's bank a slanting boulder leaned out over the slope.

Riggs nodded and used hand motions to get the attention of the healthy men around him. "Follow me! We're luring the beast that way!" He pointed east and threaded through to the back of the army to avoid the dragon's notice. A group of men followed.

Magnus made his way along the front line, dodging flame and ducking beneath archers' bows until he reached the boulder ahead of Riggs's party. The drop-off was steep here. It was not a suitable place for crossing, but crossing was not what he intended.

Crouching in the boulder's shadow, he watched Riggs lead his party at a run, as if they were attempting the crossing despite the unforgiving slope.

The dragon shrieked and flapped their way.

Magnus removed his helm so he would not be spotted. He kept his head down and used his ears to gauge the beast's nearness. When the telltale roar of flames sounded close by, he leapt upon the boulder.

The dragon hovered within leaping distance!

Magnus wasted no time assessing the health of Riggs's party. Knowing he had only this one chance, he threw his shield down and backed up to the very edge of the boulder.

As he ran toward the dragon, sword drawn, the thing shifted. It fixed its gaze to the west, as if spotting a new group of men trying to advance.

He no longer had a clear path to the creature's chest. *No!*

He had no time to abort the jump. The angle was wrong, but he made the leap anyway, pushing against the boulder with all his might. He launched into the air, sword drawn.

Danu, give me strength!

Just missing the tip of a flapping wing, he reached out and grabbed hold of a thick, scaled leg. With his sword in one hand, he scrambled for purchase, but could not get a secure hold. His sword fell and splashed into the river below.

Damnation!

At least he had two hands with which to grab hold. The pliable skin at the juncture of the dragon's leg and flank provided a handhold, but with his other arm, all he could do was squeeze the beast's thigh. He put his legs to work, wrapping them around the ankle.

Then they were soaring along the gorge.

The dragon shrieked, no doubt furious to have been taken off guard. Under Magnus's weight it listed toward the edge of the gorge. For a moment, he thought it would crash into his army, but it swiftly recovered.

Wings beating the air, the dragon angled upward. With Magnus clinging on, it climbed into the sky.

You are too late, said a voice in his head. He recognized the voice. It belonged to Hyrk. *Your children are no match for mine. You* are no match for *me. I will destroy you and your people and I will rule my Remnant while your goddess rots in a cell of her own making.*

"The only one who will rot is you, Hyrk!" He would end this abomination. He only needed to work out how.

Below, archers took aim, but no one fired. They would not endanger their king. No matter. Arrows were of little use here. It was up to him now and only him.

The dragon swooped and spun, trying to dislodge him.

Magnus would not be shaken. During hunts, he had clung to cliff sides with less to hold onto than he had at his disposal here. But he must do more than hold on. He must destroy an indestructible relic.

With all his might, he inched upward, testing how far he could reach while still maintaining hold of the dragon's leg. Not terribly far was the disappointing answer. With his sword, he might have had a chance at reaching the heart. But he no longer had his sword. All he had was a sheathed dagger and determination. While he would be able to slit the dragon's belly from where he clung, instinct told him only a direct hit to the heart would bring victory.

Hyrk's laughter rang in his head. The beast leveled off and angled toward the ground. *Take care, oh king! You do not want to slip and fall!*

Wind whipped Magnus's hair. His face burned with cold. A floating sensation took hold as the dragon dove toward the ground.

Weightlessness was replaced with a stomach-dropping surge that nearly had him losing consciousness. He bit his tongue to fight it. As they spun downward at dizzying speed, he realized something. If he were to release the dragon's leg in the moment before a dive, his momentum would carry him toward the beast's chest.

Near the ground, the dragon changed direction so suddenly Magnus's legs came loose. For a moment he flailed, but he regained his hold as they climbed again.

Almost threw you, Hyrk taunted. *Now I know where you are weakest. Say your prayers, Magnus.* Hyrk sneered his name while the ground grew more and more distant. *You are about to meet your maker.*

"You first!" he yelled. Lungs heaving, heart pounding, wind screaming in his ears, he drew his dagger and waited for the weightless feeling.

They were so high, he could easily see Mammoth in the distance. The trail they'd taken through the forest lay far beneath, appearing no wider than a hair even though they'd traversed it four-men wide. Midway between the forest and the gorge, a smudge on the snow appeared to be a herd of boar or wolves. But no. It was too large. With dread, he made sense of what he saw: the century he'd left with Danu and Anya.

No. Go back. Protect the women!

But he could shout no commands from here. He could do nothing but cling to the dragon with hands turning to ice.

His fist tightened on the hilt of his dagger. He gripped it so hard it felt fused to him.

Just when he thought his lungs would burst from the icy air, the dragon leveled out. It would begin its race toward the ground now.

He readied himself. There would be only one chance at this.

The dragon pointed its nose toward the ground, and that floating sensation billowed Magnus's shirt.

He fixed his eyes on the spot Danu's moonstone had shown him, dead center in the dragon's chest. The lone arrow still protruded, providing him a target.

I love you, My Goddess.

He let go of the dragon's leg.

The beast began its race toward the ground.

Magnus kicked off and willed himself toward that lone arrow.

Wind buffeted him. He hit the dragon's side and bounced away. A front leg came into view, and he grabbed it just before spinning out of reach. The dragon's heart was directly in front of him! And it glowed red beneath sallow skin.

Protect my people in my stead, he prayed. With every ounce of strength he possessed, he thrust his dagger deep.

It bit through thick, leathery skin and collided with something hard. The stone, he hoped, and not merely bone.

A red glare, like an angry sunset, punched from the dragon's chest. The beast shrieked.

He'd hit the stone! The heart!

But had it been enough?

Whether he'd done enough or not did not matter now. He could do no more. He had given his last bit of strength to defend his goddess and his people as best he could.

He would never sire an heir. The portrait above the queen's throne would never become reality. But if he'd done enough, his people would go on. The world would go on, and Danu would once again sit her heavenly throne.

He fell with the dragon, fist still fused to the seated dagger.

The beast's wings opened to catch the wind, but one wing crumpled. The dragon spun and twisted as they raced toward death.

The force of the fall wrenched Magnus away from the dragon, but before he released the dagger, he gave it a final twist. More red light poured from the wound.

For you, my love, he thought, and he opened his arms to his fate.

Chapter 31

FINALLY!

After hours of trudging through snow, Danu stepped from the forest into an open plain. No longer surrounded by trees, she could see Magnus's army in the distance. From here, they appeared no more than a grouping of black ants against the white ground. Still, the proof that they—and her king—were near enough to lay eyes on had her heart pounding.

Back at the cavern, Travis had told them about the Remnant, and about Vera's vehemence toward the children. It seemed Magnus's army might be up against more than a murderous demigod, but also a group of fierce cave-dwellers who longed for the extinction of wolfkind so they could rule the land. It had not taken much convincing for Verden to agree that he should lead his men to Magnus's aid. What *had* taken much convincing was that he allow *her* to come along.

At first, Verden had demanded she remain with Anya, Travis, and the handful of men he'd commanded to guard them. But when she'd refused and begun dressing herself—with Travis's help—in warm furs and boots found in the cavern, none of the men seemed willing to lay hands on her and force her obedience. So, with Verden scowling, and his men keeping their distance, she'd simply walked out of the caves behind them. Now, hours later and with aching but blessedly warm feet, she was moments away from laying eyes on Magnus.

Magnus, who had loved her last night with his whole body and heart. Magnus, who made *her* body soar and her heart rest with a wholeness she'd never felt before.

She couldn't bear to be apart from him any longer, and so she'd determined to find him and stand strong by his side while he faced Hyrk. He had her stone, true, but he did not have her eons of experience in dealing with the evil demigod. Her presence and council could mean the difference between him besting Hyrk or losing to him. She refused to allow Hyrk to win.

But something was wrong. As they neared the army, there seemed to be too much darkness on the ground, as if the snow had turned to ash…and as if fallen men lay scattered among those still standing.

"No!" she cried, running toward them. She was not the only one running. Verden's men raced ahead, swords drawn, battle cries slicing the air.

Death was an expected part of war. It should be no surprise to see men struck down in the midst of battle. But when there were so few wolfkind left, each one lost was a true tragedy. Even more distressing was the lack of a visible enemy. What had caused this charring? How had these men fallen?

Hand over her heart, she pushed her legs to carry her faster. Even as she searched for some sign of her king, she waited for the souls of the fallen warriors to seek their peace. They would enter her breast, and she would comfort them—each and every one—and see them through to their reward in the afterlife. She braced herself for them. She willed Magnus not to be among them.

But the souls did not come to her.

For two thousand years, her only connection to her people was to welcome their souls when they passed on from mortal life. It was the one thing that had remained the same in captivity as it had been in freedom. Now, it was gone.

The one who held her deity now held those brave souls. Seona. The wounded human who had nothing but bitterness for wolfkind.

Would Seona offer these souls kindness and comfort? Would she honor each one, treasure the moment each precious essence came into contact with her own?

No. She would not.

Fury and loss erupted from Danu in a scream as she reached the army and fell to her knees. All around her were men who had been burned, as if somehow the snow had caught fire. After tragically losing their lives in a battle that should have been hers alone—a battle she had set into motion with her stubborn pride—they would have no comfort. Perhaps they would not even receive their reward of heaven.

The tragedy of it was unthinkable, and yet it unfolded around her. *Death* was all around her.

But the destruction was not total. Many warriors still stood, including Verden's men. They held their weapons but they faced no opponent. A sloping bank dropped to what she assumed was a river, though the water was too low to be seen. Perhaps Hyrk was down there with the Remnant Travis had told them about.

But no. The men still standing were not peering into the ravine. They were looking to the sky.

She turned her face upward to see what captivated them, and her heart dropped to her stomach.

A great, red dragon with crumpled wings fell at great speed, and with it a single man. Her man.

"Magnus!"

While she watched in horror, her king and the dragon tumbled into the ravine. An almighty thud shook the ground. She cried out, voicing the agony of her shattered heart.

Just then, a dead man on the ground beside her moved. Fingers like charred wood gripped her arm like a vise. She tried to pull away, to run to her beloved, but the dead man held her fast. "Help me," he groaned.

§

DUFF PACED WITHIN his shadow, agitated, helpless.

Seona's cries for help intensified.

If she would not or could not let the souls pass, her agony was bound to grow even worse. What did that mean for the souls seeking rest? Would they linger in the mortal realm like ghosts? Remain with their bodies? He shuddered, not wishing such a fate on his worst enemy.

If only he and Seona were joined by Sacred Tradition already! They would be one. Her power would be his power, and her pain would be his pain. He could share in the suffering and lessen it for her. Perhaps he could even figure out how to send the souls through to where they belonged.

Of course! The bargain they'd made was to be wed in exchange for his freeing her. They had specified no timeline. There was no reason they could not speak the Sacred vows *before* she was free.

"I'll help you," he said. "But first, you must fulfill your end of the bargain. Repeat after me." He called to mind the enchanted vows of the Sacred Tradition.

Before he could say them, she screeched, "You bloody blighter!" She writhed in pain but was able to summon a tongue lashing for him. "You'll get my power then leave me. I knew you were no different from the rest—" Her words were cut off by a pained wail, as if even more souls were bombarding her.

Anger and sympathy warred in his chest. She was so jaded she mistook his intentions. "Seona, listen to me," he said firmly. "I'll not abandon you. I couldn't even if I wanted to. What I meant to say was that perhaps *I* can allow the souls to pass through. But *you* have to give me that power by saying the vows. Then I will share in your power, yes, but also in your pain. I will be able to help you."

The way she panted and wheezed concerned him. How much pain could she bear? She had the body of a goddess now, but a weakened one with a large portion of her power away from her in the mortal realm. What if the souls seeking rest became too much for her? He couldn't lose her so soon after finding her.

"Quickly. Repeat after me."

It seemed to cost her great effort to turn her head to study him—or his shadow. How he wished he could be more than a voice to her! He *would* be once they were joined. Danu's power, once inside him, would cause Arwan's curse to slough off like an old snake skin. He would be free from darkness at last, and the first to lay eyes on him in eons would be Seona.

"All right," she said, distress clear in her pinched voice. Her stomach jumped with her sharp breaths. "I'll do…anything."

"By the holy and perfect Sacred Tradition," he began, quickly but clearly.

She repeated after him.

He released a breath he hadn't known he was holding. Relief filled him at her cooperation. This would work. It had to.

"Good. Now say, By the Way of All Things."

She uttered the words between whimpers.

"I Seona of the mortal realm," he said, and she repeated. "In the body of the Goddess Danu…Bind myself to Duff, Lord of Darkness, Cursed of the Fae."

Seona faltered. "Bind myself to—*och!* I canna! 'Tis too much!"

"Say it," he urged. "Say it and mean it, and then I can help you." He grabbed the bars, heedless of his sizzling flesh.

She ground out the words.

"For now and evermore," he finished.

She repeated the last of the incantation, and he uttered his side of the vows as quickly as possible.

Heat like a shot of whisky bloomed behind his breastbone. His body bowed, and he felt a tug, like a cord going taut between him and Seona. It worked!

He had not been sure it would. The cold-iron bars between them might have created a barrier to the magic. But it had not. They were well and truly joined.

Seona was his wife, and he her husband. They were one.

Duff, Lord of Darkness, Cursed of the Fae was a bachelor no more.

He was a god.

The scent of burning flesh came from his hands, where they'd fused to the bars. With a shout of pain, he wrenched his charred flesh away. The wounds would heal, but slowly—or perhaps not so slowly. While he watched, the skin mended itself. The wounds on his wrist faded as well.

He only marveled at the speedy healing for a moment before a hundred invisible javelins slammed into his chest at once. With the pain came flashes of happy family meals, joyful celebrations, times of mourning, and tranquil moments. Wolfkind souls trying to leave the mortal realm.

Too many faces, settings, and emotions assaulted him, and they kept coming. It felt as though the very fabric of his very mind were expanding to contain the memories of these souls, and by the realms, it *hurt*.

The pain blinded him. It wiped his mind of all but agony. Falling to his hands and knees, he forced himself to remember what he'd been trying to do. Ah! He must allow the souls to pass through to the afterlife.

He tried. As he did when using his Fae powers, he concentrated on what he wanted to happen. He imagined the souls moving from his body into heavenly light. Mentally, he made a focused beam of his new power and willed it to assist the souls.

It didn't work.

He kept trying, and it kept not working. What was he doing wrong?

While he'd never been a god before, he was no stranger to power. As a Fae, he could sift through space and time with no more than a concentrated thought. He could create illusions by simply imagining what he wanted others to see. Why couldn't he do this?

Before he could conceive of an answer, the dungeon around them shook. Rock began falling from the walls. The bars of Seona's cell shuddered then crumbled to dust. The torches around the dungeon flickered out, and they were plunged into darkness. Into shadow, where he could move freely.

Long adapted to darkness, his eyes adjusted in an instant. As soon as he spotted Seona, he dashed to her and scooped her to him. He curled around her so the rocks falling from the ceiling would not hurt her.

A sudden flash of light blinded him. A crack of thunder deafened him. Then all was quiet.

Chapter 32

A SCREAM STUCK in Danu's throat.

Her lover had just fallen to his death alongside a *dragon*, and a dead warrior now beseeched her for aid. Her head spun. She could not make sense of it all. It was too much.

"Help me," the dead man said again, but he was not dead. Somehow, he still lived despite obviously fatal wounds.

"I—I'm sorry," she told him. She wished she *could* help, but there was nothing she could do. As a mortal, she had no power to heal wounds. Even as a goddess, her healing powers must be tempered with the laws set forth by The Sacred Way of All Things. Miracles, such as healing the gravely wounded, were to be rare events, and The Sacred Way must be consulted beforehand.

Charred fingers crackled as they squeezed her arm. The man's wild eyes pinned her in place. His agony was clear.

"I'm so sorry. I wish I could ease your pain." Aching for him, she covered his hand with hers. It was all she could do.

Why was this man's moonsoul still in his ruined body? He should be welcomed into the afterlife with all the comfort and praise befitting a fallen warrior. Even within Hyrk's cell, Seona should still have this one power. Or did she not know how to use it?

Of course! Of course Seona would not know how to care for moonsouls. *No* mortal would know how. Now those souls were trapped in their bodies. How many fine men lay suffering when they should have found their eternal rest?

Panic seized her. "Magnus!" His broken body was beyond the riverbank, out of sight. He must be in as much agony as this poor man.

"I'm sorry," she told the burned man. "I have to—" Before she could finish, thunder sounded.

The sky was not dark enough for a storm. Still, the clap was so loud it nearly deafened her. A flash of brilliant light surrounded her. She slammed her eyes closed against it, and when she opened them, she found herself separated from the warrior and standing within a transparent sphere. She instantly recognized it. This was one of the globes her father favored for observing the affairs of mortals.

Growing up, she would often run into his study and throw herself onto his welcoming lap. Out the window would be a shimmering sea of such globes stretching as far as the horizon and beyond. Her father would summon one forward, and it would hover within the window frame. He would explain its contents, sometimes a small scene involving a single mortal, sometimes a group of mortals, sometimes an entire kingdom or empire. With a loving but firm hand, he would touch the surface of the globe, and things would change inside. A mortal would fall to his knees in worship, a family would rejoice at a child's healing, a battle would tip toward one side.

Never did she imagine *she* would occupy one of his globes.

At once, she was overcome with shame. Her face heated, knowing her father saw every detail of this disaster. Her realm had fallen into such disarray that the most powerful and ancient member of The Sacred Way had come to—to what?

She could think of only one reason her father would pull her out of mortal time and deposit her within a globe for his scrutiny. She had proven her complete and utter inability to care for the realm The Sacred Way had entrusted to her. She had shown she was not capable of wielding the Sacred power of Creation. Her father had come to take it away from her. He had come to punish her.

Cheeks wet, she fell to her knees. "I'm so sorry." She hung her head. "*So* sorry." She could say no more. Her throat closed with regret.

"Daughter." Her father's calm voice made her tears fall faster.

She'd only wanted to make him proud, to show him how much she'd learned and how devoted she would be to her realm, her tiny little corner of the created universe.

She kept her head low, too ashamed to show her face.

"Danu, my fierce princess. Look at me." His kind, loving tone made it worse. She'd rather he lose his temper with her. She deserved his wrath.

Every millimeter she raised her eyes was a battle. She did not want to be seen. She did not want to be *known*. She never thought she'd long for the solitude of Hyrk's dungeon, but she did now. She wanted to hide. Like a coward.

No. I shall face my father like the goddess I am—or was. I will take responsibility for this mess.

Gulping down a hot lump of shame, she tilted her face to the sun. The brilliant orb broke through the wintry clouds and shone with her father's glory. She could not look directly at it, her mortal eyes weak. Instead, she kept her face upturned, but closed her eyes.

"Father," she said, and she rose to her feet, chin jutting.

From the sky, her father smiled upon her. She did not see it, but she felt it. Her whole body warmed as if she rested on the shores of Faerie without a care in the world.

"I am ready for my punishment," she said, bracing herself for her father's displeasure now that the greetings were over with.

The air around her cooled, and she imagined her father's frown tucked within the frame of his pure-white beard. "Does the vixen punish her kit for escaping the talons of the eagle?" he asked.

She frowned. "No. Of course not. But if I am the young fox you speak of, I have escaped nothing. Hyrk has won." She motioned to the bank, to all the dead men. Her aching heart pulsed with the knowledge of what lay in the river behind her, Magnus's body, possibly with his moonsoul still locked within, every bit as helpless as she had been in Hyrk's dungeon. "I have allowed the eagle to terrorize my people. To all but extinguish them. I have failed you." She ducked her head, unable to face her father's glory while she built the case against herself. She had lived for millennia, but disappointing her father made her feel like a child again.

He sighed. The wind of his breath stirred the locks of her hair. "My sweet Danu. Always longing to please. Striving for perfection."

"I am a goddess," she said. "Or I was." Her inexplicable presence within a mortal body was yet another reason to be embarrassed. "I am supposed to be perfect."

"Darling daughter, the only one to have ever expected perfection from you is *you*. To me, you are perfect in *who* you are and in the *love* you put forth in all you do. There is no other kind of perfection that matters."

Her heart wanted to soften at his words, but she did not allow the softness. Could her father not see the devastation around her? Did he not realize it had all begun when she'd accepted Hyrk's wager?

"I suspect Magnus would disagree with you," she said. If she had lived up to the perfection she expected of herself, he would be alive and well.

"Not so. Your Magnus would be the first to agree with me." The air around her warmed. "He also considers you perfect just as you are."

She snorted. "Perfect? In this human body? While my creation crumbles around me?" Tears leaked from her eyes. She swiped at them angrily. "It does not matter what he would have thought, anyway. He's gone—or nearly so." And she could not even welcome his soul into heaven. He deserved so much better.

"You sound so certain, daughter. Is there no room in your heart for hope?"

She scoffed. Hope? For two thousand years, she'd hoped for rescue, and when it had seemed to come, it was nothing but a stepping stone to more devastation.

"Perhaps, once," she said. "But I have learned that hope is an illusion, an unmet expectation. A goddess does not hope. A goddess *acts*. But my actions only result in death."

"Sweet, sweet Danu. My princess. I did not think it was possible to be disappointed in you. Until now." Her stomach shriveled. "You have learned a lesson, my daughter, but the wrong lesson."

Finally, he would voice his displeasure. She waited for it. She deserved it.

"Turn around," he said, surprising her.

Dread was a weight around her neck. If she turned, she would see Magnus's body. Would there be suffering in his eyes, or would they stare at the sky emptily? She did not want to look, but she must. Her father's commands were to be obeyed.

Chin trembling, she turned, and was instantly overwhelmed with all she saw.

Duff, with his raven hair and flawless skin visible in the full light of day, crouched protectively over *her*—or Seona, rather, in her body. Seona was no longer in Hyrk's dungeon. *She* was no longer in Hyrk's dungeon! "How—" she started to ask, but stopped when she realized the two were frozen in time, as was everything in the mortal realm.

If that was not startling enough, beyond Duff and Seona, there should have been a dragon lying in the river, but instead, Hyrk was splayed out on the rocks with water cascading over him. His blood-red hair lay limp across his brow and clung to his cheek. In the center of his chest was a gory crater with a dagger jutting from it.

Beside Hyrk, where Magnus's body should be, was her king. Not dead, not broken, but frozen above the water in the moment before impact.

She lunged toward him, clawing at the wall of the globe. "Magnus! Magnus! I thought—" A sob shuddered from her chest. He hadn't hit the ground. The thud she'd heard must have been from the dragon—who appeared to have been Hyrk. "Oh, father!" She whirled to face her father, squinting at his glory. The wetness in her eyes this time was from relief. "You stopped his fall."

His radiant smile filled her with light and happiness. "I did," he said, and she heard a note of mischief in his voice. "Why have I chosen this moment, my princess?"

How many times had she heard that question while sitting on his lap? He was quizzing her now, just like back then. The difference was that now *she* stood inside one of his globes.

Just like back then, she desperately wished to impress him. So she took great care in studying everything around her. The warriors on the bank, Hyrk, her sweet Magnus, whose peaceful face looked up at the sky, as if he accepted what was about to happen.

Hyrk must have taken on a dragon's form. The only reason she could think of for Magnus and Hyrk to fall from the sky at the same time, was if they had battled.

The dagger in Hyrk's chest. The peace on Magnus's handsome face.

Realization dawned. Her king had bested her enemy!

Her gaze fell to the dagger. She recognized the handle, having seen it in her king's hand earlier, when Duff had surprised them in Magnus's chamber. Somehow, he'd destroyed Hyrk's gemstone! He had defeated Hyrk!

She was truly free! Hyrk would harm her people no more!

Magnus had given his life to conquer her enemy. Her chest burned with love and gratitude. How she wanted to go to him and throw her arms around him!

But her father waited for an answer. She forced herself to concentrate on the question: *why this moment?* There was something here that could spark change in her realm. She was determined to find it.

She considered Duff and Seona. When Hyrk had died, his dungeon would have been rendered useless. That explained their presence here in her realm. It was what they had planned, after all, for her and Seona to be together so—so they could each return to their true forms.

Her insides went cold as the answer became clear.

"I am to make a choice," she said. "And that choice will determine what happens to Magnus."

His skin shimmered with warmth. "Perceptive, as always, my daughter. Tell me, what choice do you face?"

She swallowed the lump in her throat. "Whether I wish to return to my true form."

A few days ago, returning to her true form had been a foregone conclusion. She simply *must* return. She was a goddess. Her place was to rule over, protect, and bless her people. There was no choice involved. It simply *was.*

But in this moment, faced with actually returning to her deity… Heavens! She did not want to. She was not ready to leave.

She had only just begun to experience her realm as *part* of that creation rather than its overseer. Anya's friendship brought her happiness. Embracing children brought her joy. Attending kingdom celebrations brought her a sense of community she had never before known. Taking a mortal lover brought her tender intimacy that ran so much deeper than physical pleasure.

The temptation to remain mortal was strong. But how else could she mend all that had gone wrong except to return to her true form? How else could she ensure the safety of the children, who still faced a vicious enemy? How else could she bless her people beyond measure as recompense for all they had suffered? How else could she save Magnus's life?

"Why do you give me this choice when it shouldn't be a choice at all? I cannot abandon my people. There is no other decision I can make but to return to them as their goddess."

"You think living among them, serving as their queen, would be abandoning them?"

Their *queen?* Her father made it sound as if Magnus would live, even if she chose to remain mortal. Otherwise, Anya would be queen to Riggs's king. A glimmer of hope lit her heart like a sliver of sunshine.

"You would save him for me?"

"How could I not?" was his answer.

"But—but this is *my* realm. My responsibility." The Sacred Way was clear that a Creator god or goddess was, alone, responsible for ruling their realm. Other deities were not permitted to interfere. This rule had protected her people from Hyrk's whims, forcing her enemy to great lengths in his attempted overthrow. But what had been meant as a protection for mortals had often made her feel lonely. Even before Hyrk's dungeon, truth be told, she had longed for someone to discuss important mortal matters with, to rule at her side.

The only way to have someone like that would be to enact the Sacred Tradition, but no deity had ever made her wish to marry before.

The sun's brightness shifted from side to side, as if her father slowly shook his head. The clouds darkened except for where his glory pierced them. Fat raindrops pattered on the globe.

"You truly believe you must do it all on your own?" her father said. "That you cannot ask for help from time to time? How it saddens me that you do not call out to your father in your distress!

Two thousand years in prison, and you never once asked for my help. Still, when your beloved's mortal life is at stake, you do not appeal to me. You are grown. You have your own people—your own responsibilities. But am I not still your father? Do I not still love you? Can I not give you gifts of help when you are in need?"

Rain turned to pouring. Her father grieved, and nature wept with him.

She grieved. Her father's sadness overwhelmed her. And what he'd said—she hadn't *known*. She'd always assumed that possessing the power of Creation meant she was on her own. It had never occurred to her to ask for help.

She crumbled to the floor of the globe. Sobs racked her entire body as she understood what her father was saying. He would have helped—if only she had asked.

"I—I'm so sorry! I never thought—I never—" She could hardly speak for the regret crushing her chest. "Oh, Father, I have been so proud. I wanted to prove to you that I was capable. But all I proved was how stubborn I am. I am so sorry!"

He remained silent as she cried out her agony. When her tears finally subsided, she said, "You would have helped me? Even in Hyrk's dungeon?"

"Oh, daughter." The rain stopped, and the darkest clouds rolled back. "I *did* help you."

With his words came Duff's image. He had come to her when she'd summoned him, even though she had not been certain her summons would work within the cell of cold-iron. Her moonstone had found its way from Duff to Anya to Magnus and back to her again, completing its circle of power. Her father had done it, she realized. He'd done all of it. Sending Duff to her in Magnus's chamber, bringing her and Anya to Magnus's camp on the other side of Mammoth.

Her heart skipped a beat as she realized what else her father had done.

"It was you! When Seona fell from the cliff, it was *you* who made us swap places." Her father had been nudging her fate all along. He had sent her into her realm to live as a mortal. "You sent me to Magnus." Her mind filled with the image of the portrait over the second throne, the one of Seona holding the fair-haired child. "You gave him that vision all those years ago." It all made sense now! All the things she could not have done because she was in that cell. It hadn't been *her* power working through her moonstone but her *father's* power.

Her gaze cut to Magnus. For the first time, she realized he had his fist curled around something, something connected to his neck by a bejeweled chain.

Relief and laughter bubbled within her like the bright refreshment of ambrosia.

"Yes. It was my power," her father said, as if he had read her thoughts. "I helped you then. And I will help you now. This man, this king, has given his life for you. What kind of father would I be if I do not rescue my daughter's rescuer, my daughter's husband, when it is in my power to do so? When his living would ensure your happiness?"

"Husband?" Had she heard him correctly? "But we are not wed," she blurted.

"Your moonsoul says differently."

Her moonsoul? But that most essential part of her would only declare her wed if she shared a lifemate bond with Magnus. Her breath caught.

"Last night!" she said in a rush. "It happened last night! We became lifemates!" It had been a full moon. She'd only known because Magnus had postponed the lottery drawing that normally occurred on the night of the full moon. That explained the extraordinary lovemaking. It hadn't been because of the mortal body she inhabited but because of her moonsoul joining with that of the man meant for her and her alone.

The sun burst through the clouds, accompanied by waves of warmth. "Yes, my darling. You are no longer my princess. You are Magnus's queen. You are his moonsoul and he is yours."

I am his lifemate. And he is mine. I am wed!

"You are joined now," her father said. "You need each other. Which is why you must know this before you choose. If you return to your throne in heaven, he will suffer and eventually waste away in your absence. If you choose deity, it would be kinder to allow him to perish now. But if you choose mortality, I will bless you. Both of you. And I will guide and help the united pair who will rule over your realm in your stead."

Her head spun. Because she and Magnus were lifemates, returning to her heavenly throne would hurt him. Her choice was becoming clearer and clearer. But what had her father just said? "United pair?"

His glory shone in a beam onto Duff and Seona, and instantly, they moved. Duff straightened, his sculpted, perfectly handsome face taut with worry. How she had missed his face! What a joy it was to see him in the light of day!

Within the protective circle of Duff's arms, Seona rose to her full height, which nearly matched Duff's. Blood stained her knees beneath the hem of her shift, but the wounds healed before Danu's eyes. The crystal-blue eyes that used to stare back at her in the mirror searched the globe.

"Wha—what has happened?" she said in her burred accent. Grabbing onto Duff's arm, she looked at him, and her jaw fell open. "Why, you're—you're perfection!"

He bowed his head to her, his affection clear.

They looked beautiful together. A statuesque goddess with flowing blond hair and a dark, winsome Faerie. *United pair.* Duff and Seona must have enacted the Sacred Tradition. How interesting!

Duff noticed the globe surrounding them all. He gasped when he saw Magnus and Hyrk. When he at last spotted Danu, he grinned.

"Well, you don't see that every day," he said.

"Duff," she said on a joyful laugh, and she stepped to him. He leaned down so she could kiss his cheek.

Seona's shoulders tightened. Her nostrils flared.

"Easy, love," Duff said, jostling his new wife affectionately. "Just a friendly greeting."

Danu smiled so wide her cheeks hurt. "It is good to *see* you."

Duff's laughter tinkled around them.

"Deity suits you," she said. He had always been impeccably beautiful, but he positively glowed now.

The grin fell from his lips. "About that," he said. "I did it because of the souls. Seona could not let them through, and I thought, if I shared her power I could help—"

She interrupted him. "I am not angry. Perhaps I would have been before. But not now. I believe congratulations are in order."

He blinked with surprise. Then, typical of the Fae, he recovered quickly. Sniffing the air, he said, "Likewise, I'm sure." He could detect the lifemate scent on her when she couldn't detect in on herself.

Her heart smiled, but the joy quickly faded as the fate of those souls and the children in the fortress pressed at her.

"Father?" She would take his words to heart. When she needed help, she would ask for it, starting now.

Before she could speak, her father said, "I know, my darling. Do not worry for them. All will be set right." Her father knew her heart before she could voice what she needed. He never ceased to amaze her.

The tension in her chest relaxed. Her father would ensure those warrior souls received the peace they deserved. While she had no trust whatsoever for Seona, she did trust that Duff would rule her realm justly.

Heavens! It seemed she had made her choice.

"Thank you, Father," she said. "For everything." Gratefulness filled her heart for all he had done and all he had taught her.

A gentle pressure around her shoulder was his embrace. "You are my daughter," was his reply.

She wept, but this time, they were happy tears. When she wiped them away and could see clearly again, she blinked in surprise. Magnus stood in front of her, brows drawn together in confusion.

"Oh, Magnus!" she cried, and she threw her arms around him. "Oh, I love you! I love you so much!"

He nearly fell backward at her assault, but his strong legs kept them upright. His arms closed around her. "Danu? My beloved?" He felt her face and head with trembling hands. "Am I—?"

"You're alive!" she said, laughing and crying at the same time. And she could say no more, because her lips were kissing every inch of his face.

He received her affection in shocked silence, his gaze intense on her, his grip on her waist almost painful in its tightness.

A sudden thought made her reel back. She hadn't yet told her father her choice. She faced the sun over Magnus's shoulder. "I have changed my mind," she said with a smile. "I wish to remain right here."

Frowning, and still somewhat bewildered looking, Magnus peered over his shoulder, no doubt seeking the one she addressed.

"To whom do you speak?" he asked, gaze roving over the clear casing of the globe. With one hand—a steady hand this time—he reached out to touch its surface. A ripple started at his fingertip and spread over the entire surface like the pattern made by a rock in a calm pool.

"No, your mind has not changed," her father said. "You made your decision before I appeared." With those words, the heather-gray sky closed up around the sun, blotting it from view.

Chapter 33

Battle-lust thundered in Magnus's veins. Or perhaps it was the shock of falling from a league above the Earth alongside a mythical dragon and *not* hitting the ground, but instead finding himself within a floating sphere that seemed neither solid nor liquid but something in between. If that were not strange enough, he was not alone in the sphere. His lifemate should be leagues away safe in the caves, but here she was, shining her smile on him. And then there were the two figures bathed in light looking on.

Danu had assured him he was alive, but he could hardly believe it. "How is this possible?" He smoothed his hands over her face and hair, assuring himself she was hale. "How are you in my arms? What—" He indicated the sphere with a lift of his chin. "Is all this?" Beyond the sphere, his army was frozen. Not because of the cold, but stopped in place as if they were children's toys in need of winding.

Danu gazed at him with tears shimmering in her eyes. A bubbling laugh parted her lips. "My father has helped us," she said and kissed him again. Her mouth on his obliterated all thoughts except those centering on his love for her.

He wrapped her in his arms more securely than any cloak and tasted of her. This woman was pure decadence. The blood that raced in his veins from battle now heated with new purpose, but that purpose could not be fulfilled.

Reluctantly, he set her away from him. "Hyrk?"

"Dead." She peered into the ravine beneath their feet. Half-covered in flowing water was a man dressed in black with hair the color of blood. His eyes stared lifelessly to the sky. His chest was an empty crater, and jutting from its center was Magnus's dagger. "He must have found an immense source of power to become a dragon. But you were more powerful, my king." She stood on her toes to kiss him again. "My brave, dragon-slaying king."

He welcomed the kiss, but his stomach dropped like a stone as he realized who the figures must be. Forehead pressed to Danu's, he cut his gaze to the glowing pair. "Seona and your friend, Duff," he said. He squeezed his eyes shut. "It is time to let you go."

His chest rent in two. How would he bear his lifemate returning to her heavenly form? Hands in fists, he cursed himself for bedding her the night before. Now they would both suffer. But Danu would not suffer to the point of death, as he likely would. She would be a goddess, after all. Her power would soothe the ache of being without her lifemate.

He cupped her jaw and looked deep into her whisky-brown eyes. From this day forward, it would be Seona behind those eyes. He did not know how he would be able to look at the human without stabbing regret. He comforted himself with the knowledge that Danu would be above them all, ruling and blessing them. "How I wish—" His throat closed around a lump of regret. "The portrait," he said. "I wish—"

"Oh, Magnus," her lips landed again and again on his cheeks and beard. "I am staying," she said, and he was sure he'd heard her wrong. "I am staying." She repeated the words each time she kissed him, and slowly, he began to trust his ears.

"You're staying. Here with me?"

Her smile was radiant as she said, "Yes, Magnus, my lifemate."

Every part of his body went still. "But—" He licked his dry lips and nodded to Seona and Duff. "Then why are they here?"

"Because I had a choice to make." Her teeth caught her plump lower lip then released it. Her smile was tentative.

A choice. She had mentioned her father, who must also be a deity. Duff and Seona were here, as they had planned. Had she been given the choice whether to return to her true form?

"You chose…me?" He frowned. "But you are needed on your throne. Our people need you."

She held his face in both her hands. "They'll have me. I'll be on my throne, the one beside yours."

His heart stuttered behind his breastplate as he fell into her solemn gaze. Her words were too wonderful to be believed.

He looked to Duff and Seona. They shone so brightly he could not look directly at them. "What about Seona?" The two figures were nearly of a height. The slightly shorter one shifted on its feet. He assumed that one was Seona. He inclined his head to her. "You would give up your mortal body for Danu?"

"'Tis no hardship for me," the being said. Her voice hummed like a hive of bees if the bees could harmonize with each other. The sound was strange. Powerful. And underneath the otherness of it was the burr he associated with Anya. "If she wants that old thing, she can have it."

The taller of the figures put an arm around the shorter. "What she means to say is, thank you, Blessed Goddess for the unprecedented, unfathomable gift of deity. I will cherish it always and use this power for the good of the wolfkind people. And what *I* wish to say is this: Dearest Danu, friend of my heart, it is good to see you happy. Truly happy. As I cared for your moonstone, I will care for your realm. I will only ever be a summons away."

Waves of light shivered around the pair as they exited the sphere.

Magnus watched them float to the bank, where Duff guided Seona among the wounded. Where they walked, men shed their charred skin, and new skin was revealed underneath. Those who had fallen to the dragon's fire rose up to stand with their frozen companions. To a man, they peered around, bewildered. None seemed to see Duff and Seona, only the effects the pair had as they left healing in their wake.

The sphere moved. It lifted them out of the gorge and set them on the bank.

Magnus could scarcely believe what he was seeing. His army was whole again. Not a single man lay on the ground, even though the melted snow and charred ground remained as evidence of Hyrk's deadly fire. As Magnus looked up and down the bank, he could no longer see Duff and Seona. They were gone.

The wall of the sphere turned to mist and dispersed. At the same moment, the frozen men continued their halted motions, as if they'd never been stopped.

Battle cries rent the air. All around them, raised swords wavered and lowered as his army realized a miracle had occurred.

He gathered Danu close, using his body to protect her amidst all the blades. He trusted his men, but they had experienced the inexplicable. There was no telling how they might react in their shock.

"Lower your arms!" he shouted. "Sheath your swords! The dragon is slain! But the battle is not over!" His recent vision hit him with the weight of a boulder. "The children are under attack at the fortress!"

Murmurs replaced the battle cries. Every set of eyes turned toward the far bank.

Verden pushed through the men. "You know about the Remnant, Sire?" His brow furrowed with confusion.

"I do," he said, but there was no time to explain. There was no time to celebrate his lifemate union with his beloved. Or Danu's choice to remain by his side.

He looked to his beloved, ready to explain he must leave her temporarily. But she spoke first. "Lead them," she said, and she stepped out of his arms and moved next to Verden.

Verden glared at her. Clearly, he was not happy she had come with him and his men. "I'll take my punishment when this is over, Sire. And I'll remain with Lady Seona while you go to the fortress."

He wanted to correct Verden. This precious woman was not Seona any longer. She was their goddess, come to be with them in human form. And he was not about to hold Verden accountable for her presence, when she had so clearly needed to be here. But time was of the essence. All that would have to wait.

"Take her back to the caves," he told Verden. He kissed Danu, then jumped onto the boulder jutting over the gorge. Pointing across it with his sword, he rallied his men. "The children are under attack from a group of two dozen Larnians!" He based his guess on what he remembered from the vision. "We far outnumber them!" he called to his men, meeting several pairs of eyes. "We will capture and contain them. They shall not be harmed unless they put up a fight." He knew precious little about this Remnant and planned to make every attempt to broker peace between them. Running in with swords flying would not help them toward that end. "Absolutely no Larnian is to be killed. This is the word of your king." He looked over his army, pleased to see his men nod their understanding.

Riggs shouldered through the men and held out a sword, hilt first. It was *his* sword, the one he had dropped when he'd leapt onto the dragon.

"My thanks, friend," he said, taking it. Beyond Riggs, he spotted Verden's back as he shepherded Danu to safety. Content she would be out of harm's way, he pointed his sword across the gorge and hollered, "To the fortress!"

§

THE HEAVY-TIMBER DOORS were already open, Magnus saw, as he broke through the trees and into the shadow of the fortress. The wind had picked up, and rain would soon fall from the swollen clouds overhead. On the wind, voices carried from within the two-story structure. He had expected screams.

Curious, he slowed and motioned his men to quiet their steps as they approached.

"Stand down, Braeden," someone said. He recognized the voice as belonging to the red-haired woman.

The command was answered with a growl. A wolf's growl.

Fear for the children made a band around his chest. His hunting wolves were tame, but even they were not trusted to be near the children. Wolves were dangerous. Bloodthirsty. Wolves had no conscience.

He stepped quickly but quietly to the open door and peered within. His men hung back and to the sides so as not to be seen.

The woman, red-haired as in his vision, aimed a crossbow at a group of a dozen children huddled near the fireplace along the right wall. Between her deadly arrow and the future of wolfkind, stood a lanky, reddish-brown wolf. It bared its teeth at the woman, seemingly protecting the children.

At the far end of the hall, the scene repeated itself. A second group of children, perhaps fifteen of them, hugged each other on a raised platform. A similar number of cloaked figures with monstrous faces had the children cornered, but a single white wolf snarled and snapped at any of the figures who dared make a move toward the children.

Between the two groups of children, Magnus estimated they were nearly all accounted for, but that was little comfort considering the danger they faced. If not for those two wolves, they would likely be much worse off than they appeared.

He motioned two of his commanders forward and used gestures to indicate they should watch and listen as the woman addressed the wolf.

"They'll grow up to be enemies," she said, chin lifted. "They're outsiders."

The wolf growled and widened its stance, making it clear he was not deterred by her words—and why would he be? He was a wild animal. But then again, Magnus had never heard of wild wolves protecting wolfkind. The raised hairs on the back of his neck told him there was more going on here than met the eye.

The woman huffed. "Be reasonable, Braeden. They're only going to die anyway. They'll grow old and perish like the rest of them. If we kill them now, we'll be able to come out that much sooner. Don't you see? This is a wonderful opportunity for us. We can leave the caves earlier than anticipated."

Magnus had heard enough. "Halt!" he called into the great hall. "Drop your arms! You are surrounded by a thousand Maranners." He stepped through the doors, and motioned his men to spread out within the hall. They poured inside like swarming ants and disarmed the cloaked figures. "The wolves are not to be harmed!" he said for the benefit of those who hadn't witnessed the way they protected the children.

The woman wheeled on him, crossbow raised, but he struck it to the ground with his sword. "None of that, now," he chided, and he kicked the weapon toward one of his soldiers. The man picked it up and disarmed it, tossing the arrow to the flagstones.

The woman shook her hand as if wounded. He did not mind causing a woman pain if she was about to murder children.

One of his commanders and Riggs captured her, each pinning an arm behind her back.

Chin jutting defiantly, she met his glare. The woman seemed to have no fear.

He studied her while his men brought order to the hall. She was tall and lean. Her eyes were a pale blue that unsettled him for their resemblance to the icy gaze of King Bantus. Bantus was the only Larnian king he'd known personally, but rumor had it that many royals had demonstrated this trait. Her hair was thick and bright, youthful. Her skin was ivory. Her features were strong yet feminine. If she hadn't been practically snarling at him, he might have found her beautiful.

Where have you been hiding? He wondered. *Are there more like you?*

But he kept the questions to himself for the moment. There was much to see to before he could safely interview her, including checking on the children and ensuring the wolves did not harm anyone.

"Sire." A commander came forward. "All the children are accounted for except one. No one knows where Alexander is. I've sent a party to search the fortress."

"Sire! Over here!" another man shouted. The call came from the platform. "It's Ruben! He's hit!"

Alexander would have to wait.

Magnus ran to the platform, a rough dais that looked to have been hastily built from mismatched bits of wood. Jumping up, he met the eyes of the white wolf—a shewolf, judging by her size—who was pacing and huffing with agitation. She too had the silvery eyes of Larnian royalty.

Five of his men, two of whom he recognized as handlers of his personal hunting wolves, had her surrounded. Handler Kell had squatted onto his haunches and murmured soothing words to the shewolf. The other wolf was surrounded as well, but he sat patiently with his tongue lolling out of his toothy mouth.

Beyond the ring of men around the white wolf, Magnus found a group of wide-eyed children. He had much to tell them, but Ruben needed help first.

Magnus spotted the man who had called for him, a medic by training, and a fine soldier by the name of Derrik. He knelt by the side of a prone form with dark hair. Ruben. The warriors standing over the boy parted to let him through.

"By Danu," he hissed. A compact arrow, like the one that had been disarmed from the woman's crossbow, stuck up from Ruben's throat. A thin trickle of blood leaked from the hole. Ruben blinked, and Magnus's chest relaxed a fraction to know the boy was still alive.

He looked to Kell. "What do you need?"

Kell licked dry lips and said, "If I pull it, he will bleed out. See this?" He indicated a bluish section of swollen skin beneath the wound. "Blood is collecting here. It means the artery's been hit." He swallowed and stood to face Magnus. "I'm sorry, Sire. I cannot help him. And I'm afraid he doesn't have much time."

Everything else in the hall became irrelevant. Only Ruben mattered. This precious child, this nineteen-year-old young man who still had six years left before entering training, had done nothing more than run away with his peers in hopes of carving out a more secure future for himself, and this had been his reward. No. This could not be happening. It could not.

"Do something," he urged Kell, but the medic only shook his head sadly.

In days past, he would have knelt right there and prayed. But he was uncertain to whom he should pray. Danu was not on her throne. Duff and Seona were. Would they hear him if he prayed?

"Let me through," he heard someone say. In his state of denial over Ruben's state, it took him a moment to recognize the voice. Danu!

He turned to find her rushing onto the platform with Verden and some of his men at her side.

"She would not take no for an answer," Verden said. "She's our—" He looked equal parts annoyed and admiring— "Queen," he finished. "I could not bring myself to lay hands on her and stop her." A blush colored the skin above his beard, and Magnus understood how the commander had reached the conclusion: Danu carried the lifemate scent.

Danu gave him no time to scold her for putting herself in harm's way. She rushed to Ruben's side. For one heart-breaking moment, her face twisted with grief, but the expression cleared. She turned her face up to the ceiling and shouted, "Duff! We need you!"

In the next heartbeat, brilliant light filled the hall, and two figures appeared on the platform. The white wolf whimpered. Everyone in the hall seemed to gasp at once. Warm wind swirled around him, lifting the hair off his shoulders, twisting Danu's long hair into graceful walnut-colored ropes that licked at her face.

Ruben's hair stirred, black tufts sweeping at his brow. Before Magnus's eyes, the purple skin of the boy's throat turned to its natural color. The arrow inched out as the hole filled in. When the arrow clattered to the wood, Danu used her hand to wipe the blood away. Aside from the grisly red smear, Ruben looked unblemished. It was as if the wound had never been.

"It's a miracle," someone said.

"Ruben?" Danu said. "Ruben, can you hear me?"

Kell helped the boy sit.

Ruben sucked in a deep, shuddering breath. With shaking hands, he felt his neck and throat. "I was—I was—"

"Shhh," Danu soothed. "You're all right, now."

He stared at her, blinking, mouth opening and closing, as if he couldn't quite make sense of things yet.

Kell patted his back. "You've been healed, son," he said. "The arrow's gone."

Another warrior picked it up and inspected it. "It's the same as the ones in the woman's quiver," he told Magnus.

He nodded at the warrior, then squatted to look into Ruben's pale face. "All right, Ruben?" He looked back and forth between the boy's eyes, pleased to see understanding start to dawn. Ruben grew even paler as he spotted the two glowing figures.

"Meet your new goddess," Danu said to the bewildered boy. "Seona, Ruler of Wolfkind. And her mate, Duff, Lord of Light."

Duff and Seona stepped to the front of the platform. Their glory flooded the hall as if they were twin suns. Magnus could not look directly at them. He had to slit his eyes to tolerate the brilliance. From beneath his lower lids, he watched every Maranner in the hall kneel, even the children. Magnus knelt too, and bowed his head to their new gods.

Pride filled his heart to witness his people's worship. Wonder coursed through him at the miracle unfolding around them. Not only had Duff and Seona healed Ruben, but they were revealing themselves to wolfkind. This moment would be recorded in the Archives—Magnus would pen the words himself—and readers would cherish it for all time.

Wolfkind history was being made while he watched, humbled, awed.

"A Fae could get used to this," Duff said, and his voice sounded like wind gusts whipping through the trees, both terrifying and beautiful. "What do you say, love? Shall we stick around and sort this all out or leave it to Magnus?"

"I thought we were to honeymoon on the shores of Faerie," Seona said.

"I did make a promise, didn't I?" Duff said. "All right. We'll go. I suspect Magnus has this in hand. But first," he stretched his hand out to Danu, who still knelt by Ruben.

She took it and rose to standing. She, too, could not look directly at them. Head bowed to protect her eyes, she said, "My thanks, Duff."

"I'll always be here for you," he said. "And your people."

"Yours now, too," she said.

"Ours," he said.

Out of the corner of his eye, Magnus watched Duff extend an arm his way. He was being summoned by a god.

Heart pounding, he stood and stepped into the shining aura surrounding the heavenly pair. "My thanks," he said, head bowed. "For everything."

"Don't mention it," Duff said. Magnus thought he heard a grin in the former faerie's voice.

Around his neck, Danu's moonstone heated like a coal. It burned him, and he hissed with the pain.

"Sorry," Duff said. "Got a little carried away. Just wanted to leave you with a little gift."

Magnus lifted the hot stone from where it had been tucked into his armor. It glowed brilliant white, its amethyst color impossible to discern past the blinding light.

"Now you always have a way to reach us. You know, in case we're too distracted to hear your prayers." Yes, that was definitely a grin in Duff's voice.

Danu came to stand by Magnus's side. Duff and Seona's power gently nudged them to the front of the platform. Half-rotted wood groaned beneath his shoes as he faced the hall.

His warriors, every one on his knees, looked on. The cloaked figures, too, knelt. The children near the fireplace knelt, their smaller forms visible past the shoulders of many warriors.

Duff and Seona faced the hall as well. Duff spread his arms. "Ladies and gentlemen, children and warriors, Maranners and Larnians, I introduce your emperor, Magnus Slayer of Dragons and his queen, Danu Creator of Wolfkind."

On the heels of the pronouncement, Duff and Seona disappeared as quickly as they had come.

Shocked silence hung heavy in the hall. If a feather had alighted on a flagstone, all would have heard it.

Riggs was the first to stand. "All hail King Magnus and Queen Danu!"

Around the hall, warriors stood and shouted their honor, beginning with Magnus's commanders. Swords were hoisted high, voices higher, until cheers echoed off the walls.

Magnus wrapped Danu in his arms and kissed her soundly. Her mouth met his, and his heart took flight. Every corner of his being rang with the truth of it: she was his lifemate. His.

"I love you," he told her, feeling light of heart for the first time in many years. There would be much work to do in the days ahead, including finding Alexander and dealing with the Remnant, but hope filled the sails of his spirit. Hope for his people. Hope for the world.

"I love you," Danu said, palm on his cheek. Her lips tilted in a wry smile. "I suppose our secret is out, my lifemate." Her eyes twinkled.

Happiness made his throat feel thick. He swallowed, the sound no doubt audible to those around him. Taking both his beloved's hands, he said, "Of all men, of all kings, I have been blessed beyond imagining, for I alone have been given the honor of walking this life alongside a goddess."

The skin over her cheekbones bloomed like peach carnations. The paw-print brand that had been seared into her was rough beneath his thumb. She looked so much like the portrait that he found it difficult to breathe. How could a woman be this beautiful, this perfect?

"Wait until the other goddesses hear that I am wed to a dragon slayer," she said. Her lips twitched, as if she held back laughter. "They will all be clamoring to become mortal."

He barked out his mirth, and she followed. Danu finding humor in their situation was the most delightful thing he had ever witnessed.

He tugged her close against him and whispered, "As soon as we return to Glendall—nay, as soon as we find a night's privacy—I shall make that portrait a reality."

"I'm counting on it," she replied, and he knew she would be the mother of a new generation.

Epilogue

"*OCH,* I EXPECTED more pain," Anya said from the bed. "And should it nay have taken longer? She came so quickly."

Danu dropped one more kiss on the sweet baby's forehead before placing her in her mother's arms. "It seems having an actual goddess as your child's godmother has some benefits."

Seona had attended the birth and had only just left to return to Duff, who was busily teaching her the ways of immortals. Deity suited the former human, though she did have a tendency to let her power go to her head. Fortunately, Duff was proving more than capable of reining her in. In fact, he seemed to relish the challenge.

Duff and Seona had been true to their word. They had returned to the human realm those women who had wished to go. Surprisingly, several had chosen to remain, and of those, two were lifemated and expecting joyous bundles of their own.

With Hyrk dead, the blessing of fertility had returned to wolfkind. Not only were some of the humans expecting, but five wolfkind women were as well, including Riggs's mother, Hilda, who had thought herself past her time of breeding. All of the wolfkind women expecting births were outspoken against Breeding First's ideas. As a result, the Loyalists, who supported Magnus and his lottery, were enjoying unprecedented popularity.

But there were hardships as well. Alexander had not yet been found, and Magnus worried the Remnant may have found him and harmed him. Despite the contingent Magnus had sent to bring order to Larna, lawlessness abounded there, and it remained to be seen whether the Remnant would be allies or enemies.

Thanks to Travis, they had learned much about the underground group of Larnians. Most surprisingly, many of them could transform themselves to take on the appearance of either wolves or wolfkind. The two wolves who had protected the children at the fortress were, in fact, descendants of Jilken, as was Vera, their leader, who was imprisoned in Saroc for harming Ruben.

There was still much to learn about the Remnant, especially since Magnus wished to treat them fairly. Unfortunately, the group was not forthcoming with information. Still, Magnus was determined to include them in making plans for Larna, and Danu had learned never to underestimate her king when he determined to do something.

Danu forced her mind from political matters. There would be plenty of time for that once the sun rose. Now was the time for celebrating life.

On the bed—a new bed carved by Riggs and covered with furs he'd tanned himself—Anya held her precious baby girl at her breast. The look of love on her face as she gazed at the dark-haired cherub was matched only by the look she gave Riggs when he entered with a breakfast tray.

"I'll leave the happy parents to enjoy their morning," Danu said, but neither Anya or Riggs paid her any mind. Shutting the door behind her, she returned to the bedchamber she shared with her king.

Exhaustion pulled at her from being awake with Anya half the night, but sleep was not her highest priority. It never was when she had been away from Magnus for any length of time. Dawn would come in an hour, and she intended to spend that time enjoying her bond with her lifemate.

"See that we're not disturbed," she told her guards as she slipped into the dark chamber.

It was no surprise when Magnus rolled over and curled around her the moment she slipped into bed. Her king remained a light sleeper, even though she exercised her queenly authority to decree he never be woken before sunrise. Of course, that decree didn't apply to her. She could wake him whenever she wished, and he was always more than willing to accommodate any requests his queen happened to make.

"Mmmm," he hummed into the back of her neck. "Howzanya?" Judging by his mumbled speech, one would think he was half-asleep. Judging by the cockstand prodding at her buttocks and the warm hand stealing across her bare stomach, she could tell he was more awake than he seemed.

"It is done. You're a godfather."

"Already?" Magnus started to sit up, but she stopped him with a hand on his hip.

"Lie back down. All is well. Anya's fine. Seona eased her pain and provided godspeed to the child, who is absolutely perfect, by the way. She has her father's curls and pointed ears and the blue eyes many human children have when they're born."

He started to sit up again. "I want to see her." He got one leg out of bed before Danu managed stop him with a firm grip on his calf. The move required her to roll over swiftly, which caused him to look back with concern. "Danu! The baby!" Instantly, he was at her side, running his hands over her rounded abdomen. A lock of his golden hair hung over his brow, which was creased with worry.

She stroked the hair back and drew him down for a kiss. "Our child is fine. I'm fine."

He hadn't stopped fussing over her since she'd begun showing signs of pregnancy. Giles had examined her and declared her to be only three months behind Anya. That meant by autumn's end, Magnus would at last have an heir.

"You should not move so quickly." Her lifemate tucked himself around her and covered them both with furs.

"Then do not break your promise to me." She wiggled her bottom invitingly, content that he'd temporarily forgotten about Anya and Riggs's eventful night. "No leaving this bed before dawn. For any reason."

"Not even for a new child?" He cupped her rounded belly and kissed the back of her neck.

"Well, perhaps when it's *our* child, and he or she…needs us in the night…I might permit—" She lost her train of thought due to her lifemate's tongue tracing the shell of her ear. And his hand on her stomach inching downward.

When his fingers forked into her curls and he found her already wet for him, he moaned. "Tell me we have time yet before the day begins."

She twined her fingers with his as he grazed them over her pearl. Sensual delight made her gasp. "We have time."

"Good." He spread her with his fingers and entered her from behind, the angle bringing immediate pleasure.

Her king was an expert where her body was concerned. He used the hour well, and when dawn came, they languidly bathed and dressed each other and broke their fast in his solar. Once Magnus's needs for rest and sustenance had been seen to, she gladly went with him to Anya and Riggs's chamber so he could meet his newest subject.

Riggs met them at the door, holding the pink little bundle in one arm, like he'd been caring for an infant all his life. His mother, Hilda, was there, beaming with pride. The room was warm with the summer weather, but warmer still with affection, life, and joy. *This* was why she would not miss immortality, why she would never regret her decision to remain with Magnus.

These moments were precious. They were food for her moonsoul.

Living life from within, rather than ruling it from above, filled up a place in her she'd never even realized had been empty.

When she accompanied her lifemate to the temple that morning, she did as had been her habit since their return from Larna. While Magnus knelt at the altar and thanked Duff and Seona for the new life among them, she closed her eyes and thanked her father. Because he had known how empty she'd been. And he'd cared enough to nudge her fate toward Magnus.

Cold marble met her knees through the silk of her summer gown. Behind closed eyes, she shared with her father the image of Magnus holding little Fiona—Anya and Riggs had chosen to name the baby after Anya's mother.

In return, her father sent her an image: her, in her mortal, human body, holding a blond-haired little baby. The vision was more than an echo of the portrait, the promise her father had given Magnus while she'd been imprisoned. Because this time, she held a baby in her arms, true. But there was more. A little girl in a knee-length, frilly gown reached up to hold her hand. On the child's head was a princess's crown. And standing at her side was not just her lifemate, but also a young man with golden hair and his father's lean build.

She cradled her rounded womb. Tears of joy leaked from beneath her lashes. She no longer had the gift of deity, but she had something even better. Hers was the honor of carrying Marann's future king.

And loving its current king.

She could think of no better way to spend a mortal life.

A note from the author

Thanks so much for reading *King's Highlander*. I hope you enjoyed it. This book is number four in my Highland Wishes series, which begins with *Wishing For a Highlander*.

If you enjoyed my Highland Wishes series, check out my contemporary romances. They're full of just as much heat and heart. My newest release, *Terror Undone,* is about a woman who makes a wish that, somehow, 9/11 could be undone. The next morning, she wakes up 20 years in the past. The date? Sept 10th, 2001. It's up to her to grant her own wish. The only question is, how?

"Wow! Terror Undone, by Jessi Gage, is one of the best books that I've read in a long while."—5/5 Stars, NetGalley Reviewer Jill Tatter

"This has to be one of the best thrillers that I have read this year. Absolutely stunning... Terror Undone is a proper page-turner, a thriller that will keep you riveted to the very end." –5/5 Stars, NetGalley Reviewer John Derek

Read on for the first chapter of *Terror Undone!*

Reviews make my day. Whether positive or negative, reviews help an author immensely. Please consider leaving an honest review at Goodreads and/or your favorite retailer.

Terror Undone

Chapter 1

Lydia

BOOKS.

Printed in permanent marker, my handwriting labels the contents of the box in the simplest of terms. Too simple, actually, for what this box means to me. It's so much more than a collection of bound writings. To me, this box represents my strength, my failure, and my future.

Books. I see them when I slice open the tape and part the folds of cardboard. One after another, I lift them out and slide them into the place of honor they'll occupy here at my parents' farmhouse—my farmhouse now, since Mom followed Dad to heaven and left it to me.

The built-in bookcase frames the wood-burning fireplace in the living room. Mom used to keep trinkets and mementos here. My bronzed baby shoes. An antique die-cast tractor. Ornaments of the season. And photos. Lots of photos. Her and Dad on their wedding day. Me as a kid, me as a bride, me as a mom. The only book was the family Bible, the cover of which I dusted many more times than I ever opened.

I'll put a few of my own mementos here, carrying on Mom's tradition. I've already unpacked some pictures of my kids. They're near the top, beside the baby shoes, tractor, and Mom and Dad's wedding picture. But I plan to use these shelves for books, too. The books in this box, to be precise. Because they're special to me.

And because I'm not ashamed anymore.

That will be the tradition I begin here and now in hopes Holly and Christian will carry it on for me. I'll show them that they can be proud of their passions, displaying them for all to see. They don't have to hide their interests from the people they love, only pulling them out from under the bed when they are alone, when no one can judge them.

There should never be shame in remembering.

The floorboards upstairs are creaking. Holly is moving around the bedroom I had as a child, unpacking her boxes like I'm unpacking mine. At nineteen, Christian is a college freshman now—jeez, time flies. But Holly is still in high school and has chosen to move to Nebraska with me for her senior year.

I tried to dissuade her—she's been in the same New Jersey school district since kindergarten. But she wouldn't have it. "I'm not letting you go back there alone! Not when you're grieving. Plus, I love Grandma and Grandpa's house." I suspect she tacked on the last part so it didn't seem like she was doing this for me, as if I would relent if her intentions were the tiniest bit selfish.

The farmhouse tells the story of her movements, letting me know when she's coming down the stairs. As I'm pulling the last book out of the box, she finds me in the living room.

"It's quiet out here," she says. Beneath the hem of her cutoff jean shorts, her legs are tan from a summer in the New Jersey sun.

"Sorry, baby," I say, because it's become my habit to lead with a spirit of apology. "It's going to be a boring couple of weeks for you before school starts."

As much as I want to spend every moment of those two weeks with her, I have to start my new job. While the county hospital in Ord, Nebraska isn't overwhelmed with COVID-19 cases, like Kindred in New Jersey, it's still much busier than the norm. I'm needed there, and I've become good at sacrificing family time for patients in need.

"No, I like it." Holly cocks her hip and stares me down. "You know you don't have to apologize for things that aren't your fault, right? Having to work isn't your fault. Taylor being quiet isn't your fault. Remember, you don't live with Dad anymore."

My little therapist. Okay, she's not so little anymore. At an athletic five-foot-seven, she's three inches taller than me.

"Sorry," I say with a smirk.

She rolls her eyes, but she's smiling too. I'm proud of the way she and Christian handled the divorce. I'm proud of myself for finally taking that step.

"*The Looming Tower?* What's that about?" Holly tilts her head to read the spine of the book I'm holding.

She hasn't seen these books before. No one has. Well, Tristan saw some of them, and his reaction is why no one has seen them since.

"It's not healthy the way you're fixated on 9/11, Lyd. What is it with you and death? It's been ten years. We weren't even close with anyone who died that day. Maybe you should see a therapist."

Every generation has its *where-were-you-when* moment. For my great grandparents, it was Pearl Harbor. No matter how much time had passed, they were always able to say exactly where they were and what they were doing when they heard the news that thousands of Americans had perished beneath the bellies of Japanese bombers. For my Grandma and beloved Pawpaw, it was the day JFK was shot, closely followed by the moment Neil Armstrong planted the American flag on the moon. For Mom and Dad, it was the fall of the Berlin Wall.

For me, it's 9/11.

As a media-saturated culture, we experience tragedies of this caliber collectively, but our individual minds need to process such events in their own intimate ways. For some, that looks like volunteering. For others, it looks like social action and slogans. For others, it's getting back to normal as quickly as possible. For some, like me, processing happens by reading everything they can about the event. In that way, acute interest in a national tragedy is natural. Healthy.

But that acute interest has a shelf life, or so I have learned.

When the attacks happened, Tristan and I were still newlyweds. He worked in a law firm in Manhattan, and I was a college graduate about to start a nursing program in Brooklyn. For months afterward, the attacks were all we talked about. Me, Tristan, fellow nursing students, strangers on the subway, everyone. The attacks had left deep scars, not just on the landscape but on the city's psyche, as well. And the shelf life was long.

Nine months after the attacks I transitioned into the clinical portion of my program. Patients and other health professionals were still talking about their close and not-so-close brushes with the event that had reshaped our city and nation. I listened to wives whose husbands had been on the island or at Ground Zero, husbands whose wives had been stuck in gridlock and unable to return home until late that night, parents of first responders, and grandparents of children who were supposed to go to orientation that week but had to wait for the delayed school year to start. Everyone had a story about where they were and what they were doing when they heard the news or saw for themselves. With each telling, that day in history became more and more firmly ingrained as our *where-were-you-when* moment.

And not just for those of us in the city. The whole of the U.S. was shell-shocked. Each day, the news programs and papers examined a new aspect of the attacks. The shelf life was long here, too. Related news stories continued to dominate the airwaves long after the debris had been trucked away. Terrorism, national security, domestic policies, the lack of communication between government agencies, survivor stories, conspiracy theories, rebuilding efforts. The list went on and on.

Then one day, a newscast aired without a single story mentioning 9/11. Eventually a week passed without a related story. Then a month. After a while, people stopped talking about it, except in passing, to comment on the Freedom Tower's grand opening or to sum up a visit to the 9/11 Memorial or to mark the day's anniversary with a few somber words.

Never Forget, we were told, but once the expiration date had passed, keen interest in 9/11 became morbid. Unhealthy.

So, I learned to keep my thoughts to myself. I learned that the one person I had hoped to share all of myself with, my husband, did not like the parts I dared the most to share.

I continued to buy my books, but I read them in secret and hid them where no one would see. Until now.

Holly reaches for the thick paperback in my hands. My instinct is to clutch it to me and hide the cover. To be ashamed. But that instinct belongs to a woman who failed over and over again to stand up for herself, to *be* herself without apology.

I place the book in her hands. Watch her flip it over to read the back. I hold my breath.

"Cool," she says. My lungs relax. "Did you get this because of the anniversary? Twenty years in just a couple days." She's giving me an acceptable reason to be interested.

"I've actually had it a while. These too." I show her the shelf. I'm not ashamed that I still read these books. I'm ready to own my interest. I'm ready to stand up for it.

No more apologies. I want Holly to know that she's allowed to be herself, no matter what others think. She's allowed her own inspirations and fascinations. I will always give her space to process things in her own way.

She tips her head to read the spines lined up on the shelf. "These are all about 9/11?" She runs her fingers over them, exploring.

"Yeah."

"Why haven't I seen them before?" She's curious, but there's a hint of hurt in her voice. Her mom has kept a secret from her.

No more secrets. Honesty is the new me. "I was embarrassed," I say. "So, I hid them. Not everyone wanted to talk about 9/11. Or be reminded of it." I sigh. "I needed to know more, but not everyone shared my interest. It was easier to do my research in private."

Holly nods. "Dad," she says, and her flat tone tells me she gets it. "Not everyone" means Tristan. *Tristan* didn't like me reading books about 9/11, and Tristan can be very adamant about what he doesn't like. To the point where you just give in to stop the criticism. But for all his faults, he's a great father. He adores Holly and Christian, and the feeling is mutual. I promised myself I would never make my issues my kids' issues.

"I can't imagine what it was like to be there," Holly says. "I mean, you were actually there, in New York when it happened. No wonder you wanted to know more."

Holly's words are a balm to my spirit. But I sense a need to stand up for others like me. "Yes. I was close to the tragedy, physically speaking, but I'm not sure that's why that day captivates me like it does." I lift the last of the books from the box and slide it into place. Standing back, I admire my handiwork. The shelf looks nice. It *feels* nice to put this part of myself on display for all to see. "I suspect it has more to do with being an American than being a New Yorker. You know?"

Holly's giving me a goofy grin. "Atta-girl, Mom. Way to own it."

I ruffle her hair, reaching up to do so. We make nose-kiss faces at each other, though we stopped actually rubbing noses long ago.

"Well, my darling, I am beat. What do you say we have some lemonade and take a spin on the old porch swing?"

Holly's game. We chat about our plans for the house and the school year as we mix up some lemonade and pour it over ice.

"Hey, Jes!" When we go outside, I greet Mom and Dad's faithful, long-legged hound. Jester came to me with the house and the farm. The porch is his domain, at least when he's not doing his rounds, protecting the property.

He butts his head against my thigh as I scratch behind his silky ears the way he likes.

"You know you can come in the house, now, right? Mom's not here to chase you out with a broom, anymore." I smile at the memory of Mom's empty threats as Jes made muddy puppy-prints across the kitchen linoleum.

He gives no sign of understanding. When Holly and I set the swing into a slow, rocking motion, he turns in a circle, then settles onto his dog bed.

The chains of the swing groan quietly while Holly and I sip and chat. The sun was already gone for the day when we came outside, but slowly, the stars begin winking into the velvety sky.

I'm grateful my girl is here with me. She's really something. Compassionate all the way to her bones. I bet she'll end up in a career where she can care for others. Like me, she can't help herself.

With nothing but ice in them, our glasses rest on the porch rail. Holly leans her head on my shoulder. "It's really peaceful out here. So clean and natural, you know? So different from New Jersey."

We're looking out over the cornfield. The moon looks like a Christmas ornament hanging above the acres of harvest-ready stalks. It casts the field in hues of blue.

"Soon, it'll be loud and bustling." The harvest equipment is coming next week. I don't have anything to do with the farming anymore, other than accepting the profit after Mom and Dad's account manager processes the income and pays the renters who do all the work. "You'll miss all the action, though. It'll happen while you're at school." I stroke her long hair, a habit I'll never be able to quit.

"Maybe I'll play hooky one day to see how a harvest is done."

I start to say, no way, then consider. "That's not a bad idea." Farming is an interesting process, with all the hands and machines working in harmony. "It could be like an educational field trip, but at home. Maybe I'll make you write a report." I grin, and she snorts, calling my bluff.

We're quiet for long moments, lost in our own thoughts. She gives me a glimpse into hers when she says, "It must have been so scary, living through that. 9/11," she clarifies. "For me it's something that happened in the past, before I was born. It's something I learned about in school. But you actually stopped your day to watch the news. You walked past Ground Zero. It was real-time for you."

"I was about to start nursing school." In my mind's eye, I see the downtown skyline from the doorstep of our Spinney Hill apartment. The tops of the buildings always reminded me of an EKG. That morning, the highest peak on the readout bled black smoke into an otherwise spotless sky.

Holly has heard the *Cliff Notes* version from me a dozen times, always out of Tristan's earshot. I relate it one more time. It feels good to share an edited version of my where-were-you-when event with her, especially without having to look over my shoulder. "I was at home," I tell her. "A few miles from Manhattan, but your dad was there. Just blocks from the World Trade Center. I was so worried when I couldn't reach him. The cell carriers were overwhelmed. Traffic was a mess. The news showed people walking across the bridges to get home. I kept my eyes glued to the TV, trying to make out his face, but everyone was covered with this fine white ash. You couldn't make out hair color or clothing. There was nothing to help identify your loved ones from all the other people."

I'd felt so helpless sitting there on my couch while horror unfolded across the East River. Tristan had come home late that afternoon. We tossed his suit in the dumpster rather than deal with the ash. It was finer than chalk dust. Neither of us ever said so, but I think we both knew that dust contained more than pulverized concrete.

My husband had been spared, but thousands of New Yorkers hadn't been so lucky. *Thousands.*

It still boggles the mind, all that loss. For nothing. For anti-American, fanatical ideology. For an extreme interpretation of holy writings, as offensive to Muslims as it is to those of us targeted by the extremists.

"It's time to get over it, Lyd. It happened, yes, but it's over. Time to move the hell on."

My throat feels thick, and my heart is heavy. Old instincts prod me to shove the feelings down. No one needs to see them. They're not important because I'm physically fine. I wasn't harmed that day, so I have no reason to continue in my grief.

I ignore those instincts, because I'm not fine. The effects of that day may not be physical in my case, but they're no less real. I am still grieving, and that *is* okay.

"It *was* scary," I say. "If I'm honest, I'm still processing it." Almost twenty years has passed, and still, that day feels so *wrong.* So unbelievable. We should have been able to stop it. We, as a world power, a nation with a huge intelligence community, a strong military, and law enforcement agencies devoted to our security.

I shake my head, disgusted, distraught. I'm going to bring one of my books up to bed with me tonight. And I'm not going to hide it. I'll read it with pride, and I'll remember the lives lost.

"If you could go back and do things different, would you?" Holly's question collides with my thoughts about 9/11, and I'm confused. Images of smoking towers fill my head. As nice as it would be to go back and change a day like that, no one person could have stopped what happened. There were so many failures of communication leading up to the attacks, so many little errors and coincidences that made it possible for evil to win. "With Dad, I mean," Holly adds, and her question makes more sense. She picks at a hangnail and shrugs. "I know you weren't happy for a long time."

"Oh, baby." I hate that she was aware of my discontent.

"No, I mean, don't feel bad!" She hurries to soothe me, ever my compassionate girl. "I just wonder if you would have separated sooner. You know. Like if you had a do-over."

I've asked myself the same thing a hundred times and never settled on an answer. Honesty is the new me, but there are boundaries a mom keeps in place with her kids. Even her almost grown kids.

"That's a complicated question," I say. Honest. Safe. I pat her knee. "I certainly wouldn't want to change anything that would affect having you and Christian."

Holly accepts my answer with a wan smile, and before long, she goes upstairs with her phone to take advantage of our newly-hooked-up wireless internet. When I pass through the living room to look for the box with wine glasses inside, I notice a hole in the lineup of spines on the bookshelf. One of my 9/11 books is missing. I smile.

Glass of wine in hand, I return to the swing with a quilt to wrap up in. Jes perks up, happy to have extended company on his porch. I make a pad for him out of half the quilt and pat the swing. "Come on, boy."

He accepts the invitation and jumps up to sit with me, like he used to with Dad.

"I miss him, Jes." I scrunch my fingers over his smooth head and stare unfocused at the corn and the night sky.

He acknowledges my grief by opening his eyes to sleepy slits. Then closing them again.

Rich Petite Sirah cools my upper lip. But my blood is warm from the quilt and the alcohol. Holly's question teases at me, and I give in to a fantasy where I have as many do-overs as I want.

If I could go back and change things, I wouldn't waste the magic on myself. I would get Mom to a doctor to have her heart disease diagnosed. If she'd only known, she could have made healthy changes, taken medication. She'd still be here with me.

I would be more outspoken about Dad's smoking. Maybe I could find the right words to get him to quit, and the cancer wouldn't have taken him five years ago.

I would hire someone to cut down the tree in our yard that Christian fell out of when he was nine, breaking his leg in two places.

I would stand up for myself with Tristan. Maybe if I'd done that years ago, our marriage could have been saved.

As I reach the bottom of my glass, my fantasies grow bolder. I dare to imagine a do-over of epic proportion.

If I could go back in time, I would find a way to stop 9/11.

I nod, resolute, as I form the thought. It's utterly ridiculous and completely impossible, but I like it. It pleases me to consider where I would start, who I would contact, how I would warn everyone about what was coming.

My glass is empty. I frown at it and push out my lower lip. "No fair."

I would go back in time and pour myself a bigger glass.

I snicker at myself and start to get up to go to bed, but movement in the sky stops me.

Far above the cornfield, a pinprick of light swells in size. It grows brighter like a car turning on high beams. Then turning them up to an even brighter setting. And another. The brilliance makes me lift my hand to protect my eyes.

It's a shooting star, but no ordinary shooting star.

Pawpaw has his arm around my shoulders as we rock back and forth, back and forth. Our lawn chairs have been replaced by a brand-new porch swing that Mom painted red. I'm telling him about winning third place in the eight-grade science fair when he interrupts me.

"Look at that, Bean!" He points to the sky, and his face is surprisingly bright.

I follow his finger and see why. The moon is falling! At least that's what it looks like. But it can't be the moon, because the crescent shape hangs firmly in place off to the right.

"Do you know what that is?" he asks.

"A meteor?" I make it a question, even though I know it can't be anything else.

Pawpaw's gaze is fixed on the spectacle. It might as well be noontime for how bright everything is.

"There was a time you called them shooting stars," he says with a grin, without looking away from the sky. "Yes, Bean. That right there is a meteor, but it's a very special one. When they're that big and bright, they're called fireballs."

"Should I make a wish?" My tone is teasing, but I'm transfixed too. I've never seen anything so magnificent. It's like the sun is whizzing past the farm, lighting up everything in its path.

"Oh, not just any wish," Pawpaw says. "A very special shooting star deserves a very special wish, a once-in-a-lifetime wish."

I'm fourteen now, too old for silly wishes. Or so I think until the magic of the fireball coaxes a moment of belief out of me.

I watch the huge spotlight in the sky sink toward the horizon, taking its silvery light with it, and in my heart, I make the same wish I've been making since I was little.

Please save the ones who aren't supposed to die yet.

Pawpaw taught me that natural death is a part of life. I've always accepted that. But *un*-natural death bothers me so much that I've devoted my career to thwarting it. As a trauma nurse, I've shoehorned myself between my patients and unnatural death, a practical application of the longing I've had since my very first shooting star.

The fireball drifts like a computer cursor from one corner of the sky to the other, just like the one I saw with my grandfather, only far brighter than any cursor could ever be. It burns a trail into my retinas, and I remember smoke billowing into the sky from a pair of towers that died an unnatural death. They went too soon, and so did everyone trapped inside when they fell.

With wine on my lips and a hound under my hand, I make a very special wish for a very special shooting star. It's fanciful and impossible, and Tristan would never approve, but I make it anyway. It's a wish that would have made Pawpaw proud.

Terror Undone is available in ebook, print, and audio! Go ahead, grab it up in your preferred version and get reading!

About Jessi Gage

USA Today Bestselling Author Jessi Gage is addicted to happy-ever-after endings. She counts herself blessed because she gets to live her own HEA with her husband and children in the Seattle area.

Jessi has the attention span of a gnat…unless there is a romance novel in her hands. In that case, you might need a bullhorn to get her to notice you. She writes what she loves to read: stories about love.

Use the contact page on jessigage.com and drop her a line. There is no better motivation to finish her latest writing project than a note from a happy reader! While you're visiting her website, sign up for Jessi's newsletter so you never miss a new release.

Find Jessi at the following online haunts:

Website http://jessigage.com/
Blog http://jessigage.wordpress.com/
Facebook https://www.facebook.com/jessigageromance
Twitter https://twitter.com/jessigage